Praise for "No C]

"Futuristic and dark, No Child of Mine combines a sinister dystopian society with the terror of an unfamiliar disease to create a chilling tale you won't be able to put down." - *Indies Today*

"Intriguing Orwellian-esque story that is extremely tense and utterly disturbing" - *Commune Magazine*

"The author crafts a gripping plot that stays in the reader's mind long after the story is finished." – *Publisher's Weekly / "The BookLife Prize"*

The 57th Year of the leadership of The Ordained Liberating Party;

Or year 2273 by the old calendar.

The silence of scared, apathetic or compliant people is the reason for all evil in this world.

- Andrew Dawson ("Iron Andrew"). The opening address at the 5th Ordained Liberating Party Conference of Federation Britannia.

Chapter 1

The Broadcasting Unit burst to life, the sharp jingle of the State news intro filling the kitchen.

"Federation Britannia news at six", a deep robotic voice announced into the cement coffin of the state approved kitchen.

"Good morning, free citizen. Good morning and a glorious Liberation Day to us all", a voice of a young woman rang after the daily mechanical greeting.

"We are starting the celebratory news segment with great news, free citizens. Today, on this historical day, when our free country celebrates the fifty seventh anniversary of its independence, we are excited to report on another great achievement of our young and heroic country which wouldn't be possible without the wisdom and leadership of our beloved Ordained Liberating Party. Today, when many of us will be marching in the parades, celebrating the Liberation Day and thanking our fearless leaders for fifty seven happy and peaceful years, on that remarkable day our scientists report the first positive tests in non-biological food production", the smiling woman read from the large screen, tears of pride and joy shining bright in her eyes.

"Under the glorious rule of the Ordained Liberating Party, hunger will become a thing of the past, banished away forever. Only its memory will remain, living as a sobering reminder of what we overcame. We will be the first in the world to achieve it, and only because we live in the best country in the world. Today is a magnificent day, liberated citizens! Today we can look into the future without worry! Today we look ahead with courage and pride, knowing that our children will have a bright future with our glorious Party. Today we know that the future is ours, and it's triumphant. This is further evidence of the superior leadership of our great Party, of the freest country in the world!"

"Tom? Tom, are you home?"

Judy's voice pulled Tom's attention from the Broadcasting Unit.

"Yeah, still here. Judy, I'm in the kitchen."

The artificial daylight flooded the windowless flat fifteen minutes ago, five minutes before the energetic music of the Federal News broadcast intro had made its appearance.

The shuffling steps of feet wrapped in slippers grew, bringing into the kitchen a young woman in a greying dressing gown with messy hair and drawn face, her sleepy eyes squinting against the light in the flat set to the brightness of "midday".

"I swear, it feels as if I just dropped off", Judy mumbled.

She gave a long and wide yawn showing her tonsils and slumped on a stool at the small table.

Their kitchen was the standard, Party approved size of three square meters. One wall, where a window would have been in the tower blocks three hundred years ago, was now occupied by the wide screen of a Party Broadcasting Unit, with a ventilation grid blowing the conditioned air above it.

The adjoining wall housed the standardised grey kitchen cabinets made from imported recycled plastic, approved for use in all

7

newbuilds, an enamelled metal sink and an electric cooker. The opposite wall to the cabinets and sink was occupied by a tall and slim fridge and a small, foldable grey table with four stackable chairs around it. A vintage style round clock with two moving hands hung on the wall above the table, its ticking drowned by the constant rumbling of the Broadcasting Unit.

The uniformed tower blocks, the flagship of the Party's design and its response to the housing crisis, looked identical outside as well as inside.

Visiting friends or neighbours, one would find the same kitchen fittings made from recycled plastic and wood, the identical Broadcasting Units, a kitchen table and chairs with variations within the three approved styles, and even the crockery laid for celebratory dinners often would be the same.

In the absence of the natural light, the ceilings in tower blocks' flats were outfitted with light panels, operated distantly on the automated schedule. They'd come to life at six o'clock every morning without fail, turning off three hours later, only to wake up again at seven in the evening, then to be dimmed at ten and extinguished at midnight.

"Is there tea?"

Judy slouched against the wall.

"Sure, I'll pour you a cup", Tom called.

The groomed smiling blonde on the monitor continued with a bulletin of The Morning Federal News, and Tom had to strain his voice to be heard over her buoyancy.

The Broadcasting Unit fitted within the panes of the windows didn't have a volume control of any kind, no option to mute the unit or to turn it off. Controlled by the Central Party Censorship

Office, who made decisions on the programming content, the frequency of news segments and the volume of the devices, the Units were programmed to wake up every morning with the lights, irrespective of the day of the week, turning off automatically at eleven pm, between these hours broadcasting the country's only channel.

Tom heard that Congress members and leadership level citizens were provided with specially designed Broadcasting Units with a control panel and were able to reduce the volume, in exceptional circumstances even to mute it, but disabling or turning off the Unit was a federal crime, which would bring not only a criminal punishment, but the branding of disloyalty to the Party, none of which residents of the towers would risk.

So, the Units were constantly on.

Within factories, offices and municipal buildings, the news and announcements were played via tannoy, turned off after each news segment purely down to the fact that no worker would be able to hear it over the working machinery, carry out telephone calls or meetings above it.

But for the news broadcast, the machines in the factories would stop, nomenclature offices would pause its busy day, schools and shops would go silent, when the country as one would hold its breath and listen to the voice of the Party delivering the latest progress reports on the Party's achievements and innovations, or on uncovered conspiracies against the Party by enemy states, in particular those in Europe and the North American States, who to this day couldn't get over the fact that the country chose freedom over the royalist oligarchy.

"Where do you meet your office?" Judy called from her seat, her voice rising to drown the upbeat blonde.

"We're meeting by the Old Synagogue. Then, as we progress, our column will merge with the column of the meat processing plant and the First Textile Factory, and then, with them, we march towards the Tower Building, and from there, we're back to our factory."

Tom brought a cup of greyish tea and placed it in front of Judy.

"This year is going to be great", he said. "Can you believe it? For the first time since the Freedom War, our country had produced enough energy to fulfil its own needs, and my bureau was at the forefront of it!"

Tom's face was alight when he spoke of his Party, especially when he reported Party's achievements.

"When trams are running down our streets, when machinery is working in our factories, when lights stay on in our schools and colleges, when lights shine in flats across the city, it's all because of what we did, what we achieved. And my bureau led the way."

Judy nodded, a smile tugging at her lips. She was tired and didn't feel like smiling, but her love for her husband called for her spousal duties.

"I think, we're entering a truly great era for our country", Tom continued, as buoyant and turgid as the news presenter. "I really believe so! A new era for the country, and for us. I can feel it."

Tom's eyes shone, as he spoke.

"Everything will be great from now on. I know it. We're going to leave our children a truly great country. The greatest it's ever been."

"Don't be late, my love", Judy wedged into a short break in her husband's excitement, as he drew in his breath. "I hope to see you tonight, before falling asleep."

"Still marching with Tilly's nursery?" Tom asked, returning to the family's plans for the day.

"Yes. They needed extra disciplinarians, as this year it was decided to group all nurseries of the city together. And I wanted to spend some time with her..."

Judy took a sip of her tea.

"I'm sure pleased they signed my warrant. I feared they might not. At least, it gives me some time with her."

The blonde on the high resolution display continued reading the news.

With most of the country's factories and research facilities working overtime for months prior to the Liberation Day in order to dedicate their breakthroughs and achievements to the Party rule, the news segments on the Liberation Day were always busier and longer than usual, as the society was boldly showcasing its worth.

"After a year-long operation involving Internal Police and The National State Security, a ring of conspirators and spies was revealed."

Tom turned his head towards the Unit, watching the face of the state ratified blonde turning solemn.

"Those people, in cooperation with enemy states, plotted to sabotage the development of our nuclear systems, disrupting the country's future of energy autonomy and sustainability. A number of prominent scientists were involved, whose names will be released after a thorough and unbiased investigation."

The blonde vanished from the screen, her image replaced by the face of The National State Security Legion's general.

Wearing a green military field uniform, with a chest decorated by medals for service to the Party, he stood on the podium, a couple of black microphones of the state news outlets pointing at his chest. The Ordained Liberating Party two coloured, blue and white flag with a solitary star in the middle covered the wall behind him.

He was a large man in his mid-forties with a buzz haircut and cleanly shaven face, which accentuated his strong chin and steely blue eyes. With a heavy gaze from underneath his eyebrows, with slow and hulking movements, he appeared more a bear than a man. He was the country's favourite general, loved and respected by many, the protector of the young country.

"The nest of vipers that had wormed itself into our country, into our society and into our world was finally unearthed and brought to light", he began, his words heavy and measured and his voice deep and low. "The head on that venomous snake was cut off. The treachery had met our iron and was extinguished."

He drew his meaty hand into a fist.

"The ring of spies that threatened our freedom and peace is broken. Every conspirator was arrested and now giving evidence to their complicit affair to destabilise our young nation. Those traitors will be held accountable, and soon they'll taste our justice."

He paused. Cameras clicked around him.

"We haven't allowed that treason. We were vigilant, and we protected our country. We stood strong, and we will stand strong in the future! We'll guard our independent, freedom-loving nation from all external and internal threats. We'll guard our citizens, and we'll guard our motherland. Always have and always will. If the royalists of Frankia and Columbus' States of North America think that they can shake and subvert our small, yet mighty nation, they are mistaken. Our nation will stand! We fought for our freedom! We paid for it with our blood, and we won't let anyone take it from us. Free citizens of The Federation Britannia can sleep peacefully, knowing that State Security are guarding their sleep. Our citizens can work and raise their children, knowing that The National State Security Unit is always awake, always at work protecting them."

Tom narrowed his gaze, as he shook his head.

"I hope, they'll execute those assholes to teach every foreign spy, who thinks that they can get away with the shit like that, a lesson", he muttered past his clenched teeth.

He turned to his wife.

"Did you see that? Those bloody royalists just refuse to back down and accept the defeat. I know our president is against open war, but maybe we should kick their arses once and for all."

Judy sighed.

When following the years of the Civil war Tom's parents died, the Party, new and very young then, with passionate and truth-seeking leaders, had taken in and raised him. It fed him and thousands of orphans like him. It replaced him the family, providing a new, bigger one. It educated him. It gave him a sense of belonging. It gave him future and hope.

Tom has found his life's meaning in the Party's purpose, in its goals of bright and equal future, of uniting the broken and bleeding country which hated itself, and once out of the orphanage, Tom began attending Party's meetings, playing his part in building that glorious future, and after finishing school, he was recommended by the leader of his Youth Legion onto the prestigious engineering course. And after completing that and progressing further within the Party, he was assigned to the carefully guarded projects within the lucrative Energy Department, which required layers upon layers of security clearance, but were paid with the Party's comfort and respect.

Tom's love for the Party was apparent, his dedication absolute. And before long, he was accepted into the Britannia Legion, which in turn had sky-rocketed his career. The Party had rewarded Tom's loyalty and love with a job, flat and family.

Tom was progressing. He believed in the Party, in its policies, its leaders, and the Party rewarded him with the steady progression within its ranks and in one's professional field. If there was a new position opening, the most devoted Party member would receive it.

But Judy's life wasn't the same. But mind you, neither was her trust in the Party. She wasn't as dedicated as Tom. She had her... doubts.

During the years of unrest, and the following it Civil war, Judy's parents were of the few who spoke against the rising violence and the mass cull of royalists. They called for restraint and wisdom, saying that blood is not the cleanser their country needed, that not every rule must start with bloodshed, and that the blossoming garden of a bright future should not be built on bones.

And during the first two years of the rule of The Ordained Liberating Party, they were allowed to speak. They were listened to, and they were heard. But as the Age of Cleansing descended, progressing across the country, they were arrested and executed with the rest of the oppositionists, leaving behind the orphan, who carried the name of traitors, who was forever excluded from decent jobs and had no future.

After finishing school, Judy moved in with her paternal cousin and changed her surname, after her marriage changing her surname once again, to her husband's this time, by doing so, cutting ties with her parents completely.

But even with that, she didn't have traceable to the last breath of her relatives the biography of Tom, with hero parents who died on the barricades of New Bristol during the Civil war, defending the young country. She wasn't that lucky, and as a result, the Party didn't shower her with its love, accolade and rewards.

She knew that she should consider herself lucky that she was still alive, surviving the Age of Cleansing, but on some days, she struggled to be happy about it. And today was one of those days.

With a practiced move, Judy tried to push those thoughts out of her mind, before they had a chance to form and spill, but today they refused to go away quietly, demanding to be acknowledged, aired and shared, as only truth wants to be known. And knowing that those words would never leave her, her feelings won't be known to anyone, even to her husband, she instead decided to share something else with him, something, that any mother should be allowed to feel and say. Or so she hoped.

Judy sighed, bracing herself for her husband's outrage, for the lecture that would follow, listing the benefits of the Ordained Party's rule.

But she wanted to be heard today, even if not in everything, at least in something.

"You know, yesterday, when I came to pick her up, she didn't recognise me."

Tom turned his head to his wife.

"Who?"

"Tilly."

Judy gave Tom a small sad smile, twirling the metal cup in her hands, careful not to spill the tea.

"My own child didn't recognise me, Tom. When I went to pick her up from the nursery, she stared at me, didn't want to come, and when the disciplinarian pushed her towards me, Tilly burst into tears. My own child burst into tears, Tom, afraid of me. My own child didn't recognise me."

She felt a stab of guilt looking at him.

She knew that he loved her. She knew that he stifled his rise and his future, the moment he married her. She knew that she should be happy and grateful, but she couldn't. And today she wanted him to feel it too.

"I'm sorry, Judy."

Judy held her gaze to her husband's, taking a deep breath and braving to say something else, something that she held in for a while.

"Tom, why did we have a child, if I never see her, if someone else looks after her? What was the point in all that paperwork, waiting for years to be allowed impregnation, jumping through the hoops, if I don't see her? If I don't know her? I hadn't seen her for a month until yesterday. Between the increased hours and the deadlines at the factory..."

"Judy", Tom interrupted her. "We're luckier than some."

He pulled a chair closer, leaned in and encased his wife's hands over the mug with his.

"We were granted the impregnation licence. Brenda and Anthony are still waiting, and so are Bill and Veronica. Bill was praised for the work of his team during the winter storms, yet he and his wife were not approved for a child, and it might never come. We are lucky, Judy. We are. We have family; we love each other; our girl's healthy. What more could we ask for?"

"Yes, I know, Tom. I know..."

Judy's gaze on her husband was earnest.

"I *am* grateful. We have our little angel and doing better than some. It just..."

She fell silent, as her head dropped.

The blonde newsreader on the Unit finished the anniversary news bulletin, signing off with an energetic and future-affirming message, and a graphic image of the country's outline came over the screen, the weather forecast marking the temperatures in the country's large cities today under an accompaniment of a repetitive, and rather annoying, jingle.

After a few seconds, the tune and the "graphix" image vanished too, surrendering the screen to the images of the country's shorelines filmed by a drone. Sounds of crashing waves and calling seagulls with a background of a mellow soundtrack poured out of the Unit's speakers, its volume quieter than the news segment.

"Sometimes I wonder, what's the point?" Judy whispered, as her gaze travelled to the calling seagulls.

"Don't talk like that", Tom abruptly cut her off, and by his tone she knew that he had grown impatient with her complaints.

"Everything will be fine", he continued softer, as if apologising for his earlier harshness. "We're very lucky. We have a place to live. We have jobs, food, and now we have a child. We have far more than some people. And we can't allow ourselves to feel or speak like this. We need to be grateful to the Party for everything it had done for us. Sure, it's hard. Sure, it's difficult. But we're building better future for her."

He nudged his head towards the depth of the flat.

"Everything that the Party does, it does for us and for the country's future, and we shouldn't forget that", he added hotly.

Judy held in a sigh. The lecture and speech arrived on time, and as heated, as expected.

"You remember your history?" Tom continued. "Remember what the country was like before? We're far luckier than our grandparents ever were. We're allowed to live, study, work. Our future is in our hands and not in the hands of the fat cats, who were only interested in themselves and their profit. We're the builders of our future. We're in charge, and no one can tell us that we can't do something. Nobody will lock us up."

Judy nodded.

Of course, she knew her country's history and knew that what the country had now was far better than the enslaving of citizens that lasted for hundreds of years.

She knew of the suffering people of this country had endured, dying at a young age, watching their children replacing them as moving clogs in the meat grinder of greed, only for them to die too, with broken bodies and broken lives, whilst the ruling junta rolled in luxury. She knew how the Party came to power, how people rose up and demanded justice. With their lives short, abused, dark and full of suffering, people snapped, picked up weapons and removed owners.

"History repeats itself", history books say. "One day, the oppressed become so broken, disillusioned and hungry, with nothing left to lose, that they rise."

What happened on their small island wasn't unique. Books pointed to the rise and fall of many empires prior to that one.

"I remember my mother's stories, Tom, don't worry. I remember what it was like. How we were treated, how my parents lived. I know that we're lucky to have our freedom... It's just... Is it freedom, if I don't have time to spend with my child? Is it freedom, if I'm raised everyday by the sound of her voice?"

Judy jerked her head at the monitor.

"Is it freedom when the lights blast in the flat at six every morning, and I can't do anything to stop them? That I'm told where I'll work and what I'll be doing for the rest of my life?"

Tom threw himself off his chair.

"Judy, stop!" he roared. "Stop it immediately! Don't even talk like that."

With her gaze drawn upward, Judy studied the familiar features of the man she loved.

Her gaze met his.

But there was no anger, hate or fear in his eyes.

There was only sadness... and maybe disappointment.

"You're wrong, wrong with all of it!" he called, and his palm slammed the top of the table. "The Liberating Party is better than what we had before, and you know it. We need to work just a bit harder to build the future we want, and that means to make sacrifices. It will be hard for us, but it will be better for our children, for the next generation of free citizens that will come after us. To build something new is never easy, and you know that. We should be ready for it. We're almost there. I can see it. Our country's making phenomenal progress in raising the standard of living, in making our wonderful country better. A little more sacrifice, a few extra years, and we'll live better, better than this country has seen in centuries. Wouldn't you rather these were *our* sacrifices than our children's?"

When he spoke of their child and her future, Judy always felt guilty, remembering her own childhood.

Tom stopped speaking. His earnest gaze weaved into the tired gaze of hers.

Tom believed in the Ordained Liberating Party. It was obvious to anyone.

But Judy didn't love the Party as much as Tom did. Of course, she never said it out loud. She wouldn't dare to admit it to anyone. She was smart enough to know that it would bring consequences.

She knew to nod and smile during the meetings and tannoy announcements. She knew to listen to the speeches of the local leaders with an aghast and reverent face, smile wide and clap loud, ideally louder than the next person. She knew all of that, but for some reason, today she wanted to unburden herself, to share her thoughts with Tom, hoping for his understanding.

But, as it had been proven to her many times before, it was a silly idea, a naïve idea of some unfounded expectation that he might share her fears and doubts, heightened by the tiredness of the life they were both living.

She had felt fidgety for the last decade or so, but lately that feeling had cranked up to a full blown "unsatisfied", as if something was missing from her life. She didn't know what it might've been or where to find it. Yet, she knew that she wouldn't find any of it where she lived or worked. Maybe she wouldn't be able to find it in this country. Maybe she wouldn't find it, because it didn't exist.

She pulled her lips into a rehearsed smile, her facial muscles folding down the lines of starting to form wrinkles.

"Of course, you're right, Tom. I shouldn't be so selfish. I would rather *we* bear the hardship and tribulations of building a glorious future, than subjecting further generations to it. Please, ignore me. I spoke out of turn and was very obtuse. I'm probably just tired."

She kept her gaze open and her smile wide, and Tom accepted it, needing to end the dangerous conversation rather than believing any of it.

"Of course, darling. It's just tiredness talking. Your bi-weekly day off is coming next week. Why don't you spend it in bed? Rest, sleep, and I'll take Tilly."

She smiled and nodded, knowing that that was all she would share for a while, maybe forever.

"That sounds like a great idea."

"And if you ever want, come to the next Party meeting with me. See for yourself how much we've done so far, how far we've come, and what a beautiful country with a bright future we're building."

"That's a brilliant idea, Tom. I would love to."

She smiled brighter.

She didn't plan to go with him. Whenever the next meeting will take place, she'd be working overtime that day. She'll make sure of it.

Judy lifted Tom's hand and kissed his palm, before placing it back on the table. She rose from her chair, the smile solid on her lips.

"I'd better go and get ready for the parade."

The sounds coming from the Unit changed to the forest noises of wind rustling in the trees and the hooting of an owl, drowning the chirping of the birds.

Judy lifted her gaze to the display, transmitting a still image of pine woods.

Tom rose from his chair and gave her a quick kiss.

"I'd better go and get dressed too. Are you gonna be okay with Tilly? Do you want me to stay for a bit and help you with her?"

"In case she doesn't recognise me?" Judy thought.

But she didn't say it.

"No, I'll be alright. It's time to wake her up, anyway. We need to make our way across the city."

"Good luck then, free citizen", Tom said, calling out the universal Party address. "I'll see you later. Once we're allowed to leave, I'll come straight home. But I don't think, it will be before ten."

"That's okay. I'll see you, when I see you."

And after placing another quick kiss on Judy's cheek, he walked out of the kitchen.

Chapter 2

When the front door slammed behind Tom, Judy washed her cup and put on the kettle, chastising herself for the misguided attempt to bring up her unhappiness with her husband.

Tom would never understand. But apart from him, there's no one else she could trust with those treacherous and punishable thoughts.

The Party never took perfidy lightly.

Since coming to power and taking control over the war-ravaged country sixty years ago, The Ordained Liberating Party had promised citizens that the period of blood was over. They swore to keep the peace and preserve the country as a whole, no matter the cost, uniting its parts under the same flag and leadership, uniting the country's people too, the ones, who mourned the loss of the royals and the ones, who pledged to democracy, whilst suppressing anarchy that had begun to blossom in some parts of the smaller, post-Collapse island.

The Party had brought a ceasefire and unity, with it bringing blood and terror.

The trick to controlling a rebellious country is to become the worst on the block, becoming the most feared, the ruthless and bloodiest, all of which the Party executed flawlessly, birthing the Age of Cleansing.

The Age of Cleansing lasted for twenty years.

During that period many were killed. Public executions of political dissidents and rebels became daily occurrences. Criminal offenders that Party rounded up were dispatched to the floating prisons called the rehabilitation clinics, only never to be seen again.

The years of Cleansing simmered down the boiling pot of a country, bringing the country to heel. With the opposition quashed, the Party became the one and only undeniable controller, leaving no one to question their methods or ideas.

During those years, the demanding banging on the door in the middle of the night became the common and most feared sound. Entire families would disappear during those dark nights, leaving behind empty flats, filled with their lives and possessions, promptly occupied by another family. And it wasn't a surprise to call on a friend one day, only to find a stranger opening the door, and if that ever happened, everyone knew not to ask for previous occupants, not to ask any questions, but instead, looking dazed and confused, to mumble "oh, sorry, wrong flat" and skedaddle out of that building as fast as possible.

Twenty years of Cleansing left behind a perfectly obedient electorate, who marched in organized and uniformed columns on Liberation Day, waved blue and white flags with a large star in the middle, sang Ordained Liberating Party hymns and cheered after every slogan called to the masses from a high podium by a local leader.

Today was Liberation Day, and Judy was about to join her fellow free citizens in the country's annual march.

This year, she would walk with Tilly's nursery, keeping an eye on hundreds of children, who were reared within the walls of Party's nurseries by disciplinarians. The country's children barely saw their parents, spending nights in the nurseries, sometimes going months before the overworked parents would bring them home for a few hours.

Judy wasn't the only mother who worked twelve hours a day, with a day off every two weeks. She knew that Tilly's life wasn't any different to the life of any other child. But Judy didn't care about conformity and group sacrifices. She didn't want to suffer for the common good. She wanted to live on her terms and to be allowed to enjoy her life even a little. She wanted to know her child.

But that wasn't an option. That wasn't something they could do. If she wanted to eat, if she wanted Tilly to eat, she had to work. She had to work and obey the Party, and her love for her child was collateral damage to the rules of the country.

The owl hooted and the birds sang through the speakers.

Trying to ignore it, Judy walked to the cupboard, reached in and pulled out the tin with tea. She flipped the lid and fished out a pinch of brown leaves, which crumbled under her touch.

She sprinkled the leaves into her mug and poured in hot water. The rising steam brought the familiar smell of pine and wood.

A sharp stab of a stranger's voice came through the sounds of the Unit.

"Judy."

The metal mug in Judy's hand tapped on the side of the counter, and unable to find its balance, it fell to the floor, spilling hot water and brown leaves.

Judy couldn't breathe. She couldn't command her legs to move, or the muscles on her neck to turn, to face the voice and the danger it brought.

Ignoring the pool of boiling water, she grabbed the counter to steady herself and to make it harder for whoever broke into their flat to remove her from her life. She made a mistake speaking to her husband today, and she was about to pay the price. The arrests and the Age of Cleansing were not over.

A few short seconds stretched into eternity.

Judy's heart thumped in her ears, her body sweating and shaking, when the voice called again.

"Judy?"

This time, she heard a question in a small and young voice calling her name.

She turned on her frozen legs.

A child with dark curls and wet eyes, which looked so much like Tom's, stood past the kitchen door.

Judy drew in a shaky breath. She released it and then drew another, pushing down the panic, and hunting for the memory on how to form a smile.

"Morning, darling", Judy went to say, but her voice was quieter than her daughter's.

She cleared her throat and started again, her facial muscles and her voice responding to her this time.

"Morning, darling. Did you sleep well?"

Judy's gaze travelled to the mug on the floor, surrounded by leaves and dusty water, and after reaching for a cloth, she kneeled and began cleaning.

But as there was no answer, she glanced at her child, who didn't move.

"Slept well?"

The curls on her daughter's head moved with her small nod.

"Excellent. I hoped you would. We have a very long, yet very exciting, day ahead of us. But first, breakfast. Take a seat."

Judy nodded to the chairs around the table.

"I'm about to make us breakfast. I don't think you'd be drinking tea? Or do you drink tea? Never mind, I'll just make you a cuppa, and you can have it if you want. Or if you don't want tea, I can pour you some water... Breakfast... What to have for breakfast? Oh, I know. As we have oatmeal and plenty of time, I'll make us pancakes. We even have a plum jam. I bet it will be delicious on the pancakes."

Judy rambled on and couldn't stop. She was afraid of her own child, afraid to be rejected and didn't know what to do or say, to make her fears better and her daughter more comfortable.

This child was alien to her, an intruder that occasionally appeared inside her flat. Judy knew nothing about her own daughter: what she loved and what she hated, what she liked to eat, if she drank tea, what games she played or what made her smile. Judy even didn't know the sound of her daughter's laughter. Judy wanted to love the child, but she didn't know how to begin.

Tilly remained by the door, silently watching her mother.

Judy stopped talking and cleared her throat.

"Do you want to sit?"

She pointed to the backless chair she occupied only a few minutes ago, and as Tilly stood, unsure, Judy added, putting firmness into her voice: "Go on. Go and take a seat, and I'll make us breakfast."

Hearing a command, which good Party children were taught to obey from an early age,

28

with light footsteps, Tilly reached the chair and climbed onto it.

"That's a good girl. Do you want pancakes?"

Tilly gave a small nod, keeping her gaze on Judy, and Judy smiled.

Judy wrestled with her own body that wanted to be close to her child, with her arms that wanted to hug her tight, with her nose that wanted to inhale the soft scent at the top of her daughter's head. But she was afraid to scare her child or to make her unhappy. She was afraid that next time her daughter would beg disciplinarians harder not to let her go with the strange woman, and the disciplinarian would cave in.

"Excellent. It won't take long. And after we've eaten, I'll do your hair. We'll put beautiful blue ribbons in it for the parade. It's gonna be lots of fun, and we're going to have a great day."

Judy turned to the cupboards and began rummaging. She wanted to make sure that Tilly had a good time with her, and she was determined to hear her child's laugh, or at the very least, see her smile.

A bag of oatmeal was found at the back of the cupboard. Although called oatmeal, the flour was a mix of milled grains available at the time of production, crushed into powder fish and animal bones and herbs, which were added mainly to disguise the dusty flavour and smell and failing at both.

The old iron pan heated up in no time, and soon the oatmeal pancakes were sizzling on it.

During the breakfast, Judy tried to keep the conversation going, but Tilly's answers were so reserved, sometimes even as dry as a nod or a shake of her head, that Judy gave up with it, finishing her pancakes as fast as she could, hoping that the party atmosphere of the streets would relax Tilly a bit and make her talkative. And once both of them got dressed, Judy, in her finest, blue and black tartan dress that Tom brought from one of his supervisory business trips to Schotlandia, and Tilly, in the black uniform of the state nurseries, which was brightened up today with a white scarf tied around her collar for the occasion and with wide blue ribbons in her hair, they were ready to go.

"Shall we?"

Judy offered her hand to her daughter and was relieved when, after a glance at the outstretched hand, Tilly took it.

Once out of the building, Judy and Tilly were swallowed by the crowds of hurried people, blaring music and the buzz of excitement. The monotone chirping of the birds of their personal Unit was now replaced by elated, marching music, booming above the streets of New Bristol, delivered via tannoy propped on every lamppost.

The music bounced off the tall grey buildings, deafening the free citizens of the city.

But the citizens didn't mind.

The crowds on the streets were feverish with excitement.

A sudden guffaw of laughter would rise above the music, drowning for a moment the constant chatter, jokes and laughter of the people of New Bristol, their excitement reaching Judy's ears in waves with their arrival. The happy squeals of children pierced the air, delight lightening their faces, as they walked with their parents, waving small flags or tugging blue and white balloons behind them.

The blue and white flags with a solitary star flapped on every corner of every building. The large, blue and white banners with the Party's latest slogans were stretched above the narrow streets.

The pavements and roads were packed.

Judy pulled her daughter closer, holding her small hand tighter, as the tannoy above boomed of the "bright future for everyone in the freest country on Earth".

Smiling families walked past them. The small girls were dressed in the identical to Tilly dresses. Blue and white ribbons waggled in their hair, bouncing with their skipping. The boys in uniformed black trousers and black jackets with white shirts underneath had blue or white handkerchiefs tied to a button on their jacket or tucked into a lapel.

Laughing young couples and larger groups of young workers were overtaking the plodding Tilly and Judy.

With a sergeant ahead calling the count, the troops of young cadets of maritime and land armies marched past in perfect time, their black boots booming on the pavement, their parade blue uniforms spotless, buttons and epaulettes shining, reflecting the late morning sun.

Some people sang along with the tannoy, as they walked, some chatted, some laughed. But occasionally, Judy would notice a sombre face within the crowd, following the flow with tightly pressed lips, and when Judy's gaze would collide with the gaze of a grim stranger, his eyes would snap open at being caught, his lips would pull into a wide smile, and then a happy whistling would escape them.

The rattle of an oncoming tram came suddenly, its arrival drowned by the noises of the Parade.

"Shoot! Come on, Tilly. Let's run or we'll miss it."

Judy and Tilly arrived at the stop, as the last passengers were pushing through the tram's doors, its metal core already stuffed with human bodies.

"Come on, Tilly. Climb in and hold on to the railing."

She turned to the man ahead.

"Excuse me, citizen, would you mind to move a bit."

"There's nowhere to move, citizen", he bit, barely glancing at her. "I'm swinging, as it is."

Someone jumped on the bottom step of the tram, squashing Judy against the annoyed man, who gifted her with another glare.

The tram departed, ringing its bell, as it travelled into the city.

The closer to the Old centre the tram progressed, the emptier it became, its passengers disembarking, dispersing around the city centre, towards the starting points of their processions. And as the tram became freer, Judy and Tilly found a seat by the window.

With her nose pressed to the glass, Tilly watched the floating past the window city, mesmerised by the changing landscape, and Judy watched it with her.

The city has changed a lot under Party rule, but its change began earlier.

During the "Collapse", unable to withstand the force of the earthquake that took half of Englandia's lands, most of the twenty first century tall buildings fell, burying with it the seat of the royalist oligarchy in London, the memories of the high, glass buildings surviving only through photographs rescued and preserved in the City museum.

Anarchy and the Civil War had finished the rest, wiping the face of the city clean, leaving only a few eighteenth and nineteenth centuries buildings, and only because the bases of the opposing parties and coalitions were located in them.

With the Collapse the country became smaller, and although the loss of millions of lives was mourned, the Collapse divested the country of half of the farming lands, bringing the surviving population to the brink of starvation.

With the territory of Schotlandia covered in permanent frost, where a few remaining deer farmers were left herding their livestock, a tiny, northern slither of Englandia and Welsh Territories was all that was left for farming.

There was hunger, and there was bloodshed for the land. Farmers and landowners were lifted on spikes by desperate people, and as a result, there was no farming.

The country was eating and killing itself.

When the Party came to power, homelessness in the country was huge. The refugee tent cities covered the grounds of parks within the cities and fields around them, dotting the hills and low mountains of the countryside, sprawling across farming lands.

The answer to the housing crisis came in the form of uniformed and monolith, twelve storey residential buildings built from grey cement panels, free of frills, windows or balconies, with the large metal ventilation shafts slicing each building on the outside, at every floor, like scars.

These buildings were long and wide. Some were built in impossibly long lines, running for a couple of miles, whilst some close in on themselves in a circle. The cluster of the panelled buildings formed micro settlements on the outskirts of the cities, at first housing only the Party loyal electorate, but over time opening its doors to every worker.

As the tram progressed further, the Party's answer to the housing crisis began to phase out. The tall, panelled grey buildings were replaced by the low, red brick houses of two centuries ago, built under the watchful eye of the Last Queen.

The sturdy buildings with windows and gardens behind the picketed fences were occupied by the nomenclature elite and United Liberated organizations. The signs for a library, the typography, a shop and a few research facilities were posted on the buildings.

With every new stop more people alighted from the tram, and at the next stop, announced by the tram's bell, it was Judy's and Tilly's turn to leave the tram's almost empty belly.

"Now, hold my hand very tight, darling. It's going to be even busier here."

They stepped onto the ground and were instantly swamped by the clamorous crowd.

Chapter 3

In this part of the city, so close to Liberation Square, the crowd was denser. The tannoy boomed louder, vibrating from the ground up and into people's chests.

The Parade Organisers from the city's enterprises and factories were easy to spot. Those men and women had perpetually red faces, strained veiny necks and coarse voices, withered to an angry whisper thanks to the constant yelling over the last few hours. And of course, they wore blue and white armbands over their jackets, with the crest of the Ordained Liberating Party stitched onto them.

"I said by three, by three! How hard is it? Are you bloody deaf? Can't you bloody count to three?!"

"Keep the column tight! Stand right behind the citizen in front of you! Until you see his dandruff, you're either to the side or too far! I said, in front! Not to the left or right! In front!!"

"Pull the banner tighter! Tighter, I said! Smith, it ain't your mother's underpants so quit flopping it! Do I give a shit that your arms are too short? Then hand it over to Jackson!"

"When walking past the Liberty building, steps should be solid, decisive, march like you mean it! And remember, flags are high and waving, banners tight and straight, and when I start "Glory to our Party", you sing with me and don't save your throats! You can yell at your wifey some other time – you, yes, you, Collins! I'm talking to you. If I see you mumbling..."

"Pull those throats like you mean it! Don't spare your voices!"

"March, march – march, march, march! Keep the beat! Lift your feet!"

"Hazel, move your hand off of there..."

Judy didn't have a chance to see where Hazel's hand was, as with another tide of the bodies she was pushed past the formed columns of the textile and cement factories, past and through an unorganised crowd of freshly arrived bodies, towards the epicentre of the short crowd, where the wail of hundreds of petrified children rang with the volume of the tannoy.

"Beth! Beth, I'm here", Judy called, waving her arm above the young crowd.

The young woman carrying cosy and homely forms spun to the call, her blonde hair flying with her turn. She took rushed steps towards Judy, dragging a screaming toddler with her.

"Oh, Judy. Am I happy to see you."

Beth's face was red and sweaty, her lips quivering.

Judy looked past her.

Five more young women stood amongst the vast sea of hundreds screaming young children, who stood with their heads drawn up and their mouths open wide mid-wail, like baby birds.

"Is everything okay?"

But really Judy wanted to ask what is wrong with the children and what did the disciplinarians do to bring that behaviour to the forefront in them, in children, who from babies knew not to make noise, not to cry or to fuss, who knew that no one would come and if someone came, they'd be ignored. Those babies were raised on a diet of the strict discipline and deprivation of attention, with a ratio of one disciplinarian to thirty, sometimes forty babies.

Besides, these children were attending the Liberation Day parade not for the first time and were well aware of the expectations placed on them.

Judy couldn't understand how those toddlers were making that noise.

As she scanned the crowd of children, she became aware of the quieter atmosphere by the parade-goers around them. There was no joking or laughter, no barks of instructions, only distance and silence. She hadn't noticed it earlier, probably due to the tannoy blaring above their heads, but now she could hear the ominous hush of low voices, and she could see the glances.

That wasn't good.

Judy stepped closer to Beth and dropped her voice.

"We need to get it under control and fast, or the police will be here soon... and not for them."

Judy nudged her head towards the wailing flock.

Beth's eyes opened wider. Either she didn't consider that possibility, or due to her young age and not witnessing the Age of Cleansing, was unable to foresee that outcome.

Tugging Tilly with herself deeper into the sea of the bawling children, Judy began to sing, straining her voice above healthy lungs of hundreds.

"One, two, three, four, five,
Who is marching with that might?"

Standing in the middle of the low crowd, she let go of Tilly's hand, and cranking up her voice, she began clapping in time with the rhyme.

"Where they're marching I shall ask.
They bring freedom to all of us."

After the second line of the familiar verse, the disciplinarians joined in too, clapping in time with words of the approved poem, sang and reproduced in millions of copies for young free citizens of the country.

Looking up at her mum, Tilly began to sing the verse too, tapping her foot and clapping her hands, measuring the rhythm.

The disciplinarians began the rhyme again, and this time, bored with the lack of participation around her, Tilly turned to a boy, and scooping his hands in hers, she began clapping them for him.

The startled boy's mouth slammed shut. His head turned to Tilly, his gaze fixed on her, finally seeing the world around him.

Ignoring his gaze, Tilly continued clapping his hands, and once she could feel his hands driving towards each other on their own, she let go of him, and without her aid, his hands continued clapping, his mouth beginning to move with the words.

"Good job, Tilly."

Judy bent down to a child and picked the hands of a wailing girl.

The girl's hands were ice-cold and clammy. But not clammy with sweets' stickiness that children are known for, or even sweat, but with something else.

Judy kneeled next to the child, and lifting the girl's hands, she brought the child's palms closer to her eyes.

The skin on the girl's palms was covered in a layer of clear raised domes, which looked like tiny burn bubbles on otherwise healthy and pink skin. On the edges of the palms, where Judy's hands made contact, the tiny domes were gone, replaced by the sluggish streams, which although looked like sweat, were a tad slower and richer somehow.

Ignoring the wailing of the children and the boom of the tannoy, Judy brought her finger to a dome.

The dome's strained shape didn't burst under Judy's soft touch. Like a blister, it sat there, waiting to be pricked.

Judy moved her finger lightly over the domes, sliding it over their cluster.

"What the hell is going on here?" a male voice growled above Judy.

Startled, she whipped her head towards the voice, her hand closing over the toddler's.

"You know, it's an offence to interrupt the Liberation Parade production, don't you? We're about to march, and you have these..."

The old man pointed his finger at the screaming youngsters.

He had a dishevelled beard, beady enraged eyes above it and a red face. He wore a dark blue uniform of the military building department, with the "ceremonial master" blue and white band tied around his arm.

"I'm not gonna go down, because you're crap at your job. If the police are not on their way already, they'll be once your lot have failed to join us, and if they come, I won't be helping you there."

"Citizen, we are trying. I don't even work with these children. I work in –"

"I don't care where you work. This is your responsibility today, is it not? Then do your job and do it right. Fix it! Fix it now! We're marching in ten minutes, and if you don't bring it under control, we both know that you won't be joining me..."

He leaned in closer, dropping his voice to an angry whisper.

"And, unlike them..."

His head jerked towards the young disciplinarians.

"...you know what happens then."

And holding her gaze, he pushed through his teeth: "Fix it."

Judy didn't answer the man. There was nothing to say. Everything he said to her, she knew herself already.

He was right. She was old enough to remember the bloody end of the Age of Cleansing. She remembered it well. She knew that the methods of the Party didn't go anywhere. Those methods were never forgotten. The people, who carried out the tasks or gave the orders, were still around, rose higher within the echelons of power, carrying different titles.

The man turned on the spot and left through the crowd.

The tannoy above her head bellowed another Party approved song. This time, of the love a young man carries for a girl, the Party's monthly quota and the Party itself.

Judy returned her attention to the toddler and her hands.

The layer of the clear domes was gone, replaced by millions of sluggish rivers, and holding the small hands in hers, Judy caught a whiff of something, something that wasn't around before, and on a hunch, rather than following a clear idea, she lifted the toddler's hands to her nose.

The girl's hands smelled of the poisonous puss of a burst wound, mingled with a salty scent of sweat. And pressed for time, Judy began clapping the toddler's hands, forcing the smile to remain on her lips, as she sang to the child, ignoring her nagging confusion.

A spray escaped the toddler's hands with the first clap. The watery substance landed on Judy's face. But Judy forced herself to sing the familiar words of the rhyme, keeping her smile, her head bobbing with the song, as she wiped her cheek on her shoulder.

Finally waking, the disciplinarians began scooping the children, bouncing them on their hips and clapping their hands, adopting exaggerated smiles and happy voices.

The whisper continued to stroke the surrounding crowd, when a few men and women stepped forward. Singing the words of the rhyme, they kneeled in front of the children, clapping their hands. And lifting her head and scanning the young crowd, Judy noticed that every time a toddler would begin to clap, their face would smooth out, their mouth would close, and their gaze would sharpen, as if waking.

Judy wanted to ask someone, if they had noticed it too, to point out the weird connection, but there was no one to tell.

Leaving the calmed girl behind, she moved to another child, and scooping his hands, she began clapping them, the liquid spraying her parade blouse, a few droplets finding her face.

Within minutes the area had quietened, leaving behind only the running of the latest tannoy announcement.

"Two minutes! Two minutes! Take your places!"

Outfitted with a megaphone, the ceremonial master's voice boomed above the crowd, and letting go of the children, the men and women dispersed, leaving the disciplinarians amongst the silenced flock.

"Oh, no, two minutes", Beth whispered next to Judy, and looking at her, Judy thought that the girl might pass out.

She squeezed Beth's hand.

"You'll be fine."

"Boys and girls", Beth called to the children, "remember how we practiced. Find your partner and hold hands, or a hand, of the one closest to you. That's it."

The other disciplinarians woke upon Beth's commands.

"Jake, by two! By two, I said! Otherwise, I know you'll end up with a chain. That's it!"

"Quickly, quickly."

As pairs began to form, Beth and the disciplinarians exploded into action, shoving children next to one another, finding pairs and dissolving clusters, and tired and cried out children would shuffle their feet, keeping up with the rushed steps of their teachers, their moves exhausted, their faces checked out.

The ceremonial master came over.

He didn't say a word. He only glanced at the hype of the activity within the otherwise quiet battalion, turned around and walked away.

The tannoy suddenly died, leaving behind the buzz of radio static and silence.

The people stood still.

Not a word was spoken. Not a sneeze, whisper or hush left the people. Absolute silence covered the ready to march crowd.

Suddenly, the tannoy woke up with the voice of the country's favourite newsreader.

"Morning, free citizens! Morning and Happy Liberation day to us all! Fifty seven years ago, our founding fathers wrestled the broken and abused country from the clutches of oligarchs, criminals and murderers. Fifty seven years ago, our founding fathers rose up. Hearing the pleading of the broken country, the moans of its enslaved people, breaking under the weight of the murderous regime, they rose up, demanding justice for all – for every man, woman and child.

"Fifty seven years ago, a group of people under the brave leadership of a single man stepped forward, demanding for the people's voice to be heard, demanding equal distribution of the rewards of their labour, demanding education, healthcare, shelter and safety.

"That brave visionary was Derek Mark. He dreamt of the freedom to choose, of equality and fairness for us all. And people heard him. They began dreaming with him. The people of this great country embraced that powerful wind of change. They joined it, opening their sails under its glorious power, ready to sail into a bright future. When the oligarchs refused to release their hold on the starving country, the people rose up, replacing machinery and ploughs with rifles and guns.

"Today is a bittersweet day, free citizens. The Liberation came to us at the great cost. It was paid with the blood and lives of our fathers, with the suffering and sacrifices of our mothers, with the tears and agony of our brothers and sisters. This day should be remembered forever. It should be burned into our memory, into the memory of our nation. It should, and it will be, commemorated for generations to come, because it was the moment, when the shackles were shed, and the new world was woken, when our country for the first time breathed with freedom.

"We shall never forget this day. It shall remain with us forever. We shall pass the knowledge of that struggle to our children and children of their children. We shall remind them of the bounds of slavery we have endured, of the fights we fought, of the future we've built. We shall warn them of enemies, lurking in the shadows around our free and young nation. We shall tell them to stay vigilant, while standing brave and strong. We shall stay true to the course of our great Party! Hooray, free citizens!"

The three practiced hoorahs bellowed from hundreds of throats.

"Hooray! Hooray! Hooray!"

And expecting the obligatory response, the newsreader paused.

He gave a few seconds for the echo of the wave to die down, before he finished: "So, let's march today for the blood of our freedom fighting fathers! Let's march for our mothers who died in the prisons of oligarchs! Let's march for our future! Let's show the enemies, who are watching us, waiting for our failure, that we stand strong! That we stand united and free! We are and we always will!"

His voice faded, replaced by marching music with a sharp and punchy beat.

The wind and brass instruments roared. The decibels zinged in time with measured steps. The promising rhythm sang, inviting the free citizens to follow and praise the rule of the Ordained Liberating Party.

"Now!" The megaphone screeched, and the columns ahead began to thin out, pulling people forward.

The shuffle and movement soon reached the United Liberated nursery group, and tugging on the arms and sleeves, ushering the sombre children forward, the column began its progression.

The nursery column didn't produce the same cutting rhythm of shoes, stamping on the pavement, as the columns behind or ahead did. But the children were quiet and obedient, and it was all the disciplinarians could ask for.

Luckily for the disciplinarians, the march of their column wasn't long. The nurseries, along with other essential workers of bakeries, coal and nuclear plants and maintenance workers, walked the shortest distance, starting their march just a few blocks away from the Liberation Square.

Since the first parade fifty years ago, the processions, coming from different parts of the city, would meet in New Bristol Liberation Square, where on the erected podium, on the backdrop of New Bristol Town Hall and Free Citizens House, the leader of the New Bristol Council would stand.

Surrounded by the members of the Ordained Liberating Party, he would give his speech aimed at rousing patriotism and pride in the free citizens, listing the Party's many achievements in making the citizens' lives better and their future brighter.

The columns ahead flowed towards the centre, and Judy and Tilly, lifted by the upbeat music and following the steps of the nurseries column, moved forward, with Judy marching at the side, holding a child's hand.

Tilly walked within a row ahead, holding the hand of the child to her right, as she waved a Party flag in her left hand.

Every door and every window of every building were covered by bright blue posters celebrating Liberation Day, their blue colours matching the colour of May's sky.

The slapping of the flags on the corners of Old Town buildings, the bunting of the country's flags stretched across the streets, above the shops' entrances and wrapped around the columns of the old buildings, the posters, covering every remaining surface – New Bristol was blue and white and was celebrating.

Judy and her nursery column turned a corner, stepping onto the main square, their final destination. The tannoy burst with another startling roar of greetings in the familiar news presenter's voice, calling the Party's life-assuring slogans to the passing citizens.

The presenter, propped somewhere next to the local Party leader, announced the columns' arrival, and the columns would answer him with a deafening hooray, which for a moment would drown the tannoy and his voice.

"The column of the wool factory looks glorious today! The women of the factory have exceeded their annual quota in textile production, earning their factory another Liberating Industry Leader Award and an extra day of annual leave for themselves. This is to show what is possible with hard work! Hooray, free citizens, hooray!"

"... And now walking is the column of the multi medal winning cement factory of New Bristol. With their hard work, our buildings grow taller, and the streets grow wider. Thank you for your work! Hooray, citizens, hooray!"

As they walked deeper into the square and closer to the podium, the child's hand tightened over Judy's hand. The marching rhythm ahead faltered, as the children stopped, shocked by the noise.

But this time the disciplinarians were quick on their feet. And picking up the pace, they ushered the children forward, calling to them in their upbeat voices, encouraging their small feet to move forward, hands to wave the flags and lift the balloons higher.

"Behind them, in a happy and bright procession walks the United Column of Liberated nurseries. These children are lucky to be born in our time and in our country. They know true freedom! Their future is bright! Hooray, citizens, hooray!"

The children didn't produce the deafening call of the workers of the cement factory.

The rows around Judy remained silent.

"Hooray, hooray, hooray!" The disciplinarians called and Judy joined, their call lifted and given strength by the voices of the other columns.

Judy was relieved when she was allowed to leave. Children of that age were not expected to join the rest of the free people and stand in the square, listening to an hour-long speech of their fearless leader.

After the processions had concluded, and the tail of the last column rolled into the tightly packed square, the children were led away by the ceremony master towards the buses, which were waiting for them, ready to take them back to their nurseries.

Beth pushed through the low crowd towards Judy.

"Thank you for today, Judy. I don't know what we would've done without you. Thank you."

She jumped up and gave Judy a tight hug.

"See if you can get permission to march with us next year. I sure would be glad to see you."

Judy smiled at the young disciplinarian.

"I'll see what I can do."

Beth's attention switched to a boy.

"Jake, get on the bus. Leave the poster alone and climb in. The bus is leaving, and if it has to, it will leave without you."

And with another smile and a fleeting glance, Beth darted towards him, her threats of a punishment ringing on the street.

Judy looked at her child.

"Shall we go to the park?"

And when her daughter met her gaze, giving her a wide smile and a nod, they both walked down the city's empty streets, towards one of the few parks that had survived the artillery of the Civil war.

Chapter 4

The flat was dark and quiet. Only the ventilation system hummed, lulling the residents to sleep.

"Open up! In the name of the Ordained Liberating Party, open up!"

The door vibrated and screeched on its hinges under forceful fists.

"Open up or this door will be removed!" The demanding voice roared behind the flimsy door.

"Tom..."

Judy barely whispered it, when Tilly's cry and call for her mother rang from the other side of the room separated by a partition screen.

"Mummy, mummy."

In that moment, fear and the childish need to hide, to close one's eyes and keep quiet in the hope that whoever they are, they'll go away just by pretending that no one's home, in that moment, following Tilly's voice, the silence and fear were replaced by a rush of activity, as if set off by a starter pistol.

"Mama's coming."

Judy threw the covers and jumped out of the bed, running to her daughter.

"Coming!" Tom called to the door, running in the opposite direction to his wife.

He pressed the button to wake the weak hall light and threw the front door open.

A tight crowd of men in the black uniform of the Liberated State Security Unit stood behind the door, and after a single question: "Fellow

Whicker?" from the man at the head of the group and Tom's confirmative nod, the men pushed through, nudging Tom deeper into the flat.

The front door slammed shut behind them.

Their bodies like a black mould spread into every room of the flat, flooding it with ominous promise, absorbing light, space and air. The stomping of their heavy black boots pounded the floor.

"Where is your wife, fellow Whicker?"

"What's going on?" Tom demanded. Only the knowledge of his own stance within the Party gave Tom the courage to question the man and demand his own answers.

"We need to speak to your wife. Where's she?"

This man was in charge. He was asking questions, as his colleagues began working the flat.

The cupboards' doors opened and slammed in the kitchen. The tins and cups were singing, as they hit the floor. The drawers screeched on their runners in the family room, items of Tom's and Judy's lives thudding on the carpet.

The man expected answers with the authority granted to him by his uniform, working the fear the uniform of his department instilled.

The uniform of State Security officers was well-known and recognised. Walking down the street, free citizens would often turn around or cross the road, when they'd see a member of the State Security ahead, standing out against the grey crowd of citizens, like a crow amongst pigeons.

The Department of the Liberated State Security and Internal Police was feared. It had a reputation.

Under the decisive commitment to the country's safety and under orders issued by the department's director, the Age of Cleansing was set in Federation Britannia, spreading through the country, as free citizens were whipped in line, the murmur of the disagreeable quashed, with it birthing new electorate and dawning a new era in the history of the country.

The director of the Liberated State Security became the most influential citizen in the country, and the most redoubtable. He was able to make and break careers and lives. He decided what the country and its citizens needed. His input within the Party Committee was valued to the reverence. His troops became the most feared people, their impunity birthing permissiveness.

Nobody argued with them. Nobody questioned them. They never stood in line for food rations, and if they ever came into that line, they would strut straight to the window, ahead of the queue, and nobody would say a word. They had total and complete power, and although the Age of Cleansing had passed, the dark department hadn't lost its influence.

Without waiting for an answer, the man in charge strode past Tom.

He poked his head into the kitchen, where his officers continued rummaging through the cupboards. Then, he stepped briefly into the family room, where most of the black uniforms concentrated, with the papers and blueprints of Tom's current projects scattered over the carpet, before progressing into their bedroom.

Trailing behind the man, Tom saw his letters, books and blueprints shuffled and checked, drawers and cupboards open, their wedding tea service, the only precious item they own, shoved to the side, as an officer in the family room stroked the walls covered in flowery wallpaper, feeling for something, occasionally knocking at it in different places, his "friend" tapping with his boots on the floor, listening for hollow sounds.

"What's going on?" Tom asked the officers, but nobody granted him with a response. As much as the strangers touching his life agitated Tom, he knew better than trying to stop them.

"Judy Whicker?"

"Yes."

His wife's small voice coming from their bedroom woke Tom, and spurred on, he ran into the room.

"We have a few questions for you, if you wouldn't mind answering them."

The man sat on their unmade bed, resting his elbows on his knees, looking at Judy, who sat on Tilly's low folding bed, hugging her daughter tight.

Tom stepped forward, wedging himself between the man and his wife.

"Would you mind telling us what's going on?"

"We are here to ask you a few questions – that's all. Nothing to worry about, and nothing is wrong."

The man pulled a practiced placating smile, which didn't touch his eyes and was simply a part of his training.

He turned his attention back to Judy.

"Three days ago you took part in the Liberation Day parade. Is that right, fellow Whicker?"

"Yes... Yes, I did."

Judy's voice was trembling, her gaze fixed on the commanding intruder.

"Who did you march with? Your factory?"

52

Judy shook her head.

"No. I asked for permission to walk with my child's nursery, and my transfer was granted by the factory manager and approved by the Party member."

"So you walked with the children from the nurseries?"

"Yes."

"Who else was there with you?"

"You mean adults or children?"

"Adults."

"Bethany Taylor and a few more disciplinarians, but I don't know their names."

"Can you describe to me what happened when you arrived?"

"What do you mean?"

"Can you walk me through your day, step by step: your preparation for the march, your arrival, what you saw, what you said, who said what to you..."

He smiled at Judy, expectantly leaning closer.

"Tilly and I left the flat around nine and took a number twelve tram. We left the tram and walked to Verity Street, where the meeting point was. Once there, I and the disciplinarians arranged the children into the column, and we walked."

"So when you arrived, the children were calm and quiet, placed ready to walk?"

The man's heavy gaze was on her, studying her, reading past her sweaty face.

"He knows" passed through Judy's mind.

"Not exactly", she croaked.

"So what did happen then?"

Judy cleared her throat.

"It was very loud there... A lot of noise, so the children were stressed... Some of them were crying..."

"Some of them?"

"Most of them", Judy agreed.

"Most of them were crying", the man repeated. "I see."

He nodded.

"So what did you do?"

Judy swallowed. She turned her gaze to her husband, and for the first time she saw concern, and maybe fear, in her calm husband's eyes.

Judy's heart was pounding, echoing in her ears. Her throat was full of acidic bile.

"Nothing much. I sang to them."

"What did you sing?"

"The Marching rhyme."

"And the children calmed down after your singing?"

"Yes."

"And you didn't do anything else? Apart from singing?"

Judy's gaze involuntarily dropped to her daughter sitting on her lap and pressed against her chest. Judy draped her arms tighter around her child and met the gaze of the officer.

"I lifted up the hands of a few of them, and clapped them, as I sang."

"You clapped their hands and sang... That's interesting."

The man nodded his head at her, his encouraging smile soft on his lips.

"And as you lifted their hands, did you notice anything... Shall we say, unusual... strange? Maybe something that struck you as odd at that time? Did anything worry you? Anything that you feel should have been reported?"

He leaned closer.

"If there was something, now would be the time to tell me."

The man's gaze was unyielding, his practiced smile directed at her.

But his smile was scarier than his heavy stare.

"Not really", Judy mumbled. "Their hands were maybe a bit sweaty, but I would've expected that, as it was a very warm day, and the children were stressed."

Judy didn't know why she was hiding from the officer the appearance of the raised blisters on the children's hands, why she didn't want to tell him about them. She didn't know why. Her self-preservation whispered to her to keep quiet.

"And was there anything else? Anything, that alerted or concerned you at the time? Maybe something had made you uncomfortable? Something, that scared you or didn't look right?"

Pulling on the last slither of her willpower and composure, she managed to shake her head, trying to make it as natural as she could.

"I don't think so."

"Okay."

The man nodded again, his smile glued to his lips.

"And then what?"

"Then, the ceremonial master said it was time for us to march, so we marched."

He nodded his head again.

"So, you and five disciplinarians managed to settle one hundred ninety seven children?"

"He knows everything", Judy finally realised.

But that didn't explain his arrival.

Although, he knew what happened, Judy couldn't understand what he wanted from her. *If* he knew everything, why he was here? Is it to reprimand her for the lack of discipline during the preparation? But they walked well in front of the podium, and as much as the children shuffled rather than marched and the disciplinarians had to pick the slack on the enthusiasm with the flag waving and cheering, it wasn't bad, definitely not to warrant a midnight arrival of The State Security half a week later.

She was afraid to look at Tom, to find a sudden frost in his eyes, to see the distance he was finally ready to put between himself and the "questionable element", as The State Security loved to call suspected traitors.

Judy swallowed. Lying here, right now, to the officer might be far worse than telling the truth.

But Judy still didn't understand what had happened, or why he was here. If she knew what he wanted from her, and what he was after, she might've been able to navigate this conversation better, but right now, she was in the dark.

She looked down at Tilly and stroked the top of her daughter's head.

"No. A few people from nearby columns helped us. They stepped in, and following my actions, they sang to the children and clapped children's hands."

There was no way Judy was about to bring her child into it, no matter what it was about or how dangerous it was.

She was taught well. She knew better. She knew more than her husband, and she knew not to make that mistake. But above all, she was confident that she had done nothing wrong.

But since when did that play any role in the arrests?

The officer nodded.

"Do you know these people? The ones who helped you? Have you seen them before? Do you know their names?"

Judy shook her head.

"No."

"Excuse me, but what is this about?" Tom asked again from his corner.

The officer didn't answer, as another officer in the black uniform came in, and leaning in, whispered something into his boss's ear. The man in charge nodded, looked at both Tom and Judy and nodded his man away.

"I apologise for such a manner of intrusion, fellows Whicker", he answered Tom. "We didn't mean to cause trouble."

He turned to Judy.

"But please, continue with your story, fellow Whicker. What happened then?"

"Then, we marched. We lined up the children. They held hands, and we marched. Following the procession, we walked into Liberation square, and when we arrived at the Political History Library, the buses were already there. The children boarded. I helped the disciplinarians with that, and then, they drove off. Later, I went to the park with my daughter. Then, in the afternoon, I visited my work. Although I was given a day off, I wanted to check that my sector was functioning well and everything was alright."

"And that's how we know that you are a true citizen, fellow Whicker", the man nodded, "putting objectives of the Ordained Liberating Party above your personal time, checking on your work on your day off. The country would do well having more interested workers like you, Judy. Thank you for your work."

It was now Judy's turn to nod in a way of response.

"What is it about?" Tom asked for the tenth time.

Judy shot him a glance. Repeating this question could have been a sentence in itself, but Tom believed in the true stance of the Party, in its fairness and its leaders. And he believed that he and his wife were irreproachable.

The man turned his attention to Tom. He scanned Tom's boxer shorts and the stretched t-shirt that had lost its colour, turning a faded shade of ochre grey, with the crest of the 1st Liberated Engineering University in the middle.

"I'm not at liberty to discuss it, fellow Whicker", the man answered, "but I can assure you that there's nothing you should worry about. There's nothing *you* need to concern yourself with. If you answered all questions honestly and to the full", the man's gaze darted to Judy, "then there's nothing you should worry about. The Party appreciates your help and your time, and your honesty is the most help you can provide."

The officer's smile was back. His words are not a veiled warning.

"Or a threat", Judy thought.

A female officer in the black uniform came into the room, carrying a small black briefcase. The insignia on her shoulders was the signage of the Liberated Medics Services, which until now, Judy had never seen on an Internal Police officer.

"There's one more thing, fellows Whicker", the man started. "We need a blood sample from both of you and from your child."

"What? Why?"

The questions slid off Judy's tongue, before she could remind herself to whom she's speaking, and what could be the punishment for noncompliance. They will always get what they needed, but at the end of it, she'd lose everything: her job, her family and even her life.

The man must've been in a forgiving mood today, as his lips stretched wider, showing white straight teeth, and he repeated: "I'm not at liberty to discuss, fellow Whicker."

Judy nodded, thrusting her arm forward, indicating her willingness.

The medic placed the briefcase on the bed next to her colleague.

She released the locks, lifted the top and began looking for the required equipment within the depths of the case.

She straightened and walked to Tom, carrying in her hand a short plastic pipette with a clear tube at the end.

"Hand", she commanded.

Tom outstretched his hand. A small metal tool flashed in the medic's hand, pricking Tom's finger. The pipette attached itself to the bleeding wound, sucking Tom's blood.

The medic twisted the head on the pipette, sealing the blood sample, and returning to her briefcase, she placed it inside, scribbling on it, probably signing the sample.

A minute later, she was standing above Judy with a new pipette.

"Hand."

The procedure was repeated, after which the woman returned with a pipette for Tilly.

Protectiveness, anger and panic battled inside Judy. If she was afraid before, now she was petrified.

Whatever they were doing, whatever they were investigating, it had something to do with these crying children, with the raised blisters on the children's hands, of which she refused to speak. There was something wrong with those children. If for nothing else, but for the fact that the State Security were now involved. Nothing is ever okay, when they show an interest in a matter.

Judy had never heard of good outcomes when this department barged in with their investigations. Never had she heard of police walking away with an apology, leaving the investigated in peace. The only stories she had heard were the disappearance stories.

She knew that objecting won't achieve anything, that fighting them won't help and will only make things worse. She knew that denying them this test will seem as if she's hiding something, and as much as she was, Tilly and Tom were innocent. She didn't want Tilly to get involved. She didn't want her child's name to appear on a record in that department. She didn't want them to know of her existence. To live undetected and unknown is the safest life Judy could grant her child.

"Excuse me, citizen."

Judy rose off the bed, addressing the man in charge.

"Is blood from my child completely necessary? As you can see, she is small and frightened, but she had all her vaccinations. I have her vaccination passport, which I'd be happy to show you. She is a healthy child. She hasn't missed a day of her nursery..."

Judy was toeing the line, and she knew it.

"Fellow Whicker, we need a blood sample from every member of your family, especially your daughter."

Judy swallowed, the dread blanketing her mind.

"Especially."

She nodded. And returning to her bed, she picked up Tilly, putting her on her lap.

"Hand", the woman above commanded.

"That's okay, darling. Mama's here. Mama's here. Don't look."

With one hand Judy picked up her child's wrist and stretched it out towards the woman. With her other hand, she pushed her daughter's face away from the metal tool in the woman's hand.

Tilly's cry ripped through the silence, tearing at Judy's heart.

"It's okay, darling. It's okay. It's almost done. There's a good girl. Who's a good girl?"

Judy gently rocked Tilly, whilst holding her tight.

"Done", the woman announced to the man, who nodded in acknowledgement. Without a glance at the patients, the medic clicked her briefcase shut and left the room.

The man got up and walked to where Judy and Tilly sat.

"You see? It's all done. It wasn't that bad, was it?"

In an attempt to mollify Tilly, or more precisely, *to appear* friendly, his voice found that cooing tone, which adults use when speaking to children, although the softness of the tone did not touch his face.

Tilly would have none of that. With the honesty of childhood, she continued to wail into her mother's nightgown, ignoring the powerful man.

The man straightened.

"That will be all. Thank you for your candour, fellow Whicker. Your recollection of the parade helped us a lot, and please be assured that there's nothing to worry about."

He turned to Tom.

"Let me see, if my colleagues have finished or if they have any questions for you. And if there's nothing, we'll be on our way."

He left the room, leaving Tom, Judy and whimpering Tilly in their bedroom, the sounds of his boots echoing in the next room, followed by a muffled conversation.

Tom came over and sat next to his wife.

"What's going on? What's this?" Judy began in a whisper, but Tom placed his hand on hers, interrupting her.

He shook his head.

"No", he mouthed.

He reached out, and taking Tilly from Judy's arms, he cuddled his daughter against his chest, rocking her as he used to, during so many nights when she was little.

***

"You didn't mention the parade..."

It was the dark hours of early morning.

Tom and Judy sat in the kitchen at the table facing each other, after spending the rest of the night straightening their flat.

The State Security officers never concerned themselves with suspects' belongings, and Tom and Judy's possessions were not treated any differently.

The drawers and doors of every cabinet in their flat were open. Their contents scattered in the leisurely manner of someone not searching for something in particular, but rather perusing in the hope of finding a kompromat, with which flat owners could be nailed, of someone, who had the power to do so, and who was not restricted by the pretence of legislation or care. A few large prints that Tom brought from his business trips to Schotlandia hung on the walls at an angle.

Tom and Judy sat in their bedroom for a while after the police left. They listened to the measured ticking of the kitchen clock and Tilly's soft whimpering. The man who never gave his name promised to be in touch, if they have more questions for Judy.

Exhausted, Tilly eventually settled, falling asleep in Tom's arms, coating his T-shirt in her drool.

"We need to talk", Tom whispered to Judy, careful not to wake their daughter.

Judy nodded.

"I know."

But she didn't know how to start. She was afraid of his anger and his blame, which could only end in divorce. So, postponing the inevitable, she walked into their family room and began tidying it.

Tom allowed her that time. After placing sleeping Tilly in her cot, he entered their family room and began collecting his blueprints and papers.

"Let's go and have tea", he said after an hour of silence, interrupted only with their soft steps and the stashing of their lives back into the drawers.

Keeping her gaze to the grey marbled floor of melted plastic panels, Judy nodded and followed her husband into the kitchen, in her mind churning her survival past their divorce.

She knew he would be granted the custody of their child. Judy wouldn't have a chance of contesting it. A questionable element versus one of the regime's most loyal and loving engineers? A court wouldn't take longer than a few minutes to decide on that. She would have to leave their flat. She didn't know where she would go. There was no one left. Hopefully, he would allow her to visit her daughter.

Judy was trying not to cry.

The content of the kitchen cabinets remained largely intact and inside the cupboards, apart from grains scattered out of already opened packets, spilled tea from the knocked and opened tin, and a few broken plates.

When they were ready to talk, the two mugs of warm tea and a half-finished bottle of drinking spirit, which was left from Tom and his friends celebrating achieving the quarterly target, stood on the table between them.

Tom picked the bottle of spirit and poured a generous amount of it into his mug. The bottle glugged.

"Want some?"

He lifted the bottle slightly, offering it to Judy.

"A bit."

Since the moment they left, she felt cold. Even now, with a jumper and thick woollen trousers on, wrapped in her winter coat, she still couldn't get warm. She was shaking.

The bottle glugged again.

Tom lifted his mug to his lips and drank.

"You said nothing about that day, not a word, and suddenly, we have the State Security pounding on our door in the middle of the night, asking questions. What happened there?"

"I'm sorry, Tom", Judy began, "maybe I should've told you, but I didn't think it was important. They were children. They were crying like children do. Even now, I don't see what the issue is –"

"*They* clearly see the issue."

Tom's low hissing was evident as to how much he held inside, cultivating the calmness.

Judy took a deep sip of her laced tea.

"I didn't know there was something to tell. I didn't know it was a big deal. I didn't realise. If I had suspected it would result in it, don't you think I would've told you immediately? I have nothing to hide. It's not like I did anything wrong. Don't you think if I would've suspected it would come to this, I wouldn't have told you?"

"Okay. Sorry", Tom grumbled.

He took another deep gulp, finishing his mug.

"Tell me about the parade. Tell me everything about that day... especially the things you hid from him."

Judy lifted her eyes to her husband's heavy gaze.

"Tell me *everything*, every detail. Don't leave anything out."

So she told him.

She told him about the crying children, about Tilly discovering how to soothe them, about her touching a boy's palm, feeling that strange layer of bubbles, which burst the moment they began to clap, with it calming the children. She told him about how these bubbles felt too. She told him about the spray they produced, and how it felt on her face.

She wasn't sure what was relevant and held importance and what had nothing to do with anything, being her feelings, personal, unfounded discomfort which could not be explained, but she told him everything. The threatening outcome of that day he knew already.

They sat across from each other, Judy's guilty gaze on her hands resting on the table, and Tom's on the top of her head.

"That's all. Now, you know everything."

They sat in silence, each occupied with their own thoughts.

Judy lifted her gaze to her husband, as a sudden thought occurred to her.

"What if it's not about the parade?" she whispered. "What if they came, because of what I said? On the morning of the parade –"

Tom's fist flew and hit the table. The bottle jumped and clinked.

"Stop! Stop talking, right now", Tom roared, leaning across the table, his face close to hers.

Judy slammed her mouth shut.

Tom's breathing was ragged. His nostrils were flaring.

Judy looked at her husband. She wanted to know his thoughts, but she was afraid of what she might find.

Tom pulled back himself and his ragged breathing, and slid down into his chair.

In just over an hour, the lights in every flat will come to life, growing brighter with every minute, waking people to a new productive day. The Broadcasting Units will burst with the voice of the state newsreader, giving the customary short greeting to the citizens of "the best country in the world".

Tom sat quietly, looking with an unseeing gaze into the black display behind her.

"Do you have any sick days left?"

He turned to Judy.

"Yes. I haven't used any this year. Both are left."

"Okay, that's what we're going to do. You call in sick today, and you call Tilly in sick too. Don't go out, don't speak to anyone, don't answer the phone", he issued instructions.

Dropping his gaze and his voice, he mumbled to himself: "I'll go to work and speak to Bill, and see if I can take his rounds checking the turbines..."

"Why?"

His head snapped up at the sound of Judy's voice.

"To pop into a few places and speak to a few people."

He looked at the clock on the wall.

"It's almost morning. I need to get ready."

Tom scanned the kitchen. His gaze slowed on his wife.

She felt as if he wanted to say something, but without a word, he got up from his chair and left the room.

The lights were growing brighter, as Judy sat in the kitchen.

The first booming sounds of the Broadcast startled her.

"Good morning, free citizens! Good morning and good day!"

The upbeat voice of the newsreader flooded Judy's small kitchen.

She turned in her seat, raising her gaze to the awoken Unit.

The newsreader was a groomed middle aged man with a cleanly shaven face and neat haircut. His smile was open and grateful, as if he believed himself that today was indeed a great day, a day worth celebrating. His navy jacket was offset by the background image of the sun rising above old buildings of New Bristol.

"Let's make today another great day! Let's achieve greatness today in the name of the Ordained Liberating Party. Let's make the future better and brighter for our children!"

A short brave intro rang after his words.

At the end of the music, a sombre mask came over his face, as he settled to read the segment of the morning news.

"News at six", he announced.

"The synthetic food production continues to gather speed. Thanks to the great leadership of our Party and its scientists, synthetic food production will be expanded into manufacturing later this month. The back-breaking labour of plowing fields and peasants' slavery will become things of the past with this new discovery. Now, every farmer would be free to pursue his dreams, achieving greatness in the name of the Party, whilst freeing so much needed land for the residential developments expansions."

He paused for a couple of seconds, before moving on to another bit of news.

"The negotiations between our Party and the Royalists of the Southern Frankia hiding a fugitive, who calls himself a duke of Old England and claiming to be the last survivor of the extinguished royal family, continue..."

Judy rose from her chair, plodding into the bedroom to check on Tilly, before she notifies her daughter's nursery and her own work of their absence.

Tom walked out of the bathroom, dressed in a blue shirt and trousers. As a project manager, he was allowed to wear his civil clothes and was not expected to wear the uniform of the energy workers, only required to wear it during official meetings and parades.

He was about to stride into the bedroom, but noticing Judy in the small and narrow corridor, he turned to her, taking a step closer.

He reached and pulled her into his embrace.

"Stay in. Don't go out, just in case. I'll be home usual time."

He stopped for a moment, drew in air, wanting to add something, but changed his mind.

"Stay in", he repeated, before leaning in and giving her a kiss.

He strode into their small bedroom, already filled with artificial sunlight, streaming from the ceiling.

"Morning, cat. How are you today?"

Judy walked in after him.

Tom sat on Tilly's small bed. A smile tugged at his lips, as he watched his daughter rubbing her sleepy eyes.

"I'll be back later, but today, you're unwell. You and your mum are going to stay home."

"I am? We are?"

Tilly yawned.

"You sure are. Look how sleepy you are. I think you're coming down with something."

Keeping his voice light, he placed his hand on her forehead.

"I'm right."

He shook his head, pulling a serious face.

"I can fry eggs on your forehead."

And when Tilly raised her confused gaze to the man, of whom she knew so little, the worry knitting her eyebrows, Tom added: "But not to worry, your mama's great at mending little girls. You'll be back at the nursery tomorrow."

He leaned in and kissed her forehead.

"You stay here with your mama. I won't be long."

"Okay, fellow Whicker."

"Dad", he corrected her.

"Dad", she repeated obediently.

He leaned in, giving his child a tight hug. Her body was warm, smelling of milk and that impossible to replicate the scent of a young child.

Judy was right. They don't see her enough.

But he pushed these thoughts out, before they took hold, reminding himself that it was the life of everyone else in the country and not only theirs, and whatever sacrifices they were making, it would be worth it in the end. Their hard work, his and Judy's, will make their child's life better, and he was willing to take that, knowing that his daughter would have a better life than his.

Tom exhaled, briefly closing his eyes.

"Behave."

He got up and in two steps reached a small desk in the corner of their bedroom, at which he spent many nights finishing projects and calculations for the latest turbines, writing memos and operating instructions for the workers, on whom he relied for the functioning of his turbines.

Breakdowns of turbines were investigated. The reasons for the breakdowns were examined and scrutinized. Those, who were at fault, were prosecuted for sabotage or espionage. Tom was the third project manager on this line in the last five years.

He scooped a few papers and shoved them into his briefcase. He opened the top drawer, and after digging there for a while, he pulled out an envelope and stuffed that into the briefcase too.

"Don't leave the flat", he repeated, straightening up and closing the locks on his case.

"Please tell me, you're not angry with me", Judy said quietly, when Tom reached her on his way out of the room.

"Of course I'm not."

A smile pulled at Tom's lips without touching his eyes.

"Will everything be okay?" she asked.

"Of course it will."

And with another fleeting kiss, he walked out of the flat, the front door closing behind him.

Standing in the small hall by the front door, Judy turned her head towards the Unit, where the elastic woman bent and stretched her every limb and muscle, encouraging physical activity in the country's free citizens.

Chapter 5

"Bill! Bill!" Tom called across a long corridor. "Just the man I'm looking for."

Once through the security line at the building, which was moving surprisingly slow this morning, the patting of the bodies taking longer, the metal detectors beeping slower, only the X-ray security machine buzzed with usual determination to find spies, and after clocking in with a scanner by the door of his department, Tom walked into a large room with wide, floor to ceiling windows that his department occupied.

He strolled to his desk, calling out good morning greetings and sharing the nods along the way with engineers and their managers.

Tom pulled the papers out of his briefcase and scattered them over his desk. He took the blueprints of the new turbine farm out of a drawer in his desk and spread them too, as if busy at work, before announcing that he has a briefing "upstairs", and grabbing a thick roll of the calculations, he left the room in a search of the man he needed.

The Energy Department building was vast.

Sprawled over six floors, with an immense underground level, the building stood in the centre of New Bristol, towering above other smaller and older buildings, one of its sides pressed against the water. The network of wide passages congregated in the centre of the building, under the limitless ceiling, and wide metal stairs and large rooms were coming out of each corridor.

This building was Tom's home away from home. In this building he spent most of his days and most of his life. It held The Liberated Energy Research Labs with The Party Energy headquarters, their engineering departments and The Liberated Electric Transport department.

During The Collapse, many buildings crumbled, with many more becoming unstable. But this building stood, losing only its smaller limbs attached to the central one and the glass in its wide windows and the ceiling. Otherwise, the building remained strong.

The Party historians devised that three hundred years ago, this used to be a church for the latest monarchy, where different religions were preached on different floors and the worshipers would flock to this building on their days off to praise their deities, thanking their current rulers for allowing such different, yet agreeable, religions to coexist under one roof. The historians said that people were brainwashed in these walls every Sunday, which was apparently the day of worship for the country then.

But before the line of the Party and its history was agreed and solidified, Tom heard his grandfather's friend once mentioning that this building in the centre of New Bristol, taking prime location with its sprawling pride, used to be a trading station, where on their days off, residents of the city would go to spend their money, purchasing goods their heart desired, later stating that the entire building was stocked to the rafters with things for sale.

His grandfather's friend agreed with the historians only on one thing: this building was busiest on Sundays.

But Tom couldn't wrap his mind around the fact that a building that vast, that huge, could be filled with different produce for sale. The country had never produced that much. Tom hasn't seen, and couldn't contemplate, that amount of things being manufactured, then sitting for sale on the crowded shelves, waiting to be bought. His imagination was not able to take him that far.

When rolls of woollen fabric from Schotlandia would come on the shelves in the Party shops, or shoes for children, or suits for men, the line would gather and form immediately, the stock sold out within minutes, leaving many citizens empty handed and the shops bare again.

The notion that this huge building was a trading centre of some sort was so ludicrous, so far-fetched, that Tom decided that the building indeed was a worshiping house, and his grandfather's friend was wrong in his recollection. But before Tom could grow up and direct these questions to the man himself, his grandfather's friend stopped coming. Someone said that he had died.

The water facing side of the building was occupied by the heads of departments, who found joy in watching the river, whilst planning and organising the development and delivery of the latest energy equipment for the country's needs.

Tom marched down the corridors, up and down the metal staircases cutting through the belly of the building, his purpose measured by the wide stride of his boots. He nodded in greetings and acknowledgement to the people he met, whilst scanning the corridors and the room openings from them.

Finally, spotting the man he needed, he turned around and sprinted in the opposite direction, cutting through another staircase.

"Bill, Bill!"

The man stopped and turned towards Tom.

"Just the man I'm looking for."

Tom gave his friend a wide smile.

"How are you? How's Veronica?" he asked, when he approached.

"Hi, Tom."

The men shook hands.

"Not bad, thanks. Veronica is alright. She was sent to Carlisle to investigate the low birth rate in sheep this year, so was away for a month now, and I don't know when she'll be back. How is your family? How's Tilly? I can't believe how big she is now. I saw her and Judy at the parade. Tilly looks so grown up. She's growing into a gorgeous girl, Tom. You're a lucky man, managed to get your permission, before they paused the procreation plan..."

Bill wavered, before snapping his gaze back to Tom and finding his smile.

"But I don't mind. Hopefully, it'll be released again, and then Veronica and I will be at the head of the line."

"I hope so too, Bill."

Tom paused for a moment, before jumping to the reason he chased Bill for the last hour down these corridors.

"Bill, you are due for the wind turbines inspection in the Freedom Quarters today, right?"

"Yes."

His friend nodded, giving an indifferent shrug.

"It's a quarterly inspection there. Why?"

"Listen, would you mind if I inspect those today? You'll do me a huge favour. You see, one of my engineers thinks that he might've not programmed the generator properly. And if the turbines' exploitation starts with that fault... Well, you know...."

They both knew the investigation, and the subsequent punishment, the failure or damage of the turbine would bring on the entire department, and not just on a sloppy engineer. The department would be under the microscope for months to come.

"I need to check his work, and not just on that turbine."

And watching Bill's worried gaze, with occasional glances around them, Tom added: "Of course, I'll record the failures and discrepancies. I find and report these, along with the engineer, to Steve and the Party committee."

Bill nodded.

"You know that whatever you think might be there, I'll probably find myself during the inspection?"

"Of course, of course. It might be nothing. He doesn't remember if the controller was connected to the generator or not. It's quite possibly nothing. I've checked each approved design myself, as these were the latest to develop. If there's nothing, I'll be able to sleep at night, and if there's something... I'll do the right thing..."

Tom let the intimation hang for a while.

As Bill stood, unconvinced, not rushing to agree, Tom continued: "I'm certain, it's nothing. I just need to check. I'll carry out the inspection for you at the same time. You'd be able to do all of your work for the week today and take a train up North, and see Veronica..."

Something shifted behind Bill's eyes.

Veronica's name, the name of his lovely wife, whom he hasn't seen in months and was only able to speak three times a week on the scheduled and pre-arranged by her work call, with each conversation lasting no more than an hour, stirred him. If they had a child, Veronica would not have been sent that far, and if sent, these would have been shorter trips, and the visual communication would have been allowed to go on for twice as long.

"Okay. I'll give you the report form to complete. But if you find any discrepancies, anything at all... If there's anything..."

"Bill, I swear. I will let you know."

Bill stepped closer to Tom and held his friend's gaze.

"I mean it", he added low.

"I know", Tom answered, just as quietly. "I will."

The Party didn't forgive or excuse "screw ups".

It had no time or scope for mistakes. The mistakes were seen and presented as sabotage. Everyone was held accountable for everything they did, each citizen carrying a personal responsibility for the quality of work, he or she completed for the country.

"Fine. Come, I'll give you the forms."

An hour later, Tom sat in a rattling tram.

This late in the morning and past rush hour, the trams run empty. The announcement board under the ceiling of the tram, lit red and with white round letters running across it delivered the summary of the latest news headlines.

But the tram wasn't taking Tom into the Freedom Quarters. It carried him in the opposite direction – into the micro settlement, where he and his wife lived, and in which Tilly's nursery stood.

The weak stream of the passengers thinned out the further away from the city centre the tram went. The landscape changed, now filled with tall and windowless high risers.

Tom pressed the buzzer on the handle, asking the driver to stop, and when the tram rolled to a stop, Tom jumped off its steps, starting into the settlement, walking between the grey buildings and into the depths of their micro settlement, towards the familiar one storey building.

The nursery occupied a low building surrounded by a tall, mesh metal fence and locked within a circle of five wide tower blocks. Behind the fence, the building sprawled over a large area of weathered yellow grass, cut into slices by the asphalt pavements. The play equipment of sand boxes, metal slides and climbing frames, swings with chipped paint, which squeaked slightly with a wind, were dotted within.

This hour, the playground was free of children.

Tom came to the metal gate carved within the fence and pressed the buzzer.

The trill of the bell echoed through the intercom, before waking its black box with a human voice.

"Yes?"

"Hi, my name is Tom Whicker. I'm Tilly's dad."

"Oh, yes. Morning, fellow Whicker. How's Tilly today? Your wife called, said she's unwell. I hope she feels better soon."

The young female voice sounded familiar.

"Thank you. Sorry, is it Beth or Jen?"

"It's Jen, fellow Whicker. How can I help?"

The intercom spoke, but the gate didn't rush to open.

"Jen, can I please come in? I'm looking for Tilly's bunny. We can't find it anywhere. Tilly's ear really hurts today and she's crying, struggling to sleep, so me and my wife... well, we're at the end of our tether. We looked everywhere around the flat, but it's not there. She must've left it in the nursery..."

"I can look for you", the voice offered. "If you could come back in the evening –"

"Jen, please", Tom interrupted. "We won't survive until the evening."

Tom smiled into the intercom, hoping that his smile would translate into his fatherly despair, softening the girl's heart.

"Please", Tom begged. "What if I come in, quickly check her locker, while you check the playgroup, and I'll be out. It will take five minutes. Besides, you don't know what the bunny looks like. Jen, please, I won't be long. I took an hour off work, so I can pick up that damned bunny."

Silence and breathing took over the black intercom, eventually followed by a resigned sigh.

"Okay, fellow Whicker. Only please, fast."

"Of course, Jen, of course."

"Come through."

The intercom buzzed and the metal gate clicked.

Tom walked towards the building, marching down the narrow cracked asphalt.

When he reached the entrance to the building, Jen was already there, standing, waiting for him.

She was a smiley girl in her early twenties, with bright red hair and a faint lull of an Irish accent.

"Please come in, fellow Whicker, but please, let's be fast. We just sat the children down for lunch, so the locker room and the playgroup will be empty."

"Thank you very much, Jen. You are a life saver. Thank you."

Tom was smiling and gushing gratitude, as he stepped through the door.

He followed Jen down the familiar corridor, towards the locker room where he would take Tilly on Monday mornings, helping her to take off her shoes and her coat, settling her for another week at the nursery.

The corridor of the nursery smelled different today. It held something he didn't remember finding here prior. In the mornings, the nursery would smell of the floor washed with disinfectant, and in the evenings, it would smell of children, of the warm scent of children's skin, with a bit of brought-up milk and washing powder.

But today, a new scent loitered in the corridor.

Tom could've said it was bacon, if not for the lingering scent of a new tyre somewhere underneath, and the scent of grains, possibly pearl barley, had the drier tinge of metal to it. These could have been food smells, if not for the strange aftertaste they left on Tom's tongue as if cooked food scent was created in a lab, like perfume.

"Lunch?" Tom asked, and when Jen glanced at him over her shoulder, he waved his hand around him, lifting his nose upwards, as if smelling.

"Oh, yes. It's that new synthetic food everyone's talking about on the news. We've had it delivered and cooked for us for a couple of months now. Because of the high concentration of nutrients, the nurseries and schools were the first to receive the meals. Now it's been rolled out to municipal diners and cafes, and soon, will be available for sale in the shops. And to think that we were the first ones to try..."

"It smells...different", Tom commented.

"Yeah, I know. At first, I wasn't sure either, but once heated, the food tastes really nice, especially the grain dishes. It's been ages since the last time I had a wheat stew, but this one tastes almost like I remember it used to. The children are enjoying the meals too."

"Our Party is truly the greatest", Tom answered with the slogan that was often called out at demonstrations and meetings, this phrase serving as an appropriate response to every occasion.

Every wall in the locker room was occupied by the narrow cabinets, holding children's possessions. A child's name and an image of a long extinct animal were glued to their doors, helping the children to find their lockers, before they knew how to read. The lockers boasted pictures of an elephant, a whale, a giraffe, birds, names of which Tom didn't know, and different butterflies, which he'd seen only in his school biology book. Apparently, three hundred years ago all of these were alive, roaming the Earth.

Inside the room Tom turned to the right wall, coming closer to the locker with a drawing of a fat black and white bird, which lived somewhere up North. As a child, Tom used to question the existence of this animal and the biologist's information about it, which claimed that although a bird, it never flew, all drawings of the monochromatic creature being of the animal roaming snow-covered ground. Back in school, Tom and his mate Jack were convinced that this animal never existed, confused by the biologists with fairy tales of hundreds of years ago.

Tom tugged the locker's door open and began to rummage inside.

"Thank you very much for this, Jen. We barely slept last night. Her ear infection was giving her trouble, and she would cry and cry, calling for her bunny. We looked everywhere."

Tom's voice boomed around him, inside the slim plastic cabinet.

"Fellow Whicker, what the bunny looks like? I can check the playgroup", Jen asked his back.

"Um..."

Tom hesitated.

There was no bunny.

Tom needed to come here, needed to speak to her or ideally to Beth, but he couldn't blurt out why he was there. He couldn't tell either of them the real reason behind his visit. The metal gate would've never opened for him otherwise.

Now, he needed to think of how to bring up the State Security's interest in his family with this girl, if she had a similar visit, and what they asked her about the day of the Parade, or if officers said more to her. Tom needed to find out what she knew.

"Grey. Small, floppy and grey", Tom mumbled.

"Okay, I'll check the playgroup."

"Right, it's not here."

Tom straightened, closing the door of the locker.

"Shall I come with you? We'll be done sooner if I help."

Jen stood for a second, thinking about it, biting her lip.

"Okay. But please, fellow Whicker, if we don't find Tilly's bunny in ten minutes, I'll have to ask you to leave. The children will be back from lunch."

"Of course."

Tom followed Jen into the adjoining room filled with toys, tiny desks surrounded by tiny chairs, and cube shelves stacked around the room, no higher than Tom's mid-thigh.

"Do you want to check in the soft toys area?"

Jen pointed to the corner of the room, under the window, and without waiting for Tom's reply, she walked into the opposite corner, where more toys were scattered.

"Judy told me about the Parade", Tom began, as he moved the soft bodies of knitted and synthetic fur toys. "Sounded like a lot of hard work..."

A sudden stillness came from Jen's corner. The bodies of the toys stopped shuffling. Jen's breathing went quiet, as if she had held her breath.

"Um... yes. It was a bit...tricky. How did you?.. Oh, of course, Judy... you just said."

83

Tom continued his pointless shuffle as a heavy gaze rested on his back. He could practically taste the silence, flavoured generously with the synthetic food.

"Fellow Whicker, did Tilly really lose her rabbit?"

The question came suddenly, yet was somewhat expected.

With a carefully arranged confused expression and the ready smile on his face, Tom turned to the young woman. But collided with Jen's gaze, his face fell too. And after a few seconds of back and forth in his mind, on how to handle this situation, he decided to tell her why he came here, or at least to be honest about some of it.

"Judy told me about what happened at the Parade, and I'm a bit concerned. No, no, I don't blame you, don't worry. I know it was out of your hands. It's just... I am worried. I've heard other citizens got involved. The ceremonial master was displeased with Judy. I'm concerned with them contacting her work... or if someone comes..."

As he said the last phrase, Tom watched Jen.

The colours drained from her face. The splash of fear behind her open eyes and her caught breathing told him everything he needed to know.

"Someone" did come for them too. The State Security paid her visit, maybe even the same officer.

Jen stood silent for a moment, blinking, watching him.

"I think Judy will be alright", she eventually pushed out. "Well, of course I don't know, but I think she has nothing to worry about. They've already questioned us..."

She dropped her gaze.

"Whatever it was, it wasn't about the Parade..."

"What? What do you mean?"

She lifted her gaze to him. Her lips were pressed together, and her face had closed off.

"Fellow Whicker, you have to leave now. The lunch is over, and the children will be back soon."

"Jen, but what do you mean? Why wasn't it about the Parade? What was it about then? Do we still have something to worry about? Will somebody come for Judy?"

"You have to leave, now, or I'll report your presence as unsanctioned intervention, with breaking in."

She looked into his eyes and added in a whisper: "Please."

The young woman was upset, scared. She was pleading with him. She was already in a lot of trouble, and Tom didn't want to add any more. He always liked Tilly's disciplinarians. Both girls loved their job and the children in their care. Tilly loved going to the nursery.

"Of course. I'm sorry, Jen. Thank you."

He turned around and walked out of the room, past the lockers, towards the main entrance.

The corridors were still empty, but the children's laughter and chatter rang louder past the closed doors. Lunch was about to finish.

Jen's light steps sounded behind him.

He turned to face her once again.

"I'm sorry, Jen."

Her eyes met his, but she didn't say anything else.

She nodded and pressed the button on the door. The lock clicked, and Tom stepped out onto the cracked asphalt.

The door closed behind him as he walked down the steps, then turning the opposite direction from the way he came.

The metal fence around the nursery had two gates: the main one, through which he came, and another gate, at the back of the building, opening onto a narrow footpath, leading deeper into the settlement.

From this location, if stepping off the pavement and slightly to the right, Tom could see a corner of the blind tower where he lived, and where Judy and Tilly were waiting for him.

He would see them in the evening, but for now, he would take a tram to the other side of the city, to inspect the wind turbines, as he had promised.

He buttoned his jacket, lifting the collar against the May wind, which promised impending rain and thunder, and pressing the release button on the gate, he stepped through it.

Chapter 6

Tom managed only a dozen steps down the path and was almost under the cover of a nearby tower block, when the revving of engines and screeching of tires cut through the quiet of the midday.

The engines grew louder, belonging to different vehicles. The lighter sounds of two cars were interlaced with the deep rumbling of trucks.

The cars and trucks were an uncommon sight in the settlement.

Every Monday morning a rubbish truck would come, collecting the rubbish from the communal bins that sat on the ground floor of each building. But apart from that, vehicles rarely came into Tom's domain.

Only when residents moved, a hired packing truck might come, carrying their belongings, and maybe a couple of times in his ten years living here, he saw a department car bringing a neighbour, who'd been working on a time-sensitive project and was allowed to collect clean clothes, and give his wife a fleeting kiss, before disappearing again in the depths of his work for a few weeks.

The simultaneous arrival of a few engines alarmed Tom. The rumbling sound of their engines was out of place, and following his own survival rulebook, the one that he perfected during his childhood, Tom ran the remaining distance to the nearest tower and pressed himself against its concrete side.

The sound of the engines grew closer, and for a moment Tom thought about turning and walking away, not to be seen here, not to have any association with whatever might be happening. But he didn't know where the engines were going. What or *who* was their destination. Running in that situation was as dangerous, as staying in the open.

Tom shuffled along the wall, until he reached a cluster of low shrubs filled with soft, oily green leaves. He slid down behind them, now shrouded by the shadow of the building and the foliage of the bush.

The sounds of the arriving vehicles burst into the opening, bouncing off the surrounding buildings, before stopping by the main gate of the nursery through which Tom had walked not so long ago, under the pretence of a lost bunny.

But one engine kept rumbling, its noise moving around the low building, and soon, a large military grade truck with a green tarp over its bed has turned a corner, stopping by the back gate.

The truck's black metal body and its green tarp were void of any insignia, not allowing Tom to assign it to any department.

The buzz of the intercom whizzed in the distance, followed by the prompt swing of the main gate.

A few pairs of heavy boots struck the pavement.

A voice called a command, followed by the scattering of the boot laced feet.

The bushes in front and the truck by the back gate obstructed Tom's view.

Now, knowing the destination of the vehicles, he argued with himself as to whether he should move away whilst he still could, or if he should stay here and wait, to see what the trucks wanted.

If it were any other place or any other building, he probably would have left. But this was his daughter's nursery. It was the place that was connected to him and his family, and after the Parade, with the subsequent midnight visit of the State Security unit, leaving his hiding spot and not finding out what was going on was out of the question.

Tom knew that if he was spotted in this place, he would be done for sure. He would be arrested, especially if they didn't want witnesses, or arrested because he simply was not supposed to be here. But he went into the nursery to find things out and now was his chance.

The footsteps, fanning around the nursery's perimeter, brought into Tom's view a State Security officer. His sealed in the black uniform body moved along the metal net fence, taking up a post within the nursery's grounds, with another officer progressing further behind the fence. The long black rifles balanced in their arms.

Tom's heart pushed against his ribcage.

The nursery was encircled. His child's nursery, the nursery, where Tilly would've been today if not for his decision to keep her home, was surrounded by State Security troops.

The situation was no longer "too close to home". It had walked into his home, making Tom's life its business. For the second time in the last twenty four hours, his life was invaded.

The State Security arrival into his home last night felt like an oversight, a misunderstanding of sorts that would clear up any time now, a huge and scary mistake, which will go away, vanish, if he stayed quiet and worked hard, behaving and not stepping out of line.

They would see what a great citizen he was, how much he loved and respected his Party. They would see it in his heart. They would appreciate everything he has done for the Party. How he never believed any of the lies whispered by the Party haters, how he knew that these stories were disinformation spread by enemies of the state, and how the Party wanted only what is best for its people. If they knew the trust, the complete and utter trust he had in decisions of the Party's leaders, they'd know that there was no agenda and that he had nothing to hide, because he has done nothing wrong. He only did his best. He loved the Party as much as he loved his family.

But now, watching this, he was confused. He was lost. He didn't know what to do or how to explain the arrival of these officers. The black uniforms of State Security and Internal Police had no business in a nursery.

There was nothing for them there. They should not be here, let alone with those cars and trucks, encircling the building, while carrying rifles, *weapons,* around the building filled with young children.

Tom's heart was beating fast, his fear and confusion spilling out.

The nursery was quiet. No cries or screams were coming from the closed doors of the building, and Tom hoped that that was a good sign. Maybe the troops went inside to ask for directions, and having received them, were about to leave.

But something deeper inside him told Tom that it wasn't true, that his wishful thinking was far off the mark.

For the first time in his life, Tom cursed the sealed tower blocks design. He wished that the sounds of the engines would have been heard in the flats, that their arrival would have been seen and noticed, maybe questioned.

But the blind buildings were shut off to the outside world. At this time of day, only Party Broadcasting Units kept sick and elderly residents company.

At the exact time when Tom wished for visibility and transparency, for witnesses, a door into a tower block opposite the nursery swung open, letting out a middle aged man in a tartan jacket and black trousers, with a hat on top of his head and an orange flat briefcase in his hand.

Tom felt elated as if his wishes were granted. He was about to smile.

The man was a nomenclature worker. They were always easy to spot.

They had a different posture and look to other citizens. With their straight backs, with gazes drawn down to the rest of society, with lips fastened into a tight disapproving line, they were above the rest. With higher security clearance and above average access to the government's plans, and coming with those associated perks, these free citizens carried themselves with self-worth and importance that oozed out of their every pore – from the way they glanced at the world, to the way they interacted with it. They carried themselves with pride. They were the only group of citizens carrying permission for a late arrival into work.

Of course, this man didn't work in a ministerial position, otherwise he would have been residing in the Old Town, but he worked for The Party nonetheless.

"Mind you, we all do", Tom thought.

The man's wide body froze on the top step, his head moving from side to side, as his gaze scanned the State Security trucks, cars and the uniformed officers past the mesh metal fence. Tom couldn't see the man's face.

The man was immobile only for a moment, before with unexpected for his large frame speed, he turned on the spot, and ripping the door open, disappeared inside the building as if he was never there.

With the man's disappearance, something slacked inside Tom.

By the hushed conversation and dropped glances, he knew of the fear some free citizens had for the State Security and Internal Police force. He remembered the stories he'd heard, shared in whispers and abruptly stopped the moment he walked into the room. He remembered the glances citizens would give him, when he, as a child, marched amongst the column of the Liberated Youth Squad in the Liberation Day parade. He saw their fear.

But Tom thought that as much as the Party was strict – how could it not be, when it was surrounded by enemies wanting its collapse? – the Party was fair.

It was fair in everything and to every citizen. Its laws were transparent and just, everyone receiving a fair trial and given a chance to explain and defend themselves.

His childhood righteousness and loyalty awoken, Tom chastised himself for hiding in the shadows, as if he had done something wrong, as if he was against the Party and no longer trusted its decisions, when a sudden thought came forward, bursting with poison: *"Maybe I* have *something to hide. Maybe last night meant exactly that? That I should hide, that I've done something wrong, if not me then at least my family."*

"But what did my daughter and wife do that was so bad? What?" he was arguing with himself. *"If anything they helped the situation at the Parade. Judy sorted it. Without her help, it could've been much worse."*

Tom rose from behind the bushes. He straightened his back and lifted his chin, about to leave the embarrassing hideout, returning on his way to the tram station from which he'll go and do the promised inspections, when the double doors of the nursery opened.

The two young disciplinarians, the ones Tom had seen before working in parallel with Tilly's group, came out of the building and descended down the stairs. A man in the black uniform of the State Security followed them, telling them something.

Both girls nodded. And turning to the open doors, they called something into the depths of the building, the wind carrying only one word to Tom: "us".

The nursery children, in twos and holding hands, appeared through the doors and descended the stairs. They came out following the instruction of the disciplinarians – the women who they knew better than their own mothers, the young women who loved them too.

The two disciplinarians waited for the children at the bottom of the stairs and once the children joined them, the disciplinarians turned, walking down the path that weaved past the sandpits and swings, leading the children towards the main gate. And the children followed them, in a thin stream of soft bodies and shuffling steps.

Turning the corner, the stream disappeared.

The wide open doors stood empty, but not for long.

Beth and Jen came through them, out and down the stairs, leading their children after them.

Another officer ran down the stairs, joining the disciplinarians at the bottom. As the young women turned, about to follow the direction of the previous group, the officer waved his arm in Tom's direction, towards the back gate, saying something to the girls.

Tom's mouth was dry and his head spun. His decision to rise up and walk away had long since dissolved.

The earlier panic came back, a dark and hidden at the back of his mind, the dusted and forgotten memory coming forefront. Tom felt as if he was witnessing something bad, but he couldn't understand why or what had brought that feeling.

The exercised logic of the Party-led education told him that he had no evidence to back up his fear. But something inside him didn't let the panic to loosen its grip. Was it the quiet of the escorted children? Was it the out-of-place contrast of black uniforms next to the blue slides and the squeaking red swing?

Nothing bad has happened, nothing worth worrying or panicking about. There was nothing tangible he could present to anyone should someone ask, apart from the fact that it was State Security.

He was telling himself that maybe the children were going on an excursion, a trip, organised or sponsored by the State Security department. The department can't be only about dark whispers and disappearances. The department was about keeping the peace too, and the visit to his flat last night was purely a coincidence.

But no matter how many times he repeated those qualifiers in his mind, the awful gnawing wouldn't leave him.

He was pacifying himself, and he knew it.

What he didn't know for sure, was how bad it was. Tom kept watching.

Beth and Jen nodded to the officer, and calling to the children, they waved their hands towards the back gate and the children followed.

The back gate buzzed, clicked then swung open, letting through Beth, then Jen, and then the children, in pairs and holding hands.

Tom recognised the children. These were Tilly's playgroup friends, her classmates. Some of them came to the door of their flat a few times, calling Tilly to come out and play. Tom knew the parents of some of the children and most of them were their neighbours. Some of the parents worked in Tom's building and some worked with Judy.

There was no laughter between the children, no hushed or excited whisper. They weren't chatting, laughing or singing, something that Tom witnessed every time he passed a crowd of small free citizens on their way to a museum or a theatre. The children were concerned and unsure, maybe even scared. The faces of their disciplinarians were guarded too.

When they came closer, Tom could see concern and fear on the young women's faces. He could see their gazes darting up the blind, grey buildings – maybe looking to be saved, maybe for support or instruction.

An officer jumped out of the cabin of the truck, and unbolting the back panel of the bed, he lowered the steep metal ladder. The ladder hit the ground, vibrating for a few seconds.

An officer came through the back gate, bringing up the rear of Tilly's class, and strode towards the back of the truck.

Tom's eyes were consuming the man's face.

It was the same officer who came into his flat last night – the one, who was asking the questions and the one, who never gave his name.

The officer marched past the lined up children of Tilly's class, and swinging his hand at the truck, he said something to both disciplinarians.

After a quick glance at him, both women nodded. And with another scan around the quiet area of the micro settlement, Beth ascended the metal ladder, disappearing in the back of the truck.

Fumbling with their feet and holding tightly to the vibrating stairs, the children climbed up after her, one at a time. Jen stood at the base, smiling softly at the children and saying reassuring words in a hushed voice, as she helped them climb.

But the progression was painfully slow. And after picking up a radio at his waist, the officer issued an instruction.

Following his command, two officers came running towards the truck, strapping their rifles onto their backs. With a short nod at the officer in charge, they began picking up children by their waists, lifting and throwing them into the truck's bed. The soft bodies hit the wooden planks and cries began to ring.

Faster now, the children began disappearing inside the black truck.

Jen shuffled backward, but her arm was caught in the vice of the officer's grip. With a smile he said something, nodding at the truck, and she climbed up the ladder, following her children.

Another group of children came out of the nursery's back gate, following Beth and Jen's group. More children were thrown unceremoniously into the truck.

The children in the truck were crying now. Their panicked wails were answered by the cries coming from the truck at the main gate.

The driver turned around, asking something the officer, who then nodded with permission. The driver lifted the back of the truck's bed and, slamming it against its sides, he bolted the edge into its original position, sealing in the cargo.

Unrushed and ignoring the cries, the midnight interrogating officer walked around the truck and climbed into the black cabin, the driver jumping into the cabin after him.

The engine revved, echoed by the deep rumbling of the truck on the other side of the nursery. Clumsily, the black truck turned in a wide circle and drove off, leaving the settlement and following the fading sounds of the other engines.

Tom no longer could deny what he had seen. He couldn't pull his eyes away from the nursery.

He knew that he needed to move, to go somewhere, to tell someone, to do something, but he didn't know what to do or where to go, his mind and his body frozen. Instead, he sat on the dry soil, his unseeing gaze pinned on the low building.

"...*Tilly could have been there...*"

Tom rose up on his numb legs. Stumbling, he turned and walked, striding towards the building where his child was, still protected by him and his wife.

Tom's steps widened the closer to the building he got. And before he realised it, he was running full speed towards his tower block.

He flew up the stairs, into the dark and narrow lobby and pressed the button of the lift. But he couldn't stay still, he couldn't wait. An irrational fear of being locked in a metal cabin, unable to reach his child had made the decision for him, and no longer waiting for the lift, he kicked the door to the staircase and began running up the grey stairs.

He was out of breath when he reached his floor. His heart was punching at his throat and his legs were weak.

Tom fumbled with his keys. But unable to stem the jitter of his fingers, he jumped at the door, his fist thumping on its smooth surface.

"Judy! Judy! It's me, open up. Open! It's me!"

The lock clicked and the door cracked open.

Tom pushed it wider and stepped through, pushing Judy into the flat with him, slamming the door shut.

"Tom? What's wrong? Why aren't you at work?"

The flat was filled with a white noise coming from the Broadcasting Unit. This time it was joyful flute music, with sounds of trees rustling in the wind and chirping birds weaved into the background. Never being at home during the day,

Tom wasn't sure if that music was normal or if it was something else he should be worried about.

He marched into their bedroom, Judy trailing behind him.

He reached to the top of the wardrobe, yanking the two worn suitcases.

"Pack! Now!"

He threw the suitcases to the floor.

"What? Tom, what do you mean?"

"Pack, now. Light, a bit of clothing, not much, all of the money we have and anything we can sell."

"Tom, wha –"

He spun to her, and grabbing her by her shoulders, he brought his face close to hers.

"Pack. Now. We're leaving."

"Tom, you are scaring me. What's going on?"

Tom let go of her and began opening the drawers, throwing clothing into the suitcase they used for their last biennial holiday that is approved for all free citizens. Last summer they spent two weeks in Welsh Territories.

Tom span towards the door. His daughter stood by it.

Tom pulled his lips into a smile.

"Hi, darling. Shall we go on holiday, huh? The three of us? Wouldn't that be exciting?"

Tilly nodded, aware that it was the answer expected from her.

"Then grab your favourite teddy, pack two jumpers, trousers, a toothbrush, a hairbrush and a jacket. There's a good girl. Off you pop."

But Tilly stood where she was, her gaze jumping between the two strange people.

Tilly never packed her suitcase. She didn't know where her clothing was in this house. She knew where her belongings were in the nursery, but not here.

Tom turned, and leaving the bedroom, he strutted into their family room, to pack their documents and whatever little money they had saved.

Judy followed him, pleading with his back: "Tom, please, please stop. Tom, what's going on? What holiday? What's going on with you? Stop for a minute. Can you explain what's going on?"

Tom stopped and turned to her, only now realising how pale her face was.

He walked to the door and closed it, keeping his daughter out of what he was about to say.

"We have to leave the city, now. Last night, the visit... they will be back. They'll come again, and something... something isn't right. I just saw the State Security unit encircling Tilly's nursery, packing all of the children and all disciplinarians into the trucks and driving them off somewhere. Our last night visitor was there too."

Judy's hand flew to her mouth.

"We need to tell someone", she whispered, her voice was quiet and suffocated.

"Who?"

Tom gave a dry huff.

"I don't know... Someone", his wife insisted. "How about the children's parents? Someone should tell them..."

"It's not my problem. I have more important things to figure out."

"But, Tom..."

"They might've been told already, and if not, they will be told soon."

Saying these words, Tom suddenly realised how true they were. He didn't proceed to tell his wife that the parents might have been rounded up like their children already, packed into the black trucks and taken into the unknown too.

He held his wife's gaze, before saying it again, quieter this time and with more force: "We need to go, Judy. Now."

"Where are we going? Where *can* we go? There's nowhere to go, nowhere to run. We won't be able to get far. Our documents..."

She didn't need to finish that sentence.

They both knew that they'd need their documents to purchase tickets, along with a permission slip from their work for authorised absence, which they don't have and no one will issue them one. Their attempt to leave the city would be futile, and that if they were not already wanted. Then, they wouldn't make it past the first ticket office.

"I don't know, Judy. I don't know. But we must try, hear me? We must try."

He raised his gaze to his wife.

"I don't understand any of this myself, but we need to at least leave the city, put some distance between us and that." He waved his hand to the side. "And then I would be able to think. I don't understand what's going on, but whatever it is... something isn't right. It wasn't..."

He pulled his gaze from hers, dropping it to the floor.

"It's not the Party. I can't believe it", he said quietly.

Judy began crying, her whimpers muffled by her hand.

"They will find us. There's nowhere we can run."

"Judy."

Tom came closer and lifted her chin.

"If you want, you can stay here. Tell them that you know nothing, that I took the child while you were out, or better still, wait a few hours after we leave and call the police, report Tilly missing. That way, they won't do anything to you. You had nothing to do with it."

Tom hoped so.

His gaze slid around their family room.

He hoped that if Judy stayed behind, they wouldn't hurt her, that they wouldn't take it out on her.

Judy shook her head.

"I'm not letting you take Tilly from me. Nobody's taking her from me, neither you nor them. She's mine. She will always be mine."

Judy wiped her face with her hands. The gesture was rough, as if she was trying to wake herself or ready herself for something.

"I'll pack my clothes", she said. "You, figure out where we're going."

She pulled the door open and walked out of the room.

"Find money, pack our documents and figure out where we're going", she yelled back into the corridor, before the bedroom door closed.

Tilly stood in their bedroom, where Tom and Judy had left her, hugging her teddy to her chest.

"Okay, let's pack", Judy said as she walked in.

She arranged her face into the brightest smile she could muster, and after opening the zip on their suitcase, she began shoving her and Tilly's clothes into its esurient core.

Judy walked into their tiny bathroom, consisting of a toilet, a small sink and a narrow shower stall. There, she picked up their toothbrushes and a rough brown brick of soap.

Tom began the packing of his own.

102

He flung open the glass doors on the cabinet that occupied an entire wall in their family room. Out of the stack of neatly folded papers, he fished out their identity documents, containing their photos, fingerprints and a black strip at the corner with their DNA samples. He pulled out the release papers for last year's holiday, Tilly's medical card, his fifth level security clearance, and after a moment of thinking, he pulled out the ownership document for their flat and his Party award from last year.

One by one, he scanned the documents in the pile, weighing in his mind what might come in useful, to sell or to fraud, when he came across the paperwork for his parents' small house in a remote village on the Schotlandia Borders.

This could be it. This could be the place, where he could go and take his family.

He pulled the papers out, folding them with the rest of the papers, he was taking with him.

Tom opened a drawer. In that drawer they kept whatever little money they could save from their salaries, whatever was left after their bills were paid. It was the money they had put aside for their next holiday. The stash was low and pathetic, not enough to take the three of them to their destination, not that he would be able to board a train.

"We're ready."

Tom turned towards Judy's voice.

She stood by the door, holding their suitcase in one hand and Tilly's hand in the other, both of them wearing light raincoats.

Doubt flooded his heart at the sight of his family, the family he thought he was saving. He wasn't sure if he was overreacting. If he should have trusted his Party and let them take the lead, as they've done his entire life.

The Party has never failed him. The Party made him the man he was today. He trusted his Party implicitly all his life and suddenly, he didn't.

Now, without any solid proof, just through fear, a pathetic childish fear, he was going against his Party and its decisions, and it hurt him, hurt him more than the thought of possible retribution.

He swallowed.

It wasn't too late. They hadn't left the flat. They hadn't become wanted fugitives yet. It wasn't too late to fall into the open embrace of the Party and accept its judgement as his own. It wasn't too late to show how deep was his love for the Party, how absolute was his faith in it. He still could change his mind and no one would find out about his treacherous thoughts, and his moments of weakness.

He looked at his child, at the girl who needed to be told to call him "dad", the child he barely knew. Would he give up everything he worked for so long for her? Would he sacrifice his stable life for her?

Her open gaze held his, her eyes watching him.

"Dad?"

The word startled him.

That's right, he was a dad. He was her dad. If he didn't protect her, then who would?

Throughout his childhood, the Party told him that it protects the vulnerable, and so should he. He was told that standing up for the weak and voiceless was an honourable thing to do. He was told that he must right every wrong he saw, fight for the future of the country, which was its children, and protect its future with his life. And realising that at this precise moment, he was following the Party's line, he felt better. The metal constricting his chest opened up a little.

Looking after his country's future was exactly what he was doing.

He nodded.

"Ready? Let's go then."

He ushered his girls out of the room, out of the flat, and with a last quick glance at his abandoned life, he shut the door, turning the key.

"Do you know where we're going?" Judy asked in a whisper.

"I have an idea, but we need to leave the city first."

Chapter 7

The tram rattled down the line, shaking its metal guts.

The only passengers were the three of them and two old people, seated at the opposite end of the tram.

With the tidal wave of waking indoctrination, Tom's earlier determination dwindled, exposing the propagandised mind.

His mind cried logic and slogans at him, begging to turn back while he still can, whispering that in these moments of turmoil the true citizens are known, reminding Tom of everything the Party had done for him.

When his parents died, he was taken into one of the Party's orphanages, which began to sprout after the bloody years of the Civil war and unrest. He was a part of the "orphaned generation". The streets then were teeming with youngsters fed by crime and begging and the young government stepped in, adopting them all, providing them with food, education and shelter. And Tom hadn't forgotten his Party's generosity.

Tom's head spun. The nagging doubt sank in its claws deeper, questioning if he had done the right thing by running away. Before he left the city, and before his absence was discovered, he would be able to return. He can bring his family back, put the documents and clothing back in the drawers and live as if nothing happened.

But every time these waves swallowed him, the image of the scared children marching to the trucks rose in front of his eyes, of the officers with rifles around the perimeter, of officers throwing the soft bodies of the children into the truck, as if they were cattle.

It was wrong. It was cruel. It wasn't the Liberating Party he knew. And the more he thought about it, the more adamant he grew that if anyone in the Leadership Committee knew about what had happened, they would have stopped it.

He was confident that his Party didn't sign off on this.

Tom reached into his briefcase and pulled out a piece of paper, a pen followed. He clicked his briefcase shut, and resting the piece of paper on it, he began to write.

"To the Central Committee of the Ordained Liberating Party. The Freedom Square, Cabinet 1", the first words read. And following those, Tom wrote everything he had witnessed; everything he had seen.

He wrote fast, the pen ripping the paper.

He ended the letter with a request: *"As a loyal and trusting Party member, I can't stand idle and watch the destruction of the Party's good name that some officers of the State Security have committed. Their unlawful actions would bring years of unrest onto our fine land. It would set back our development by dozens of years. It will risk our goals and will rob us of our bright future, as we all know: the children of our country are our future and in their hands our country will rest. I urge our brave and wise committee to step in, to investigate and suffocate the attempt of the treacherous element to sabotage the work that our wonderful Party had carried for many years."*

The pen froze above the paper for a moment.

No self-respecting free citizen would allow himself to write an anonymous complaint letter. From the early years of his childhood, Tom was told that he needs to own up to his words, needs to be brave to stand up and voice his concerns, speak up against injustice and sabotage, that every objection and whistle-blowing should have a name to it, a name to which the accused could respond, which is only fair in a country where everyone was equal, in a country that treated everyone fairly.

But Tom couldn't bring himself to sign his name to this letter. It was a risk he wasn't prepared to take. He made the decision to protect his child. He made a commitment to his wife and his daughter, and he feared that with a light scribble of a truth-searching signature, their moment of safety would end.

Tom put the lid back on his pen, leaving the letter unsigned. He then folded it twice.

Tom fidgeted in his seat. He scanned the passing landscape, inspecting the buildings and pavements on both sides of the carriage, whilst glancing at the moving news line ahead.

So far, everything was quiet, and there was nothing out of the ordinary on the news. Black cars of the State Security or Internal Police hadn't surrounded the tram.

On that rushed walk from his front door to the tram stop, when he almost broke into a run more than once and had to restrain himself, he had searched through his mind and memory, picking and discarding names of the people he knew, his wife knew.

Both orphaned at a young age, neither had family apart from the one they had built.

Tom knew that he needed to bide his time, to figure out a route out of the city, maybe on foot, up North, through smaller villages, or bypassing settlements completely, sleeping and hiding in the woods as they travelled. Tom knew that the legal routes were closed off to him and his family. Their photos with the word "wanted" might be circulating through ticket offices.

Yet, the only local people he and his wife knew were their colleagues. Tom was aware that workplaces were the first to be updated on newly detected quislings, with suspects' desks impounded, stripped and searched, colleagues and heads of their departments questioned. The gossip and news would then spread like a virus through the building.

Tom wouldn't risk going to any of his colleagues, no matter in how many Parades they have marched together or how many department barbeques they had attended. He knew that he would be handed over to the State Security the moment they knew his location. As much as he would have loved to blame them, he knew he would have done the same.

Today, Tom had chosen between the two things he loved the most: his Party and his child. He made his choice. But only now the weight of his decision dawned on him, the unwinnable battle he had entered. He feared that his choice would bring death to him and his Judy, stripping his daughter of her future.

Many couples lived happily without children. Some wanted children, but were declined the impregnation licence, whilst some chose not to have children at all.

But Tom and Judy were lucky. They wanted a child, and they were given permission.

They were lucky.

Tom had repeated those words time and time again, to himself and to his wife, but now he wasn't convinced of their truth.

"Where are we going?"

Judy's warm whisper stroked Tom's earlobe, pulling him back from his thoughts.

"I have one place in mind, but I'm not sure if we'll be allowed in."

After discarding dozens of names, Tom arrived at the unlikeliest of them all. The name which he almost forgot, the name that the last time they'd seen each other, he'd sermonised with nothing but the "bastard of the traitors".

That name would be the last to be associated with him, because he made sure to cut ties between himself and that man. The last time they spoke, when Tom had said all these things, both of them were twelve. It was when the barracks of the orphanage were divided into the barracks for "children of enemies of the state" and "children of true citizens", the Party waking to the poisonous influences of the "bad element" and encouraging the separation, whilst promoting active hate and divide.

A lot of water had passed since then. A lot of time had gone by. The crack that the resentment and hate had opened grew, distance and time widening it.

Tom didn't know if his childhood friend would be alive or if following the fate of his parents, he would have been shot as a traitor.

To Tom's surprise, he found the familiar name through the phone directory. The man lived in the old part of the city, which thirty years ago was a separate town to New Bristol, but now, with the expansion, was consumed by the new developments and Party control.

Tom and his family had changed trams twice over, before arriving into The Purlieu.

The buildings behind the tram's windows began to change. The grey cement skyline of the Party's smokescreen lowered, exposing the red evening sky.

The residential monolith of the Party's buildings vanished, replaced by lopsided short houses, built of mismatched salvage from the post-Collapse. They were half of brick and half of wood – the Frankenstein's monsters of real estate.

The piles of rubble were common too. Some were as large as a collapsed corpse of an entire house, whilst some were small. The little islands of tall grass waved between the low buildings, and nature began to claim the old pavements too, grass and flowers breaking through the cracked asphalt.

Tilly was glued to the glass of the tram's window, watching the unfamiliar landscape.

"The Purlieu?"

Judy's whisper of disbelief rang in the empty carriage.

Tom couldn't blame her.

This place was a shameful mark on the Party's development of New Bristol. This was the last place left to "conquer and clean", as leaders called the modernisation process of bringing the Party's comfort and control to its citizens.

In their annual appearances, the members of the Party presidium pledged to bring order to the streets of The Purlieu, as grey high scrapers marched towards the low shacks, closing the circle tighter around the remaining residents.

The Purlieu wasn't lit as well as the rest of the city, and once they took a few steps away from the tram stop, Tom's family was swallowed by the dusky shadows.

"Hold on a second."

Tom turned and walked to a blue post box nailed on the wall of the tram stop.

"Liberated Postal Service" was printed in white round letters below the solitary star.

Tom's letter slid into the narrow opening.

"What did you post?" Judy asked when Tom joined her and Tilly.

"Nothing; something for work."

They started deeper into the settlement.

"Where are we going?"

"Not far now."

Stray dogs jogged past them into the darkening late evening. The streets and overgrown gardens behind the toothless short fences were empty, the residents of The Purlieu hiding inside their reconstructed abodes.

Tom marched down the street, a suitcase in one hand and the hand of his daughter in the other, Judy keeping up with his long strides to the side of him.

He was afraid to slow down, to shorten his steps, to be caught here after nightfall or to change his mind, to turn and walk away without asking – no, begging! – for help and shelter. He marched forward, stamping out his pride, preparing to fall to his knees in front of the one he hurt many years ago.

He knew that most likely he would be sent away, with a kick in the shins and a string of colourful profanities to endorse the message, but he had to try.

If that doesn't come to anything, Tom will find an abandoned house to spend the night in, before figuring out the logistics of escaping the city the following day.

The air smelled of grass and cow's dung. It was crisp and clean here, clear of the factories' black smog which swaddled the city, including the part they lived in.

Every day, the smog would settle on the town in a layer of black residue, coating buildings, trams and pavements, leaves on the trees in the parks and on children's playgrounds, which the machines of Liberated Cleaning Services were sent out every night to clean. The machines would run their routes, spraying façades of the buildings and pavements, playgrounds and parks. The black streams would run down the city's streets, leaving behind streaks, which would disappear the following day, dusted with a fresh layer of black grit.

For the first time in ages, walking down the street, Tom could hear the chirping of birds in the evening sky and not the pre-recorded squawking of seagulls through a Broadcasting Unit.

The house he was after stood at the end of the last street at the farthest end of The Purlieu, the back of the house opening onto a field.

Although the brick house still held its structural integrity, it leaned slightly sideways, as if resting on its own broken fence. Thick cracks ran through the house's façade, through panes of the broken windows, where the glass had been replaced by black plastic sheets flapping in the evening breeze.

The house didn't hold a number plaque or the name of the street, but checking on the Party's

Street Map prior, Tom knew that this was the house.

Three wooden steps cried under Tom's feet, wobbling slightly, as he climbed up and knocked on the door.

The door opened without delay, questioning whether the owner was waiting for someone.

The man standing past the door was burly, his body taking most of the space within the doorframe. The weak light from his house leaked around him, touching Tom's features and keeping the owner's face in shadows.

"Yes?"

The shadow had a deep voice and didn't pretend to like the idea of the late arrival.

"James? James Colman?"

"Yes, and who are you?"

The man's gaze slid past Tom and onto his wife and daughter, standing at the bottom of the stairs.

Tom stepped forward, closer to the man and deeper into the puddle of light.

Now, he was able to see the man's face better.

"Thomaās Whicker. Tom Whicker."

Indifference slid off the man's face overtaken by surprise, which in turn gave way to raging hate. The man's eyes narrowed into slits, his nostrils flared, as the recognition had brought memories.

Watching the man's face, Tom was sure he would be punched. He was certain of it, until James took a step back, inside the house, his breathing short and hateful. Without a word, the man nudged the door, pushing it closed.

Tom threw himself towards the door, thrusting his arm and foot past the threshold, grabbing hold of the frame and preventing the door from closing.

"Please, don't. James, please. Please, I beg of you, give me a moment. Listen to me. If not for me, I beg you for my family, please. For my daughter, for my wife. I beg you. Please, just listen to me, just one moment."

The door suddenly flew open. The man's body pressed against Tom's, his hot breathing stroking Tom's face.

"I was begging you too, remember? I was begging you. I was begging everyone. I was on my knees, and do you remember what you said to me? Do you? Do you?!" the man roared.

"Because I do, to this day I do. You stood there, watching with everyone, and then said: "The bastard of traitors should be executed too". And when I saw you a week later and asked for food, do you remember what you told me then? Do you?! You told me to help myself to the pig's swill. And then you said that even that is too generous for a traitor, and the more traitors are killed, the better it will be for everyone. So don't you fucking come here with your begging. I will give you exactly, what I received from you. In fact, I will be more generous: I will spare your life. Now, get the fuck out!"

The large body pushed Tom down the stairs, Tom barely noticing the usage of profanity, punishable under the law.

Under the barrage of accusations, of memories and hate, Tom began moving backward, when the loathing spittle landed on his face.

Tom wiped his face with his sleeve, as he backed down the stairs, his gaze on the man ahead, each step forward of James's met by Tom's step back.

They stopped the descent upon reaching the ground, and standing there, next to his wife and his child, Tom no longer could move further away. This was the farthest he could retreat.

"James, please", he tried again.

If only he could apologise, to explain that whatever happened in their childhood was in the past; that they needed to move on, to grow up, "forgive and forget". Tom was ready to apologise, was ready to stand on his knees. He needed help, and he was prepared to do and say anything to save his family.

The once best friend of Tom's, the man leaned into him, searching for something in Tom's eyes, and either not finding it there, or maybe finding the reminders of his past, of the pain he had locked away and covered, he took a step backward and swung his fist.

"Dad?.."

Tilly's little voice came to Tom as a frightened plea.

Tom turned his head to his child, pulling his lips into a soft smile, about to reassure her, to tell her that everything will be alright and there's nothing for her to worry about, when the power of a train hit Tom in the right temple, exploding with a sudden pain in his head.

Judy's scream filled the dark air and Tom's knees buckled underneath him.

Tom's body was already unconscious, when it hit the ground.

* * *

Tom's senses crawled forward, as the world crouched nearby, waking Tom inch by painful inch, bringing with it unfamiliar smells, the hush of low voices and the unavoidable mumble of the newsreader in the background.

A male voice asked something and a female voice answered, and Tom was about to question the lucidity of his own mind, when the ownership of the female voice barged in, waking him, bringing with it the memories of the hateful stare of James.

Judy!

Tom opened his eyes to the murky shadows of a dark room, lit by flickering candlelight dancing on the wooden planks of the ceiling. The planks of rotting wood were nailed sloppily, not parallel and crossing in places.

Tom raised his body up, pushing with his arms on the lumpy bed, commanding his muscles to move and his body to turn.

"Tom! You're alright. I was so worried."

Judy's voice cut in from somewhere to the side, and her soft arms came over Tom's shoulders, helping him to sit up.

Tom's gaze swung with his rise, in turn coming to James, who sat at a table in the middle of the dark room.

James's right elbow rested on the table hidden under an old tablecloth. His hands were clasped over his stomach, and his legs were stretched ahead of him.

Tom's feet touched the cold floor, as he sat up on the worn-out sofa.

117

Judy fussed around him, touching his head and shoulders, then coming to kneel in front of him.

"How do you feel? Where does it hurt?"

"I'm okay, darling. I'm okay."

Tom reached out to his wife and stroked her arm.

Ignoring James's narrowed glare, Tom's gaze travelled around the room.

The room was small and dark, with only two candles fighting the shadows and failing at it miserably. One candle stood on the side table, next to the bed, and the other was placed on the top of a wooden chest of drawers. Tilly sat on a fraying rug next to it, scribbling something on a piece of paper.

A breath of relief left Tom. He lifted his gaze to his wife, and closing his hands over her wrists, he brought her hands to his face, kissing them, suddenly realising that it's been a few months, since he touched them.

Her hands were dryer. The cracks that used to bleed regularly from the chemicals she was exposed to at her work, were carved deeper. The thin skin is ready to break again.

"How's Tilly?"

"She's fine, busy drawing something", Judy answered.

Tom nodded.

"Can I please speak to my friend?"

James huffed from his seat at the word "friend" but made no comment.

"Of course", Judy replied, and after a moment, she added quieter, "are you sure you're alright?"

"Sure."

"Okay, then. I'll see if Tilly needs any help."

She leaned to Tom and kissed him lightly on the lips, before walking over to their child.

The voice of the newsreader mumbled the latest government news.

Tom scanned the room again, but the glowing display was nowhere to be seen.

"No Unit?" he asked his oldest friend.

"No", James bit. "The residents of The Purlieu aren't worthy of the fruits of the Party's progress. The radio transistor is all that we're given: to keep us informed, but without spending Party's resources."

Tom didn't want to go down that road, so after clearing his throat, he changed the topic.

"You're still in the city... I thought you would've gone by now..."

James gave a short bark of a dry laugh, keeping his heavy gaze on the one, who once was his "brother".

"Where would I go? Who would want me in this country? Not everyone has a perfect, clean past and Party approved biography. Not all of us are worthy of education, engineering jobs or a new flat in the Party towers..."

He turned his gaze to Tom's family.

"And not everyone's allowed to marry and have a child. Some are not as lucky, as others. Clearly, the distance from the tarnished reputation and "children of enemies of the state" served you well."

"James, I –"

"Funny how fast life changes, isn't it?" James interrupted, resting his elbows on his knees and leaning closer to Tom.

"One day it was me, who was starving, pleading for help, without friends, nowhere to go, and then suddenly..."

James's face bloomed with a wide smile, as he gestured at Tom.

"It's you. The country's most exemplary citizen arrives at my doorstep, out of graces and on the run. How weird, how... unexpected."

He paused for a moment, keeping his heavy gaze on Tom, before shaking his head.

"I don't want you here. We are no longer friends, you made sure of that. You made a mistake coming here. I won't help you. I don't know what trouble you are in, what you've done, but it must be pretty hefty crap if you ran to me of all people, especially dragging your family with you. I want nothing to do with you and your problems. I have no obligations to you. I don't owe you anything and I want you to leave, first thing in the morning."

James turned his gaze to Tom's family.

"If not for your child, I would've let you lie where you were and let the dogs piss on you. But contrary to the Party's propaganda, we are not animals, not all of us and not towards everyone. The three of you can spend the night here, but I want you gone in the morning."

"James, please..."

Tom unsteadily rose off the sofa. Swaying, he took a few steps forward.

But the floor was moving under Tom's feet, and his last step was a lunge. He grabbed a side of the table to steady himself, but it wasn't enough, and still weak, he fell to his knees in front of his once friend.

"Please, James. I need help. *We* need help."

James laughed.

"Of course you do. Otherwise, you wouldn't be here. But I'm not interested. I will not get involved in your mess. Whatever is left of my life, whatever the Party had allowed me to keep, is mine and I won't risk it for anyone, let alone you."

"James, I'm sorry for everything I've said, for everything I've done. We were children... please don't hold it against me. I'm sorry for everything. I need your help. James..."

"This is your mess, so I'll let you deal with it the way you left me to deal with mine. The difference is that I had no say in who my parents were. My mess was not of my making. Consider yourself lucky that I didn't report you to the authorities. Tomorrow, I want you gone, all of you."

James got up, and without a glance at Tom kneeling on the floor, at Judy or Tilly, he left the room, the old stairs creaking under his heavy frame, as he climbed up.

The footsteps boomed above Tom's head. The screech of old springs on a mattress followed.

Judy came over, and pulling Tom by his arm, she helped him to the chair.

"It's okay, we'll manage. Whatever happens, we'll manage. We couldn't stay in the city anyway, so we'll leave tomorrow and figure things out as we go. It will be fine. *We* will be fine. We'll figure it all out, as long as we're together."

She pulled his head against her chest, stroking his hair. He could feel her lips on top of his head.

Tom was lucky to have met her. She was the only friend he needed.

"You and Tilly take the couch", Tom said into the enveloping shadows of the shack. "I'll sleep on the floor. We'll walk a lot tomorrow, so you need to rest."

Chapter 8

"I'm hungry."

Tilly's small voice pulled Tom out of his thoughts.

For the last two days, the three of them were hiding in the barn Tom spotted in a middle of a field on their way up North.

The abandoned barn had a well nearby, and they were surviving by eating berries that Judy and Tilly gathered, and game that Tom managed to hunt.

But neither of them were raised on the land, with the countryside being furthest from their lives, so to say that they were hunting and gathering, whilst sustaining themselves, would be an exaggeration. They were barely surviving, and Tom knew that the time was coming for him to make a move and make another decision.

When they awoke the following morning in James's place, James was already gone, and the place was empty. Two hard boiled eggs and two large slices of fresh bread sat in the middle of the table. It was a breakfast for his wife and his daughter, and not a veiled message to Tom. But Tom was okay with that. He understood. He wasn't angry. At least his friend was gracious enough to look after his family.

Pushing through waist-high grass of the field behind James's house, they walked further away from the city.

Their decision not to risk freedom by asking for help was set.

Tom had finally accepted that nobody would risk their neck for him.

But admitting the Party's failings? That still hasn't come.

Somewhere, in the depth of his heart, Tom carried a seed of hope that all that had happened was an oversight that would be cleared up any day now, a mistake, which would be rectified, only if Tom trusted and believed, and stayed alive. It might take a day, a week, a month, but the true way of the Party would shine through, finding overzealous commanders guilty of misinterpreting directives, taking it upon themselves to threaten good citizens in days of peace.

Tom was reluctant to show that precious seed to his Judy. He didn't want to hear her doubts. He didn't want any criticism of the Party to leave her lips.

Tom felt that voicing his reservations about the Party might give Judy carte blanche to badmouth the Party as others did, and he wouldn't be able to stand that. He blamed himself for that too. He knew that she never carried that absolute love for the Party in her heart as Tom did, and he didn't want to feel her discontent.

He'd had a moment of weakness, and he knew it. He failed to trust his Party. That impulsive decision was now breaking his heart, and might one day lead to their deaths.

During his long, and often empty, food scouting trips, Tom's mind would churn over the decision to go up North, looking for the refuge in the house of his late parents.

Tom would play his plan backwards, looking for threats and pitfalls, analysing the trip lying ahead. He would imagine their lives in the village, although not big, but probably with residents.

Would they ask questions about the new arrival? They more than likely would.

Would they ask who he was? Of course, they would. He would lie. But between the key to the house and his face, which resembled the face of his late father so much, he won't get away with it.

What if a particularly upstanding resident decided to alert the local Internal Police about the new family, Smith or whatever the name Tom would give them, then what? Where would they run then? Would they manage to escape again?

But Tom feared that answering these questions might be too late, if his house, the only option for their safe life, is being watched. His ownership of that property was documented within the Property Registry, and his trip there might be expected. State Security might be already waiting.

These were the dangers of arriving at their final destination, but there were hundreds more threats, for the hundreds of miles that lay between the house and their hiding barn.

With heavily populated towns between them and his parents' house, with regular Police patrols and patrols of the Farming Agency, with scouting for food for a month and sleeping on the ground in the woods, exposed to the elements and wild animals, they might not make it to his parents' house at all. As the fugitives that they are, they could no longer expect a comfortable and easy life within this country, and Tom knew they won't survive for long here.

Tilly crawled closer over the bed of straw, tugging at his arm.

"I'm hungry, dad."

"Of course, darling. Let me go and find you something. Is mummy still asleep?"

Tilly nodded, smiling, pleased at having someone's attention. During the last few days, with constant interaction, she relaxed around her parents, her guard falling, and the words "dad" and "mum" began sliding off her tongue with ease.

"Let's wake her, and see if she wants to have breakfast with us."

Tilly's smile stretched wider.

"Mum, mummy", Tom called inside the barn, keeping his voice low, so it wouldn't be heard outside. "Wakey, wakey, time for breaky."

The last night was fruitful. The trap that Tom had set held a strangled rabbit, and although Tilly was horrified at the sight of the lifeless body of a "sleeping bunny", Tom was pleased. Their dinner last night was rabbit stew, after days of eating only Judy's nettle soup.

On their first day out of the city, Judy came into the barn hugging a large bunch of stinging nettle to her chest, announcing that her grandma had told her that before the revolution, with the subsequent establishment of the Party, when hunger swept the country, she used to make a soup out of nettle.

The soup had turned out surprisingly palatable, although missing salt.

But the price for that dinner were Judy's hands. After collecting the nettle, they were swollen, covered in red and angry bumps of the nettle stings, and after dinner, Tom spent the evening washing his wife's hands in cold water, calming the itch.

The sun sat above the barn, its rays seeping through the gaps in the old roof.

"Say, "wakey, wakey", Tom whispered to Tilly.

"Wakey, wakey", she lisped in her thin voice.

Tom crawled under the low rafters along the straw bed.

Judy was there, lying peacefully, her eyes closed, her chest rising and falling with her breathing.

"Rise and shine, sleepy head", Tom called in a sing-a-song voice, leaning over her.

He stretched on the straw next to his wife, gently lifting her head, turning it to him, his hands stroking her hair.

"Sleepy head, wakey-wakey."

He pressed his lips to hers, expecting her eyes to open the next second, her breath to draw and her chest to rise with soft moans, followed by the familiar stretch.

But none of that came.

Judy's eyes remained closed, her body motionless.

"Judy. Judy."

His hand flew to her shoulder, giving it a light shake.

Her head lolled to the side.

"Judy?" Tom's voice rose. "Judy? Can you hear me?"

He was on his knees now, touching, stroking, shaking her body, desperate to wake his wife, to prompt any response or reaction, and was getting no luck.

Her head lolled side to the side with his shakes, her limbs flipped with the movements of her body.

"Judy!"

He tapped her cheeks, her skin turning burnt red where his fingers made a contact with it, as if his fingers were hot iron. Now, he was afraid to touch her, yet needed to do something.

"Judy!"

Tom's voice rang under the roof of the barn.

He laid his head against her chest, listening to her heart. Her breathing was shallow; the beating of her heart was slow.

He slid his hand around her shoulders, about to slide one under her knees, to lift her and following the established muscle memory, take her to the nearest hospital, to get help, when he remembered where and who they were.

With his arm draped over her shoulder, he pressed her body closer to him. Her arm dragged after her, and that's when he noticed it.

The skin over her hands was raw, redder than after the stinging of nettle.

Carefully, Tom laid his wife down, and pulling his arm from under her body, his hands found her hand.

He brought it up to his eyes.

The skin was raw and swollen. It was covered in the red bumps, which as much as it could have been mistaken for a rash of sorts, had nothing in common with the itchy rash he saw yesterday. Whatever covered her hands today stretched the skin over her swollen hands. Her fingers were twice their usual size; her knuckles disappeared within the swelling, nails turning purple-blue.

Her palm felt odd to Tom's touch.

His moves were slow and gentle, as Tom turned her hand.

Judy's palm was covered in a layer of small greyish bumps, tightly nestled next to each other. Their round dome shapes were uniform, covering the palm from the tip of each finger up to the wrist, their layer then tapering off, disappearing under the sleeve of her blouse.

Tom tugged on the sleeve, pulling it higher.

The sleeve slid by a couple of inches, revealing more grey bubbles, and when Tom tugged again, to see how far the bumps went, restricted by the button, the sleeve stopped its slide, and something burst with a wet sound.

A thin stream of blood flowed down her arm, when something else smacked once, twice then thrice, the sickening noises birthing more blood streams. They flowed faster, merging, dripping onto the straw, and his wife moaned.

This moan was the first sound he heard from her.

"Judy!"

He was about to place her hand down when more domes, those closer to her wrists, began to burst under the internal strain, one by one popping in front of his eyes, producing miniature geysers and sending the small fountains of blood into the air, opening her skin.

Judy's moans grew, her cries accompanying the bursting of the geysers.

Tom couldn't leave his wife to suffer. He couldn't let her die.

He can't lose her. He can't be alone again. She is his whole life. She is his family, and he is hers. He won't be an orphan again. And scooping her in his arms, he carried her towards and then through the door.

With his wife in his arms, Tom pushed through the green line of the shrubbery, marking the borders and ownership of the field. The brook, from which they drank for the last few days, babbled nearby.

He walked through the familiar fields they had crossed together only a day ago. His daughter trailed after him. Tom could hear a crunching of twigs under her state issued shoes. He marched through the weak ash forest, listening to the singing of the birds that had startled him when he heard it for the first time.

He walked for hours.

His arms were on fire, and his knees were buckling underneath him. But he pushed through, counting his steps, closing his mind to the pain, finding power in the rhythm, knowing that if he stopped, he wouldn't be able to get up.

The familiar red brick buildings of The Purlieu came forward. A field was between Tom and help. Not far now, only a field.

The waist-tall grass opened around him, as he pushed through, his feet finally stepping onto the asphalt.

The dilapidated houses were quiet, the neglected street empty.

"Please, help!" Tom called into the sunny morning.

"Please, help me! Someone!" He cried into the still air.

But the houses remained silent. The doors didn't open, and nobody came out to his call.

"Please, someone! Help!"

He stood in the middle of the street, pleading and calling. He spun on the spot, looking for help, when a figure scattered at the end of the street.

"Please! Citizen!" Tom called. "My wife needs an ambulance. She needs a hospital."

But ignoring Tom, the figure darted into the shadows behind a building, leaving Tom roaring hateful curses into the empty street.

Tom turned his head to his child, for the first time looking at her and finding strangled fear swimming in his daughter's wide eyes.

"Don't worry, darling. Mummy will be fine. We'll take her to hospital, and she'll be fine."

Tom's body screamed at him. His muscles and joints were alight. He adjusted his hold on his wife, before continuing his march forward, towards the line of tall grey buildings cutting across the horizon.

"Not far now. Not far", he mumbled. "Stay with me, girl. Stay with me."

He repeated these words, at one point convinced they were for his wife, and the next that they were directed to his daughter. Once bent, his knees refused to stretch, demanding to fold and to bring his body down with them.

"Not far. Stay with me."

A few streets further, Tom spotted a few people in their front gardens, behind their broken fences.

A woman hung laundry. A man carved something out of wood, and an old woman peeled potatoes.

But none of them rushed to Tom's aid, neither showed any concern to a small family, marching past their wonky fences, and when Tom took a lungful of air to call for their help, they pulled their gazes away from him, returning to their business, paying Tom and his bleeding wife as much attention, as they would to a stray dog.

Tom got the message. He had learned his lesson. Keeping his gaze fixed on the grey tower blocks ahead, he marched forward.

"Don't worry, darling. Not far now."

Tom repeated these three words like a mantra. He was assuring himself and their daughter, who trailed behind him without a whimper or word.

Judy's arm was dripping with blood, leaving behind a dotted trail on the cracked pavement.

There must have been "domes" over Judy's back too, because after hugging her close to his chest, Tom's arms grew wet, the shirt over his chest became soaked, and the metallic scent of blood wafted into his nose.

Tom knew he threatened the safety of his family by returning into the city, but he couldn't stand by and watch his wife bleed to death. He won't be choosing between the life of his wife and the life of his child.

Tom was aware that by now they'd be wanted.

The State Security would have visited their flat by now, and finding it empty, with the occupants and their documents gone, the dogs would have been called, and the chase would have been on.

But after churning over the situation in his head for the last few days, Tom decided that their crimes would never be made public. Whatever was going on, the Party would want to keep it a secret. The Party would never allow that leak of embarrassment. The Party wouldn't admit that their citizens didn't obey, and worse still, managed to escape and hide from the Party's over-reaching hands and its watchful eye.

Tom didn't expect for their faces to be broadcasted, their names splashed in white writing against the red tableau of trams' news lines. Not yet.

The State Security and The Internal Police would be looking for them, but quietly. They won't involve the public as yet. They will try to keep it under wraps, as they had done with everything up to this point.

The Party would initiate the first stage of the chase, but the fabrication of lies would come later.

But what Tom feared, what he thought might present an issue, it's their names flagged in the system, marked as say, petty thieves wanted by the Internal Police, or non-compliant farmers, refusing to surrender their lands into government hands. Whatever crime would be written against their name, it would be small and non-political, something that won't portray the State Security and Internal Police Department as incompetent fools, outrun by an engineer.

Once in the hospital, if he gives them his real name, the trap will shut.

Somewhere at the back of Tom's mind, a happy denial whispered the future-assuring nonsense of disobedience not being a big deal, their disappearance unnoticed, because nobody was looking, calling Tom's unfounded fears, a product of confused imagination of a scared man, who has no evidence, apart from what he saw and then concluded, the denial proclaiming that maybe the last few days won't turn into an avalanche of problems.

Tom questioned his decision to bring their daughter with him. He was thinking of leaving her in the barn, with instructions to sit quietly, waiting for him and hoping for the best, but he couldn't abandon her. As long as he was with her, he knew she'd be protected.

He couldn't leave her alone, so small, young and defenceless, but now, as the grey towers ahead swelled, bringing her along felt like the worst idea.

Tom's legs grew laden. Every new step he took shot the searing fires to his muscles and his back.

But he couldn't stop. He can't stop here, not here and not now. The Free citizens' Medical Services won't be called from here, and he doubted they would come. He needed to get a bit further, past the grey tall buildings ahead.

With his hands awash in her blood, Tom suddenly wondered, if maybe it is too late for his wife, if her blood loss is too severe to curb, and the risk he is taking, would be futile.

But he shoved the thought out.

If he lived long enough, how would he look into his daughter's eyes and tell her that he chose their safety over her mother's life? He needed to be able to say that he'd done everything he could. He needed to be able to say it in order to live with himself.

But the doubt nagged.

What if he doesn't save her? What if something happens to him? Tilly would then grow up an orphan, raised in one of the Party's Children Centres, which he endured.

The memories of his childhood in the orphanage came back.

Most of the boys in the centre were orphans, but there were a few, who came into the centre from Young Offenders' facilities.

They didn't stay in the centre for long. They always absconded, jumping over the fence in the middle of the night, disappearing into the depths of the city. But a couple of these boys returned. Then the director of the orphanage would call a meeting, making a big speech about forgiveness and second chances, whilst the offender would stand next to him, with his head down. But more often than not these boys would never come back, vanishing from the list of attendees, just like the ones who had absconded for a second time, and the orphanage wide gossip was going, debates raging after the lights were out on where these boys had gone and what had happened to them, with some boys were betting that they've signed up on a trading ship as seamen and were now cruising around the world, whilst some said that they were assigned to new families.

But once, Peter, the nastiest and angriest of the boys transferred from the Young Offenders facility, screamed into the darkness that the boys were morons, if they thought that the Party would have excused or tolerated such behaviour. He yelled that those boys were either dead or working in coal mines, or cleaning nuclear waste from the plants, and we are all idiots, for not realising where we are and what's going on. He yelled that it was a warning for everyone who didn't obey or follow the rules. He screamed into the dark silence, calling other boys "sheep", making "baa" sounds at them, growing angrier by the minute, taunting them to stay in line or have their lungs dissolved from nuclear waste.

Then, Tom shrugged it off as lies. In fact, he remembered being so angry with Peter that it was the first time he had the bravery to confront the angry and beefy boy, telling him that he should stop lying about things he didn't know. That was the first time Tom fought. Tom was ready to defend his Party to the last breath.

Tom never trusted those boys, the offenders. He thought of them as good-for-nothing, telling anyone who'd listen, that the Party should not have wasted their time on them, that them, being in the orphanage, was their second chance, a bigger chance than they deserved.

In the wake of the memories of the orphanage, Tom was confused even more by the appearance of the black trucks.

The parents of those children were unwavering Party members, serving the regime for years, honoured with flats and many gratitude certificates. The parents of those children applied for the Procreation licence and were granted one. They had followed the rules. They *obeyed* those rules.

But Peter's words from years ago rang a different tune in Tom's mind now. The words of the boy held not lies, but rather a promise of the future. Those words suddenly tasted of truth.

Peter spoke these words before the Party had divided the orphans into the "children of loyal citizens" and the "children of enemies of the state", before the line was drawn, dividing the country into "us" and "them", then progressing into exterminating those who looked to "destabilise the country", and everyone associated with them.

Tom turned his head and glanced at Tilly.

He knew what she'd be named in that division.

The years old memory turned in his chest, making him uncomfortable.

Tom was at a loss where to hide her or whom to trust with her.

There was no one. Nobody else who would protect her like he would, who would lay their lives for her. No one would, and he knew that. Going against Party wishes had drawn a target on his back. Tom wondered if his daughter would be allowed to survive in this country.

He passed the outer city limits. The tall grey Party designed skyscrapers rose ahead, crowding him. It won't be much longer, before he will be spotted by free citizens, who will rush to help him, calling medics from the emergency box at an entrance to their flats.

These last few steps would be truly his last, the last when he could turn back and change the future.

Chapter 9

The wailing medical truck drove through streets of New Bristol, en-route scaring off trams and rare municipal cars. Occasional citizens would stop and stare, following the truck with their gazes, wondering what had happened, in their minds thanking their lucky stars that they are not the ones inside that truck, behind the white curtains.

"Name?" a female voice demanded above the crying siren.

Tom turned his attention to the nurse sitting on the opposite to him bench.

Zipped into a white gown of the Liberated Medical Services, with the Party insignia stitched onto her breast pocket and a white medical cap balancing on her voluminous hair, she looked irritated, as if blaming Tom for disrupting her otherwise perfect day.

"Sorry?" Tom mumbled

But the wailing of the siren drowned his voice, so he cleared his throat and called louder: "Sorry, whose name?"

"Patient, of course", she snapped.

An open notebook rested on her lap, a pen hovered above, ready to record the information.

Tom turned his attention to his wife lying on the white plastic stretcher inside the rolling truck, her head bouncing in time with its turns.

The nurse's colleague, a male nurse in a white medical jacket and white trousers sat on a bench next to her, inspecting Judy's arms, then turning her slightly, lifting the blouse over her back.

The nurse had as much patience as the siren.

"So?"

"Veronica. Veronica Edwards", Tom answered.

"And who are you to the patient?"

"I'm her husband."

"And your name?.."

"William Edwards."

Tom decided not to risk giving their real names. Instead, he borrowed the name of his colleague. Knowing that with Bill's wife out of the city, she is unlikely to be a patient in the City hospital.

"Do you have any identification with you?"

"No. Sorry."

Tom shrugged his shoulders, giving the woman in front the most charming smile he could muster, the one he had perfected over time, bargaining for extra time or resources for his department or "access to the body" from female secretaries of the Energy Department.

"We went to visit a relative, and my wife fell ill. She felt unwell overnight, and these spots have appeared. Then they began bursting…"

Tom mumbled, taking on the role of a distressed husband, although not needing to pretend the concerned part.

"You know, you're supposed to keep identifications with you at all times?" The unimpressed and unmoved nurse interrupted Tom's rambling. Her lips turned thin and her face went sour.

"It's a civil offence and you might be prosecuted."

"Yes, I know, and I'm very sorry."

138

Tom hugged Tilly closer.

She hasn't said a word for a while.

When Tilly first saw her mother, she asked what was wrong with her, but once she had noticed the blood-drenched arms, she began to scream, her shrills turning hysterical, before turning fearful after Tom shook her, his yelling meeting her shrills.

After that, she went catatonic. Without a word and with a checked out gaze, she followed him through the fields and streets of The Purlieu, now sitting next to him, staring at her mother's face and not making a sound.

"I'll register her under this name, but you have to present her identification to the hospital admission within twenty four hours, after which, if you fail to do so, your offence would be reported."

"I will", Tom nodded.

He didn't plan to leave his wife in the hospital for twenty four hours, and he didn't plan to stay there for that long either. Tom needed doctors to stem the blood loss and figure out what was wrong with her, ideally fixing her within that timeframe. If not, Tom would think of something. He would figure something out.

Twenty four hours was a long way away. He will cross that bridge when he comes to it. He didn't think that far ahead, but he knew that one way or another, he'd find a way. He would carry her out. He would steal an ambulance. Whatever it will take, but he will find a way.

All that he wanted from them now, is not to let her die.

Inside the rolling truck and hidden behind the white curtains from the outside world, Tom didn't know how close they were to the hospital, when suddenly with another sharp turn, the medical truck stopped.

The doors clanked outside, thrown open the next second by sure hands.

The two beefy male hospital workers in the pale blue uniform with identical jackets and trousers with the Party insignia on their breast pockets stood outside.

Following the procedure, the male nurse pushed the stretcher towards the door. The stretcher was pulled out, picked up by both men, then briskly lifted and taken towards the hospital entrance.

Tom climbed out after his wife, reaching into the truck and dragging Tilly with him. He was trying to move as fast as he could, afraid to let Judy out of his sight.

Carrying Tilly in his arms, he marched after the stretcher, catching up with his wife inside the admissions ward.

A young doctor with a Party ID card on his lanyard came to meet the new arrival, ushering the men with the stretcher into an adjoining room. He stepped in front of Tom, blocking him from entering, when Tom was about to follow his wife.

"No. You can't go in there, citizen. Please take a seat, and our staff will update you, once we know more, or when you're allowed to see her."

He didn't wait for Tom's answer and didn't expect one. Party authority figures expected absolute compliance from their citizens, and doctors weren't any different.

The doctor turned on the spot and left through the glass double doors covered in white paint to give the other room privacy, leaving Tom standing in the middle of the admissions hall, with Tilly in his arms.

A simple desk painted white was pushed against a wall. A young nurse sat behind it, writing in papers and checking something on the monitor fixed to the left corner of her desk. Against the opposite wall, a row of wooden chairs was placed, for the relatives who were waiting for a doctor's verdict on their loved ones. Currently, only two chairs were occupied: one by a young woman with tear-washed cheeks and the other, by a middle aged man with a closed off face, seated on the opposite end of the line of the chairs.

With Tilly in his arms, Tom walked and sat on a chair in the middle of the row, sitting his daughter on his knee.

The City hospital was located in the old part of the city, occupying a large, yet low building that sprawled over a thousand square meters. The building was very low by the Party's standards, only four floors. It was an inexcusable luxury in today's world and would have never been given architectural approval. The Party history books said that the building was a three hundred years old market, where ancient farmers, traders and rich authoritative elite would come together to trade goods and humans.

The walls of the admissions room were painted white, the paint smeared over the old tiles, which went up to the middle of the walls. Silver ventilation shafts and wiring hung exposed under the ceiling.

Once repurposed by the hospital, the humongous room was divided by new walls. The ornate design that ran along the top disappeared behind a newly constructed wall, cut rather abruptly.

The three tall windows in the room were covered by white paint too, blocking the outside world for the anxious relatives and them from the world.

Sealed in the white room, Tom had nothing to do, but to watch the large Broadcasting Unit, through which the sounds of nature were transmitted.

The seaside creatures wailed, cried and screeched from the speaker, relaying the Party executives' creative imagination on the sounds our ancestors would have found at the seaside, before most of these animals disappeared.

Blocking the cacophony of noises, Tom turned his attention to his daughter.

"Sweetie, everything will be alright. I promise you, everything will be alright. Mum will be fine, and then we'll go back to our holiday. Everything will be alright."

He stroked his daughter's soft hair, but she didn't respond. She wasn't crying or talking. No millions of questions, so common in children, were coming from her. She didn't even raise her gaze to him.

Tom hugged her tighter, rocking with her slightly. He didn't understand what was happening to Tilly and didn't know what to do or say. For years, he was removed from his child, and now, he was paying for it.

He hoped, it wasn't something he yelled at her, but it could've been. He worried that whatever has happened to Tilly would stay.

Tom thought that unlike him, Judy would've been able to fix their daughter, finding a way to reach her. But Judy wasn't here, and it was up to him to figure it out and fix it.

Tom's gaze travelled back to the Broadcasting Unit, scanning the running news line at the bottom, where a summary of the latest news was replayed on a loop between the state news segments.

He was on edge, checking for any mentioning of his name or of Tilly's nursery.

But there was nothing.

The running line was busy with reports of the Party's synthetic food production achievements, which were dominating the news as of late, and a few segments on foreign affairs.

Suddenly the sound of the sea creatures dimmed.

Tom pulled his gaze away from the Unit and onto the nurse, who was speaking into her earpiece connected to the Medical Service Network.

"How old is the patient?"

She listened for an answer then shrugged her shoulders.

"You know we won't provide medical help and hospitalisation for her. She's too old."

The nurse listened again.

"Where does she work? What does she do?"

Another pause followed by a huff.

"Does she have dependants?"

The nurse paused again, as she listened.

"You see? You know, as well as I do, that "No hospitalisation or extensive medical treatment for anyone over age sixty five and no treatment for pre-existing conditions. Exclusions apply only to citizens with dependants or to citizens in the Party's essential work positions, which must be validated", she recited, "and she is neither. Why did you pick her up?"

She listened again.

"I'm telling you, she won' be admitted. Listen to me, Justin. All you can do for her is to take her back and provide on the spot emergency care. No, I don't care how you tell her husband. You should've thought of it before loading her in. You know the rules."

She listened for a second.

"Don't take that tone with me!" the nurse snapped. "Shall I record your insubordination and breaking the law, or are you going to fix it?"

Her voice went softer again: "Listen, just tell him. He should've known the law. It's not like it's all on you."

She dropped her voice, spinning her chair and facing the wall, and Tom had to strain his ears to hear her.

"I warn you, if you bring her here, against my instructions, I will have to report your insubordination. Whereas if you sort it yourself, right now, nobody would know of your misguided attempt to help, and there will be nothing on the record, apart from the "on the spot" emergency help. Think about it."

The adjoining doors, through which Judy was taken earlier, flew open, slamming on both sides of the wall, startling everyone in the admissions room.

The nurse whipped her back straight, pressing a button on her earpiece, disconnecting the call.

A group of nurses and doctors in white uniforms rushed out of the doors, the edges of their jackets flapping, lanyards swinging on their necks. Without slowing, the group threw another pair of doors open and disappeared through them.

Just as the pneumatic doors began to close, another group of doctors appeared, scurrying through the doors, which had taken Judy.

Edging closer in his seat, Tom scanned the closing doors, before his gaze swept to the nurse at the desk, but her face was lost. She looked as shocked, as he was.

After a moment of watching the doors together with the startled relatives, the nurse swung her chair towards the screen, and pulling out a short keypad, began to type.

Tom rose from his seat, and with Tilly in his arms, he shuffled closer to the entrance door.

Nobody looked at him. Nobody stopped him.

The doors opened, and he walked through, pausing at the top of the steps.

The streets were the same, the same, as he'd seen them many times before. A few office workers in crinkled suits hurried along the pavements, their briefcases swinging with their steps. A tram rattled past, currently empty, but soon to be filled with their kind, when the working day will end, and offices will close.

There were no black cars, no black uniforms.

Tom took a step down, then another step.

Nobody jumped out of the bushes at him. Nobody called his name.

The entrance door banged open behind his back, making him jump.

"Fellow Edwards? William Edwards?" a male voice called.

Only on the third call Tom remembered that it was his name.

He turned.

"Yes?"

The male doctor in front of him was in his late forties, with silver hair on the top of his head and goatee beard on his chin, his medical gown draped over his pinstriped suit as if thrown on in a rush.

"Fellow Edwards, can you please come in? I need to ask you a few questions."

"Um... Yes... sure."

With another careful glance at the street and at the door ahead, Tom put his foot on the stairs, ready to bolt should he need to, when the doctor added: "I have a few questions about your wife."

Apprehension forgotten and caution discarded, Tom flew up the stairs, meeting the doctor at the top.

"Please", the doctor said, pulling the door open and guiding Tom in, stepping in after.

In a few minutes of Tom's absence, the admissions room had transformed.

It was now crowded with medical personnel, senior doctors barking orders at juniors, whilst they and nurses run from one door and into the next, fanning out following the given instructions, doors slapping behind them. The young woman with wet cheeks and the middle aged man must've been escorted out of the room, as the admissions hall was without them.

The young nurse at the desk was pushed aside. The papers on her desk were appropriated. A dozen doctors stood above the papers, pointing at something, arguing, one of them jabbing his finger at the monitor.

With a bang of the entrance door, their backs snapped upright, their gazes turning to Tom.

Tom hugged his daughter closer.

"What's going on?"

"Please come through."

146

The doctor ushered Tom in.

One of the nurses grabbed a chair from the row against the wall and placed it in the middle of the room.

"Please."

The doctor pointed to the chair, inviting Tom to sit.

Tom took the seat, sitting Tilly on his lap, only now noticing that the Broadcasting Unit was muted, spreading the unusual silence.

"What's going on?" he repeated, scanning the tight crowd of doctors in front of him.

The doctor with the goatee came to join his colleagues, taking his place at the head.

"Fellow Edwards", he started, after clearing his throat. "Can you please walk us through the events that took place, before your wife fell ill? Where were you? The notes say you were visiting relatives. Where? What did she eat? What did she drink? Did she comment on her health? Did she complain of any pain or aches? Anything you can remember, no matter how small it might seem. Can you please walk us through the last few days?"

"I don't understand... Is she alright? Is everything okay with her? I need to see her."

Tom rose off his chair, his gaze darting to the double white doors, his feet turning to walk.

The doctor stepped closer to Tom, blocking his path.

"I'm sorry, fellow Edwards, but we can't let you see her at this moment. She's currently in a critical, non-responsive state."

The two beefy medical assistance officers in pale blue uniforms, those who helped to bring the stretcher in, took a few steps forward from a line of medical personnel next to another wall. The doctor waved his hand, and both men took up a post at both sides of the white double doors, past which Judy was laying.

"What's wrong with her?" Tom tried again. His head was swimming.

"That's what we're trying to figure out. We have a few questions for you and would appreciate if you answer them."

"Appreciate if you answer our questions" was a well-known phrase, used mainly by officers of the State Security and the Police, but now adopted by other Party departments.

It was the code for "either you answer the question voluntarily or we will make you answer", and every citizen knew that more often than not, it's exactly how it followed.

With no State Security in sight, Tom didn't worry about the doctors or hospital staff, but he was cautious not to invite the trouble with his emotions, bringing the State Security with it.

"I will be glad to help", Tom answered, sliding back into his chair.

"Let's begin from the end. How did you come to discover your wife's condition?"

"We were on our way back from Carlisle, where my wife had been conducting research. On the way back, as we both had two days left of our holidays, we stopped to camp in a forest, in a tent. We spent the night, and in the morning I found her like that. I thought she was asleep, but when I came to wake her, she was unresponsive, and that's when I discovered the spots over her hands. Because we weren't far from the city limits, I carried her until the medical services could be called."

The doctor nodded and a few of his colleagues scribbled something in their papers.

Tom wasn't about to tell them exactly where they were or what led to their "camping" holiday. Ducking and diving, whilst bending the truth, revealing only as much as required, or as much as he could get away with, was the only way to avoid the State Security's arrival in the next twenty four hours, and he had twenty two of those hours left to help them to fix Judy, and for him to figure out a way to sneak her out.

"Did she eat anything this morning?"

"No."

"What about last night? What did she have then?"

"She ate. We both had a bit of stew that we brought with us from Carlisle."

"Who is this?"

The doctor pointed at Tilly on his lap.

"My niece. I promised to look after her this weekend."

The medical personnel around him scribbled some more, recording his every word.

Tom had no clue if Bill had a niece, but that was an issue he would have to deal with later.

"Any medical history to note?" The doctor continued his questioning.

"No."

There were none. Judy hadn't held a position important enough within the Party to qualify for the wide medical coverage, so any pre-existing illnesses, any medical issues worth noting, would have killed her by now.

But Tom knew nothing about Bill's wife and hoped that she was healthy too.

"Can you tell me what's going on with my wife?"

The doctor held Tom's gaze and sighed.

"We are running tests. Although her work position excludes a few testing methods, I have authorised them, as we haven't seen anything like this, and we need to understand what we are dealing with."

So, Veronica's coverage wasn't any better than Judy's.

"Can you at least tell me how she is? Can I see her?"

Tom rose from his chair again, taking a few steps closer to the doctor.

The doctor scanned Tom's face, his gaze lingering on Tilly in his arms, before returning to Tom.

"I'm not going to sugar coat it, fellow Edwards. Her condition doesn't look good. What doesn't help us is the fact that we don't know what we are dealing with. She is losing blood, and we're unable to stem the flow and close the wounds. There are many of them, and they are all over her body. I have authorised to open the next level of policy cover for her, and she was given a blood transfusion, but it is limited to thirty litres, before I won't be able to give her anymore. Of course, you are welcome to donate your blood, but I looked at both of your medical records, and you're not her blood type."

Tom's throat went dry. They're going to be found out when her body rejected the transfused blood. Tom didn't know what the blood type Veronica was.

Giving them Veronica Edwards' name, he didn't think about their access to her medical files. In his defence, he didn't think it would be so bad. He didn't want to believe it. No one goes into a hospital, whilst planning a funeral for loved ones.

"Can I see her?"

"Of course, but as she is in intensive care, I would strongly suggest for you to leave the child here. One of our nurses will be able to look after her, while you are visiting your wife."

A female nurse in her forties stepped forward, following the doctor's words and the wave of his hand.

She was about to stride towards Tom, when he shook his head.

"No. I'll keep the child with me."

The doctor shook his head in disapproval but didn't argue.

"As you wish."

Tom adjusted his hold on his daughter, shifting her weight on his arm. Although still quiet, she laid her face against his chest, and whereas before her head was tucked in, her eyes closed, now her gaze with open eyes scanned the room and the medical personnel that popped into her line of vision with Tom's movements.

Tom followed the doctor through the set of double doors, their footsteps ricocheting within a tiled narrow corridor.

Tom glanced behind. A couple of doctors and both beefy men were following them.

The white lights of the corridor buzzed and crackled above Tom's head, closed single doors floated past him.

The corridor turned sharply right, and their medical party turned with it.

After a few more steps, the doctor paused outside a closed door, before pushing it open and stepping inside. Tom stepped through.

Judy lay on a white plastic stretcher, the stretcher's tall legs ending with wheels. Her head rested against a wall saturated with machinery dials. A silver apparatus beeped next to her, measuring her life. Three IV bags were propped on the metal rods coming out of the wall, drip tubes disappearing under the white plastic sheet that covered her body.

Tom's gaze slid over his wife, stopping at her face. He clenched his teeth.

Judy's beautiful face was marred with small patches of missing skin, exposing the raw wounds underneath.

But apart from those, her face was hers.

However, the skin on her arms, or more accurately, the absence of skin, is what incited Tom's gasp. The skin over her arms resting on top of the plastic was completely gone, as if dissolved.

The bloody, meaty stumps that were once her hands and arms seeped with blood. The stretcher under her body was smothered in her blood.

Tom gulped.

As fast as he could, he pushed his daughter's face against his chest.

"Don't look, baby. Don't look."

He wanted to ask the doctor how bad Judy's condition was, but he feared he wasn't going to hear the answer he hoped for, so he said nothing.

He knew himself how bad it was. Not medically trained, he had enough common sense to realise that it was bad.

"Stay like that, Tilly. Close your eyes and keep them closed. Close them, I said."

He nudged her head closer, keeping her wrapped in his arms.

"What's the prognosis?" Tom croaked eventually, pushing past his closed throat.

"Until we can understand what's going on with her, and why her skin has... disintegrated, I can't answer that question. The confusing thing is that we ran tests and there's nothing unusual on her skin. Her pH level is perfectly normal, which would indicate that whatever it is, it comes from within, which is a most bizarre reaction, nothing I've seen before."

The doctor's gaze met Tom's.

"I've never seen anything like that. At this moment, all we can do is replenish the blood loss, as we're unable to stop the bleeding. However, I fear internal bleeding. I have requested the medical scanner, and when it arrives, we'll know more."

"Can she hear me?"

"We have sedated her, so I doubt it. But of course, we can give you a minute with your wife, if you wish."

"Please, I would appreciate it."

With the doctor's nod of agreement, the medical crew funnelled through and out of the door, leaving Tom with his daughter alone in the white room.

Tilly fidgeted in his arms. He could feel the straining of her body under his hold. He knew it would be only a matter of time before she managed to sneak a glance at her mother, and he needs to leave the room before that happens, before his child becomes scarred by that sight.

But Tom wanted time with his wife. He needed it.

He wanted to stay with his Judy, to stay longer. He wanted to take her hand in his, but he couldn't. He wanted to hug her body to his. He wanted to touch her, to disperse the lonely feeling that was with him all of his life, until he met her, and which began spreading again; its memory fresher than he thought.

He wanted to kneel next to her, talk to her, cry for her, beg for her forgiveness that he didn't protect her, that he failed her. He wanted to strike a bargain with whatever old deities might be there, begging them to take him instead, leaving his beautiful and soft Judy alone. He wanted to wail, to mourn, to scream and let his fear loose. He wanted to release the feeling of dread and pain that had crawled into his chest, tearing at his insides, before settling on the bloody ruins of his heart, making it their home.

Sorrow, an utter sorrow blanketed him. He didn't want to mourn his wife, and he couldn't stop. He wanted to tell himself that she will be alright, that they will fix her, and he will leave this hospital with her, soon, but those lies wouldn't form and wouldn't touch his heart.

He stood frozen, facing his wife, Tilly in his arms.

He wanted to knock on the door and call for the medical personnel, to tell them to take the child, knowing that this sight is not for her, but he couldn't move.

He couldn't draw his gaze away from his wife. He couldn't command his body. He couldn't bring the reasoning of his mind, his other needs becoming secondary to the need to be with her. He felt that if he were to leave the room, the moment he left it, Judy would die, that his presence here is what was keeping her alive.

Tom's throat tightened, squeezed by an invisible hand. Tears slid out of his eyes, rolling down his face, his body slacking, the ringing in his head intensifying.

He felt his daughter turning in his arms, before his mind registered her movement.

154

By the time his arms had tightened around her body, it was already too late.

A piercing scream ripped the rhythmic buzz of the machines.

The shrill ran on one note, bouncing off the walls, finally waking Tom.

"Tilly, no! Don't look! Tilly! Turn away! Don't look, Tilly! Look at me!"

Tom pushed his daughter's head against his chest, but the scream continued.

"Tilly, she'll be alright. Do you hear me? She'll be alright. I promise you. These men are very good doctors. They'll fix her. She'll be alright."

But Tom didn't know how much of his words had sunk in, as Tilly's shriek morphed into a cry, becoming the wailing of a desolate child.

Tilly screamed, wriggling in his arms, struggling in his hold, wanting to be set free. She fought him, screaming and bawling, about to fall out of Tom's arms.

"Tilly, no. Tilly, you can't go to her", Tom called, when a sudden thought hit him.

His daughter didn't know the woman who was lying on the stretcher under the plastic, the woman who birthed and nursed her.

The child didn't want to go *to* her.

She wanted to get away *from* her, out of this room and away from the disfigured woman that scared her. This woman was a stranger to her.

Scooping his daughter in his arms, pressing her fighting body closer to his, binding her kicking legs and flailing arms, Tom kicked the door open and walked out of the room.

Chapter 10

A small crowd of the medical staff of the two earlier beefy men in pale blue uniform and two female nurses waited outside the door.

The older nurse came forward.

"Please come with us."

"What? Why? What for?"

Tilly screamed and writhed in Tom's arms.

"For a medical interview. We need to run a few tests on you two, as you have been in contact with the patient when this happened."

Tom adjusted his hold on Tilly, who was sliding out of his grip.

"I don't think we need a medical interview or testing", Tom snapped. "Neither of us even have the spots."

Tom jerked his head at his arms, visible under the rolled-up sleeves of his shirt, his exposed arms wrapped around Tilly, flaunting the smooth skin.

"That was deemed necessary by the Lead Medical Officer, when he was notified of your wife's case."

Tilly's cries and screams grew duller, yet her struggling remained strong.

"I honestly don't think –", Tom began for the second time, his voice rising, when he heard the clipped strides of heavy boots coming from the admissions room.

He slammed his mouth shut, listening.

Voices accompanied the boots barked orders, and although their words were inaudible, they

156

held plenty of the decisiveness and authority of someone taking the charge. The noise of the Broadcasting Unit in the admissions room had extinguished.

In the unusual silence and among the commandeering bustle of the takeover, suddenly a familiar voice came.

"As of this moment, this hospital is under State Security management. All personnel will remain under my direct command until further notice. Please provide officer Stone with the medical information on the patient, and assist her with any further requests she puts to you. Please notify your staff."

"Where's the patient?" the voice demanded, his words crisp even against the march of the military boots on the tiled floor.

"Room thirty four", the doctor's voice answered. "Down the hall, then right; the fifth door on the right."

"Where are the relatives?"

"They were escorted into examination room C for a medical interview."

"I'll see the patient first and then speak to them."

"As you wish. Would you need..."

Tom didn't need to listen any further.

He knew that voice.

"Where's your toilet? My child needs to go to the toilet. And I'd rather have a moment to calm her before we begin the interview."

"I can take her", a younger female nurse started, stepping forward.

"That won't be necessary. I could calm her faster, and we would be able to proceed then."

The medical staff exchanged glances.

But as they didn't make a move to agree, Tom added, nodding his head toward the corridor, leading to the admissions room: "The State Security's here, and they'd want test results and pronto. And the faster she's calm, the faster you'll be able to report back to them."

The female nurse in charge gave a short nod.

"If you please follow me."

Tom hadn't seen a yellow sign for the toilets in the admissions room, so he hoped that they were in one of these corridors, away from the State Security officer.

The nurse walked ahead, leading the way, and for a moment Tom's mouth dried, as he followed her towards the corridor they had come from.

But the nurse walked past that turn, taking the corridor on the left instead.

Tilly's screams withered into a soft whimpering interrupted by hiccups. Her body, no longer struggling, slumped in Tom's arms.

The yellow sign was lit above the next turn, indicating the toilet rooms ahead.

The nurse escorted Tom to the white door, and after watching him step through, she took her post by the door, folding her arms over her chest, her back against the wall.

For now, Tom walked free, even if escorted, with guards posted at the door. But he knew that with the arrival of the familiar officer, it would be only a matter of time, before handcuffs were introduced.

"Thanks."

He nodded to the nurse and walked through the door.

Once inside the windowless white room, with two stalls behind ajar doors and a wider area with two washbasins, Tom kneeled on the floor, releasing his daughter out of his hold.

"Stay here, darling", he whispered.

Tilly stood, swaying on her feet, her gaze frozen and lost.

Tom held her for a moment longer before he rose. He spun on the spot, his gaze sweeping the small room with the buzzing bright lights above.

Tom strode to the stalls, pushing the doors open, making sure that they were empty, whilst scanning the brickwork, searching for an escape.

He marched to the opposite wall, looking for a fire exit, a window – anything – and finding nothing, he returned to the centre of the room, to his daughter.

The room was sealed like a tomb.

Tom marched towards the cubicles for another, this time closer, inspection, scanning the small spaces inside.

Although both cubicles were windowless, behind the metal grid, the ventilation system roared in the last one, its opening above the toilet seat blowing the air on the head of an unfortunate patron, who would've chosen that stall.

Tom climbed onto the toilet seat and reached to the metal grid.

The grid vibrated in his hands, the air blowing into his face. Tom shook the grid harder, listening to its rattle.

He leaned closer, and after a quick inspection of its sides, he slid the unsecured plate to the right, then up, the lock clicking, the plate of the grid coming away in his hands.

Tom knew the Party's ventilation systems as well as he knew its turbines. The government energy infrastructure in its entirety was known to him. He studied it all, and he worked with it all.

It was the way the Party raised its specialists. The Party was keen to have specialists with transposable, interchangeable skills, who would be able to step into a role at a moment's notice, should the Ordained Liberating Party ask them to.

But the Party never asked. The Party commanded.

The specialists would be lucky, if they were transferred within the same department, or where they could utilise their skill sets, as more often than not, the Party would plug emerging holes with an available body, even if the said body had little knowledge of the sphere they were thrusted into.

The Age of Cleansing gave birth to the most common Party's phrase, widely used to this day: "There are no irreplaceable people". Everything and everyone could be, and would be, if needed, replaced. Everyone was equal in the eyes of the Party. Their position and knowledge are not a guarantee or protection from reprisal.

Engineers were expected to fix turbines, as well as trams. Farmers were expected to grow crops as well as herd sheep, and teachers were expected to teach every subject.

A broad generalism had replaced narrow specialization.

Following this established course of training specialists, Tom worked within the ventilation maintenance department, before receiving his management assignment into the wind turbine division.

With years of serving ventilation systems, Tom knew that the maze of the ventilation throughout the building would be wide open, with pressure and suction increasing dangerously towards the fan on the outside of the building. But if he went through the ventilation tunnels into another room, he might be able to find a way out.

But only if he moved fast. Tom was aware that he was running out of time.

He strolled to his daughter, who sat on the floor, her legs folded underneath her.

"Come."

He scooped her in his arms and carried her towards the open vent.

"Climb in. Tilly! I'm talking to you! Climb in."

Her wide eyes were locked with his, fear swimming in them. Her body was frozen.

"Now! Climb in!" Tom hissed. "I'm not kidding. Climb in immediately. Do what you're told!"

He nudged her deeper into the opening and she gave in, her body, together with her whimpering, worming into the hole.

"Now, crawl. I'm coming too. Go!"

He nudged her bum, listening to her cries going deeper into the shaft, her knees and hands rattling the metal.

"Daddy's coming", Tom whispered into the opening, and lifting himself up, he shimmied into the tight space of the ventilation shaft.

"Tilly, I'm behind you. Stop crying and listen to me. Listen to me!"

Tom's angry whisper echoed in the metal tube.

"Stop crying and listen. Are you listening?"

"Yes", a soft lisper ahead answered.

"You need to crawl and listen to my instructions. I'll have to whisper them to you, so you have to be very quiet. You need to move as fast as you can, while staying as quiet as you can. Can you do that for me?"

"Yes", the little voice whispered.

"That's a good girl. Then go, go straight ahead. I'll tell you when to turn."

The arrival of the State Security had changed things, amending Tom's plans spectacularly.

He no longer had twenty two hours to come up with a plan to save his wife and his child.

Now, he had only minutes to save one.

He would crawl through the ventilation, until he came to a corridor with a fire exit or an empty room, with a window that he could open, or coming across an old vent opening within an outer wall, which was possible too, due to the building's age.

But before heading towards an exit, he needed to do something else. He needed to say goodbye and apologise, to ask his wife for forgiveness for abandoning her, for choosing their child over her.

He knew that if she was awake and was able to speak, she would've told him to look after Tilly, to protect her. At least he hoped that this what she would've said. But he needed to say his goodbye. He knew that it would be the last time he would see his wife.

Even if she came around, even if she recovered, she wouldn't be allowed to return to her old life. She went against explicit instructions. Both of them had disregarded the clear command they were given, and that would never be forgiven.

The Party doesn't allow tales of disobedience to live on. This little stunt of theirs would be branded as "enemies sabotage", punishable by imprisonment within labour camps, where she would live out her short life, atoning for her sins, with her life spent working for the Party's needs... unless they go for death.

Tilly's and Tom's feet and hands rattled the metal shaft.

"Right, Tilly, right", he whispered to his daughter, when she stopped at the crossroads of the metal tubes ahead and turned her head back to him.

"That's a good girl."

She followed his instruction, and he followed her.

They have veered three more times, before arriving into a tunnel, where by Tom's calculations should be Judy's room.

"Stop. Tilly, stop."

He crawled to his daughter.

"Darling, you stay here", he whispered. "Sit down and wait for me. Stay here, really, really quiet."

He bent down and placed a quick kiss on Tilly's forehead, before squeezing past her in the tight space of the metal shaft.

He turned and glanced at her. Her fearful gaze was glued to him.

To lift the mood, he winked at her, pulling the funny face he used to make, when he tried to make her laugh, this time producing no result, not even a polite smile.

He slid as lightly as he could along the metal, taking his time placing his knees and hands, and after a couple of painfully slow meters, he could hear voices, with the doctor's voice leading the way.

"... not patient zero? Why haven't I received any paperwork from the Medical Officer?"

"Doctor, if you haven't been notified, then there must be a reason for that. The Party knows what it's doing, and it's not for you to question its decisions or methods", the voice of the State Security officer cut the doctor off.

Although calm and low, his voice rang with a scope of authority much higher than of the lead doctor in the City hospital, and the doctor knew it.

"Of course, of course, my apologies", the doctor backpedaled. "But if I had known, then we would've been prepared. We would've isolated the patient... Now my personnel is exposed, nurses, doctors... I was exposed... Please let me assure you that we followed the Party guidelines, and following those, I have reported any suspect or unusual cases to the Lead Medical Officer..."

"While admitting the patient into the hospital, without checking her paperwork", the officer interrupted. "If you had done what you were supposed to do, and *followed the guidelines*, you would've been aware of the immediate need to notify the State Security of your new patient. So, you see, doctor, you haven't followed the guidelines. If I were you, I'd be more worried about failing at your citizen duty and allowing the negative element to sneak into your great hospital, where they could've infected more of our citizens, and not just your staff. Your dereliction of duty will be noted, and let's hope it doesn't lead to more deaths... of which you are concerned so much."

"But how was I supposed to know?"

The doctor's voice turned tearful.

"They were picked on the outskirts of the city, giving the correct data, associated with the given names. Who would have known? I informed The

Lead Medical Officer the moment I inspected the patient and had my suspicions..."

"This will be taken into consideration, when the sentencing is issued by the Federal Court."

"Please", the doctor whispered.

"Where are the relatives that came with the patient?" The officer asked, unmoved by the doctor's plea, returning to business. "Still in the room C?"

Tom didn't hear an answer, but it must have been satisfactory, as the heavy boots marched across the tiled floor. The door opened and then closed.

Engulfed by silence, Tom realised that the room, which by his calculations should have been Judy's, is void of the beeping of medical apparatus.

Tom belly-crawled forward, bringing his face closer to the metal grid of the vent, and scanned the room.

It was Judy's room. It was quiet, and it looked empty.

Tom found the doctor. He was sitting in a chair between the white stretcher and the door, his elbows on his knees, his grey haired head in his hands, as he rocked from side to side, mumbling to himself.

Tom's gaze slid from the man to the stretcher, his breath catching in his throat.

The white stretcher still stood next to the wall of the medical equipment. The three bags of fluid, one of which was blood, still hung on the metal rods above it. But the machines were no longer lit. The IV tubes no longer ran towards the body.

The body on the stretcher was covered fully by the frosted plastic. The face, with which Tom fell in love, was no longer visible.

Chapter 11

It was Tom's turn to lead.

"Follow me and stay quiet."

Tom looked ahead inside the dark tube of the roaring ventilation shaft, but all that he could see was the image of the slim body lying on the white gurney, covered by the rigid stained plastic. And every time he blinked, the image would be replaced with the smiling face of his beautiful wife, the face he knew so well and loved so much.

The air was blowing into his face, watering his eyes.

Tom insisted that it was the wind that made him cry. He couldn't afford to stop, to sit down and mourn the love of his life. He didn't have the luxury of time, or safety. If he wanted to make sure that his wife was the last loss he or his daughter would suffer, he needed to move.

He crawled as fast as he could, whilst producing as little noise as possible.

He knew that about now, the officer would've opened the door into interview room "C", and having not found them there, would've alerted his colleagues. Before long, the whole building would be alight, searching for them. Tom needed to escape the building before this happens, which gave him five minutes tops.

Tom knew that the officer had recognised Judy. He was certain of that.

Tom knew that following that recognition, their treason had become obvious and undeniable, and if he wasn't branded a "traitor and spy" before, Tom would have been placed on that list now, and Tom knew that if he was caught, his path would lead only into the nuclear reactors, to top up the cleaning crew made up of sad bastards like him.

He glanced back at his daughter.

She was crawling behind him. Her face is a frozen and distant mask. He knew that he needed to speak to her, to talk to her, tell her about her mother's passing, then allowing her to mourn her mother, as loud as she needs, to mourn her for as long as she wants, but he couldn't allow it now. He couldn't allow his child to be a child.

But he wasn't sure if his daughter would mourn her mother. How could you mourn someone you didn't know?

As a result of his decisions, they had become traitors, and when sentencing comes, the Party won't look at her age. Wherever the nursery was taken, Tom was sure his daughter would follow, and he couldn't allow that.

Although remaining a grey and uncomfortable topic, The Age of Cleansing was somewhat touched upon from the podiums in the last decade, the tone of discussion set by the Party. The New Party Leaders danced around it, softly mentioning the "wrongful and overacting" nature of it, although, not condemning the mass executions, but suggesting that not all of the "traitors" were such.

The New Leaders wanted to distance themselves from bloody and clumsy methods of open terror. Having a more obedient and placid electorate on their hands, they wanted to appear softer, friendlier, more open and non-discriminatory, promoting equality for everyone under their thumb.

"We're all in this together. Let's build a bright future as one" was their favourite slogan that was called out regularly from podiums.

But in the last few days, Tom began to wonder if the Age of Cleansing was bloodier and more ruthless than anyone knew, and if the New Leaders were not that different to their predecessors.

Tom was scared. He had jumped overboard into the dark waters of political reprisal without thinking or investigating prior. He jumped, hoping for the shallow waters of the shore, yet finding himself drowning in the icy ocean of retributive justice.

Without planning or a conscious decision, he changed camps. Suddenly, he became the same, as the traitors he hated and despised, the ones, who were sent into his beautiful country to destabilise his new and fair world.

And now, there was no way back. No way to come back, to say sorry and return to his earlier life, to pretend that none of it happened.

"There was no way."

As he said it to himself, he realised, with absolute clarity, the enormity of what he had done, the implications of the decision he had made in a heady rush.

Tom realised that the course of the last few days was measured by the single question: "Can I go back?"

That question sat around his neck like a chain. The possibility of coming back measured its length.

On that fateful day, when Tom decided to run, the chain rattled behind him, for the first time announcing its presence. It was attached to Tom's approved life. And the further from the life

Tom went, the harder it strained. Tom toyed with the line of the Party's expectations, and the closer to the line he went, the harder the chain stretched, strangling Tom.

But the chain held.

Tom wondered if today, it had fallen off.

But the release from the chain didn't mean freedom. Instead, it announced the start of the open season for a wild animal. No longer assigned to a keeper, Tom had become the plague-bringing vermin, to be shot on the spot by a shepherd herding its flock.

He blinked through the gaze of his unfocused eyes, sharpening his mind. He then decided to turn right within the ventilation shaft.

They needed to get out of this building, and the fact that they were still here, with the State Security troops crawling around it, was Tom's failing.

He stopped for a second, waiting for his daughter to catch up with him, and once her little body appeared around the corner, he progressed forward, this time slowing by each metal grid and checking the area and rooms beyond its metal bars.

Muffled by distance, the barking of commands and the pounding of dozens of boots on the floor suddenly wafted into their shaft.

Their time was up. Their absence had been discovered.

Tom hoped it would have taken them a bit longer, but that was not meant to be. There was no more time left for crawling about and hoping for the gift of a quick and easy escape. Whatever decision he needed to make, he needed to make it now.

The corridor below was quieter than the bedlam that rang around. Tom touched the walls of the ventilation shaft. Its left side was cold. It must be sitting next to an external wall. Being so close to the outside of the building was as much as he could hope for.

"Stay here!"

Tom crawled ahead as fast as he could, glancing past the grids of the metal bars, scanning the rooms and the corridor, and soon, one grid revealed an empty room with a closed window.

That had to do.

Tom crawled back to his daughter.

"Follow me, Tilly."

But as she didn't reply, her glazed eyes staring into space, he hissed louder: "Tilly, now!"

She blinked, then turned on the spot and followed him.

Through the metal bars of the grid, he swept his gaze over the empty room once again, and finding nothing unusual, he turned in the tight space of the ventilation shaft, and with one swift kick, he booted out the grid, the metal grille landing on the floor with a bang.

Tom wasn't worried about the noise. He hoped to be gone before State Security officers came to investigate the sound coming out of this room.

He spun within the shaft again, and poking his head through, the top of his body slid out of the hole.

The empty white room was someone's office.

An empty desk sat against the wall, with a chair tucked behind it. One wall held a small white wardrobe and a glass cabinet next to it, with shelves filled with medical, possibly surgical,

171

equipment and small bottles of brown glass. Next to the closed door, a hat rack stood; a white doctor's jacket hung on it.

Tom wriggled to the edge of the opening then dropped down, landing on his feet on the floor.

"Tilly, come here", he whispered.

His daughter's face appeared through the hole.

"Come, sweety, come. Don't be afraid to jump. Daddy will catch you..."

Tom hadn't had time to issue another instruction, to tell her to turn around within the vent and slide out legs first, like he did, when Tilly stared at him for a split second, and then, without a warning, launched her body towards him.

She fell out of the ventilation opening, head first.

This child was raised under one strict commandment that was implemented with head-bashing compliance in her nursery, which would help to create another generation of the pliable electorate. That commandment she would carry into the future, throughout her life, no matter where she would go.

That law was called "obedience".

It came with the demands, placed upon them from an early age; not to question anyone in a position of authority: be it their parent, a disciplinarian or the Party itself.

Tom had caught his daughter, awkwardly, by her legs. He pressed her body to his, as she hung upside down. Wrestling with his breathing, he gently slid her down, before kneeling and laying her on the floor.

Looking at her petrified face, he restrained himself from reprimanding her for not following his orders, for not waiting for his full instructions. She followed his orders; she did what he had asked.

Instead, he stroked the top of her head, scooping her into his arms.

Tom strolled to the door, trying it. The door was locked.

He took the medical jacket off the rack, and after sitting his daughter on top of the desk, he took off his blood-soaked shirt and shrugged the jacket on.

He tried the drawers of the desk. The two slid open, revealing a few books, newspapers and some papers, but the top one was locked.

Tom didn't have much time, and even less time to rummage in someone's drawers, in the vain hope of finding something useful. But if he were to find money in there, the delay would be worth it.

He turned to the glass cabinet, to the shelf with the medical instrument.

Tom slid a scalpel and a couple of sharp scissors into a pocket of his medical jacket, scooping some beefier-looking instruments off the shelf and strolling back to the desk.

He wedged the instrument into the narrow gap around the drawer. He leaned on it. He wiggled it, probing for the tongue of the lock, but the iron lock, fitted into the solid wood of the desk, wouldn't budge.

His daughter followed his manipulations with interest, his activity distracting her, her eyes coming alive.

"Dad?" she started, her crisp voice bouncing off the tiled walls.

"Shh", Tom hissed, interrupting her then adding with a smile and in a softer whisper: "What is it?"

"What are you doing?"

Her dramatic whisper tugged his smile wider.

"Engineering something."

He pulled both bottom drawers out. Then sliding under the desk, he reached upward, towards the base of the drawer, with a shiny metal saw.

The base of the drawer was no thicker than cardboard, holding the weight of papers by a narrow wooden plank across. Tom began sawing the cardboard, utilising the same instrument used by someone to saw a bone. He saw along the back wall, sliding the instrument down the sides, up to the plank.

Within a minute the cardboard was ripped. The papers and belongings of the office owner were scattered on the floor, some landing on Tom's lap.

Paper banknotes of the Ordained Liberating Party, scraps of paper and a handful of illegal boiled sugar treats dusted Tom.

He scooped the treats and money into his pocket, before reaching into the vandalised half-open drawer with his hand, blindly searching there for a moment and ushering the remaining content towards the opening.

Letters in orange envelopes came out, longer sheets of paper filled with the scribbles of a rushed hand. The last thing to fall out was a thin paper with a photograph glued to its corner.

The reward was better than Tom had expected. He would have been pleased with just money, but Frankish sugar treats, which could be sold on the black market, and an ID were the winnings beyond his dreams.

Tom picked up the ID papers, folding them down the original crease lines, and pocketed that too.

The rush of running boots suddenly came into the corridor past the office door.

Doors were kicked somewhere in the distance. A man's voices barked, demanding for every room in this wing to be searched and nothing missed.

Tom slid from under the desk. He rose, and placing his finger to his lips, telling Tilly to be quiet, he scooped her into his arms and walked, as softly as he could, towards the window.

The latch on the old window was rusty in places, but after a few seconds of tugging and wiggling, it slid, releasing the panes.

Tom threw them open, climbed onto the white windowsill and out of the window.

Chapter 12

"Stop! Stop where you are! Don't move! Hands up!"

A young shaky voice called behind Tom's back.

Tom hoped that the encircling of the hospital hadn't taken place yet, but clearly his hopes were in vain. He was too late.

"In the name of The Ordained Party, hands up! Hands up, I said!"

The young voice spiked with hysterical notes, whilst digging deep for resolve.

"I can't. I'm holding a child", Tom said. He was willing to bring the calmness into the situation, even if the boy couldn't.

"Turn around and don't try anything funny!"

Tom began turning.

"Slowly!" The voice called, catching the new highs of panic.

In front of Tom stood a teenager, no older than fifteen, skinny, with a layer of red pimples covering his face.

The boy was clearly a new assignee to the Internal Police squad, coming with this year's wave of fresh work assignments.

The black uniform hung like a sack on the boy's slim frame, and the gun in his hands that was pointed at Tom shook wildly.

"Can I please put my child down? Please? So we don't do anything stupid that we'll regret?"

Without waiting for permission, whilst keeping his gaze interlaced with the boy's, Tom bent his knees and placed his daughter on the ground. He pushed her against the wall, away from him, before raising his arms.

"Do you want to see my papers?" Tom asked.

The boy's eyes danced over Tom.

Tom doubted that the boy's instructions were to check papers, more likely it was to intercept anyone who leaves this building, especially a male with a child, maybe even their orientation was given, but Tom needed to confuse the boy and buy himself time.

Tom's feet slid closer.

"My papers are in order, and whoever you're looking for... it's not me. I'd be happy to show you my papers."

Decisiveness took over the boy's face, brought forward by the logic of something that he knew was part of his job and was within the procedure.

"Papers... Yes, let me see your papers."

The boy took a step closer, his open palm reaching out to Tom.

Tom's hand slid into the pocket of his medical jacket, as his feet took a step closer to the fresh officer.

"Of course, of course", Tom gushed. "One moment please. It's in my pocket. You'll see that I have nothing to do with whoever you're hunting here. I'll show you... I will prove it..."

Another step closer.

Tom could see the black muzzle of the barrel of the gun on him.

"That's close enough!"

The boy's breaking voice betrayed his fear, as it touched the new heights of falsetto.

"Close enough", Tom mumbled, nodding his head, as his hand closed over the handle of the scalpel.

"Close enough", he repeated, exhaling one long breath, as his feet took the last step.

Tom's hands flew out.

His left hand closed over the barrel of the black gun, tugging the body at the end of the gun closer, whilst the right hand with the scalpel shot out, ripping a hole in the pocket of his medical jacket on the way out, before speeding towards the boy's neck.

But the moment Tom's hand closed over the barrel of the gun, the boy had awoken too.

His eyes flew open, shock replaced by a survival instinct, as his other hand closed over the gun handle, tugging at it, wrestling it out of Tom's hold.

The boy's finger found the trigger.

The bullet shot out, hitting a wall, the noise of a gunshot ringing within the narrow back street. Tilly screamed behind Tom's back.

The boy twisted his neck further away from Tom, and remembering his training, he began to scream: "Post three-two-eight needs help! Post three-two-eight needs help!"

But unable to reach the radio, the boy was yelling into the well of the backstreets.

Another gunshot rang.

The bullet flew upwards this time, as Tom twisted the boy's hands, and in a desperate attempt to silence the boy and his gun, Tom jumped up on top of the boy, throwing him on the ground, both of them collapsing on the cracked asphalt, air leaving the boys crushed lungs with a "huff".

Tom felt the boy's body underneath him, his bent arm pressing into Tom's solar plexus. He felt it straining there, wriggling to be free.

Tom felt the metal of the gun pressing into his side, and pushing himself with his feet, Tom pressed harder on the boy, aware of the loaded gun underneath him, realising that if fired now, it would take Tom's life.

But that was the only way to reach his target. And leaning down harder, reaching higher, Tom sunk the scalpel into the side of the boy's white neck.

The boy's eyes snapped open. His head jerked under the scalpel still held in Tom's hand, the scalpel cutting a longer and deeper line across the neck, blood spilling. Tilly's scream rang from somewhere behind Tom, coming through the haze of the spectacle of the dying child in front of him.

Tom scrambled off the body, rising unsteadily, struggling to draw his gaze away. He took a few steps towards his daughter, when his mind finally registered that amongst the sea of screaming, she was calling his name.

He ran the last few steps. He kneeled in front of her and scooped her in his arms.

"Are you alright? Tilly, Tilly! Are you hurt? Where are you hurt?"

He turned her in his arms, but he couldn't see any blood.

He threw her against his chest.

"Shh, darling, shh. Don't look, just don't look. Hush, child. Quiet now."

Tom twisted at the waist, and picking up the scattered documents, sweets and money that fell from the ripped pocket, he stuffed them into another pocket, before picking up his daughter. He rose to his feet, and without looking back, he started down the alleyway that snaked behind the old building.

The narrow backstreets of the Old Town twisted between the low buildings.

Tom knew that he wouldn't be able to return to the barn they were hiding in. He knew that it would only be a matter of time before his favourite officer sanctioned the search of a few miles radius from the area where they were collected by the ambulance, and a matter of time before witnesses were found, before the State Security arrived at the door of James's house, their previous connection unearthed.

Maybe James will tell them everything, but maybe he won't. However, irrespective of the supplied information, as a registered "child of the enemies of the state", James will be arrested and executed, that was for sure.

James's connection to Tom won't be seen as coincidental. His past would speak for him. His birth in the family of traitors would be the final sentence in that brief hearing. Tom knew that James had nothing to do with it, but he knew that no one would care or listen. James's objections and plight for fairness would fall on deaf ears, as Tom began to rack up the crimes.

Tom not only disobeyed the direct orders of the Party's representative – the State Security officer – to remain in his flat, but today, he committed another horrific crime, unimaginable by any citizen – a crime of killing a State Security officer. On top of committing treason punishable by death, he threw another death sentencing charge, becoming the country's most wanted criminal.

The silence held by the state would be lifted. His photos would be splashed across news outlets, informing the country's residents of the cold-blooded killing of the officer, committed by an enemy element, a saboteur.

With this killing, Tom had crossed the line.

He untied their hands. They will no longer need to bring children into it or his decampment. Now, they have a body and a brutal, non-political crime.

Tilly had stopped her shrill a while back, now slumped in his arms. A few hundred meters away from the hospital, Tom had to slow down to pull her away from his chest, to see if she was alright.

She was, although only physically. What was happening inside her, Tom couldn't tell, as she fell into another comatose trance, her glazed eyes staring into space.

Tom turned another corner, bringing the backstreets of the Old Town to an end.

The main street ahead teemed with busy administrative workers from nearby ministries, which occupied the wide buildings of the Old Square. In their crinkled suits, a few secretaries and ministerial support workers jogged between the buildings and entrances, wads of papers clutched to their chests. They didn't pay attention to Tom, busy with their own obligations.

Past these open streets, past the bloated buildings of the forgotten royal reign would be a park.

Tom knew that park. The summer demonstrations and entertainments for the free people of New Bristol were held there every year, and when he was a student, he laid the electric cables through its underground tunnels, connecting the lights and the public address system with a new energy box.

When the new country was born, surrounded by enemies seeking its demise, the Party had very

181

little in terms of resources. But the places of state importance, like this park, were given only the best of people and resources. Tom remembered the deep tunnels that were dug hundreds of years ago under the park, updated and lined by the Party, the tunnels that covered the entire length and width of the park, some of them finishing outside of the Old Town. And that's where Tom was heading.

The park is where Tom wanted to get to, before he was spotted.

Tom crossed the wide road at the next set of lights, listening to the tram clattering behind his back. His steps were rushed, and he had to amend his stride time and time again, when his feet would burst into a mad run.

Tom could already see the tips of the hundred year old tall trees of the park ahead, when he noticed the black uniforms of two officers turning the corner. The officers headed directly at him, the stars of the Ordained Liberating Party shining bright on the front of their peaked caps.

"Shit!"

He turned and was about to cross the road, disappearing into a nearby building or a street, when another tram rattled towards and past him, slowing down outside the stop, blocking his escape.

"Shit!"

He spun back.

"Tilly, come on. Darling, stand up. Stand up and walk."

He put her down on the pavement. She stood, swaying lightly.

"Please, darling. Let's walk. Come on, baby. Look how bright the sun is today, look at the sky.

Isn't it the bluest sky you've ever seen? Look, there's a magpie."

Tom smiled, as he spoke to her, pointing at their surroundings. With his head bent down and his voice soft, the bottom of his face and the medical coat were the only noticeable things about him.

"Come on, baby. Let's walk."

Tom pulled her with him.

She didn't respond, her gaze directed straight forward, and Tom could only guess what her face looked like.

But maybe he could get away with it. He could just as well be a doctor, implementing some sort of therapy, taking his patient outside as a part of their treatment.

"That's it, Tilly, one foot ahead of the other. Keep going, darling. Keep going."

He moved forward and looked at his daughter. Seeing her frozen face scared him more than the two approaching officers ahead, his smile falling off.

But he would deal with that later... If there's a later.

He kept his head down, as he moved. The voices of the officers were getting closer, their radios mumbling on their belts, ignored. Their radios were too quiet and too far for Tom to hear, but the officers didn't pay attention to them, deep in their conversation.

The pavement moved under Tom's gaze, his daughter's black state issued shoes, approved for use in all nurseries of the country, moving with it.

Holding his daughter's hand in his left hand, he slid his right hand into the pocket of his medical jacket, stroking and sorting the metal equipment there, until he found a pair of long and slim scissors, his hand closing tightly over them.

"...and I'm telling her: "Citizen, that's not my problem, if you've lost your place in the queue for curtain fabric. To steal a queue place is not a crime, whereas hitting another citizen with a newly acquired frying pan is.""

Both males burst out laughing, their young laughter echoing off the three hundred year old buildings, which survived the Collapse and the Civil war.

"That's it: one foot ahead of the other. That's it."

Tom was mumbling soft nonsense to his daughter, not listening to it and not expecting her to listen or reply. His hearing was strained towards the approaching men, as their black heavy boots beat the pavement painfully close.

Tom could have sworn that he could hear their heartbeats too, until he realised that the loud banging of the pulse in his ears was the beating of his own heart.

"Fuck!"

The old fashioned word that Tom picked up in the orphanage left him in a breath. Tom hadn't said that word since childhood.

The word was barely audible and not heard by anyone. The penalty for that outlawed word was as heavy as for adultery, punishable by four weeks of unpaid state service.

Tom was introduced to the word in the orphanage by Jeff, one of the "children of the enemies of the state", who was quick to get into fights and whose hate always bubbled close to the surface.

Tom had forgotten that word. He never used it. But the sudden memory of how succulently

184

that word felt on the lips, the slap of it when it met the air, those memories must have sat at the back of Tom's mind, coming forefront in that moment.

Tom enjoyed the sharpness that word delivered. He liked its taste, the release it had brought.

"F —"

With an exasperated roll of his eyes and dismay at his own mind, Tom caught himself in time, before the word slid out again.

"Oh, yeah. I remember in my first year of service, when they put me on crowd control. That year I witnessed the bloodiest fights, all in queues and all by women. Do you know what I learned then?"

Tom couldn't see a shake of the head by another officer, but there must have been one, as the officer speaking barked a laugh before continuing: "Stay well clear, don't get involved and enjoy the show."

They both burst out laughing.

"Of course, if executives are nearby, you have to do the active crowd control and break up those fights. But if they're nowhere to be seen, staying out of the way is safest."

The officers fell silent, their boots walking past Tom.

"Women get crazy when queuing", one of them continued behind Tom's back, once they were at a distance. "Even mine can go nuts in those, be it queuing for coats from the Finnesse state or a foldable pine table from the North Oligarch republic. I'm surprised she hasn't come home with a black eye yet."

Another guffaw followed.

Suddenly, the radio screeched with hysterical screams, although its volume muted. Tom couldn't understand a word that far away, but the urgency of something happening was evident.

The officers slammed their mouths shut mid-guffaw. One of them cranked up a volume on his radio.

"I repeat: extremely dangerous! Wanted by the State for espionage, sabotage of the power plant and killing a state officer. White male, medium height and built, has a child with him."

"Shit!" Tom spat.

With his head bent, Tom glanced over his shoulder.

His searching gaze collided with one of the officers', who nudged his colleague with his elbow, both of them now looking at Tom, their eyebrows drawn, as they continued to listen.

Tom turned away and resumed walking, this time faster, pulling his daughter along. He could feel the gazes of the officers on his back, the wind bringing to him their hushed voices mumbling into their radio, probably sharing Tom's description.

A newsstand stood two meters ahead.

Erected across the city centre, these stands dotted the pavements of all major streets, stood in the parks and outside municipal buildings. The newsstands were mobile and transportable. No larger than one square meter in floor size, the upright standing shoe boxes of information propaganda had their three sides plastered with posters of the latest Party directives, new Party approved movies and concerts and plans for the upcoming volunteer "Working Sundays". The fourth side of the newsstand had a window, behind which a vendor would sit, selling for a few pence the fresh Party's newspapers: The Liberated Guardian, Free Times and The Two Coloured Star.

This time of day, the street was empty. There were no eager patrons outside of the newsstand window, wishing to purchase their portion of the latest news.

Turning a corner, Tom darted to one side, and lifting Tilly into his arms, he dashed through a low wall of shrubbery.

The sharp branches tugged at his medical jacket. Tom heard the ripping of the fabric, but he didn't care to stop. He ran around the newsstand, ducking behind it.

"Tilly, hold on to daddy. Hear me? Hold on, I said."

His command came out in a low hiss. Once he could feel her soft arms locking around his neck, whilst holding her on his left arm, Tom reached to the metal ridge of the newsstand with his right hand, and pulling himself up, he stood with his right foot on the metal handle on the back door.

His head rose above the metal corrugated roof, and without slowing down, he rolled his daughter onto it, before throwing his arms over and pulling himself onto the roof too.

Tom rolled to his child, and with his face next to hers, he placed his finger over his lips, indicating to her to be quiet, as his hand held the back of her head, ready to press her to him should she become frightened and decided to scream.

The second the metal on the roof had stopped vibrating under his body, the two pairs of military-issue boots of the "street-beaters" ran past, their voices clamouring over each other, yelling.

"He must've run ahead...There's a side street... leading to the Council..."

"Unit six-one-eight are in pursuit of a possible suspect, heading north down Unity Road. The suspect's not identified but possibly wanted in connection with espionage..."

Their voices disappeared with the thunder of their boots.

Tom lifted his head.

From this vantage point, he could see the green boundaries of the park ahead, the park in which he knew they could hide, to bide their time before he decided what to do next.

He climbed down first, his daughter followed, obediently throwing her thin legs over the sharp ledge, pushing herself off and diving forward, hoping to be caught by the one she is supposed to trust.

He kneeled in front of her, and keeping his voice low, he instructed: "We are going to run, Tilly. Run as fast as you can, as fast as your little legs let you. We are going to run."

Holding her small hand in his, he nodded to her.

"Now."

And they run.

They ran as fast as they could. They ran, across the pavements and wide streets, darting between people and trams, no longer worrying about being found out.

Tom knew that their survival was reliant on their speed and ability to reach the park, and the hope that they don't meet anymore "street-beaters".

Now, he was wanted.

There were no two ways about it. They both were. His entire family had been named as

188

saboteurs and spies. Not a common alcoholic or parasite that bounced between the drunk tank and work communes, that were ordered to work on government needs on a volunteer basis, for shelter and meal, but a murderer and a spy. He had entered another level, of which he knew nothing about. And whatever the little he knew, he was confident that all participants of that level exited life promptly, courtesy of the State Security service.

Passers-by scattered out of their way, stopping, gaping, following the two mad runners with their gazes.

"Almost there, Tilly, almost there. Come on, darling. We're almost there."

The grass areas of the park were encircled by low, mid-shin metal railings, dividing the greenery and the pavements. A large yellow sign was propped nearby, warning anyone off from walking on the grass, promising a penalty and state community service.

Tom slowed down his run before the railing. He bent down, and after scooping his daughter into his arms, he jumped over the metal hurdle, running across the grass, adding another crime to his ever-growing rap sheet.

He headed towards the metal doors of which only the servicemen knew, and which were hidden in the base of the statue of the founding fathers and obscured on the other side by a wide bush.

Tom nudged the leaver and pushed the door open, listening to the commotion behind his back and the screeching whistles of traffic officers.

Chapter 13

The metal tongue of the lock bit the door behind Tom, submerging them into the darkness.

Preparing for Tilly to scream, Tom leaned in and whispered: "Daddy's going to find a light. I won't be a minute. There's nothing to be afraid, Tilly." And then to himself: "It should be somewhere here."

He stroked the wall on his right, as he spoke, knowing that the metal exchange box would be housed there.

His fingers cut through cobwebs, brushed by smooth bodies of something that crawled in the dark, before suddenly stabbing on a metal edge.

"Shit", he mumbled.

His hand travelled upwards along the left wall of the metal box, feeling for the release button, which would open the energy box with a soft click, the metal door swinging open on its hinges.

"Here we are, Tilly", he added louder, "lights are coming right up."

Swinging his arm wider, Tom's hand dived inside the box, gripping the handle of a large leaver located above a dial of buttons, and threw the leaver up.

The immediate area by the door awoke with the light of two light bulbs, although still keeping the corridor ahead in the shadows.

"Here you are. Let there be light!" Tom called, repeating the phrase his physics professor would say, when he managed to successfully complete an experiment, which wasn't that often.

He stood his daughter on the ground and kneeled next to her. For the first time, since she had seen the broken body of her mother, he was able to take a moment and speak to her.

"How are you doing, Tilly? Are you hungry? Maybe thirsty, tired?"

Tom tried to meet his daughter's gaze, but she kept it fixed on the ground.

He reached into the pocket, and producing a Frankish sugar sweet, he outstretched his palm, flaunting the offering to his daughter.

"Would you like it? Look what daddy's found. I was told these are very sweet."

After a few seconds, Tilly's head rose up. Her gaze travelled toward his hand.

"You're supposed to put it in your mouth and suck on it."

Tom kept his voice smooth and soft, encouraging his daughter to relax, and hopefully, talk to him.

"Come on, take it."

Her head rose some more. Her hand followed, reaching for the sweet, her fingers brushing its smooth surface, before her hand closed over it. A second later her teeth were scratching over the sweet's hard surface.

"Just don't swallow. It's too big, and you might choke."

Tilly's wide open and concerned eyes were on Tom.

"Oh no. Don't worry, darling. It's okay. Keep it in your mouth. Push it to a side, against your cheek or under your tongue. Just be careful and don't swallow."

Tilly followed Tom's instructions, her eyebrows drawn and her gaze directed upwards.

"Nice, right?"

Tom smiled, watching his child discovering a new flavour for the first time. But how many of those moments were left for him and her? How many of those would Tom witness, before he is dead? How many before they're found, and she is pulled out of his arms?

Tom wasn't able to block those thoughts, as his mind circled back to his current situation. Every breath he took, his mind asked how many more were left in him. Every word, smile or cry he received from his daughter, his mind taunted him, wondering if that was the last one.

Tom wished he had been a criminal, before he stepped onto this road, as maybe then he would have had the required contacts and had known what to do or where to run. If he was a criminal, maybe he would have known how the State Security operates and thinks.

Now, the "law-abiding citizen Tom" was lost and chased into a corner like an animal, who at the last moment managed to scurry into the dark tunnel of the city.

But he didn't know where to run next. From the moment he made his first and fatal decision to run and protect his child, his desire to escape hadn't progressed as he had wished or planned. His plans for the next stage of the escape were shattered or amended at every turn, without Tom's input or knowledge, dependent on the will of other people, ignoring Tom completely, as if it wasn't his life.

The turmoil that followed that first decision dismantled Tom's future, throwing him under the moving knives of the Party's meat grinder.

Tom's rational and problem-solving brain screamed at him, demanding to get a grip and begin making uncomfortable and challenging decisions, but decisions nonetheless. It cried at him, warning that without a plan, a solid plan that includes a final stage of that escape, a destination of sorts, his running would always result in capture.

But Tom didn't know what to do next or where to go. He was precluded from seeing ahead in his life by the constant hunt and danger or threats coming from other people, which were hurled at him and were out of his hands.

He wasn't experienced in breaking the law or running, and after almost being caught time and time again, he began to wonder, if that's indeed how running from the authorities goes. Maybe you're never ahead, but rather darting, hiding. Your every move is a response to theirs.

Tom couldn't allow the doubt in his ability to survive and outplay the authorities to enter his mind. If he folded now, that would have been the end. Tom repeated to himself that he simply needed time to think. He needed to think about their final destination, which currently was as detailed as "out of the city".

But then, he argued with himself, he knew the city like the back of his hand. He knew places to hide. He knew the backstreets and shortcuts. Working in every part of it for the last twenty years, he knew the city well. He wouldn't have that advantage in a new place. There, he would be caught within minutes.

Tom reached into the metal box of the power switch, taking a portable flashlight off its charger and turning it on.

"Here you are."

He handed the flashlight to his daughter.

"A personal light just for you..."

He reached into the box again, producing an identical light.

"...and the light for me."

Tom clicked the switch and the white circle of his flashlight joined Tilly's.

"Let's go."

He offered his hand to his daughter. And as soon as she took it, he stepped into the darkness of the corridor, the small circle of his light dancing over the arched ceiling and curved walls ahead.

He would get deeper into the tunnels, into one of the wider openings that connected three or four tunnels, and pitch his camp there. It would provide him with multiple routes for escape should he need it.

Life on the run and the lack of planning were not the only topics occupying Tom's mind. He was worried about his daughter and the effect the turbulence of the last few days had had on her.

Tom knew that she was affected by it. Her tears, her moments of checked out gaze directed inward, her fearful eyes on him... All of it told him that she struggled, and he couldn't blame her for that. He struggled with his new life too.

She was ripped from the measured safety of her nursery, thrown into whirl created by strangers, who told her to trust them and call them "mum and dad".

Tom knew she had been affected, but he had no idea how badly. He wondered if she was afraid of him.

He didn't know how to find out the depth of her grief and fear, or what to do with it once he discovered it. He was afraid of the small stranger he loved, afraid of her rejection and her hate.

194

Tom didn't know how to tell her of her mother's death. He was afraid that the moment when he said those words to her – "your mother is dead" – they would become a truth somehow for him too, opening the gate of grief and acknowledgement which he wasn't ready to confront, not just yet. He was afraid that after saying those words out loud, he would crumble and would fall.

He didn't want to bring up Judy's death with a stranger, even if that stranger came from him and carried his last name.

How could he speak to his daughter about his beautiful wife, about the one who he knew and loved his entire life and who was taken away from him, ripped from his arms, leaving him bloody and dying. How could he speak to his daughter about the love of his life, when he wasn't ready to say the words himself?

But he was more afraid of his daughter's indifference to her mother's death. Judy's words on the day of the Parade were haunting him. He didn't want his beautiful Judy to be forgotten, her sorrow and pleas with him for missing time with her child becoming his fault.

The memory of that day came to mind: Judy sitting in the kitchen, protesting to the expectations the Party placed on them, leaving little or no time to spend with their child they loved so deeply and waited for so long, while the Broadcasting Unit gushed about the glorious day.

Tom was a familiar stranger to his own child. They have never built that deeper connection that Tom remembered having with his own father. But in fairness to him, his parents lived at a different time. Before the Party became greedy for their citizens' lives as it was now.

"We're going to stay here for a bit", Tom said into the murky darkness smelling of mildew. "Not for long, just for a bit. Remember how we camped in the woods? Well, now we're going to camp in these tunnels."

Tom knew he needed to support his child, and he tried his best.

"Please, don't worry, Tilly. It will be fine. Everything will be fine. In fact, we're going to have fun. Did you know it was your dad who did the work in these tunnels?"

He looked down at her, and in the shadows, he saw her looking at him.

He smiled.

"That's right. I laid cables in this tunnel, probably laid dozens of kilometres of the cables within these walls. See these?"

Tom shone the light to thick black cables tied with plastic bands and running along the left wall.

"These are the cables, the black ones. They power the lampposts in the park and in another tunnel. I can show you later, if you want. I installed more of the cables, some for the audio system."

Tom pointed to the ceiling above them.

"When the lights come on at night in the park or speakers talk... Remember, like that day at the Parade? It's because of these cables, and I laid them. Exciting, isn't it?"

Tilly didn't answer. She walked by his side, occasionally glancing at him.

"And if you want, I can take you into the corridor where I installed the power exchange. I can show you how we can make the light go on and off in the park. We can make the lights dance."

Tom knew that he sounded pathetic, but he wasn't versed in talking to children, and the prospect of a conversation with his own child, of whom he knew so little and who was hurt, daunted him.

"When I see the sun rising behind mountains
I think every time
How lucky I am to have you and how glorious is your shine..."

Tom began singing softly, the song that Judy loved so much.

The song wasn't propaganda department approved. But it was so old, loved by so many generations and was about love, that the Party, deeming it was glorifying the love for the motherland, left the song with the people.

"We'll run through the gold fields together
And I'll follow your call
As you've stolen my heart and you have my old broken soul."

Tom fell quiet, his memories invading him.

"Your mama loved this song. Do you remember her singing it to you?"

He glanced at his daughter, who lifted her eyes at him and softly shook her head.

"I suppose, you wouldn't. You were very little then. When you wouldn't sleep at night, when you were tiny, she would rock you, as she would walk around the room, singing it to you. In the first three months of your life, I must've heard that song a million times."

He smiled at the memory.

"Oh, how much I wanted to hear anything, but that song. But now? Now, I'd give anything to hear it again... and her voice..."

Tom choked.

He promised himself not to go down there, not to think, to keep his cool and his shit together, and here he was, his resolve as weak as him.

They walked in silence for a while, Tom taking turn after turn, leading them away from the entrance. The flashlight in Tilly's hand danced over the walls and the ceiling, as she explored the tunnel.

The hush of a low voice came unexpectedly from the tunnel ahead.

Tom froze on the spot, pulling his daughter towards him. He brought his finger to his lips, telling her to stay quiet. He reached and turned off her flashlight, shoving his light into the pocket of his jacket, dimming it.

Holding his daughter's hand, Tom progressed forward.

The closer he came, the louder grew the voice.

The voice was old and raspy, belonging to a man. It was talking to someone with a grandfatherly softness and patience, although its fellow participant wasn't answering.

"You truly have great skill here, Josephine: to kill it without damaging the fur, and skin it so smoothly... I wonder what you were doing before we met..."

The voice laughed.

"But of course, I won't ask and you won't tell. Oh, Josephine, oh, Josephine", the voice sang. "Sometimes I think how different we are. But then sometimes, I wonder if we are? We're both here, have found each other, and getting along rather swimmingly, definitely better than I fared with some of my intellectual peers, which in turn could attest to wisdom measured not only by education..."

The voice was relaxed and talkative.

Tom stopped, thinking about going back, but there was only the entrance behind him. If he wanted to find a safe place for himself and his child, he needed to push forward, past the chatty stranger and into the wider tunnels.

During his inspections of the city's tunnels, Tom would often find scattered or abandoned belongings. He would report his findings, and a "street-beater" would come to collect those, inspecting them, searching for a name of a contumacious vagrant.

But Tom had never seen one. Back in his day, when discovering those tatty possessions, he would wonder who these people were, who were so crazy as to prefer to scatter in the shadows of tunnels like rats, rather than live in the open, contributing to the Great Party and society.

And now he knew. They were people like him.

The voice babbled on, occasional soft laughter interrupting the one-sided conversation with "Josephine".

Tom shuffled closer, pulling his daughter along the corridor, filled with the smell of cooking meat.

The sharp medical scissors had left Tom's pocket and were tightly gripped in his hand, when he turned the corner.

Chapter 14

In the middle of the floor of the vaulted room, a small fire was burning.

A tiny carcass of an animal roasted above it, producing that mouth-watering smell. A dark figure sat next to the fire, the rags and shadows hiding its face.

"...As the ancient philosopher Nietzsche once said: "There are no facts, only interpretations", the familiar crazy voice recited, and the seated figure threw his finger upwards.

The openings to the tunnels behind the figure gaped with inviting blackness.

Tom stepped from the shadows, the fire illuminating him and Tilly.

Reacting to his approach, a large dark shape scattered towards the fire, throwing its hand at the arrival with a low growl.

"Josephine, what –" the seated figure began, as it turned to face them.

It was an old man with a dishevelled, unkempt grey beard, grey hair on his head poking from under a blanket that swaddled his body.

His eyes flew open. His gaze came over the newcomers, wrinkles over his forehead deepening, before a smile took over his face, carving more wrinkles, this time around his mouth, opening it and flaunting a few missing teeth.

"Oh, my... That is highly unexpected, I have to say. We don't usually receive visitors", the old man said. "Come, dear friends. Please come, come closer. There's nothing to fear. Not from two old people like us, anyway."

"We're not going to bother you", Tom answered, sliding around the fire and giving a wide berth to the crazy. "We're going into those tunnels, and we'll be gone."

Tom jerked his head behind the old man and his companion.

"Nonsense, young man, nonsense. A guest is like a prince when he comes..." the old man began to recite in a singing voice.

"...And a rare phenomenon in our humble abode", he finished brighter, smiling at Tom, as he swung his arm around, indicating at the small room.

"Take a seat by the fire please, warm yourselves up and share our meal with us. How could we let you and your little one go without sharing our hospitality?"

The smell of cooked meat fought the stench of mildew, winning occasionally, but it would dissipate with a gust of a draft coming through the tunnel behind their backs.

"It's really not necessary", Tom answered, skating wider around the crazy man.

"I can promise you that neither I nor lovely Josephine would do you any harm."

Tom drew his gaze to "Josephine".

It was a large, dark figure, taller than Tom and wider. The body was swaddled in rags, with only a face, with glistening eyes that glared at Tom from under the eyebrows, visible.

"Dad", Tilly squeaked next to him. "I'm hungry."

"Come, little one. Come closer."

The old man rose from the low stool, which he occupied. But the rise didn't add much to his height. His folded back remained almost parallel to the ground.

He twisted his neck and looked up at Tom.

"You can keep your instrument handy, young man, if you like."

The old man nodded at the shiny scissors in Tom's hand.

"But I assure you, there are no bad intentions towards either of you."

The old man shuffled forward, leaning on his cane.

"Josephine won't mind sharing her squirrels. How much could two old people need?"

Tom glanced at the tenebrous shape past the fire.

Concealed by the dark, Josephine hunched her shoulders, turning slightly, as if hiding behind her own back. Only her eyes shone in the shadows, like eyes of a wild animal.

It didn't appear that Josephine was happy at uninvited arrival, let alone to share fire and food with them.

"No, it's okay. We're just..."

Tom didn't know how to finish that sentence.

They are what? Lost? On an excursion through the city's underbelly by themselves? There was no plausible way to finish that sentence.

"That's okay. You don't need to tell me why you're here."

The old man kept walking around the fire, coming closer to Tom.

"I won't pry, but please, spare me unimaginative lies. I'm too old, and I'd like to think, I'm too smart for that, young man."

The man laughed softly. He stood in front of them now, his face hidden by the shadows from the glow of the fire behind him.

"Sightseeing has not brought you here, especially with a child."

The man took one step closer, and resting his hands and his folded body on the cane, he leaned to Tilly.

"Are you hungry, little one?"

Tom pulled his daughter behind him, as he stepped forward.

"We're okay", Tom repeated.

The old man straightened as much as his bent back allowed him.

"You're a very stubborn young man. Suit yourself. The invitation is here, and what you do with it is completely up to you."

Slowly moving his feet, he turned, and taking his time, he shuffled back to the fire, before perching again on his stool.

"Dad?"

Tom looked down at his daughter's small face and pity squeezed his heart. Her world had turned upside down in the space of a week. Everything that she knew had been taken from her. Because of Tom's decision, she was thrown on the streets, now starving and scared, and today she saw her mother die.

Tom felt guilty.

"Okay, sweetie, okay."

Tom smiled at her, and squeezing the medical scissors tighter, he took a step towards the fire, the smoke rising to the ceiling, carried out of the room by the draft of the surrounding tunnels.

"Thank you for your hospitality", Tom said. "If your offer still stands, we would love to share your fire with you."

"And as I promised, you are welcome to share our dinner too", the old man answered, smiling.

"Thank you, that's most generous of you."

Tom's gaze slid to the body of a little animal grilling above the flames.

The old man followed his gaze and laughed.

"Oh, no, don't worry. I'm old, but I'm not senile. I'm not proposing to share one squirrel between three adults and a child. We have more."

He nodded somewhere to the side of him.

"Josephine is an incredible hunter", he announced louder, turning his head to his friend.

Tom glanced at the dark, amorphous figure past the boundaries of light.

Meeting her without an introduction, Tom would never have guessed that the large pile of rags, with a wild mop of hair on the top was female, and when she glared at him from underneath her eyebrows, she looked even less feminine.

... That not to take anything away from her, Tom thought, *as there's no saying how I would've looked, if I had lived here for however long these two have.*

"But only with my help", the old man continued, dropping his voice. "You see, I make poison for her traps. Her knot tying is atrocious. Squirrels laugh at her traps, as they jump in and out of them. She'd never be able to tie a shoe should she need to. But with a bit of help from science, we make it work."

The old man gave a soft laugh.

"In a previous life, I was a biologist. And once a biologist, one's always a biologist. You don't forget the trade, to which you dedicated half a century."

He smiled.

The old man claimed he wasn't senile, but after the remarks about "beautiful" Josephine and claims of being a "biologist", Tom began to wonder, his hand involuntarily tightening on the handle of his scissors.

"There are small crates over there, if you want to grab a couple and sit next to the fire."

The old man waved his hand to the right of him, where against the wall drinking water crates were piled.

There was no doubt that these two called these utility tunnels their home.

Dark laundry hung on a cord against a wall. Pallets were stacked in width against an opposite side, creating something that resembled a bed, pieces of fabric draped over it. An old cabinet stood next to it, leaning heavily to the side as if drunk. Wild flowers and bushy plants in jars were strewn over that single piece of furniture, adding a homely touch to the bunker, with a mishmash collection of random things spread around the area. The tied bunches of dried herbage hung off a string stretched between the two rusty nails in the wall. And surprisingly, a stack of books sat underneath it.

Holding his child's hand, Tom walked over to the crates, and picking up the one with the most of structural integrity, he brought it to the fire.

"Let me introduce ourselves properly", the man continued, when Tom returned. "My name is Felix and this's Josephine, our fearless hunter and gatherer. She doesn't speak much, but she is the loveliest of people you'll ever meet. So please, don't let her appearance confuse you."

Tom nodded, remaining quiet.

The following introduction pause stretched for a while.

The societal convention called upon Tom to introduce himself, but he wasn't in any rush of doing so.

"You don't have to tell me your names if you don't want to", Felix interrupted the silence. "I presume you are here because circumstances led you to these tunnels, and we're all aware that circumstances rule a man, and a man cannot control circumstances. That's fine, young man. You don't have to tell the old man your name, who you are or what brought you here. In the end, we're all supporting actors in someone else's play, and when tomorrow comes, you'll move on and Felix Rose, once the Party's most decorated Lead biologist, will become your supporting act."

"Lead biologist?" Tom asked. "What would the Party's Lead biologist be doing here?"

Tom hadn't intended for his scepticism to escape, and although he tried to veil it, it transuded in his tone.

"You don't believe me?"

The old man smiled.

"No, I –" Tom tried to smooth the situation.

The old man lifted his arthritic hand, interrupting Tom.

"That's okay. I wouldn't believe it either. If someone living in these conditions would have told me that he once occupied one of the most coveted science position within the Party, I would've laughed, and I would not have believed that man either. Why would you, young man? Why *should* you? What do I have to prove it?"

The old man spread his arms, inviting Tom to take in the full glory of his current residence.

Tom didn't need to be invited. He was aware of where he was and what position he was in, where the chain of decisions had brought him.

"Nothing", the old man answered his own question. "I have nothing to prove it, because I have nothing now. I have no means to prove my words to you. But once, young man, once I had everything."

The Lead biologist paused. His gaze glazing, as his memory emerged, reminiscing on the times passed.

A few seconds later, he snapped back to the present.

"But I need to know how I should address you and your little angel. Would you like me to choose names for you or would you like to come up with those yourself?"

"My name is... Bill, and this is Tilly."

"Nice to meet you, Bill and Tilly."

Felix bowed his head, down and slightly to one side. His hand flew to his head as if looking for something, and finding nothing, it fell down to his lap.

He turned to his companion.

"Josephine, please meet Tilly and Bill."

Tom glanced at the woman. But she hadn't relaxed with this new piece of information, her eyes still drilling him from under her low hanging forehead.

Felix turned to face the fire and his guests.

"Josephine is not big on talk, which suits our tandem rather well, because as you can see, I am. In fact, I don't even know if that's her name, as she has never shared it with me. To this day I don't know her real name. But once, when I was telling her stories of ancient military commanders, and in particular of the life of a French military general whose name was Napoleon, she became rather animated, when I mentioned the name of his beloved wife. So now, she is Josephine for all intent and purpose. And if I have my Josephine, I guess that makes me Napoleon. Although, god knows, I am far short of his bravery and thirst for power."

Felix laughed.

"I think the squirrel must be ready."

The Napoleon of the underground turned to his Josephine.

"Dear, can you please find our guests a plate and put another squirrel on?"

Without a word, the pile of rags rose to its feet, eclipsing with its height the glow of the fire.

Josephine plodded forward, her heavy footing delivering a faint vibration to the concrete floor of the tunnel.

She reached out, and with a hand wrapped in a rag, she took the metal rod off the supports, striding back towards the wall, where their crockery lived.

Tom followed her large frame with his gaze, realising that within the single organism of this duo, Felix was the brains and "beautiful" Josephine was the muscle.

She returned to the fire with a large metal plate in her hands. The plate's sides were bent and the enamel that once coated its entire surface was largely chipped, coming off in blotchy spots.

"Here you are", Felix announced for her, as she stretched the plate towards seated Tom.

"Thank you", Tom nodded to both of them.

He stared at the bowl in his hands, his mind suddenly changed regarding accepting the dinner, now thinking of an excuse to avoid the moment when a rat would slide down his throat. Tom was skittish. His trust in humanity and society had evaporated in the last few days.

But his stomach had a different idea, growling within the quiet of the tunnel.

"Looks like you haven't eaten in a while", Felix commented, and rising to his feet, he shuffled towards Tom, and keeping Tom's gaze, he pinched a bit of the squirrel's side and placed it into his mouth.

"The poison that I give them leaves their bodies a couple of hours after they drop dead. If you don't eat their internal organs, you'll be fine. It's all in timing and careful calculation. I know how much to give. So Josephine's hunting is more like gathering fallen apples after a storm."

Felix took another piece of meat, placed it into his mouth and walked back to his stool.

Josephine came over with the same blackened rod, now holding a fresh pink body, and set it above the fire.

"Thank you", Tom repeated.

Tilly had found the idea of eating a rodent far less repulsive than Tom had. Whilst he was staring at it, battling with disgust for control over his face and lips, Tilly reached over and pinched at a crispy side, swiftly putting the winnings into her mouth.

"We don't have many visitors", Felix said, as Tilly continued to chew, and Tom tentatively put a piece of a squirrel into his mouth. "Not many, in reality the exact number is zero. So please forgive me, if I disturb your dinner, but my curiosity is getting better of me. I hope you'd understand it. How are things out there?"

The old man lifted his eyes toward the ceiling.

"Is Bosman still the Leading Father to his children?"

Tom nodded.

The old man must have been here no longer than five years, if he knew about Bosman, unless he read newspapers. It would have been plausible for him to leave now and again, or for the trusted wife of Napoleon to dig for newspapers through recycling cans, scavenging for those along with fallen squirrels' bodies.

Felix acknowledged Tom's information with a nod.

"Bosman's not stupid, but he is greedy. Mark Derek would have hung him, if he had lived long enough to see, what these bastards are doing to his dream."

Tom stopped chewing at Felix's assessment of the most powerful men in the country.

He has never heard anything like this. Such words were never spoken. An unfavourable appraisal of a Party leader has never left anyone's lips. No one dared, not in those brazen words. Even criticism of the Party leadership in its mildest form was unheard of, let alone the cavalier evaluation like that.

Involuntarily, Tom turned his head, glancing over his shoulders – a habit from years of living in his country dying hard, and probably never.

Were it not for arriving into these tunnels by chance and finding this crazy old man and his Josephine here, Tom would have suspected a foul play on behalf of the State Security department.

Everyone in the country knew that State Security had agents everywhere, infiltrating layers of society, their saboteurs initiating talk of mistrust of the Party in the bid to unearth conspiracies against the country, the Party and its rule, and Tom was always supportive of these tactics. How else can you catch a quisling? You need a lie to catch a liar.

But this couldn't be that scenario, Tom reasoned with himself. The old man couldn't be a State Security saboteur. Tom didn't know he would end up there. He hadn't planned it. Not many knew of his knowledge and experience of the tunnels, but some might, and the possibility of the old man being placed here to find and report on the country's ill-wishers and renegades was a plausible one.

Tom kept his mouth shut, in his head already planning a prompt escape.

"Once, the Party was glorious", the old man continued, gazing into the past. "Once, it was everything we dreamt it would be."

He snapped his gaze to Tom.

"Do you know your Party's history, young man?"

Tom gave a brief nod, keeping quiet.

"Of course you do. And although your medical coat is stolen, I can spot an educated man."

As Tom's back straightened, his muscles tightening, the old man waved his hand dismissively at Tom.

"Don't worry. Who am I going to tell? Who is Felix Rose going to tell, and who is going to listen to Felix Rose? But do you know how I knew? Your hands are too large for a surgeon and covered in old blisters. Not many may have spotted it, but I have. Surgeons' hands are soft, limber and often small."

Felix watched Tom over the fire.

"And "educated" you might ask?" he continued, although Tom didn't say a word. "That's easy. It's the way you speak, young man. If it's okay with you, I would rather not call you Bill, as we both know that it's not your real name. Whereas your child's name is truly Tilly."

Tom's muscles were pulled like a string, ready to snap and ready to intone. He was ready to bolt, to jump, to fight. The food forgotten, his hand found the scissors in the pocket, as his other hand hugged Tilly's little body closer, who, oblivious to the danger, continued to chew.

"You won't need whatever you have in your pocket, young man. And you won't need your nifty scissors. If you're thinking of robbing us, you will be sorely disappointed, as apart from a few pelts that will be exchanged for food tomorrow, we have nothing of value."

Tom began rising to his feet.

"I can promise you one thing, young man. You would be better off spending the night here, with us, so your child has somewhere safe to sleep, and if you still feel like this..."

Felix gestured over Tom's rising.

"...by all means, feel free to leave."

With her mouth full, Tilly turned her head from the man to man, watching. Josephine was quiet too, hovering by the side of her brave general, like an ominous cloud.

"To ease your mind, I swear to the Party and everything that free citizens hold sacred that no harm would come to you from us."

The old man recited the first part of the Party oath that free citizens would say when they'd pledge to the Party, when admitted into the Youth Legion and later, into the Party's Liberated Citizens Congress Organizations.

Felix changed the ending of the official pledge to suit his needs, but he held his hand on his chest, as pledging citizens used to during their swear in.

"Although, I don't know why I would swear the oath to you, as we both hide from the Party that created that oath and made us."

He glanced at Tom, narrowing his gaze on him.

"I hope, you won't be asking me how I know that, as it's pretty obvious. And I would be very disappointed in your observational skills if you haven't figured out that only a free citizen who fears the Party would come to these tunnels."

"Dad?"

Tilly's concerned voice pulled Tom to his daughter. Her large eyes were on him.

"That's alright, darling." He smiled at her. "That's alright. There's nothing to worry about. Are you enjoying your food?"

He hugged her closer and stroked her arm.

"Don't worry. Everything's okay."

Generic notions and generic words were all he could find at the moment.

"Do you like cookies?" Felix asked, leaning closer to the fire and addressing Tilly.

"Do you know what a "cookie" is?" he asked, when he received no answer.

"Josephine", he called over his shoulder.

The woman shuffled around the fire, and leaning in, she opened her hand under Tilly's nose.

On her palm laid an almost empty small packet of Party approved, low sugar content baked goods. "Golden sunrise cookies" was written on the side of the brown plain wrapping. The packaging held no colours or decorations, the Party not believing in a frivolous flounce.

Everything produced in the country, be it food or machinery, was required to have only the essential amount of material to function or to relay a message, and everything above that was royalists' bourgeois behaviour. Necessity and laconicism were the two pillars of the Party manufacturing rule.

But that never applied to Party leadership speeches. Those were animated, dramatic and eloquent, as well as long-winded and, at times, ambiguous.

The packet looked empty. Only when Tilly cautiously reached and picked it up in her hand, Tom realised that something was in there.

"Feel free to inspect it", Felix interjected, addressing Tom, and without waiting for an answer, he continued. "I remember when cookies were real cookies, and not those compressed dust circles. The peanut cookies were my favourite. They had roasted peanuts sprinkled over them, and when you'd bite into one, you'd have that ear deafening crunch. When I used to eat them, I wouldn't hear anything but my teeth crushing the nuts. And these?.."

He waved his hand at the packet in Tilly's hand.

"That's what happens when there's a shortage of farming land, and food production is left to spineless scientists, who to save their hide would agree with an idiot playing the leader."

The old man huffed. And again, a breath caught in Tom's chest at his blasphemy of the Party.

Carefully, as if it was the most precious gift, Tilly opened the grainy brown wrapper, exposing two small, brownish circles within.

"These can't be called cookies", the old man continued, "not due to their ingredients or their nutritional value. They're the pressed sawdust at best, but..."

214

The man fell quiet into a concavity of sadness from his earlier outrage.

"That's what it has become. That's what the Party and country have become. That's what people have been reduced to", Felix mumbled to himself.

"Josephine was given these for five pelts, which a woman said would be a shawl for her daughter, for her wedding", Felix added louder, before changing the subject. "Would you like some tea?"

"How do you have tea? Here? And biscuits?"

The words spilled from Tom's mouth, before his stunned mind registered what he was saying and how ill-mannered he sounded.

Tom's position within the Party was solid, favourable, but even he had trouble finding tea and biscuits, seeing the latter only in the End of Year celebration packages that his work gave to its best engineers and architects. And whereas tea could still be found in the shops, biscuits were an unobtainable luxury.

"I'm sorry. I didn't mean it like that..." Tom mumbled for the second time.

Felix waved his hand at Tom.

"Please, don't worry about it. I would be asking the same questions, if I was in your position. This place is not a norm for Party living. Yet Josephine and I have a few things here too, thanks mostly to my saving angel's resourcefulness. You see, Josephine exchanges squirrel pelts with women who work in the park, for tea, milk or grains. The women's desire to look good knows no limits, and no regime would ever stop that, I'm afraid. This winter the pelts from Josephine's squirrels would decorate the collars of their coats."

Although, it was Felix who offered the tea to his guests, it was Josephine who set to work, their connection obvious.

She stood up and plodded on her large feet into a corner. After the rattling of metal pots, water glugged and a black pot had been brought to the fire and hung above it.

Chapter 15

"Do you know that I built the Party, young man?"

Felix raised his gaze to Tom, the light of the fire dancing in his eyes.

"Yes, yes; that's right. Your humble servant had a role to play in the rise and establishment of the Party. The Party of today was built by me and my friends. I was at the beginning of it. I was at the source. I lived under the royal oligarchs and witnessed their fall. I was there, in London, on Saint Andrew's Day, when the Windsors slaughtered that demonstration. I survived, but my brother didn't. Like many others, he lost his life on that day."

Tom nodded.

"I know the history."

"You read about it, young man, whereas I lived it."

Felix smiled, showing the missing teeth, and again Tom wondered, if the man was who he claimed to be.

"Do you think the Party has always been what it is now? No. At the beginning, it was soft and young. But it was brave, and it was pure. It was clean. It was everything we dreamt of and more. It was our salvation. It became the saviour for the broken country and its abused men. It was a shining hope for our new future. It was everything, we had hoped for, and could have been so much more, not only for us, but for many other countries. Yet today, it has turned into a caricature of its former glory and its former self, made so by the idiots occupying the office.

"Power corrupts everyone, and total power corrupts totally", Felix recited.

"And the Party hasn't survived that curse, I'm afraid. The taste of power births the thirst for total control, which in turn gives the ruling few a misguided idea of infallibility. They begin to believe themselves to be gods. Standing one step above others, one begins to think himself better. That confused supremacy is like bacteria. It eats at everything pure and human within us, until nothing is left, but the shell of a being. People are never satisfied with what they've got. We are greedy. We always want more: more power, more blood... more life."

Felix sighed and shook his head.

"No ruler or government has ever escaped it, all eventually falling to the same affliction. History is full of them. One needs to be aware of it to avoid it. But our Party isn't. They were struck by that disease too. They grew avaricious, and they wanted more. They wanted the luxury of the fallen days, their gold and silk. They confused the placed in their care trust to lead equals, with the submission of the enslaved. And as always, the little man is the one who pays the price for their venal..."

Felix's criticism of the Party made Tom extremely uncomfortable, making him squirm on his crate. But Tom wanted to hear more.

The old man sighed.

"I fear they will destroy everything we built. Our dreams and ideas would be lost, tarnished by their greed and bloodshed. Our sixty years of equality would only serve as a cautionary tale for new generations, a warning to anyone who thinks to search for fairness again. It would be "remember what happened there? Would you subject people and country to that, when you can clearly see that it doesn't work?" Our quest for equality will be smeared."

The old man was arguing with someone invisible, and Tom knew that he wasn't a part of it.

Resigned, as if he wasn't being heard, Felix waved his hand, before falling quiet, gazing into the flames.

"I was fourteen when my brother took me to my first Party meeting. The meetings were conspiratory then; the Ordained Liberating Party and its members were outlawed by the rule, meetings taking place in abandoned buildings outside the city, in factories between shifts, with only a few trustworthy people invited. The royals screwed the people and the country tight then. I had already been working in a factory for the last four years, sleeping there too, fed by the owner, although a bowl of rice hardly could be called a meal for a teenage boy. Once a week, on Sunday, I was allowed to see my parents, as we went to church. But my mother was a baker. So she worked every Saturday and Sunday, baking fresh cakes that neither we nor our neighbours could afford. Between her work and the compulsory church worship, I didn't see much of her. I don't remember her."

The man fell quiet, his mind roaming his past.

"I have that grainy image in my mind of a woman with no smile and tired eyes, her hair always pinned on the top. I don't know if she ever smiled. But I don't know if it's her I remember, or if it's someone else. I don't remember her voice or her touch. I don't remember her smell, although she must have smelled like fresh baking. But I don't have those memories either. Every Sunday I would be released for nine hours, before I'd need to get back to the factory again. I had to be there by six in the evening. I remember once, a friend of mine, Mike, was late coming back, not by much, twenty minutes maybe, so the following Sunday he was not allowed to leave. He stayed behind, maintaining the machinery instead."

Tom knew the history of his country, his schooling covering the rule that preceded the Ordained Liberating Party. But what he heard now was far more vivid and alive than books' dry accounts, so Tom sat, listening.

"Back then, every child at the age of ten was required to join their parent at the same factory, farm or wherever their parent worked. Girls would follow in their mothers' footsteps and boys, their dads'. The children born to parents in service became the property of the owner. They became the property of a business, like a lamb on a farm or a pair of shoes that father made in the factory...or a loaf of bread that his mother baked."

Felix lifted his gaze to Tom.

"There was no way out of service, young man, let me assure you. Signing oneself to "service" was the only way to survive. With the land divided and owned by the few, with factories and properties owned by them. Roads, rivers, lakes, forests... Everything was theirs. They charged people for everything, for the use of everything they owned. There were tolls to pay to use the roads and only a "gratis paper" from another owner could waive that off. There was rent to pay to live in the rooms of their "living houses". There was a duty payable to be able to fish in their rivers or hunt in their forests, and of course, money to pay for food that was grown on their farms by their people. Many were locked in that cycle, that unending cycle of birth, servitude and death. And each generation was born with less hope of breaking free, and each generation would die, submitting their children to an owner, die watching their children stepping into their shoes, taking on their lives, miserable and grinding, as the lives they had lived themselves.

"But one day my brother told me of a man called Mark Derek, the man who said that everything in this country should belong to the workers and farmers, to those on whose blood and bones things were built and run. My brother spoke of the man who spoke of equality, of everyone having their fair share of the rewards – not enough to survive, but enough to live. He said that the man spoke of freedom, freedom to choose one's life and destiny, life for their children, freedom from subjugation to an owner, and I have to say, that notion, that idea sounded so bizarre to me, so unreal and implausible, that I had to go and hear the man. And then I saw him."

Felix's eyes twinkled, a reverent smile tugging at his lips.

"Oh, young man, you should have seen him. I was one of the first to see the ideologist of our Party speak, and I was enthralled by him. When I saw him for the first time, he was your age, and when he stood on the podium of empty crates and factory rubbish, addressing our workers, he was truly glorious. The energy, the voice, his shining eyes... He was so honest and real, and when he was addressing us, I felt as if he was speaking to me personally. He spoke of his dream, of the future, and I believed him. I wanted it for myself. I wanted it for everyone, and on that day my allegiance to the Party was born."

Tom didn't interrupt the man's memories.

"For the following three years I attended every meeting I could. At night, I would copy Party fliers by hand, distributing them the following week. I spoke to other workers about Mark Derek and his vision. I'd heard of sabotage work that the Party was doing, but I wasn't allowed near it because of my age. My brother did some saboteur work though. Once, AI machinery at our factory produced faulty sets of wrenches, which had to be melted, and at another time, the factory produced an entire batch of faulty drills.

"A lot of accidents happened to the royalists oligarchs' enterprises over those years. It had done a fair amount of financial damage to them. But it hurt us too. I heard of the poisoning of an entire village, when a fabric treating acid spilled into a river from a nearby factory. The villagers, most of whom worked in that factory, died. The source of the young river was moved by the government. The Party never claimed responsibility for that, and with insatiable owners worshiping profits above everything, it could just as well have been them. They were murky times. But no matter how hard we tried, the damage that we inflicted on them was like mosquito bites to them. They shrugged it off and moved forward, their regime imprisoning and killing our saboteurs."

Tom couldn't stop listening to the strange man. He was engrossed by the power of history coming alive.

Tom remembered the daily lessons in the orphanage, containing the Party's history, the history of Rebellion, touching on the last monarch and his selfish and egoistic rule, and the Rise of the oppressed people, who wanted equality in their world, a better life for themselves and their children. He remembered the school books filled with stories of exploitation, starvation and death, and the eventual rise of hungry people. He learned about the Party uniting people, who dreamed of equality and freedom, about following that years of fighting, repercussions and the prosecution of revolutionaries by the powerful elite, who refused to surrender their power and money, about the exiles of some and public executions of others.

"Then came the Collapse. One day, we found out that London, with the Windsors, Buckingham Palace and its corrupt parliament were no more. All, but half of Englandia had disappeared, and with it, millions of lives were lost. The country had no government. There was a power vacuum. With the loss of the Southern farming lands, hunger had descended. The country began falling apart. And that's when Mark Derek stepped in. That was the moment when everything had changed. We received the new party as our Government, and with that, we got ourselves a future. The young country that emerged from the Collapse was smaller, but it was freer. Mark Derek had made sure of that. He united the country once more, only this time, it was united for people."

Felix's memories brought Tom's own memories to the forefront.

The mornings of singing the Ordained Liberating Party's hymn in the dining hall, before being allowed to sit down for a meal, stories of the forefather of the Party, of the great Mark Derek, of his bravery and his vision, but above all, Tom remembered the love he felt for the Party, the pride he felt in being born a free citizen, born in the best country in the world, a country that inspired pride.

When the hymn would sound, amplified by the large dining hall, goosebumps would cover Tom's body, and he would fight tears that threatened to roll out of his eyes, as pride, love and trust in his Party would swaddle his heart.

Josephine came over with two dented metal mugs. She took the boiling kettle off of the fire and poured water into the mugs, offering one to her "general".

"Thank you, dear."

She plodded around the fire and offered a mug to Tom.

With mumbles of gratitude and a smile that were ignored, Tom took the mug, instantly assaulted by the homely smell of tea that brought memories of his wife. Tom closed his eyes, breathing deeply, swallowing back the rising sorrow.

Tilly was still chewing next to him, ignoring the old man's stories and her father's turmoil.

"The young country had enemies, young man. Of course we had", Felix continued after a loud slurp. "You can't imagine how many enemies we had, as we began. Every surviving oligarch that managed to flee the country was throwing his money at drowning us. The tables had turned, and now our young, blossoming government was sabotaged. You should've seen how much was thrown at us..."

The old man shook his head.

"The crime, fires, damage to the remaining power and rail network, embargoes, blocked borders, refusal to trade with us, while the propaganda of the old regime called the citizens back into the fold, asking to submit once again and be fed for that. Half of our remaining factories stopped, as we couldn't get raw material into the country. Nobody would buy our products... It was tough. Famine took hold of the country. Many died."

The old man took another sip.

"Mark Derek and his Party had to innovate, restarting the factories. The country had to learn how to rely on itself and provide for itself. We had to raise our own specialists with the help of professors, researchers and engineers that we had left, who were loyal to the cause and to the Party. We had to do everything from scratch. We had to build our country from the base up, laying foundations. And that's how I ended up at the university."

The old man smiled.

"Would you believe me, young man, if I told you that as a boy I could barely read and write?"

Felix looked at Tom, his eyebrows raised, as he animatedly nodded his head.

"It's true. All that I've become, my life, education, achievements, my research, I owe it all to the Party and Mark Derek. Within the first few years, he had established the education communes and re-opened universities and schools. During those years, the Party educated every citizen, *every*, and not just the ones who could afford it. Evening schools for workers were organised... "They can't take our pride, freedom and our knowledge". Remember that? That's what Mark Derek said during the June conference and what became the motto for the country for the next sixty years. But he was right. Look at me now. Even as I fell out of favour, my knowledge remains with me. It's something no one will take away from me."

The old man sighed.

"The progress we made... You should have seen it. We restored and extended the damaged, post-Collapse rail network. We built houses that sheltered refugees and survivors. We educated the country. We fed it. We were locked in by the enemies, but we learned how to be self-sufficient and self-reliant. Finally, after years of death and turmoil, I began witnessing the rise of the new order, and I couldn't have been happier. We began to make a serious difference. The change finally became palpable."

Tilly slumped against Tom, and when he dropped his gaze to her, he saw that her eyes were closed. She was ready to slip into her first peaceful sleep in a while, as Felix's voice and warmth of the fire brushed over them.

"Many brilliant minds that shared our dream and wanted to contribute to the building of the new world came here to teach. Many had defected from their countries, leaving selfish regimes behind. Mark Derek had even put the sailors of the collapsed Maritime Guild to work, establishing a dangerous, yet vital to our country charter service, smuggling scientists across the channel from Frankia.

"And the higher we rose, the deadlier became the assaults on our country. It was relentless. Our small country was under constant attack. Our little fire of change needed to be stamped out so nobody else got any ideas of freedom from the ruling few. Many countries in the world didn't like our coup, especially the states with a deep-rooted, centuries-long divide. And when I say we were surrounded by enemies, I do not exaggerate. It was an uneven fight. Combined, they had a wealth of the world behind them. The money that we had made for them for centuries meant that they could outplay and outwait us. All that we had was a desire for change, determination and a refusal to walk under an owner again. The people who believed, those who were with the Party, they stood strong. They were unyielding. And over time they grew hard."

Felix raised his eyes to Tom, and over the light of the fire, Tom noticed a darkened gaze, the light of excitement extinguished.

"The Party grew stronger and tougher, young man. Every life form adapts to its environment if it wants to survive, and the Party wasn't any different. They had to. *We* had to. We were surrounded. The State Security department was formed from the most committed, yet ruthless followers. The Party grew teeth and claws. The country refused to roll over and die, as it was wished by so many. The Ordained Liberating Party and Mark Derek grew tougher. At first, it was directed outwards. But as the raging sabotage within the sealed country wouldn't smoulder, it came for its citizens."

Felix fell silent, holding Tom's gaze with a heavy gaze of his own, and Tom knew, he was talking about the Age of Cleansing.

"The Party grew unforgiving, no longer differentiating between their own and an enemy. It turned merciless. Anything that dared to threaten it was extinguished, everything. Then anything and anyone who chose to disagree... But I stuck with my Party. I stood by it, by its every

227

decision, through thick and thin. I never, not once, betrayed my Party or its vision. To this day, I believe in Mark Derek's dreams. Through that period, I hoped that it was a moment of weakness brought on by fear. The short period of our history that would teach us about ourselves. But ultimately, it would be a period that would pass, as we would find the wisdom and strength to forgive. The strong ones don't need revenge and don't hold grudges. I hoped it would pass the stronger we grow. I hoped that the paranoia and fear, that gripped the country, would dissolve. I hoped it would get better... And it was getting better, I suppose... until recently..."

Felix looked straight at Tom. His gaze was so fierce and powerful, touching deep into Tom's own memories and life, that at that moment, Tom believed every word the old man had said.

"I remain loyal to the country and to the Party", Felix said. "I am and I always will. It's my heart. It's my life and my family. It's the only religion I need, the only promise of a life to come. I don't care about the mystiques of the afterlife. My life is here and now. I don't want to live later. I want to live to the fullest now, but I want my life to mean something, to me and others. "Thus of life which delivers hope to those who lost it and light to those who live in the darkness", Felix recited someone's words.

"I was prepared to die for my Party. I would never have betrayed it no matter what. I couldn't breathe without it. So tell me, young man: how have I ended up in here?"

Felix leaned closer to the fire, his face coloured red by the flames.

"How did we come to this?"

Felix waved his arm, either indicating at the catacombs they were in or at the regime above them.

"I've spent countless nights thinking about the moment when we became alienated from the Mark Derek's dream, when it became tainted, moulded into something more sinister and deficient, and I cannot pinpoint that moment. When did the country change, young man? When what we held once sacred had lost its meaning? Tell me."

Felix's voice was rising.

"Was it the time, when we turned on ourselves and excused the means, as long as they delivered results? Or was it always inevitable? Is greed stronger than love? Is fear stronger than liberty and trust? Tell me! Could we have done something else? Different, better? Did *we* make it happen, or was it the natural evolution of every regime, the rise and fall of every empire? How have we failed ourselves and our future?"

The old man was yelling. His wide eyes were on Tom and his words were pouring. Tilly jerked awake next to Tom, and he hugged her closer.

Felix cried out his questions, but he wasn't looking for Tom's input or opinion. He didn't need it. Tom realised that he was a soundboard, an audience, against which the crazy man was testing his theories.

"I've heard that now, the same people who once risked their lives bringing free-thinking scientists and scholars into our country, are smuggling citizens *out* of the federation, this time for a fee, of course. When it became so bad that people would risk their lives, pay extortionate amounts in a bid to escape our beautiful country?

When did this happen? When did we become the poison?"

Felix's head fell to his chest, as his voice dissipated, and Tom could have sworn he heard the weak whimper of a cry.

"I don't know who or what to blame. Are our new leaders to blame, their greed for luxury? But if so, how could they become so? Is it our fault? Is it how we raised them? How the men, who were raised right and true, raised in our free-thinking country, with deep-seated desire and dreams of equality, how did they become so selfish, greedy and stupid? Where have we failed them? What did we do wrong? I see their avarice, but I don't understand where it came from. Or is it human nature to dominate one another, and we were on a losing track from the onset? But how can that be? It can't be. I refuse to believe that we are only looking to subjugate and manipulate, that we are all no better than savage animals! That can't be right. That can't be all. What did we do wrong?"

The exhausted man fell silent, his head falling into his hands.

"Maybe it's human nature to tarnish anything clean?" Tom said quietly. "Maybe selfishness is hardwired into all of us? Maybe it's stronger than any good intentions?"

Tom felt raw with guilt. He listened to the old man, and in his accusations, he saw himself. He heard his own name. Look at him now. Look at what he had done. Like the leaders Felix debunks, Tom chose his small, personal world above the wider one. He chose his child above the country.

The country of the last forty years is all that Tom knew. He didn't meet the founding father of the Ordained Liberating Party, Mark Derek. He

230

didn't see the country it was before. Until the last week, he wouldn't be able to say a word against his country, and not because of fear, but for his deep love. Deep in his heart, he believed his country to be the greatest country on earth, his love for it infinite.

But what had become of his love now?

The ruins of his life's purpose and sense of belonging withered his sense of self, bringing doubt, hate and confusion. By losing love and connection with his country, he had lost himself.

"Why are you here, Felix?" Tom asked the top of the grey fallen head. Tom had battled with this question since the moment the man began to talk, but Felix's desire to share pushed Tom to air it.

Felix raised his head.

"If you love this country so much, why aren't you there?" Tom asked, jerking his head upward.

With his gaze on Tom, Felix huffed a bitter, mildly resentful laugh.

"When was loyalty ever rewarded, young man? I'm here, because I refused to betray my Party."

Tom stroked Tilly's arm, lulling her back into sleep.

"How so?"

"I refused to do something that would kill it, killing everything that so many have fought and died for. I refused to sell out, to go along with the stupidity of the new owners, who put their demands above the country's interests or the interests of its people. I stood up for Mark Derek and his dream."

Felix rose off his stool.

Josephine rushed to him, helping him to get up.

"I think I've chewed your ears for long enough, young man. It's late. Let's get to sleep. Josephine will help you to arrange a bed."

And without waiting for an answer, Felix plodded to the covered plateau of the pallets, and with heavy sighs and breaks to catch his breath, the man, who built the Party, climbed up onto his bed, rolling to the wall and settling for the night.

Chapter 16

"I'm going into the city today."

Tom stood next to Tilly, who sat on a crate around the fire, eating the porridge cooked by Josephine. Tom had declined the offer of breakfast. He would accept food for his child, but that was about it. He was not a parasite.

This morning, when he had to hold Tilly over a bucket that Josephine and Felix used as a toilet, that exposure to this smell and sight was a clear declaration of how far Tom fell, washing over Tom in a fresh wave of self-loathing and doubt.

"I'll find us some food", Tom continued. "We can't keep eating yours."

"Nonsense, young man", Felix waved him off from his stool. "As our Party says, "We won't grow poorer by sharing with others", and neither would we. Please don't worry about that."

Tom didn't want to dive into a debate on his moral principles and his need to contribute, so in order to pacify the old man, he nodded.

He didn't want to share his real reasons to go up, but the lack of food wasn't the only issue concerning Tom. He needed to find a way out of the city for himself and his child. He wanted to go North, maybe into the sparser populated mountains of Schotlandia. But for now, it was back to his original plan to leave the city.

"Come on, Tilly. Finish your food and let's go."

"I apologise in advance, young man, if I'm overstepping my boundaries, but is it wise to bring the child with you?"

Tom turned to the man, raising his eyebrows.

"Excuse me? Why not?"

"You see, from what I know of the Party's Internal police, and I believe that I do know enough, your BOL would have been circulated across all of the city's divisions by now, and as much as a middle aged white male without noticeable marks might not be much to work with, the same male with a female child, walking the empty streets during work and school hours... Well, that might be a bit of a red flag."

"She is coming with me."

Tom could have told the man that he knew all of that, that he was aware of the dangers and of State Security and Internal Police operations. He knew that a child of any age on the streets in the middle of the day, when they are expected to be in an appropriate Party institution, would attract attention. The police were on high alert, after he killed that young officer.

Tom had no illusions. He knew he was wanted. The killing of that officer was a mistake, which had played into the State Security's hands. Tom knew all of that.

But Tilly was his child. She was his flesh and blood and the last thread that connected him to his wife. In his world that had turned upside down, she was the last thing he could hold on to, and he wasn't about to leave her in the care of complete strangers.

"I'm very grateful for your hospitality, Felix, for everything you've done for us, but I won't let her out of my sight."

"Completely understandable, young man, but very misguided. You won't manage to go far with her. I would've imagined, you'd be looking for ways to leave the city, and for that, you'd need either papers in someone else's name or a connection to someone who can smuggle you out. But not many free citizens would risk getting involved with people like us. So, you'll need a criminal. Or papers..."

He paused, looking at Tom.

"I don't think you have either, otherwise you'd be gone by now. So, you'd need to find a way to leave the city... Maybe stealing yourselves onto a train or perhaps bribing a train station worker... But before finding somebody, who'll risk breaking the law for you, whichever mode of transportation you chose to employ, you'll need to have money and a willing person, and that might take some time. And not only will she be noticeable, but she'll slow you down."

Felix shuffled closer to the fire and perched on his usual stool.

He raised his eyes to Tom and held his gaze, before he added quieter: "I think this child would be the end of you."

Tom was impressed with the old man's assessment of the situation, and slightly unsettled by his insight into Tom's plans, as if Tom himself had told him. But Felix's last sentence got Tom's back up. That comment riled Tom.

"I'll take that risk", Tom snapped.

He had a plan. Having to tend to his daughter would limit his reach, but he knew that if he managed to hide her somewhere, he'd be able to work within that radius, coming back to check on her now and again.

"Thank you very much, Felix, for your hospitality. Just in case if we don't come back, it was nice meeting you. Josephine."

Tom nodded to the large woman behind Felix's back, and taking his child's hand in his, Tom and Tilly walked into the tunnel, pressing themselves closer to the tunnel's walls, away from the wide, insulation wrapped pipes that run through the corridor's core.

They came to the door, through which they had walked a day ago, the lights that Tom had woken with a lever, still shining in the corridor's darkness.

He turned the lock and cranked open the door.

The sunlight blinded Tom, and shielding his eyes, he scanned the area beyond the door.

Something was different. Something was wrong, and Tom felt it.

Slowly, he shuffled past the threshold, keeping Tilly in the tunnel, whilst holding the door open behind his back.

Judging by the position of the bright sun, it must be mid-morning.

The air was quiet and heavy like a blanket. It was free of the usual sounds of the city centre's traffic: the chatter of distant human voices, the rings and rattles of city trams and constant mumbling of news, broadcasted through the street speakers.

The screech of static above suddenly cut the silence, making Tom jump.

Tom lifted his head up.

A black metal megaphone fitted to the top of a "talking" lamppost vibrated with life and was ready to spill a message.

"Free citizens of The Federation Britannia", it began. "As of midnight of 2nd of June, under the urgent Directive Three Ten issued by the Liberating Ordained Party, an absolute curfew has been imposed on the city of New Bristol. All municipal organisations will remain closed. Work on all Party enterprises is suspended until further notice. The curfew is implemented across the city with immediate effect. All free citizens of New Bristol are ordered to stay indoors until further orders. For your safety, the streets of New Bristol will be patrolled by Internal Police troops. Under Directive Three Ten, Internal police have the right to shoot without warning. Anyone found outside after the curfew hours will be executed on the spot. Await further orders and stay indoors."

The pre-recorded message in a robotic voice ended. The megaphone cut off with a click.

The booming sound of a few pairs of heavy boots rose ahead, approaching from one of the park's paths, and not thinking for too long, Tom stepped back, pulling the door closed, leaving only a hair-thin crack.

"Be quiet, darling", he whispered.

The beat of approaching feet grew louder, its rhythm slower than the pumping of Tom's heart.

A minute later, three uniformed police officers came into Tom's narrow view.

The officers weren't dressed in the usual police uniform that Tom knew. The three wore black all-in-one latex suits of protective gear. Their faces were covered with black masks. Heavily stocked ammunition belts encircled their waists, as their gloved hands rested on the rifles suspended off the belts across their necks. In his forty years, Tom had never seen Police like that on the streets.

237

Silently, without a word or the usual chatter that Tom had witnessed from "street-beaters" before, the trio marched down the path, past the entrance into the tunnels, their measured strides loud.

Tom swallowed.

That was new. It was something very new, unexpected and dangerous, more dangerous than Tom had expected to encounter, and something that he hadn't thought existed in his country.

The trio's presence looked like a foreign invasion, of which the Party warned their citizens often and which they worked tirelessly to prevent, and Tom would have thought it was an occupation by an enemy state were it not for the star and the two coloured flag that was sewn to the sleeves of the officers.

"Free citizens..." the megaphone above clicked, starting again.

Carefully, Tom nudged the door closed, with it cutting off the commanding voice.

"Darling. Baby girl... sweetie."

Tom kneeled in front of his child. He reached out to her, stroking her messy plaits. Judy had plaited her hair that evening before she fell sick, and Tom couldn't bring himself to touch those plaits.

"Sweetie, my lovely girl", he cooed. "Daddy needs to go out, but you have to stay here. I'll go out, but not for long, and you have to turn the lock behind me, like that."

Tom turned the metal nob, and the lock clicked.

"Don't let anyone in, only daddy. I'll come back. I will knock and say that it's me. I won't be long. I promise. Only a few minutes."

The moment he said that he wanted her to stay here, alone, Tilly's eyes snapped wider, and the longer he talked, the more distraught her face grew. The corners of her mouth fell and began to quiver.

"No, darling, no. Please, don't cry. Daddy won't be long, I promise. You stay here, and I'll be back very, very fast. You won't even notice me gone."

Tears welled up in her eyes, slashing at his heart, but Tom needed to go.

"Tilly Whicker", he called stricter, "you need to be brave, brave like I know you can be. And you know how I know that you're brave?"

His daughter shook her head, her wet eyes on him, holding her father's gaze, begging.

Tom pushed through guilt and smiled at his child.

"Because you are your mother's daughter. She was the bravest woman I ever met. She was fearless, and you're as fearless as her."

Tom leaned in, hugging his daughter tight.

"Stay here, close the door and wait for me. I won't be long. You will be safe in here. Be brave, darling."

He took her face into his hands, wiping the fat rolling tears with his thumbs.

"I'll be back. I promise."

Before Tilly broke down with her childish distraught wails, which Tom knew would break his resolve, he rose to his feet, and with another fleeting glance at his young child, he cracked the door open, scanned the park beyond, listening to its noises for a moment, before he threw the door open wider and stepped out.

"Tilly, lock the door", he whispered.

The click of the lock answered him.

"Good girl", Tom mumbled.

Crouched down low, Tom ran to a nearby bush and from there, he sprinted to a closed newsstand with the drawn metal shutters.

The park was deserted.

The same Party message that was repeated via megaphone ran on the red illuminated news line above the closed newsstand window.

Tom had already heard the message. Now he needed to understand what has prompted it.

With another glance at his empty surroundings, Tom darted to a tall metal urn next to a nearby bench.

He bent over it. Moving papers and rubbish inside it, he was looking for the latest newspaper, a Party leaflet, a notice given to someone or posted through someone's letterbox, glued on their door and then ripped off, read and discarded, anything that would shine a light on the unprecedented development of a sudden curfew and the latest directive. He needed more information than that dry threatening demand, to understand what was going on.

Towards the middle of the rubbish pile Tom found an issue of the "Two coloured Star" dated 1st of June. He fished it out, reading the front page.

The entire page held a story of a farmer, who by exceeding the Party imposed norm on wool production, had earned himself the "Honourable citizen of the Ordained Liberating Party award". The man posed proudly for the camera. A gold star pinned to the lapel of his baggie tartan jacket shone as bright as his smile.

There was nothing more on the front page. Nothing about the curfew or its reasons.

Tucking in the newspaper at the back of his trousers for a detailed inspection later, Tom jogged to another large tree.

The earlier plan of acquiring documents and leaving the city was crumbling with this new event. The curfew has changed his earlier plan, making Tom wonder if he'll ever leave this city, or survive.

Was the curfew implemented because of him? Was the city locked down to catch him?

Although that could be the case, it didn't make sense. Surely, there were renegades and criminals before him? Surely, he is not the first in the history of the Party to break the law? And if they are not hunting him, then whom?

Running in short bursts broken by pressing against tree trunks and the sides of newsstands, crouching under greenery of shrubbery, Tom progressed to the main road encircling the park.

The road was deserted. No people, no trams, no cars.

The seagulls floated in the cloudless sky, calling into the still air, landing on the buildings and benches, walking on the empty pavements with an arrogant sense of exemption to freedom. A Party speaker on the nearby building broke the silence of the street, reciting the same announcement.

Tom crossed the wide open road, darting to the old buildings on the other side.

With his back pressed against a wall, he scanned the windows of the buildings around.

The windows of the municipal building of the Road Maintenance department and of The Library of Political History remained dark and lifeless. The buildings stood empty, obeying the law and the announcement.

With another glance at the road, Tom was about to turn around and rush back to the utility tunnels, when the roar of heavy vehicles entered the street.

Although concealed by shadows cast onto the pavement by the overhung balconies of the three century old buildings, for fear of being spotted, Tom slid deeper around the corner, away from the face of the building and the road, when the noise of the large engines grew louder, and the first vehicle came into view, followed closely by the second, then the third, as the fourth turned the corner at the bottom of the road.

Trucks progressed down the street, their dark bodies swelling, as they approached.

Tom's throat dried at the recognition.

The black vehicles without insignia were identical to those Tom had seen outside Tilly's nursery. They had the same square black cabins of military trucks and the beds hidden under black tarpaulin stretched on the metal overhead bars.

But this time, a masked driver in the black uniform sat in each cabin, and two armed officers with rifles stood on the footboards, at either side, their faces hidden by the black masks too.

The convoy crawled forward.

By the time the first truck reached Tom's hiding spot and drove past, a fifth vehicle had turned the corner, appearing at the bottom of the road. It was the last one.

Tom couldn't breathe. Unable to walk away or draw his gaze from the trucks' slow beetle bodies, his eyes were drinking in the sight.

As the last, fifth truck rolled by the building where Tom hid, Tom shuffled closer to the road, following the disappearing convoy with his eyes, when the truck dove into a pothole that the country was riddled with, jerking upwards and sideways, as it climbed out.

At the same moment, a sudden gust of summer wind came, showering the black truck with pink soft petals and scent of cherry blossom... and lifting a flap of the black tarpaulin.

Tom's heart, giving the last pump, jumped to his throat, his chest suddenly constricted at the heart's absence. Tom leaned onto the building, his fingers digging into the cavities of loose cement between the bricks.

Rows upon rows of young children, some younger than Tilly and some older than her, sat on the low benches, their small bodies packed tightly within the truck. The children's frightened faces, black and white, belonged to both boys and girls. Black uniformed dresses and suits of schools and nurseries interrupted the greyness of clothing, adding darkness to the abyss of the space.

The children's tear-welled eyes shone with pure fear in the void of the truck. Their soft cries and calls for "mummy" drifted past the open flap, and seated on the benches, older children were hugging the crying youngsters.

Tom couldn't tell how many children were there. He couldn't see them all. Only the first few rows were illuminated by June sun, which snuck in past the tarpaulin. The back rows of the captives, shaded in grey, disappeared in the depths of the truck. A masked soldier stood inside, just past the flap, with his back to the street. His rifle was trained on the scared cargo. His stance is a clear attestation, as to who is the enemy.

The next second, the truck straightened. The wind passed and the black flap fell back.

The convoy proceeded forward down the road, turning right on the lights, which were flashing a constant orange.

Tom shuffled back into the alleyway. Unable to stand any longer, he slid along the building's wall and on to the ground.

Chapter 17

The high-pitched buzz of static screeched, filling the street and slapping Tom awake.

He didn't know how long he'd been sitting here. He couldn't tell how much time had passed.

Tom felt weak and lightheaded. He felt the same way only once before, when he had pneumonia and had no energy for any movement, his body only concerned with drawing a breath, which hurt and exhausted him, every new shred of oxygen lacerating his lungs.

Tilly was waiting for him – his child, his life.

His hands travelled up the rough wall, his legs pushing him up.

Tom rose.

"Free citizens of The Federation Britannia..."

The robotic voice began a new wave of the announcement.

Like a diver before a jump, Tom took another deep breath, steadying himself, before he shuffled towards the road.

The road remained empty, the Party announcement bouncing off the buildings, drowning the cries of the seagulls in the sky and the ones, strutting about and demanding food. After a quick dash across the wide pavements and the road, Tom would reach the park, where his daughter waited for him.

He paused, readying for his run, when his gaze slid across the road and to the right, where the building of the "Ministry of Forestry" stood, flaunting its white corner of polished stone.

Last year, during the final step of the delivery of his energy project, Tom and his department leader were summoned into the "Federal Ministry of Energy", to receive praise from the deputy energy minister for timely delivery of their latest project, whilst at the same time, updating him on the progress of upcoming projects.

On that visit Tom learned that the large ministry buildings were independent, self-sustained towns within the city, created to meet any, and every, need of ministers and their staff, from exercise and sleeping rooms, to a laundry service and restaurant. With a unique level of access to the luxury of the Party lifestyle of its top nomenclature, ministers were left wanting for nothing. And now, Tom wanted crumbs of their comfortable life.

With another set of short zigzagging sprints, bouncing from building to building and corner to corner, Tom reached the ministry building and slid around, towards the back of it.

The white stone building was over three hundred years old, boasting pompous decorative façade of arches, columns wrapped in curved designs of glorified flora, none of which would have made it into an architectural design of the buildings of today's utilitarian Britain.

Tom turned the corner.

The back of the building faced a paved yard with white lines slicing it across, marking parking spaces for ministerial cars. The backyard was encircled by three other buildings, turning it into a stone and cement echoing well.

There was no pomposity here.

The back of the building was riddled with cracks running its width and length, loose and chipped stone, with chunks of missing grandiose glory. The green "fire exit" plaque was nailed onto a door under a metal porch, its brass handle shining in the daylight.

Tom rattled the door. It was locked. Made centuries earlier and reinforced by the Ministerial Security, it was no match for Tom's kicks or stubbing with his trusty scissors. Tom wasn't skilled in lock picking, and ramming that thick door would be totally pointless.

There were no other doors, nothing shabbier, no delivery manholes that Tom had hoped would lead into the basement and were secured only by a cheap padlock.

But a row of small windows poked above the ground.

Tom kneeled in front of one, trying to see past its dusty surface. He crawled in front of each, glancing into it, until one finally revealed what Tom was searching for.

The room past the window was large and dark, but the sides of metal stoves glistened in the weak light.

Not willing to waste any more time, Tom crouched closer, and yanking down the sleeve on his jacket and holding the fabric in his fist, he drove his hand through the glass window.

He paused, listening to his surroundings, but the announcement drowned the crisp sound of the shattering glass.

Tom knocked the shards around the frame, and with another glance over his shoulder, he dropped to the ground and slid into the opening.

It didn't matter how quiet Tom had tried to be or how much he tried to muffle and cushion his fall. The window positioned high above the tiled floor was too high for Tom to make a quiet entrance, and knocking a row of pans stacked next to the sink under the window, Tom fell.

He mumbled his favourite curse, as he rolled to his stomach, before rising to his feet, expecting the arrival of the Police any moment now.

"They might come, but they might not", Tom conciliated to himself.

He didn't know if this building was wired for security alerts or if someone might've been nearby and heard him, but he was here for a single reason – food. He needed to find what he came for and get out, ideally in one piece and not hand in hand with a State Security officer.

With no time to lose, Tom began working the kitchen.

He threw open cabinet doors along the wall occupied by a huge stove with twelve burners, only to find crockery, pots and glassware.

An impressive selection of cook's knives hung on the same wall. Reaching out, Tom scooped the two largest knives, tucking them behind his belt.

He was about to walk away to continue his search, when changing his mind, he reached out, and picking up a small knife, he shoved it in his trousers pocket.

Tom walked to the opposite side of the large room, and after throwing open the double doors of a tall and wide cupboard, which looked more like an oversized wardrobe, he froze.

The "wardrobe" was filled to the brim with the rows of neatly stacked fat packets wrapped in the brown packaging paper. Each packet held the Party star on the front, stating below in small letters what the product was inside the packet. A stamp of large red letters ran across the writing like a fresh bleeding brand, announcing: "FOR MINISTERIAL USE ONLY".

Tom shuffled closer, his fingers dancing over the packets.

There were tea, pearl barley, oats, dried fruit and more. Tom reached deeper into the pantry, moving the precious stock around, exposing tins of fish and meat.

An involuntary smile spilled over Tom's face. He had found what he came for.

There was more food than he needed, and more than he could carry.

He began picking up packets, placing them on the metal table behind him. A bag of pearl barley, a couple of tins of fish and meat, tea, the pile began to grow.

Tom turned to the pantry, ready to scoop another bounty, when he realised that he won't be able to fit even such a limited amount of food into his pockets and carry.

He spun on the spot, looking for something he could use as a bag. Methodically, he threw the rest of the kitchen's cupboard doors open, searching now not for food, but for bags, whilst cursing himself for not thinking of it before setting off. But there were no carriers of any kind in the room.

Two white doors in the two, nearby walls led away from the kitchen.

Light on his feet, Tom moved to the nearest door and pushed at it.

The door creaked and opened.

Tom moved closer, glancing through the gap.

The room must have been living quarters for a cook.

The bare walls and a naked light bulb under the ceiling, a metal bed under a grey blanket and a bedside cabinet next to it were the only fittings in the room, taking almost all of the space in the cubicle. The food pantry was larger than this room.

Tom stepped into the room, coming closer to the small cabinet and opening it. A glass container with tooth cleaning powder, a toothbrush and a comb were all that sat inside.

Suddenly, with the corner of his eye, Tom caught a light movement coming from under the bed.

Keeping his body still and his back bent, as if engrossed in studying the content of the bedside cabinet, Tom slid his right hand to the back of his jeans, finding the handle of the knife and tugging it free. Keeping his feet in the same position, Tom twisted at the waist, and once ready, he dived forward and under the bed, grabbing a fistful of something and pulling it free.

A shriek pierced the small room, ringing on a hysterical single note, as Tom pulled out a slim body.

"Shut up! Shut up, shut up!" Tom hissed then screamed, but the shrill tolled.

The sound of a slap rang out next, cutting the shriek mid-wail, bringing with it silence.

"Keep quiet and you'll be alright", Tom growled.

A young woman in her early twenties stood in front of him, holding her stinging red cheek.

"Why are you here?" Tom asked, and receiving no answer, he shook her slender shoulder to induce cooperation.

"I –... I work here. I was working the night shift when they closed the city and locked the building."

"Do you know *why* they've locked the city?"

250

The woman shook her head, her curly brown hair bouncing around her face, her eyes bulging at Tom.

She was abandoned, sealed in the hull of a damaged submarine, as it began taking water. Tom wondered how many more like her were locked around the city, and what had prompted that immediate lockdown and abandonment, with troops patrolling the streets, carrying rifles and a threat of shooting anyone on sight.

"Don't scream, don't jump me and don't run... Don't do anything stupid, and you'll be alright."

Tom brought the knife to her throat.

"I'll take some food, and I'll leave."

Her gaze was fixed to the knife, as she nodded.

"Good."

He exhaled.

"Do you have a bag here? A backpack, a shopping bag, anything?"

Careful not to cut her neck with a rushed movement, she nodded again.

"We have delivery bags", she said. "They're in the changing room."

"Where is it?"

"The next room off the kitchen."

"Come on. You'll show me."

Grabbing her by her shoulder, Tom shoved her forward, out of the room and through the last, unexplored white door.

The adjoining room was indeed a changing room, with tall, floor to ceiling lockers running along two opposing walls, whilst a wooden stall with railing hooks cut the room in the middle.

A couple of forgotten white cook's jackets dotted the railing, and judging by their size, belonging to different people. But there were no bags.

"Where are the bags?"

"There."

She pointed to a set of double doors.

Keeping a tight grip on her shoulder and dragging her along, Tom strutted forward and opened the door.

The height of the cupboard was cut by four railings, holding navy blue bags that hung off metal hooks, their cross-body and shoulder handles dangling underneath. Some bags were bigger than others, whilst some looked insulated.

They were a part of the privileged service for the top Party elite that Tom had only heard of, but never witnessed himself, or knew of anyone who used it – a courier food delivery service. That perk was strictly for the upper echelons of the Party and was rarer than a house with a garden behind a low, white fence within the city limits.

Tom reached in, and after pushing a few bags out of the way, he pulled out a backpack and a cross-body bag off their hooks. The "Party delivery service" was written on the front. The Party star shone against the backdrop of the two coloured flag.

"Come."

He turned the woman around, nudging her back into the kitchen.

"Move it."

Once in the kitchen, he walked with her to the pantry, and with a warning glare, he pushed her aside, towards the cooker.

"Stay here."

He opened his new bags and began scooping the packets of food into them.

"Not that", she said behind him, as he picked the next brown packet.

"What?"

Tom turned, raising his gaze to the woman who stood nearby, watching his manipulation with the food.

"These beans require twice their weight in water and three hours of boiling, before they are edible. And this," she pointed to a row of tins in the cupboard, a few of which he had already shoved into his bag, "is a salty fish paste. It's flavouring. You only need one spoon for a twenty litre pot. You won't need three tins of that."

She pointed to his bag.

"You need something with higher nutritional value", the woman continued. "Maybe something that can be eaten by itself; or ideally, choosing a few ingredients that can go together as a meal."

She shuffled closer to the pantry, and stretching her neck around the open door, she glanced inside.

"Like a corned lamb, for example, or tins of pre-cooked butter beans, reconstructed dry potato flakes, dry fruits, rice flakes, corn kernels."

She pointed to the tins and brown paper packets as she announced her choices, and after listening for a few seconds, Tom began filling the bags with the food she was pointing at.

"And a box of synthetic food", she added, announcing the final ingredient to her shopping list, her finger moving to a tower of brown boxes in a corner of the kitchen.

Tom's gaze followed her finger.

"Each pouch contains three thousand calories, more than most meals. There are chicken and beef flavours."

Tom heard the whizzing of an object cutting through the air before he saw a pan coming at him.

He jerked sideways, but not far or fast enough.

A shiny stainless steel pan landed on his shoulder.

Tom roared. His hand opened, releasing the bag. The tins within the bag clanked against each other and the tiled floor.

Tom spun. Forgotten, the knife in his hand drew the trajectory of his turn, searching for the person responsible.

"I said, nothing stupid", Tom growled, barely holding his rage, the leash on it slipping, calling for reprisal.

"Do you want to die? I can arrange it", Tom hissed, mindful of the need to be quiet.

The woman pressed herself against the cupboard, waiting for his strike.

"You might as well kill me. I'm logged in for this shift. I'm responsible for that stock. When the curfew is lifted, they'll sentence *me* for theft", she spat at him, her eyes were narrow slits. "I'm not going into labour camps for you. You might as well kill me."

"Someone will kill you, you stupid bitch, but it won't be me."

Tom pointed the knife at her.

"Drop it. Drop it, I said!"

His gaze travelled to the pan in her hand.

But her stance and her glare oozed with defiance.

Tom pushed his hand forward, the knife's edge kissing the skin on her neck.

"You're dumber than I thought. Drop it. Now."

A few seconds later, the pan met the floor with a hollow ring.

With his knife trained on her, Tom grabbed her shoulder, and once again, dragged her across the kitchen, now in the opposite direction. Her feet ran, keeping up with his long stride.

Tom opened the door to the room where he found her, and shoved her in.

Pushed, she almost flew, landing on the bed.

Tom stepped out, slamming the door. And before she was on her feet, ready to jump at him and at the closing door, he slid a handle of a meat cleaver through the door handle, jamming the door shut.

The pounding and the kicking rattled the door.

"I'll tell them what you look like", she howled behind the door. "I'll tell them everything. They'll find you. Do you hear me? You're dead! For the theft of Party property, disobeying the curfew, you'll be dead! Hopefully, you'll be dead when you leave this place. I wish, they'll see you and shoot you. You'll be lucky to see the inside of a labour camp. You'll be hung! You hear me? You'll be hung!"

With her shrills muffled by the door, echoing behind his back, Tom walked across the room and scooped up his bags, before throwing a few more tins and packets into them.

He hitched one bag over his shoulder and slid one across his body. And after picking up a box of synthetic food, he climbed onto the chair, onto the steel sink, and out, through the window.

Chapter 18

Weighed down by the two bulging bags, with the large box of synthetic food balancing in his arms, Tom's return to the utility tunnels was less smooth and took longer.

Loaded with his loot, Tom was slower. The sprints across the open and wide pavements and the road were trickier, the breaks between those bursts of mad rush longer.

Once, he managed to avoid a patrol of masked officers only by an inch, by diving behind the nearby bushes, then sitting there, wrestling with the jitter in his legs and arms that were not only a result of physical exhaustion.

Tom contemplated dumping the box of synthetic food here, then being lighter, run towards the safety of the tunnels. But he decided against it. Not only the box would alert the Police to the presence of a fugitive in the area should it be discovered, but it would also rob his daughter of food.

Tom's muscles sang. His heart punched at his ribs. But he managed to make it to the metal door of what is now his home, a few times saving the bulky box in time from hitting the pavement by catching it with his knee.

Tom adjusted the box in his arms, and after leaning one side of it on the metal frame and propping it with his body on the other side, he freed his hand and tapped softly on the door.

"Tilly. Tilly, darling. It's daddy", Tom called in a hushed whisper into a narrow gap between the door and its frame. "Open up, sweetie. It's daddy. Open, Tilly."

"Daddy?"

A barely audible stammering whisper came past the door. It was so quiet that Tom couldn't say for sure, if it was his daughter who asked, or if it was his imagination.

He scratched at the door again.

"Tilly, darling, please open up. It's daddy."

The lock turned, its springs resisting the command of a weak hand, eventually clicking.

Tom nudged at the door, and it opened.

He stepped into the dark shaft.

The two light bulbs on the opposite walls were still lit, illuminating the small frame of his daughter. Her eyes were large and scared, her face awash with tears.

Tom dropped the box on the ground, turned and locked the door, before allowing himself to relax. He fell to his knees in front of his child and pulled her close.

"Daddy's here. Daddy's here. I'm back, darling. Daddy's back", he mumbled, as he hugged her, stroking her soft hair, her back, rocking her gently, as he had seen Judy doing so many times.

"Daddy's here."

As he continued stroking her back, relieved at seeing her again, finding her safe and being able to return to her, finding food for her, ensuring her survival past today and knowing that she will be safe and fed from now on, that his child would stay with him for longer, much longer, maybe even escaping the city, finding life past these walls and past the black trucks, he couldn't stem his mumbling, his relief pouring in those repetitive words, tickling his nose and itching at his eyes.

But he refused to cry.

He was a man. He was a strong man and a Party member, raised in the toughest country in the world, the country that fought enemies every day of its existence, the country that promoted resilience and strength at all cost, that demanded nothing less from its citizens.

Tom was raised tough. The Party made sure of that. The guidance of the Party was to never show feelings, stomping on them, not just hiding them, but preventing them from surfacing, controlling them, as one was expected to control his destiny and future. That guidance was clear. It was weaved through Tom's life, and Tom wasn't about to fold.

Tom wouldn't allow the weak softness of a bourgeois to enter his heart, debilitating him, pulling him off his course, crumbling him and his resolve. He won't become soft.

He maybe was on the run from the Party, but he was a Party member nonetheless. Who he is now was down to the Party, and that will never change. In his heart, he was as the iron as the forefather of the Party – the Iron Andrew.

And he was doing well, until he felt the small arms rise around him, moving behind his back, settling there. And Tom realised that for the first time since her birth, his daughter was hugging him.

Her small body was pressed to his. Her head rested on his chest, awkward at first, until he gently nudged her closer, cupping her small head in his hand.

He remembered how she used to fit in his hands, when she was born, perfectly and safe, how her head rested in his palm, as if it was made for him. He remembered how well she would nestle in Judy's arms, how perfectly Judy fitted in his embrace, when she leaned on him.

Sudden memories of the early evenings of the first month after Tilly's birth resurfaced.

He would come home, and that new, alien feeling of happiness would wash over him the moment he would step through the door. That feeling was gentle, yet intense. Every organ of Tom's body would be soaked in it. He would feel it inside of him. He would feel it with his skin, as it would surround him, like air.

The three of them were the pieces of the same puzzle, fitting perfectly, as if made for each other, the other two puzzles created and shaped only for him, for his arms and his heart.

Now, he had lost a piece. It was torn away, taking with it a chunk of his life and his heart, although, on most days, it felt as if he had lost his entire heart. It was very hollow in there as of late. Were it not for breathing and standing upright, Tom often wondered, if he had any heart left at all. His chest felt empty.

Tilly's body shook next to his, her sobs muffled by her personal, indoctrinated demands placed by the Party. She was suppressing her emotion, as she was told to do from the moment she slotted into the Party's fold. She wanted to share her fear and relief with her father, her fear of something as trivial, as being left alone in an unknown place, her relief at his arrival, yet she didn't know how, and she wasn't allowing herself to.

They were the two broken and hollow people, each missing the same piece of the same puzzle, forever left empty, searching for something, anything, to fill that hollow spot, the Party demands of strength haunting them both.

And either in a need to aid Tilly's release, to avail her healing, or maybe desperate for her closeness, wanting her to share her pain with him, allowing him to be the father he was never given the chance to be, or maybe selfishly wanting to finally mourn his wife and not be alone during that moment, but Tom's guard slipped – no, he allowed for it to slip – and the tears began to flow, as the sorrow took a hold, raking his body, as he bit on his lip, stifling his cries and his screams, finally finding a release.

Tom rocked his child, his soft words flowing past his guard and reasoning, coming from somewhere deep, until he realised what he was saying.

"I'm sorry. I'm sorry. I'm sorry."

He spoke these two words repeatedly. He was apologising to her, apologising for everything that was wrong in her life, for everything that he had done to contribute to it, and even for everything that wasn't his fault.

Tom's tears flowed.

But the release they brought scared him.

The questioning of himself and his life went deeper, lifting the rocks of his past, glancing underneath them, searching for a starting point, asking if this outcome was a prerequisite, if it was set in motion years before Tom's rash decision.

He couldn't allow it. The demons that lurked in his past were not made for this day.

Tom pulled himself away from his daughter, wiping his face with the palm of his hand, taking a deep breath and shaking his head.

"Let's go, baby. Let's go and see Felix."

Tom rose to his feet.

But before setting off into the tunnels, he took a backpack off his back, and after scanning the area around him, he shoved it on top of the insulated pipes, nudging it deeper, pressing it against a wall.

Pulling a newspaper from behind his belt, he took out the middle page spread and placed it over the bag, tucking in the corners between the pipe and the bag.

"Sweetie, can you please hand me that brick and that piece of metal?"

Tilly's gaze followed the direction of Tom's finger.

Sniffling, she wiped her nose on her arm and plodded to the corner, bringing the items her father asked for.

"Thank you, darling."

Tom smiled at his child, and taking the two rough objects from her hands, he placed them on the top of the newspaper.

Tom took a step back, admiring his work, before scanning the area and picking up a few more pieces of metal junk and placing them in front of the bag, covering it completely.

He was satisfied now.

"Let's go."

He reached out to his daughter, and she took his hand.

"Ain't I pleased to see you again, young man."

Felix rushed over to them the moment they walked in, as if he was pacing the dome room, waiting for them.

"Can you please explain to me, what's going on up there?"

Felix jerked his head sideways. The agitation shook his voice and his weak body.

"Josephine went to exchange the pelts", he continued, shuffling closer, "but not ten minutes had passed, as she comes back, with pelts, shrugging her shoulders then pointing up and shaking her head at me, with not a word of explanation. Of course, brevity is completely in Josephine's style, but that doesn't help me. If you hadn't have come back, young man, I would've had to go up there myself, to figure out what's going on."

The old man was next to Tom now. Animated, he spoke faster than usual, his distress at the new development evident.

"What is happening, young man?"

Felix's gaze raked Tom's face, skipping to Tilly, darting back to Tom, before stopping at the bag with the star on the front.

"What is this? Where did you get it? What's going on?"

Whilst holding Tilly's hand in one hand and the box of synthetic food under another arm, ignoring the flustered man, Tom marched to the fire.

He placed his haul on the ground and sat his daughter on the crate he occupied himself only a few hours ago.

"I'm not quite sure myself, Felix, that's why I'm here. I was hoping you'd be able to tell me. Maybe you've seen something like this before, because I haven't."

Tom kneeled next to his daughter, and taking the Party delivery bag off his shoulder, he opened it, and after searching inside for a moment, he produced a small packet of dry fruits.

"Here you are, sweetie."

He smiled at his daughter, as he handed her the fruits. He stroked her hair, which was so much like Judy's.

He looked at his daughter, but all that he could see were the faces of the children within the truck. No amount of blinking was able to wash them away. Tilly's face, as he had seen it on his return, tear-washed and scared, rose within the image, slotting into a row of children's faces within the truck.

Tom gulped.

The world Tom knew started and ended with the Party. Anyone, who refused to follow the rules, tended not to live well, or long.

A sense of betrayal and confusion skulked nearby, as denial questioned his eyes and his feelings, his patriotism demanding to know, if his love for the Party was ever real, if the love for the country should be absolute and infinite, above personal feelings and Tom's love for his child. Shouldn't we all sacrifice for the greater good? Isn't it his moral obligation to his country, as a true Party member and citizen?

With Tilly occupied with food, Tom turned his attention to the old man.

"The streets are empty, and an announcement is playing on a loop, saying that a curfew was imposed on the city from midnight last night, and that all citizens must stay indoors, and anyone who's found outside, will be shot on the spot by the patrols."

Felix drew himself back at the Tom's last words.

"Really? Shot? On the spot?"

Felix's forehead was moving, wrinkles setting deeper.

Tom nodded.

"Is that it?" Felix asked, as Tom stood silent. "Nothing more? There must be something else, young man. There must be..."

"Nothing. That's it."

"But have you looked around? Have you checked – "

"What? News? The news lines don't run. Newspapers? I found one, but there's nothing in there, and there are no people on the streets for me to ask questions."

Tom was short with the old man, and he knew it, but he didn't like to be treated like an incompetent fool.

"Of course, of course, young man", Felix mumbled, as he took his seat by the fire.

"Honestly, I don't understand why I'm surprised", Felix muttered to himself, "sounds about right. No explanation, no communication. The Party has made a decision, and the people are expected to fall in line and follow without a question. But that's harsher than anything I've seen from them in a while... Since the first decade..."

"That's not all", Tom interrupted the old man's contemplation. "Something else I saw there."

Felix leaned his head to his shoulder. His smart, deep set eyes were on Tom.

"What?"

Tom took a few steps away from the fire and Tilly next to it. With a groan, Felix rose off his stool, and in his short, shuffling steps followed Tom.

"I saw a convoy of black trucks", Tom said, when Felix finally reached him. "Five of them drove down Freedom road, through the town. They could've been military, could've been

Internal Police or State Security, but I've seen those trucks before."

Tom paused, holding the old man's gaze.

"Trucks like that came to my child's nursery. The men picked up the children from the nursery, packed them into the trucks and drove off. But I recognised the man in charge. He came to our flat the day before, asking my wife questions about the Liberation Day Parade this year, about the children from the city's nurseries, about what happened there."

"And what's happened there?" Felix interrupted.

"I'm not really sure, but nothing that I could see to be connected to the children, although it must be. In the Parade, my wife walked with the nurseries column. The children were not behaving, crying. She cheered them up, sang them a song. A few people from nearby columns stepped in... But everything was fine. The nursery column walked, which is why that visit feels even more confusing, the State Security coming to question me and my family in the middle of the night... Their visit, then the following day, the children being taken..."

Tom was mumbling.

"That's why you ran", Felix concluded, the relief at opening the secret bringing a satisfied smile to his face.

"But today", Tom continued, "today, when the trucks drove through, I saw more children inside. Dozens, hundreds of children inside."

"Children?"

Felix's eyes narrowed and deep wrinkles marred his forehead.

"Children", Tom nodded, speaking faster, the alarm at the last few days coming fore. "There was a soldier inside, with a rifle, guarding them. He wore a mask and all the other officers I saw, including the ones patrolling the streets, they all wore masks..."

"Hold on a minute, young man. Let me think."

Felix turned and shuffled away, his hand rubbing his forehead.

He turned, his attention back to Tom.

"Where's your wife now?"

Tom swallowed.

"She's dead. She fell ill, and she died."

Unable to look at the man, to see his pity, Tom dropped his gaze.

"I am very sorry for your loss, Bill. I'm truly sorry. The little angel is without a mother now... Now, I understand your protectiveness even more."

Felix's gaze flew to Tilly, but he didn't add anything else. Instead, he walked to the other side of the room where his books were kept, and bending over the pile, he fished out a book, opened it and flipped through the pages, before placing it back and picking another one out from the stack.

"What have you brought with you, young man?"

Engrossed in his book, Felix waved his arthritic hand towards the brown box and the bag that sat next to the fire. He licked his fingers and flipped a few more pages.

"Food."

Felix nodded absentmindedly.

"That's very useful, young man, especially in the current situation."

At the word "food", Josephine, who stood in a corner of the room during the entire exchange, strode over to the loot, and without asking, scooped both, the bag and the box, in her large arms, taking them into the corner, where their food supplies were stored. Placing it there, she opened the bag and began rummaging through its content.

"Excuse me", Tom called after her. "That's our food."

Josephine ignored him, but Felix raised his head to Tom, and with a glance at both of them, answered on her behalf: "Of course, it is for all of us."

Watching Josephine's manipulations with food, her possessive stocking of the tins and brown packets in her corner, Tom had to suppress the need to walk over there and ripping it all out of her hands. His hand even slid to his belt, where the handle of the knife sat, but he forced his breathing and his hand to calm down. There will be more time for that.

"What are you looking for, Felix?"

Tom walked to the man.

"Books hold far more answers than you might think, young man. Of course, not all books and not Party books, but there are some books that have escaped censorship or a shredder. I have a few of those with me. You know, contrary to what our great Party leads us to believe, their advances in science and technologies are the old inventions that they unearthed... probably found in those books."

Felix shook a book in his hand.

"...Which they then revamp, delivering as their own advancements to the country's people, who in turn applaud to each new discovery. And let me tell you, their innovations are banal or stolen. Their operations and ideas are copied, and more often than not, not copied well or correctly, sometimes missing important nuances, especially in genetics. And whatever they "develop" themselves", Felix huffed and rolled his eyes, "are shocking in its disregard to the laws of the universe. Or damage it does to the world, and even the Party's own people."

Felix turned to Tom.

"Did I tell you that I was a biologist?

Tom nodded, wondering if that man can be trusted if he forgets a conversation that he had only twelve hours ago. Maybe he is a crazy man after all.

"Once upon a time, I was their leading research biologist", Felix continued. "I would develop and implement ideas that state ministers would bring from their diplomatic missions. But some bright ideas that the Party leaders came up with, were just outright bonkers, ideas of someone, who has no knowledge on how nature, the world or science work, who comes up with a maddest of the solutions to Party issues, and then, holding on to their name, peddling their madness further. Sometimes, I would be able to work with their ideas, amend, change something, make something worthwhile and palatable out of them, but more often than not, it was just the crazy drivel of a mad man. And they had the audacity to call me mad!"

Felix was on a roll. His face was growing redder, and his eyes were frantic.

"Just what was their idea of synthetic food production worth? I spoke against it at the presidium of scientists. I told them that they've done no tangible research, that they're playing with genetically modified synthetic organisms that have nothing in common with the natural food and don't interact well with natural organisms. I told them that my research showed mutations within the organisms exposed to it, that more modelling and research needed, before it's allowed to be mass produced. I pleaded with them to pause the rollout, to give me more time. God, I wouldn't wish ingesting that product on any human in its current state. I told them that it creates a by-product that enters the bloodstream, tangibly modifying the human genes. But did anyone listen to me? No! Instead, they branded me mad and locked me away in their asylum. If it were not for Josephine, for my saving angel, who was a janitor there, I still would be lying there, strapped to the bed."

Felix flipped through the pages of another book.

"Synthetic food?" Tom asked. "This one?"

And when Felix lifted his head, Tom pointed to the box expropriated by Josephine.

Felix's neck turned, following Tom's finger, and when his gaze arrived at the box, his face dropped, turning white as if suddenly washed of all colour.

Felix closed the book, and without drawing his gaze away from the box, keeping it on it, as if it were a snake that could bite him at any moment, he placed the book down on the stack of others.

The book fell, bringing down with it the entire tower.

But Felix didn't pay attention to it.

Hypnotised, he shuffled towards the corner.

Felix bent over the box on the ground and poked at its brown cardboard with his cane.

"Open it", Felix demanded.

Tom was about to step in – he wasn't sure, if he was the one, who was asked to perform the deed – when Josephine moved forward, kneeling next to the box and ripping the cardboard open.

The silver pouches poured from its brown core, scattering on the ground.

"Give me one!" Felix demanded.

He was a surgeon, and she was his faithful assistant.

Josephine picked one up and handed it to him.

Felix turned the pouch in his fingers, examining its shiny sides, reading the writing, inspecting it, as one might inspect a weapon. He held the pouch in his hand, weighing it then turning, before tearing the top off along the perforated line.

The pouch dropped to the ground, its slimy brown guts spilling, filling the room with a smell of beef gravy.

Felix staggered backward, his eyes wide.

"Don't touch it! Don't touch! Don't touch!" he screamed at Josephine, when she bent over to pick it up.

Felix continued stumbling backward.

His gaze was on the pouch on the ground, horror washing over his face.

"Don't touch! Don't touch!"

Felix screamed, as if he was possessed, and Tom again wondered, now with a stronger conviction, if this man is truly mad.

Felix spun to Tom and his frenzied shrill filled the room.

"Where did you get those?"

"In the place, where I got the rest of the food. It's the Party's synthetic food. I told you about it. Its development was announced on the day of the parade and must have been released into circulation –"

"The one I just told you about?"

Tom forced himself to keep his voice quiet and calm.

"Look, I didn't know if that was the one, you were talking about. And if it's the one, you didn't say anything about it, until I had already brought it here. If you don't want it here –"

"You didn't tell me it was already in circulation", Felix interrupted Tom. "Nobody did! Did you eat it? Did you eat any of it?"

Felix was hysterical.

"No, I haven't."

"Why did you bring it here?"

"As I said before, because it's food."

Tom was speaking slowly and calmly, as if reasoning with a petulant child or a dangerous and unpredictable stranger, as this man was.

"It was in the storeroom, with other food."

"You have to take it away! All of it! Now! You have to take it away!"

Felix now was on the opposite side of the room from the open pouch and its silver mates.

"You have to take it away and get rid of it! Now! Get rid of it! Get rid of all of it!"

"Okay."

Tom nodded, pacifying the madman, at that instance deciding that he and Tilly would leave this place this night.

"Wait", the old man called, as Tom bent over the mess. "Wait, wait. Tell me something else, young man. Your wife...What had she died from?"

Tom straightened, leaving the beef gravy and the rest of the pouches where they were.

"I don't know. I wasn't told."

Felix was lucid again. He was calm. His eyes shone with inquisitive knowledge.

"But how did it progress? What symptoms did she exhibit prior to her... departure?"

Tom was tempted to tell the man to get lost, but that crazy man was a scientist and there was plenty Tom didn't know about what had happened to his family.

"Her skin was covered in spots. They were raised. They looked like watery blisters. Some were as big as a republican eagle. Her entire skin was covered in them. Then, they burst and began to bleed."

Felix watched Tom's face, and his eyes grew wider.

"They have rounded up the children from your daughter's nursery and now have done the same to the other children in the city?"

After a moment of confusion at the sudden change of the subject, Tom jerked his head with a short nod of confirmation.

But his calm gesture created more outrage and paranoid fear that Tom thought could be possible.

"You two have to leave, immediately! Take those pouches away and leave! Leave now! Both of you! Now! Right this minute!"

From across the room, Felix shook his cane at Tom, shuffling away from him, putting more distance between himself and his once warmly greeted guest.

"Get out! Get out immediately! Get out of my home. Take your child and get out! Get out and never come back!"

Tilly's soft voice snaked past the old man's hysteria, reaching Tom.

"Dad? Daddy?"

Tom glanced at her.

She was still on the crate. The packet of dried fruit was on her lap. The panic in her eyes was matching Felix's.

"That's okay, darling. Don't worry. It's all fine."

In a few short strides, Tom was next to his daughter, standing next to her and stroking the top of her head.

"Forget your way here!" Felix shrieked, froth forming around his mouth. "Forget that you've been here. Never come back again. And if you want to live, you will abandon that child!"

Felix threw his finger at Tilly.

"Leave her behind and save yourself. Leave her and go, go as far away from her as possible! You will run from her, and you'll keep on running! There's nothing that can be done for her, nothing!"

Felix suddenly closed his mouth, cutting off his hysterical cries.

"But it might be too late for you", he added quieter. "It might be too late for you too... You might be already gone... gone like your wife... Soon to be dead, as she is."

Tom launched forward, covering the area between himself and Felix in three large strides.

"Don't come near me!" The old man screeched. "Don't come near me!"

Felix shrieked, as he shuffled backward, around the fire and away from Tom, fear spilling from his eyes onto his face.

Josephine jumped in front of Tom, blocking his way to the old man.

"Get out of my way!" Tom roared at her.

"Daddy!"

Tilly's cry grew louder, urgent and petrified.

"It's okay, Tilly", Tom answered, without looking at his daughter, stepping closer to Josephine.

But the large woman wasn't about to back down.

Keeping her gaze locked on Tom, she reached to the side, yanking out of the ground the metal rod, on which the pot used to sit, and without a word of warning, she swung the rod in front of herself.

Tom jumped back, out of the way of the swinging metal, tripping over something, stamping out the weak fire with his shoes. Tilly's scream entwined with Felix's howls.

Although the room turned darker with the light of the fire gone, there was still enough light for Tom to see the woman progressing forward, pressing her advantage, the metal rod in her hand slashing and stabbing.

Tom's hand flew to the belt of his jeans, finding the handle of the cook's knife and whipping it out.

"Put it down! Put it down, and get out of my face, Josephine", Tom growled. "We're going. He wanted us gone? We're gone! Don't be stupid now. I have a knife, and it's more dangerous than your pick. Back off."

Ignoring Tom's reasoning and warning, the woman advanced, her shoes walking over the hot embers.

Suddenly, Josephine lunged forward, stabbing with her rod, aiming its flaming tip at Tom's throat.

As Tom watched the red end of the metal coming towards him, the survival instinct awoke in him, taking control. And following the muscle memory of many childhood fights in the

274

orphanage, Tom took a step sideways, diving and twisting at his waist, then slicing his knife at the body next to him.

The knife slowed its flight, cutting at flesh, filling the room with Josephine's throaty roar, joining Tilly's high-pitched scream.

The metal rod clanked to the ground. Cries and wailing, that could have come from a child, if not for the deep timbre of the voice, rang off the cement walls, dissipating into the flue above.

"Step back. Get away from me, Josephine. I don't want to hurt you."

"Josephine, my dear, come here", Felix's calm voice cut the cacophonous room.

"Come here, love. Come", he cooed to her, coaxing his friend to come over.

Whilst sobbing and holding her hand over the bleeding gash on her arm, Josephine glanced at Felix.

Her gaze shuttled between the two men for a few seconds, before with another glance at her "general", she plodded to him, her cries quietening, leaving only Tilly's screams to ring around the room.

"Good. Stay there, the both of you."

Keeping his gaze on the old man and his friend and keeping his knife trained on them, Tom strode over into the corner, where the food was stored.

"We're going, but I'm taking my food."

Scooping the brown packets and tins, Tom filled the Party delivery bag.

But he left a few tins and a few packets behind. He didn't need them all. He had more, and with whatever was going on up on the surface, these two might need it.

Tom threw the bag on his shoulder, and striding across the room, he picked up his daughter, who instantly went quiet at the proximity of her father, although soft whimpers still raked her body.

"Come on, darling", Tom murmured to his child.

"You have to leave her", Felix screeched after Tom, in the silence of the abused room his voice ringing high. "You can't have her near. You can't touch her. She will kill you. She is the death! She will kill you, like she killed your wife!"

Felix was incessant. He screamed his insane prophecy over and over again, on a loop, like the robotic announcement above.

But Tom wasn't about to placate the old man, to answer or to listen, and with a last glance at the odd couple, and under the accompaniment of the hysterical preaching of the once beloved Party biologist, Tom and Tilly left the tunnel.

Chapter 19

Tom and Tilly sat within the tunnels for a few more hours, waiting for dark.

Worried about Felix or Josephine coming after them, Tom wanted to leave the tunnels immediately, escaping the claustrophobic belly the same instance, but he knew he had no choice but to wait.

He won't be able to move during the day, not with his daughter and under the curfew. Although Tom's feet were itching to run, he needed to think. He needed to find another place for them to stay, another hole to hide in, but that would only be a short term fix.

With the country in lockdown, with armed troops policing the streets, with the black trucks packed with the country's youngest generation, Schotlandia's mountains were no longer a safe haven of the destination, where his daughter could be safe for the rest of her life.

The moment Tom ran, he had made his decision.

He stepped onto a path, from which it would be impossible to deviate, and he accepted that. He knew that a labour camp or the needle were waiting for him at the end of this road. He knew, and he tried not to think about it. He knew he would pay sooner or later. But he hoped it would be later, when his daughter is older, when she could survive without him.

But now, it looked like that might not happen either.

The parting words of the crazy scientist bothered him too. He didn't know what to do with it, how much weight to put by them.

Tom's thoughts were jumbled, his attention bouncing from subject to subject.

He knew that his exemplary life would open channels of progression for his daughter. He hoped that with him playing by the rules, she would be sorted too. At the end of the day, they were approved for a procreation licence, and he knew that his stance within the Party had something to do with it. He was almost confident that he would have a comfortable and easy ride on his boat under the Party's flag. He thought he had made it... until it collapsed around him.

At the beginning of the journey, when that officer came into their flat, Tom wasn't scared, not at all. He was calm. He was assured, and his trust in the Party's justice was complete. He was sure that his love and lifelong contribution to the cause, his life full of good deeds and his complete alliance would count for something.

When he chose to save her, against the Party's wishes, he felt raw and sick with the betrayal he was committing. That first step, to come home and tell his wife to pack their belongings, was made in a rushed heat of conviction, his instinct taking over his beliefs and reasoning.

But every waking moment that came after had become agony.

Tom felt alone. The feeling that crept into his heart over a week ago rang with the tune of the emptiness of his childhood and abandonment, the cold that the Party had pushed out, replacing it with trust, belonging and hope.

But there was no way back into the fold.

There was no redemption for those who put themselves and their wishes above the Party's.

Not many were asked for the ultimate sacrifice. But when they were, the Party expected to receive it. The sacrifice was expected to come, promptly, in full and in the way it was requested.

Tom always said that the Party's needs were greater than his own. He called it from the podium to his colleagues and subordinates, and to some extent it was true. He was ready to give anything of himself to the Party. He would have done anything for it and its just cause.

But the sacrifice the Party sought this time wasn't Tom's to give. His daughter wasn't his to give, not in the sense the Party and people saw it.

She was above him. She wasn't his. She wasn't his life. She was more than that.

She was above him and above the Party. She was a miracle, and miracles were above his world.

If the Party would have asked for his life before she was born, he would have given it, gladly, the same instance, without a second thought and without asking for anything in return.

But back then, his life belonged to himself and the Party. Now, his life was no longer his to give.

Its ownership had transferred to Tilly. She held his life in her small hand, her needs becoming his own. The Party had lost him, as far as complete sacrifices go. Only his child could demand and receive those.

That transference of ownership came slowly. It hadn't happened overnight.

Tom couldn't pinpoint a day or a month when it happened. He wouldn't be able to remember what he was doing when that transference took place. But it happened, and it was irreversible. In Tom's eyes, his life belonged to her, and she belonged to no one.

Yet now, his wonderful country was against his child and Tom couldn't figure out why. He didn't know what to do with it. He didn't know how to process that feeling of betrayal, confusion, sadness and disbelief. It felt too surreal.

The plan of raising her in peace in Schotlandia, surrounded by the rolling hills and mountains of its landscape, under the sounds of winter storms and the bleating of sheep, under a cover of snow and away from people and the Party's all-seeing eye was more delusional than ever. That plan was driven away with the cargo of the black trucks.

His country had initiated a war against its children, although that war had not been announced. There was nothing in the newspapers.

Tom couldn't understand it. He couldn't wrap his mind around it. He couldn't' believe it was happening. He couldn't believe that his fair, honest and generous Party would do something like that.

His original thought, nurtured by the wishful thinking, came to the fore.

Maybe it wasn't. Maybe his Party wasn't at fault after all. Maybe the Leader of CKKPSS didn't know what was going on, what was happening. Maybe it was orchestrated without their knowledge. Maybe the Party and the people of the country didn't know. The people didn't know what was going on, as surely, there were parents looking for their children, inconsolable mothers and fathers running down the streets, calling for their children, children who had disappeared without a trace, taken and driven away in the trucks. Maybe it had nothing to do with the Party, but to do with that officer.

It must've been him, him or someone on his side, who organised that for some treacherous reason. Children were the Party's future. The Party repeated it often, and Tom believed it to be true. How could it not be?

But the sobering reasoning barged into his mind, pushing away the chimera.

Then the curfew didn't make sense. No single man was powerful enough to orchestrate it on his own and without the Party's knowledge. To steal a nursery full of children is one thing, but the curfew was quite another.

Tom couldn't figure out, why the lockdown was happening. Why it was so severe, promising the final brutality to anyone who risked disobeying it. Of course, the Party had a habit of doing things without the citizens' knowledge, insisting that the leadership knew better, and Tom was happy to accept that, he trusted the Party and its leaders, but today he wanted answers. He needed to know what the curfew had to do with the trucks full of children, or if they had a connection at all.

A new thought ricocheted off a blue and white wall in his mind.

The parting words of the old man were not giving Tom's mind a rest: the questions Felix asked, the last hateful words he screamed. How could a sane person blame a child, a healthy, happy child, for the death of her mother, calling her the "death", prophesying death to everyone next to her? How could it be? The old man must've been crazy. There must've been a reason why the Party had locked him away in the asylum.

Tom glanced at his daughter in his arms.

She looked healthy. She *was* healthy. There was not a sneeze on her or a cough. Her skin was pink in colour. After crying for a while, she fell asleep, curled up against his chest, her face sad as she slept. Her even breathing soothed Tom, as her strong heart measured a steady rhythm.

But the lucidity of the Felix's words, the coherence of his thoughts for the last two days that Tom had known him, bothered Tom. Prior to this news, prior to questioning Judy's death, the old man seemed sharp and strong of mind, yet suddenly he slipped?

Tom's thoughts spun.

The usual organization of the thought process that he had grown accustomed to and which he expected from himself, the logic and chain of command that he knew he possessed and which were sharpened by his engineering training and work had turned into the irrational disarray of a crazy man.

His thoughts jumped and darted from one improbable explanation to the next, from one impossible idea to another, confusing Tom, questioning his every move, every decision, his loyalty, his life, his love.

They won't be able to travel under the curfew, fake documents or not, and waiting it out could be the only way forward.

There was only one place in the city, where he would be able to hide for a long period of time, buying their safety. That place was the dock's quarters.

The watch on his wrist beeped softly, informing Tom that it was midnight.

Tilly smacked her lips, producing that wet noise many babies and young children do when they sleep. She stretched, curving her back, her arms rising, as she gave a wide yawn.

She pouted her lips a few more times, before turning her sleepy face to her father.

Tom softly laughed.

"Morning, darling. Slept well?"

Since the day she was born, he discovered that he could watch her sleep for hours, watching her pink round face rest or frown, or pulling her lips forward, smacking them, as if she had a mother's breast between them.

The thought of Judy dampened Tom's single second of happiness, making him feel sadder the longer he looked at his daughter.

"Do you want something to eat, before we go?"

Tilly nodded.

Tom produced a packet of crackers, and after ripping at the seal, he handed the packet to her. His hand dived into the bag, conjuring a can of peach flavoured water, laced with vitamins and minerals, developed by the Party to enhance its people's performance during work, the Party's slogan written on the side of the can: "Higher, faster, further!"

"Finish your breakfast and we'll go."

Tilly nodded.

Tom was worried about her. The stress of the last few days on such a young child must be crippling, and to reassure her, he leaned in, giving her a brief hug, taking that moment to inhale her babyish scent from the base of her neck, the sweetest smell in the world.

"Don't be scared, darling. Never be scared, and if you're ever scared, never show it to anyone", he said.

Tom gave his daughter a light squeeze.

"Nothing bad is ever going to happen to you. Daddy won't allow it", he whispered into her skin, although knowing that it was an impossible promise, one nobody will be able to keep.

Tom straightened.

"Right, ready to go?"

"Yes, daddy."

Tilly turned on his lap, lifting her face to him.

"Let's go then."

She climbed down and Tom rose, throwing the Party bag across his body, yanking the backpack from its hideout and shrugging it on.

He turned the lock and tugged the door, leading his daughter out.

Outside, it was pitch black and quiet.

Although having never been in the city centre or in the park after midnight, Tom knew that the security protocol of the energy grid dictated that the illumination of the streets and the centre is to continue throughout the night. Violation of that directive is not permitted. Yet here and now, the street lamps in the park were out, the roads past it immersed in darkness, as well as the buildings behind.

"Okay, we're going to walk. We need to be as fast as we can, while staying as quiet as we can. Can we do that Tilly? I think we can."

Tilly didn't answer, and in this blackness of the night, Tom couldn't see her usual nod.

The docks were on the other side of the town, a buffer between the city and the port.

As an honourable citizen, an engineer and a long-standing Party member, Tom hadn't come across the criminal element in his life. He didn't think that those good-for-nothing seamen served any purpose to the country. Tom often said that their active disregard of the law should've been stomped out years ago.

But those seamen must've been useful to the regime in one way or another, as overlooking their self-policing freedoms, the Party hadn't extinguished the dock's area, allowing them to quietly carry out their dirty business.

Tom heard of stories about the docks – a town within the city that lived under its own rules, a dodgy place where counterfeit, illegal and banned goods could be purchased at an extortionate price. A few people from Tom's work had visited the place, Tom overhearing their hushed gossip.

The docks was the place where one could find remnants of silk or satin for a wedding, sugar treats, if spare cash was burning a hole in a pocket, occasionally old and non-Party issued books and foreign music. There was even gossip of the possibility to purchase tobacco and foreign liquor there, but Tom decided that it was a far-fetched lie for sure.

Upstanding Britannia's citizens would arrive at the docks during the day, carrying their full briefcases, pretending to have business there, the less brave sneaking under the cloak of darkness, but each time utilising the New Bristol Liberated tram service, with the tram ride taking a little over an hour from the city's centre.

But the trams didn't run during the curfew, and scanning the darkness, Tom wondered if they would ever return. If he wanted to get to the docks, he and his child would have to walk.

The blackness of the curfew and its empty streets hid their progression. Tom knew that they would only be able to move under the cover of night, and when the sun wakes, he would need to find a safe place to spend the day.

Twice they came very close to being discovered by the night curfew patrols, but the bright lights on the officers' vests had forewarned Tom, and pressing closer to the buildings or hiding behind its corners, Tom managed to avoid both.

The patrols walked past, the radios on their shoulders mumbling. The chatter of the officers was muffled by their masks. The occasional bursts of their laughter were loud on the empty streets, and once the white lights of the torches left with the patrols, Tom and Tilly continued walking.

The old and ornate buildings of the Old Town were soon replaced by the red brick buildings of the municipal leaders, short picketed fences encircling their manicured lawns.

The patrols in the leaders' residential area were more frequent, and after the constant diving behind the corners of short buildings and trimmed bushes, after spending long periods hiding in the shadows of the outer buildings of the leaders' housekeeping staff, Tom decided to stay away from the main street, following the narrow passages of the back lanes instead, zigzagging past parked there rubbish bins.

After hours of walking and after a couple of stops, when Tom had to hold Tilly as she went to the toilet, using newspapers he found in the recycling bins as a toilet paper, after walking next to her and then carrying her on his shoulders, they finally exited the red brick paradise of the

Party approval, entering the residential sector of the universal grey tower blocks, identical to the one he used to live in.

When the blind grey towers come to an end, the docks area will begin.

Sooner than Tom expected, the black sky began to lighten, dissolving the night, leaving the last tendrils of shadows to linger on the ground and between the buildings.

It was Tom's cue to find shelter, before they were exposed.

It won't be long before the Broadcasting Units will come alight in the flats, waking the servants of the regime, summoning them for another day of productive work. The absence of windows on the tower blocks and the lack of patrols on the streets in the grey development might buy them some time, but it won't be much.

Tom veered towards a tight cluster of grey buildings, with the small squares of grass and network of pavements within. An empty playground sat in the middle of the grassy area, the wind pushing colourful swings that screeched into the silence of the morning.

Dragging tired Tilly behind, Tom rushed to a corner of adjoined grey buildings, where he knew a small utility cubicle would be, which a local street sweeper would use to store his cleaning equipment, and in which the electric and gas exchanges were located.

The shabby wooden door, painted grey on the day of the completion of these towers, flaunted scales of chipped paint of years of neglect.

It was locked. A padlock rested next to the handle.

Tom rattled the door, wishing for a heavy hammer to drive this padlock free, when he realised that the wooden door was riddled with woodworm holes.

"Stay here, darling."

Tom tucked his daughter deeper into the shadows around the building, and tugging the knife from his belt, he slid the blade between the latch and the door.

The screws came out easier than Tom expected, the rotting wood giving away its inhabitants. The padlock swung on the latch, as the door unlocked.

Tom pushed the door open, and after a quick inspection of the room's bleak and tiny belly, he ushered his daughter forward, walking in after her and pushing the door shut.

Chapter 20

The room was small.

Transmitters and generators hummed, occupying most of its area; a shovel, buckets, a broom and a rake rested against a wall, leaving very little free space in the cubicle, maybe enough for a handful of people to huddle together standing up, but that's about it.

But the room wasn't any smaller than Tom's room in the University of Energy dorms, in which he spent five years of his life, and it certainly was something Tom could work with. It was only for a few hours.

Tom pulled the belt out of the loops of his trousers, and hooking it over the broken tooth of one of the wooden panels, he strapped it to a pipe next to the door. Now, the door was held closed by his belt.

Tom hoped that during the curfew a street sweeper wouldn't be carrying out his morning tasks, at least not today, but should he arrive, the belt would give Tom enough time to eliminate another threat. He stroked the handle of his knife.

Tom took his jacket off and laid it on the dirty concrete.

"Come."

He patted the area.

"Come, darling, and try to have some sleep."

They will be travelling again at nightfall, and right now they needed to rest.

He slid down the wall, placing himself between the door and his daughter, his body a wall of flesh between her and the threatening world, a wall, which is prepared to die for her.

Tilly shuffled closer. Awkwardly and unsure, she kneeled on the jacket.

"Lay down", Tom whispered, and tugging his child closer, he hugged her, placing her head on his chest.

"Try to sleep. We'll be walking again soon", he said, and holding her soft body next to his, they fell asleep.

Tom jerked awake.

For a moment, he couldn't figure out where he was or how he had gotten here, but as the sleeping fog dissolved, Tom remembered. He reached out to his dropped knife, squeezing its handle.

They hadn't been sleeping for long. The bright light was still streaming into the utility cupboard past the cracks in the door.

Suddenly, a commotion of noises and screams barged into the cupboard.

"As per Urgent Order Ten-Four-Six, issued by the directive of the Party's presidium, your child's coming with us, for everyone's safety, including yours. Step away", the commanding voice bellowed next to the door.

Tom raised his knife, pointing it at the door, listening. Now awake, Tilly shook next to him, but she kept quiet.

"Step away! Step away, I said", a male voice roared, but it was drowned out by the woman's screams, entangled with the clipped and roaring barrage of commands of a few more voices, the sounds of a struggle, of a boot and something heavier meeting human flesh, and then the groans of a man.

Tom reached to his child's face, placing his hand over her mouth, leaning to her, he whispered: "Not a word, Tilly. We must be quiet, absolutely quiet. Don't listen. Close your ears."

She nodded under his hand, her hands flying to her ears.

Tom's relief was short-lived, as a new assault of voices pushed past the door.

A man bellowed.

A woman shrieked.

The shrill of a young child tolled.

But the young voice didn't ring for long, cut off soon after it was born by the slam of a metal door.

Suddenly, machine gun fire ripped the morning air, waking Tom like a slap, silencing the pandemonium of noises, leaving behind a single wailing cry.

"Anyone else, who takes it upon themselves to disobey the order and prevent officers of State Security from doing their job, will be executed without further warning", the voice barked.

Tom leaned to his daughter, mouthing into between her fingers: "Stay here."

He moved to get up, but the grip of the small hands strangled his biceps.

Tom turned.

"Tilly, darling", he whispered, her wide eyes glowing in the glum room. "Don't worry. I won't go out. I just need to see. Let go of daddy. Please?"

He stroked her head, as he whispered the words in her ear.

"We're safe here. Please let go. I'm here. I'm not going anywhere. Please?.."

291

He tapped on her hands, and after stroking their soft skin, he pried her fingers off, until they fell, and she let go.

On his knees, Tom shuffled to the door, and his head leaned against a crack in the old wood.

"Rot in hell, crow", a female voice shrieked from the side.

Tom couldn't see its owner.

An officer sealed in black uniform was within Tom's line of vision.

He stood a few meters away from the cubicle and next to the entrance into the nearby block of flats. The bright midday sun stroked the metal of the carbine in his hands pointed somewhere at the entrance, his black uniform stark against the light air. More black uniforms fanned behind him, with a convoy of black state cars parked along the pavement and behind their backs.

"Shut your mouth, bitch, unless you want to follow your husband", the officer hissed, stepping closer to the entrance, and following his movement Tom shuffled, tilting his head, until he could see the bottom half of a body on the ground, judging by the large size of work boots and worker's trousers, a man.

"Labour camps might like to welcome another worker tonight", the officer added.

Tom still couldn't see the woman.

"Anyone else feels stupid this morning?" the officer barked, swinging his gun, pointing it at the entrance.

The question was met with silence.

There must have been more people there, but Tom couldn't see anyone apart from the officers and their cars.

"Medical services were dispatched to test this building", the officer called louder, as if addressing a crowd. "If I were you, I would sit home, waiting for their arrival, and follow their instructions to the letter. Right now is not the time for selfishness. This is for your safety and for our country."

The officer turned.

"Round up and out!" he called to his comrades, and following his call, one by one the officers jumped into the cars, their doors slamming and their engines starting.

A minute later, the rumble of their engines dissipated past the grey concrete and the woman's cries rang out, calling after them.

The cries were so heartbroken that they echoed in the emptiness of Tom's chest, her loss mimicking his. Tom wanted to come out, to hold the mourning woman, to tell her that he knew, telling her about his own loss, which was as brutal and as raw as hers, but he knew that he couldn't.

He couldn't expose his daughter's hiding place. He will never risk her safety.

On his knees, he shuffled back to where Tilly sat, and hugging her tight, he stroked her small body, her hands, which were still pressed to her ears.

The disillusion and shock at what he witnessed heightened his sense of despair.

He rocked her, and he rocked *with* her, finding comfort in her warmth.

The sudden shriek of a woman made him jump. His daughter's body strained. Her whimpers grew louder.

"Shh, shh."

His hand hovered next to her mouth, ready to muffle her screams should she finally burst.

"Shh, shh."

The female voice disappeared, as suddenly as it came.

The fast beating of footsteps sounded within the building. The banging on the doors, screams and further shouting followed, and before long, the area outside of the Tom's and Tilly's hiding cubicle was filled with strangled gasps and hushed voices.

"Oh my..."

"Poor Jon."

"What's happened?"

And then quieter: "Is it them?"

A siren blared in the distance, its wailing growing closer, now only a couple of streets away.

"Keep your hands on your ears, Tilly. That's it, darling, that's it. Don't listen to it. Don't listen. Shh, shh. Don't listen..."

Tom rocked his child, mumbling into her hair, but she didn't need his instructions. He could feel the sharp angles of her elbows, as she pressed her hands to her ears.

The siren burst onto the grounds, its cry echoing within the well of the buildings.

The brakes screeched. The doors opened and then slammed.

"Give way, give way."

Tom didn't need to see to know what was going on.

The medics were here.

Tom knew how that would go.

They would push past the crowd of bystanders. One of them would kneel next to the body.

A medical bag hit the concrete.

After a long silence, the gasp of many voices was louder. It was followed by the renewed wave of woman's wails.

There must have been a shake of the head from the medic.

A heavy and thick sheet of plastic rattled, probably the unrolling of a body bag.

"Stand back."

"...distance... Give the medics some space."

"I'm not going to repeat... Stand back."

Bodies pressed against the cubicle door, stretching Tom's belt.

"Poor Jon", a man's voice said beyond the door. "Poor Mary."

"Of course, poor Jon, poor Mary, but if you ask me, they brought it upon themselves. Yesterday's order was clear: under the martial law directive, all free citizens under the age of twelve must be surrendered into the authority's custody due to the outbreak of an unknown disease. The Party ordered as such and we, as true citizens, must follow the law, including Jon and Mary. The law is the law, and it applies to everyone."

"Come on, Viv. It's people's children. How do you expect them to give them up, just like that?"

"It's the order, Dave. The orders are there to be obeyed and not discussed. Didn't you see the presidium briefing?"

"Of course I saw, but −"

"It's the worst threat our country faced since the Frankish crisis", Viv interrupted the man. "The children are the ones who carry the disease. The Party said so. Many citizens have died already, and many more would die, unless we do what needs to be done, unless we make difficult choices."

She sounded, as if she was reciting someone else's speech.

"Many more will die unless the danger is eliminated. You can die. I could die. The whole country could die. Everyone will be dead, just because we were not strong enough to do what was needed to save the country."

Tom couldn't see the woman, but judging by her voice, she must have been in her fifties.

"Besides, it's not like the government are killing those children", she huffed. "They will be isolated until a cure is found, and with our country's best minds working on it, I'm confident it won't be long."

The man must have rolled his eyes, as her voice rose up a notch, ringing with righteous indignation.

"I saw their son only the other day. He walked up the stairs, touching the railing, door handles... Can you imagine what he left behind? You're not the scientist. You don't know how bad it is! They said it's fatal. So far not a citizen over the age of forty had survived. For all we know, I might already have it. Thanks to their son, I might be infected. I might be at risk."

She grew the more hysterical, the longer she spoke.

"Viv, they are children, and these people are their parents. How can you expect them to give up their kids? What are you talking about?"

"If they are real Party's citizens, if they are true liberals and worthy of our great nation, they will hand over their kids, for everybody's sake, for the greater good, to save their country, saving you and me, saving other citizens. The Party gave them those children, and Party can take them away, if it pleases."

"Viv, what you talking about? Can you hear yourself?"

296

Dave sounded appalled and so did Tom. Tom couldn't believe what he was hearing.

Viv's voice responded, carrying an agitated tone, although she was whispering: "So what are you saying exactly? That those children are more important than me? That I should protect them, because they're kids? I should die for them? I don't think so! They are rats that carry the New Plague and they need to be isolated... eliminated, if necessary. It's that simple."

"Children are our future", Dave argued.

"Lethal future", the woman rebuffed. "There will be no future, if they're left to roam around, infecting us all. Whereas, when this threat is resolved, the citizens can go ahead and have more children."

"You're a bitter woman, Viv."

Tom could almost see a sad shake of the man's head.

"You're only talking like this because you don't have kids of your own, Viv. You don't know what it's like to be a parent. If you were a mother, you'd understand."

"No, I wouldn't", Viv bristled. "For me, the Party would always be above my personal needs, and if the Party came to me, told me that my child places the entire country in danger, I would trust the Party to do what's right. I would have complete trust in my Party, like *they* should've had. "

"Viv, you're neither stupid nor naïve, and old enough to know how the Party deals with its threats."

He put emphasis on the word "how", lowering his voice.

"That's what enemies of the state might say, Dave. I never pegged you as one."

Her voice was saturated with implications.

"Viv, your imagination is too wild for this morning", the man rebuked, a forced smile coming into his voice.

"You never know..." Viv said in a low tone, her voice full of poison and threat.

The footsteps walked away from the door, followed by a heavy sigh, when the heels of another pair of shoes clicked on the cement, coming towards the door.

"Can you believe that bitch?" Dave asked someone quietly.

Viv must be the one who has left.

"Who? Viv?" A new voice asked. It belonged to a younger woman. "What did the cow do?"

Another long sigh sounded past the door.

"I won't be surprised, if she was the one who reported them to the authorities, for not handing in their son."

"Yeah", the woman agreed. "I wouldn't be surprised either. Poor Mary... lost her entire family in one morning... Jon, Steph..."

"It must be bad", the woman added quieter after a pause. "Coming like that, rounding up children, killing the parents... What's going on? How bad is it?"

"Must be pretty bad", Dave mumbled, then sighed. "Curfew, now that..."

"What do you think is happening to the children? Do you think they're being treated?"

Tom wanted to hear the answer too, but the answer didn't come. The footsteps of Dave and the woman moved away and into the building.

New voices spoke past the door, asking Mary to get up, to get into the flat and lay down, to have a rest, mumbling empty reassurances, speaking to what was once "a mother and a wife" and now was a broken woman.

The voices began to fade.

The entrance door slammed.

Slow footsteps shuffled on the staircase above Tom's head, the sobbing disappearing with the footsteps.

The doors of a car opened and closed, two sets of heavy boots marched towards the entrance of the building, walking up the concrete stairs, booming above Tom's head. These must be the promised medics, ready to test the residents.

Memories of the last week rose in Tom's mind like a photomontage.

The memories were made of images, small and grainy, with the dark emptiness between them, as if Tom's mind fell asleep or blocked them out, delivering only brief and clipped notions, possibly saving Tom's sanity.

The visit of the State Security officer in the middle of the night, the image of his colleague, the medic, taking blood samples, the black trucks outside of Tilly's nursery and the tight lines of children ushered in, the bleeding blisters over Judy's white skin, the outline of her body under the murky white plastic, the convoy of black trucks filled with children, their scared eyes, shining in the darkness and an officer, facing them, his rifle pointing at them, and finally, the parting screams of the crazy Felix, although, with every passing hour, Felix seemed less crazy.

Tom's head swam.

Felix claimed that his Tilly was the disease – his love, his life, his air, his everything... she was the poison. He said she killed Judy and she would kill him. Then, the children were outlawed overnight by the Party directive. The betrayal of it was inconceivable to Tom, questioning the whispers of the long list of the Party's contentious deeds, pushing Tom through a door, through which he wasn't ready to walk. The possibility, the implications of the Party's wrongdoings were too grave. With his wife dead, Tilly and the Party, for which his parents fought and died, were the only two things Tom thought he could hold on to.

He could survive being a traitor, but he couldn't survive to be deceived, especially by the one he trusted unquestioningly.

The image of the Party began to rust the moment the State Security officer walked out of the nursery, ushering the children into the trucks. It had tarnished, but it stood.

The titan of the Party shook when Tom ran, choosing his daughter over his Party's obligations. But that only brought the personal guilt, the colossal image remaining upright and intact.

But now?!

The titan's feet of clay began to crumble under Tom's searching and questioning. The cracks on the monumental image of the Party that Tom had erected were running in every direction, and Tom was afraid to turn, to look at it, at the image he held. It would be the end of him too, of his life.

The Party could not be killing its own children.

Tom couldn't explain why he drew a line at the children, whilst every citizen was aware of the existence of the forced labour camps for the traitors and the enemies of the state. But they were traitors. They did wrong. They spoke wrong, whereas the children did nothing to invite this annihilation.

Everyone was equal in the eyes of the Party. Every life is worth the same, irrespective of their background, achievements or age – that's what the Party preached, that's how the country lived. In the eyes of the Party, the children should be and will be treated like any other citizen, and Tom knew it, the law of equality dictated so, and as much as it was wise in every other instance, it was unthinkable in this. If Tom tried to explain it to any of his friends, to other Party members, even if he had a chance, he knew he would fail, that they wouldn't understand.

Equality means equal, everyone. Viv's words, whoever she was, had proven it.

But Tom knew that Viv's words had little to do with equality and more to do with self-preservation. She was a bitter old woman, who was never granted a chance to be a mother, and who resented the motherly happiness of other women.

But the Party's decision had nothing to do with the small-mindedness of Viv. Their decision was driven by something by far larger and scarier – scary enough to sacrifice an entire generation, and Tom knew it. Apart from Felix, he was the only one who knew.

The idea of children being sentenced to death, just because of the disease, seemed unreal and cruel to Tom, and he knew that if he was to accept it, to acknowledge it and take it into his heart, it would set the image of the Party he had constructed up in flames, the titan would finally fall and crumble, its clay shards scarring the remaining pieces of Tom's broken life.

Tom looked down at the soft body in his arms, lit by streaks of sunlight, seeping through the door's cracks.

Viv's words came back: *"If they are real Party members, they would hand in their children...for everyone's sake."*

It's not like Viv cared for those children, not like she showed them any compassion. Unlike her, Tom saw the trucks. He saw the soldiers with rifles.

But even if they were right, if all those allegations were true, would Tom hand her over? If she were to become the death of him, would he hand her over to save himself?

Tom knew the answer, and as it turned out, he wasn't as devoted Party member, as he thought. He realised that he didn't care about everyone's sake. He cared only about his child.

Tilly's arms flopped by her sides, as she fell asleep, tiredness and stress claiming her body.

Tom lifted his finger and stroked his daughter's face, when suddenly, a thought punched at him: *"One of them will die soon"*.

There will be no "happily-ever-after" for the two of them, no peaceful life in the country. He wouldn't see his daughter grow. One of them won't be here. One of them is going to die, and if the Party and Felix are correct, it will be him. He would be dead pretty soon.

He won't see her grow. He won't watch her become a young woman. He won't be there. If he is to believe everything he heard, he has no more than a week, before it will be his turn to lie under a plastic sheet or in a body bag. It won't be long at all, and if he stays with his daughter on the run, he will die on the streets, under a bush like a dog, and she'll die with him, soon after.

Without him and his protection, she will be loaded into the trucks. People like Viv would make sure of it.

For a brief moment, a thought of what would happen to her if he surrendered snaked into Tom's mind.

His mind went with it, imagining his surrender, the masked police officers taking her, Tilly crying in their arms and calling for him. His mind added a picture of him, lying on the gurney in the City hospital, maybe in the same room where his wife was, doctors looking after him, maybe even saving.

But the doctors didn't save Judy. Maybe because they didn't know what they were doing or maybe because there was nothing to save, maybe this New Plague, as the Party called it, is final, and nothing can be done.

This idea of surrender was detached, not a real contemplation of a possibility. It hasn't taken roots. It was as ephemeral, as Tom's dreams of a personal car. He will never have it, especially now, but as the dreams of a car were only the dreams, thoughts of surrender were just as removed from reality.

The moment when the chain of the possibility took him away, drawing the images of her crying, his daughter's inconsolable face and her small body in an officer's arms, with another officer pointing his gun at her, Tom knew that it wouldn't be something he would ever do.

He knew that irrespective of his impending doom, he won't subject his child to that.

Tom kept rocking, rocking his child and himself with her, the repetitive motion soothing him, as it did when he was a child, when he learnt how to look after himself, how to soothe himself, when he learnt that there was no one else in the world for him.

That was before he found Judy.

Today the rocking numbed his pain, guarding him from his hate, his mind occupied by keeping a rhythm, refusing to process everything that he knew.

Once the memories of the last few days came, and Tom had greeted them, he felt scared, petrified. But now, as he pushed them out, replacing them with the metronome motions of his rocking, measuring only time, nothing but the time that was left for him with his child, he accepted his world, accepting with it his future.

The monotone motion helped Tom to detach, the decision about which one of them is going to live has formed, followed by the images of the future, in which he won't be.

He imagined Tilly's life after he's gone. Not twenty years down the line, but the first year, maybe a first few months, maybe a week, and the more he thought, the more he was convinced that it couldn't be in this country.

Here, the future for her was painted with the black and white colours of a labour camp and State Security uniforms, stained with the colour of the freshly spilled blood.

Leaving the country...

It sounded so... implausible, unimaginably ridiculous, like a plan to take a flight to Cassiopeia and establish a colony there. Nobody ever left the country, nobody. Nobody Tom knew or had heard of. Of course, ministers and diplomats left the country on official visits, but again, a minister and Tom the "wanted fugitive" were not of the same calibre and could not be compared.

A ridiculously implausible thought – leaving the country. It seemed the only way out, and the unlikeliest of them all.

Chapter 21

"Dad... Daddy..."

A weak voice and a touch of the soft skin on Tom's face woke him. He opened his eyes to Tilly looking at him.

"I'm hungry", she whispered, her eyes wide and wet as if sharing a secret, and Tom felt a smile blossoming over his lips, as he looked at her.

"Let's find something then."

He yawned.

It was quiet past the door. No voices, no pressure on the belt.

Tom shuffled away from it and towards the bags.

"Today for our special camping dinner we shall have", he whispered.

"Corned beef and beans!" he called after a pause, with the enthusiasm of a circus ringmaster, announcing attractions at a show.

But Tilly didn't laugh at his silly voice.

"I need the toilet", she added in apologetic lispy whisper.

"And we can fix that too."

For a brief moment, Tom thought of their flat, where his happiness lived, where laughter held, no matter how hard the going was, and where his child could go to the toilet, where the comfort of the Party was to be had.

But this was their life now. He chose it. He made it what it is, and he had no right to repine, and if she was about to go to toilet in the smallest

306

room in which they've been locked in, than that was his doing too and he shall take it in his stride.

"Let's do it there."

He picked up his daughter, and after helping her to take down her tights, he held her on his arms, her butt lowered towards the ground. The sound of piss hitting the concrete followed.

"Done?"

"Done", she squeaked.

He shook her slightly, then released her on a drier spot on the floor and pulled her tights up.

But as his arm brushed over her leg, he felt something.

A new pain in his arm, somewhere within layers of his skin, tingled with a weird sensation. It stretched his skin, and it twisted and burned his muscles.

Releasing Tilly, Tom walked to the door.

With a shaking hand, he unbuttoned the cuff of his shirt and rolled it up under a ray of evening light, passing through the cracks in the splinting wood.

He didn't need to roll far.

Straight past the wrist, the murky blisters began.

They were small, stretching his skin with their tight cluster, in the dim light looking grey. They weren't uniformed in diameter or in height, but they held the same colour of decaying flesh as Judy's did, before they began to bleed.

He looked at the greyish blisters, and he couldn't pull his gaze away. His chest was tight. His body was shaking.

The earlier thoughts, reasoning and plans suddenly fled his mind, leaving behind a ringing emptiness. If someone asked him his name now, he couldn't say for sure if he would remember.

Tom exhaled a shaky breath.

He reached out, blindly shuffling closer to the door. He needed hold on to something, to stop the spinning in his eyes and the weakness in his legs, but as soon he rested on the wall, his legs gave way and he slid.

"Daddy?"

Tilly's voice came through the fog, and Tom couldn't command his own voice to answer his child. Somewhere deep in his mind, the parental response called to her not to worry, that daddy's fine and everything will be okay, but it couldn't push past the shock and Tom's frozen lips. He couldn't make his body to obey him.

She called to him, moving closer, her voice rising, when her small hand landed on him, touching his arm, jolting Tom and waking him.

"That's okay", Tom managed to push out.

But the coarse voice of an old man in the cubicle didn't belong to Tom. But quite frankly, Tom wasn't Tom anymore.

Now, he was a walking corpse, only days away from the grave.

Past the hopeless distance of his fear, Tom reached out to his child, pulling her closer, hugging her tight, encasing her small body with his, his fear, pain, dread, resentment, sorrow... and hate burning his body.

His wise daughter didn't pull. She sat in his embrace, whilst he rocked with her, biting on his lip to stem the wounded roar that vibrated in his chest, threatening the rupture.

The earlier realisation of impending death was not as accepted as he thought. It hadn't had a chance to seep into his mind and his heart. He hadn't had enough time.

He thought he wasn't done in yet. He thought he had more time to save his child.

His head pounded.

Tilly relaxed next to him, leaning closer, resting her head on his chest. And that human response, that empathy and love made Tom feel so happy, so loved and so... angry, angry at himself, at Viv, the Party and the world, who stole that tender love from him, that he pulled away from his daughter, choking on his pain, afraid in his agony to hurt her.

"Let's eat", he croaked, and to take away the sting from his distance, he placed a soft kiss on the top of her head.

He reached for the bag, producing the promised tins of meat and beans, and opening those with his knife, he handed them to Tilly.

Taking the tins, Tilly looked up at him, blinking.

"Oh, spoons", Tom whispered.

"Sh –", he started, but catching himself under the gaze of his child, he finished, "shire! Let me find you a spoon or something. Hold on, darling."

He patted himself. His pockets were empty of anything that could serve as a spoon, but the internal breast pocket on his jacket rattled with a familiar jingle, and reaching in, Tom pulled out the keys to his flat.

These were the keys to his previous life. He had forgotten that they were there.

The two narrow cylinders with indentations shone on his palm, roped by the key ring that Bill gave him three years ago, when Tom got his promotion.

"Now, you are always on call", Bill joked, handing him the small metal box, housing the two Allen keys, the corners of the box serving as spanners heads. "Every tool you need to access a power exchange wherever you are. Now, like a hero, you can rescue the country's energy supply twenty four seven. With a tool like this, we'll be celebrating your new promotion in no time."

Tom laughed then.

Now, he looked at the metal box in his hand, his burning enmity finding an outlet in a crazy idea, promising retribution and soothing of his hate.

He slid the keys back into the pocket and exhaled.

Suddenly he felt better. The metal ring over his chest has opened slightly, and he drew in a deep breath.

He will die, but he won't be the only one who will.

**

The air in the room grew darker with the encroaching evening, but Tom waited for the night.

As he couldn't find spoons, he fed his daughter off the palm of his hand, his fingers diving into the tins, placing the food onto his palm, and she is picking it from there.

They would leave around midnight. The docks became the only viable option. He will hide his daughter there until he calculated his next step, until he figured out how to take her out of this country – a crazy task – and how to protect her from beyond the grave.

About an hour later, voices came around and stood nearby, discussing today's occurrence.

Sometime later, a car drove in, and under resisting screams, a woman was loaded in and driven away.

An hour after that, a wave of residents returning from work descended. The constant banging of the entrance door and stomping of feet on the stairs rang above Tom's and Tilly's heads. The residents of the tower had returned to their mundane lives.

When dusk swaddled the air, virtually no resident entering the building spoke of today's incident that took lives, soon to be completely forgotten.

As the air seeping through the door turned jet black, the tower grew slower and quieter.

If it wasn't midnight yet, it must be nearly.

Untying the belt, Tom cracked the door open, listening for a minute, before pushing it wider, scanning the dark and empty pavements beyond.

"Let's go, sweetie."

Taking his daughter's hand in his, he stepped on the black asphalt.

Walking down the dark road, Tom's hand slid into his pocket, finding what he needed, as he led his daughter to the farthest side of the building.

He swung open the metal door on the tall utility box. The internal metal mesh door was locked. The box's insides past it buzzed, filtering the air for the tower blocks.

The cube of Tom's key ring spun, releasing bolt after bolt, its corner unlocking the metal lid on the cistern containing the purifying liquid for the ventilation system for the blind homes.

Tom twisted and lifted the lid.

The liquid inside the silver cistern shone like black oil. And glaring into its void, Tom pulled the knife out of his pocket and sliced at his hand.

The sharp pain took his breath, briefly catching in his throat and then releasing. A new calmness took over, as he watched the fat droplets of his blood hitting the dark surface.

Tom huffed a bitter smile remembering the letter he wrote on the tram, pleading with his Party, asking for assistance and help, thinking that what he had witnessed was the subversion, carried out by enemies of his wonderful country, without the Party's knowledge, put in motion to undermine his country's rise.

Now, he couldn't believe how stupid he was.

The night was quiet, and the moon was hidden behind the June clouds.

The streets were empty. Faithful workers that received their flats from the Party's feeding hand sat behind the closed doors, obeying the orders.

But Tom and Tilly walked.

The line of the identical grey towers soon began to wither, taking with it asphalt pavements and any notion of infrastructure, leaving behind a single road surrounded on the both sides by the heaps of dumped rubbish, broken brick and concrete strewn over unkempt fields, occasionally interrupted by broken shrubbery and trees.

Tom kept away from the lit road, walking around the mountains of rubbish and through the fields mined with cow dung.

It was a couple of hours of trudging around the debris, before the yellow flashing lights on top of the docks' cranes blinked in the distance.

The landscape has changed to include containers repurposed as storage, and low, one storey, metal buildings with the Party star on them, before growing into two storey brick or concrete warehouses, factories and workshops.

The large, long buildings stood in darkness along the road, their doors closed until the next morning, when they swing open, taking workers into the fold of another day of labour.

The street lamps appeared. Some were with working, yet dim light bulbs within, whilst some, although dark, had a string of round bulbs wrapped around them, stretching between a few lamp posts.

The crusty layers of government posters plastered one on top of another, covered every lamp post and the occasional tree, some posters as much as three years old.

The port rose in New Bristol practically overnight. The post-Collapse Britannia threw all of its scarce resources at creating a port within the new country and the new landscape, the port and docks expanding to the current size within a year and becoming a bloodline for the young country. It became a means of survival.

But as the autonomy and autocracy of the country grew, the stream of ships dwindled. As the country turned inwards, sealing itself, maritime transportation dissipated to a trickle of occasional ships, taking with it the port's importance and influence, and following the years of distance from the Party's hand, which could hit as well as feed, the port's buildings began to decay, its infrastructure to wilt, crumbling with each passing year without Party's love.

But the folk of the docks liked it like that.

This side of docks never bowed low to the establishment, workers and residents seeing themselves "freer" than the average free citizen. The docks trifled with the Party, exchanging their freedom for the required dedication and work.

Tom didn't know how the docks managed to get away with that sort of behaviour for decades, or what cards it might have held that without too much of a ruffle, the Party waved their hand at the docks, allowing it to live the life they choose, as opposed to the rest of the country, who lived the lives chosen for them by the leaders of the Party.

Tom had never been here, seeing himself above the dock's filth. But as the life of a criminal had settled in, Tom resigned himself to a visit.

Two days ago, he planned to come onto these streets seeking to buy documents, to go up North, exchanging for those the food he held. But today he wanted more. Today, he wanted the impossible; something he wasn't sure he could get and knew would cost him more than he could offer. He would be asking for a ticket out of the country.

Until Felix's comment about people smugglers, Tom didn't think they existed. He had never heard of anyone who had defected from the country. The people he knew never dreamt of leaving Federation Britannia. They would never conceive such a treacherous thought, and not only because there was no point in trying to escape the inescapable, but because they were satisfied with the lives they were living.

But evidence of the thinnest stream of illegal goods that trickled into the country pricked Tom's suspicions, and Felix confirmed them. Tom figured that if there was a way into the country via the docks, there must be a way out, and more than likely through the same channel.

Tom realised that that request might be crossing the lines the docks would risk to venture. It was bigger than a remnant of silk. It could be the line the docks won't cross with the Party, quite possibly being the one agreement between themselves and the regime: to hand over traitors to the authorities in an exchange for an uninterrupted black market.

Maybe. Tom didn't know. But it was a chance he had to take.

Tom decided to walk into the docks alone.

With the announcement that children carry the disease and the Party imposed hunt, with the precarious request he planned to put forward, Tom had no choice but to hide Tilly, until he could survive long enough to ask questions and strike a bargain.

He didn't want to do it. But it was the only way he knew.

Human fear knew no Party allegiance. Tom was afraid of what scared people would do. He had seen plenty of that in the last few days. He feared for his own and Tilly's safety should they walk down the streets. Maybe not surviving to see inside a nuclear reactor, he and his daughter stoned to death on the streets of the bandit's enclave.

Straying from the main lit road, occasionally Tom and Tilly would appear within a weak pool of street light, but abandoning that circle almost immediately, ducking into the darkness of the pre-dawn hours, Tom thought he had managed to sneak into the docks unnoticed.

He thought wrong.

Chapter 22

A lever clicked in the distance and the round pool of a searchlight blasted the area, blinding Tom.

He slammed his eyes shut.

Tilly cried next to him in fright and surprise, and throwing herself to him, she pressed her face against his thigh.

"That's far enough!" A voice called from somewhere above. "What are you doing here? It's a bit late for official business. Or early, depending on how you look at it."

The male voice laughed. He was a philosopher.

Tom spun away from the light, away from the voice, blindly stepped sideways, tugging Tilly with him, when the metal muzzle of a weapon pressed into his stomach.

"Don't be stupid", the voice barked, losing its good mood.

"And you have a child", the voice tutted. "Haven't you heard that you were supposed to surrender your children into Party's custody?"

Tom could feel bodies around him and he could hear the shuffling of their feet on the dry ground.

Shielding his eyes with his hand and turning slowly, his eyes scanned the ground, watching the boots and shoes that encircled them.

There were many of them. A dozen of pairs he could see, but maybe more. Tom didn't want to test how many of them had weapons, even one that uses his gun well and shoots straight, was one too many.

"What do you want?" Tom called.

"No. It's me, who should be asking you, and I have. What are you doing here?"

Here it goes.

"I have something to sell. I need to speak to whoever's in charge. He will be interested in what I have to offer."

The voice laughed.

"What? Your child?"

The men around Tom laughed too, and Tom felt his daughter's body pressing tighter to his leg.

"No", Tom growled, barely holding it back. "Not the child. What would you want her for? I have something better."

"Better?" the voice mused. "Better is good, because I didn't want to tell you, but your kid is too old to sell. There's no market for children as old as her. No market for children now, period."

"Are you interested in my proposal or not? Or is there someone else I should be discussing the transaction with? Someone, who can actually *make* a simple decision?"

Tom didn't receive any answer. The following his remark silence lasted for a while.

Keeping his eyes on the ground, Tom hugged his daughter closer, turning again, looking for a break in the shoes on the ground, wanting to cover her body with his, if the bullets begin to fly. But the shoes have closed the circle.

"And what do we have here?" The earlier voice asked closer, now within the circle of the feet, startling Tom.

A hand, covered in dense black hair, reached to Tom and tugged at the handle of one of Tom's bags.

Tom resisted, yanking his shoulder out of the grasp of the greedy hand.

"Don't be stupid, mate", the voice growled.

The metal barrel of the sawn off shotgun pressed into Tom's stomach, then strangers' hands dived towards Tom, cutting the straps of his bags, freeing Tom of his stuff.

"Party delivery service", the voice read, as the zip screeched. "Very interesting."

Seeing the stranger's hands in the bags of his food supplies, felt like a violation and a mortal loss. Tom wanted to jump up on the man, snatch his bags, protecting them with his life. But he had his daughter to think about.

After inspecting the bags, the stranger's hand dived to Tom's waistband, freeing him of his knives too.

"Very interesting..." the voice mused, before commanding: "Now move! And don't even think of doing anything stupid. Even dead traitors are well received by State Security."

The switch clicked again, the blinding light gone, leaving behind the soft glow of hand torches.

"Follow me."

Tom dropped his hand, and turning his head, he swept his gaze over the crowd, assessing the situation.

He was surrounded by a tight group of men, with two of them holding hunting rifles and a few more holding handguns.

The men kept their distance. A few were glancing at Tilly with evident fear, taking a step back for every step Tom and Tilly took forward.

Tom was right. The news had spread, and they were afraid of her.

"Hold my hand, darling. Open your eyes and hold my hand. There's nothing to fear. We're just going to take a short walk."

Tom's soothing voice stroked the air, trying to reassure not only his child, but the jittery men with guns.

"We're going to walk, calmly and slowly."

"Look after your kid. If she bolts, if she touches anyone, she'll be shot right here. Got it?"

Tom lifted his head to the familiar voice and nodded.

The man standing outside the circle was roughly Tom's age. He was shorter than Tom and beefier. His large arms past the rolled-up sleeves were hairy and hung low, belonging to a man, whose entire life consisted of demanding physical work.

The man turned and walked.

"Move!"

Metal shoved into Tom's back, and Tom followed.

After crossing the single main road, their group dived into a network of warehouses and workshops, and snaking between dark buildings, they headed deeper into the network of docks. And the deeper they went, Tom realised that he would have a hell of a time trying to find his way back out of this metal and brick maze should he try to escape.

But Tom didn't plan to escape. There was nowhere else left for him to run.

Tom followed the man, taking turns between the buildings and watching the sunrise lighting the roofs around them.

They came to a two storey, grey building under a metal roof. Its windows were dark, and the single door at the front was closed.

"Ordained Liberating Party Customs Control and Border Protection. The free nation we serve!" was written on the long, polished sheet of metal that was nailed above the entrance. The sheet was painted in the colours of the flag, light blue and white; a solitary star shone in the corner of the sign. This sign was newer and shinier than the building it adorned.

But instead of coming to the main entrance, Tom and Tilly were led around the back of the building, where the man threw open two large metal bulkhead doors at the base of the building and took steps down.

Tom shuffled unsure, but with another nudge at his back, he followed.

The basement of the building was dimly lit by the yellowish crude light fixtures suspended off the low ceiling at even intervals and generously covered in cobwebs and flies excrement.

The basement may have been large, but Tom stood in a small room with doors to his left and a narrow corridor to his right.

"Move!"

Prompted by another shove, Tom walked down the corridor, following the orang-utan of a man.

Unexpectedly, the corridor ended at an open door, and Tom and Tilly stepped over its threshold.

The room they were in was small, the ceiling low. A single light bulb hung above the desk that sat against a wall, with a chair behind it and two chairs in front of it.

"Take a seat."

The man gestured to the two chairs. Tom sat in one, then picked up Tilly and sat her on his lap. Once Tom assumed his position, the man left the room, closing the door behind him, a key turning in the lock.

"That's okay, darling; that's okay", Tom mumbled, as he stroked his daughter's head. She was frightened and Tom could see it, but apart from these meaningless words of reassurance, he couldn't do anything else to elevate her fears. For now, he was as powerless, as she was.

He was methodically stroking her head and her back, mumbling those words, when a burning wave suddenly touched the skin on his arms and his legs, rippling with a strange tingling to the surface.

Moving his arms away from his daughter, careful not to startle her by showing her his destined end, Tom reached, and with his shaky fingers, he unbuttoned the sleeve on his shirt.

He forced himself to look down.

The muted yellow light illuminated a white mass of raised domes covering his arm.

The domes had grown. They were larger, and there were more of them. Now, clear at the top, with the sloshing darker centres, they looked like a layer of frogspawn.

Tom tugged his sleeve higher. The domes went up, past the elbow, disappearing under his shirt.

He yanked his sleeve down, fumbling with the button on the cuff, when the key scratched the lock, and a moment later, the door opened to let a man in.

The man strutted forward, the orang-utan man trailing behind him.

The newcomer had short grey hair on top of his head and a cleanly shaved face, which exposed his heavy jaw and thin, tightly pressed lips. He was older than Tom, yet younger than Felix, and the grey eyes under his eyebrows shone with a calculated metallic sheen.

The authority pulsated off of him. He was the one in charge.

"What are you doing here?" he started without a preamble. He perched on a corner of the desk, one foot resting on the floor, whilst the other swung slightly.

"I came to sell something", Tom answered.

"Sell something", the man repeated. "And what made you think that we're buying?"

"I heard you might."

"You know, there's a lot of gossip and lies going around the city about the docks, being that dangerous world of cut throats and outlaws..."

He dropped his gaze to Tilly.

"And of children, who, according to the Party, carry diseases..."

Tom swallowed.

"She's not your issue and not your concern", he bristled.

"Au contraire. She is here, isn't she? Now, she is my concern for many reasons. But I'd really like to hear what you have for sale that required a midnight arrival, and with hot goods in tow."

The man got up, walked around the desk and slid into the chair behind it.

"I have information and I have goods, both are for sale", Tom answered, following the man's movement with his gaze. "But I want something for it."

The man laughed.

"Of course you do. If you didn't, you wouldn't be here."

The door behind Tom creaked open, then closed, and a pair of boots marched across the floor.

Absentmindedly, Tom's gaze slid onto the new arrival.

It didn't plan to linger there. It ventured there only to keep tabs on the danger in the room, but confronted by the familiar features, which tugged at Tom's memory, Tom's gaze refused to move away, held in place by the newcomer's surprised glance, and then the glare.

The two men stared.

"Do you know each other?"

The old man's voice cut silence and the tension, and as Tom turned his head to the man in charge, he saw him waving his hand between the two of them, two deep wrinkles cutting his forehead, as his eyes narrowed into slits.

"We've met before", the newcomer answered, and a smile tugged a corner of his lips, as his eyes narrowed. "In another life. A long time ago."

The man took his post by the desk, a loyal lieutenant to his general.

"What's the Party's most subservient rat doing down in the gutter with the unwashed?" he asked.

"I didn't expect to see you here either", Tom bit back, "although, I can't say I'm surprised. You always had a predisposition for a life of crime."

"Better than breaking my back for twats, who don't give a shit about me", the man retorted.

"So many pleasantries", the old man huffed. "The love between you two truly warms my heart."

"Now, how do you know each other?" The old man demanded, not impressed with being out of the loop on the tension, his earlier sarcasm set aside.

"Sharík, let me introduce you Thomaās, the Party's most obedient rat and exquisite arse licker, who's probably for those talents alone flying high right now. We were in the same orphanage together, only I starved in my barracks, while he enjoyed the best the Party had to offer."

The man leaned his shoulder on a wall behind the desk, reached into his pocket and, under Tom's stunned gaze, produced a cigarette.

He leisurely lit it and took a deep drag.

Cigarettes were more illegal than guns, overtaking the next illegal product, sugar, as Federation Britannia kept a close eye on the population's chaste health. Tom hadn't seen cigarettes, never smelt one and didn't know anyone, who had tried it. They were impossible to acquire.

The old man turned his attention back to Tom.

"So, you know Jeff? That's good. If we're all friends here, it would make our transaction more friendly... and honest."

The old man turned to Jeff.

"Your friend's here to sell us something. We began the discussion into the goods and price when you arrived. Your presence might help us negotiate."

Jeff's eyes snapped open, feigning shock.

"Selling? Thomaās Whicker is here to sell something? To us? To break the law and sell *us* something? Us? The political dirt and saboteurs?"

Tom sat silently, watching Jeff, who turned more animated with every passing minute and every spoken word.

"Who would've thought", Jeff continued, "Thomaās, the one who started a brawl because someone had the audacity to say bad things about his wonderful Party. That Thomaās is to make a deal with *us*? I must be hallucinating."

Jeff threw his head back and laughed, finding Tom's presence in their bunker amusing.

But his good mood was short-lived.

He pushed himself off the wall and strode to Tom. The flicked cigarette flew out his hand, drawing a flaming trajectory, before falling to the concrete floor.

"And do you remember how you started that petition, to reduce the food portions for "the children of enemies of the state"? Remember?! The Party was only happy to oblige and they reduced our ration, bringing children to the brink of starvation, and the stronger ones were taking food from the youngest and the weakest, and within three months five young boys in my barrack died, do you remember that?"

With every word spoken, Jeff moved closer, his voice rising, and by the time he reached Tom, he was roaring, hovering above him, his spittle flying, his eyes burning, filled with hot hate.

"Is that the same bootlicker Thomaās Whicker here now, breaking the law and trying to sell us something? Is that him?"

Tom's orphanage past had caught up with him again.

Tom covered his daughter with his arms, hiding her with his body.

"It's okay, darling. It's okay. It's nothing to worry about. Daddy won't let anything happen to you. Don't worry", Tom mumbled in a low voice, whilst keeping his gaze on the hateful man above.

"Daddy?" Jeff's eyebrows rose. "She's your daughter?"

Jeff shook his head in disbelief and pulled back.

"I should pick up that fucking phone and call State Security and give them both of you. I don't give a shit, if the news about the disease is true or a new perverted experiment the Party is cracking on the country, I should just hand you both to them, knowing that you'll rot in the camps, while your daughter will die in the orphanage, on the half portion that you advocated for!"

"Daddy."

Tilly was crying. She was shaking next to Tom's chest. She was rocking herself, her hands pressed to her ears, failing at sealing away the world.

"That's okay, baby. That's okay. This man is daddy's old friend. That's how he's joking. Shh, shh."

"Fucking joking", Jeff mumbled.

He shook his head, turned and walked away.

"Shh, shh", Tom murmured.

"So what is it you're selling and what's the price?" Sharík interjected from his chair.

"I came to sell you food, the food that I had in my bags and that was stolen by your man", Tom hissed, turning to the old man.

Sharík lifted his hand, silencing Tom.

"That wasn't stolen, Thomaās. We're not the criminals that rob good free citizens in the middle of the night. No, no, no. Let's consider it a payment for my time... a toll, collected on arrival."

Tom gritted his teeth.

"Fine. That *toll* was a part of the deal. That food was for sale, but that was not all. The food that you... seized, I can get you more of it, the same nomenclature quality, and a lot of it, not the synthetic crap, but real, naturally grown food. I can get a lot more of it. But most importantly, I have classified information for sale, and I think you'll find it very useful. The Party hasn't released it, and now I think they never will. They more than likely will bury that information, and anyone who knows it. The only person, apart from me, who knows about it was branded crazy and was locked away, although, he's in hiding now. I can promise you, you'll need that information, at least for yourself... if you want to live."

"Okay", the old man nodded. "And how much do you want for it?"

"I don't want money. I want something else."

"And here we are", Jeff chimed in. "Of course you want something else. Why don't you ask your fucking beloved Party to grant you your wish. I'll tell you why. Because you want something they can't provide. That's why you're here, dirtying yourself with the filth of the earth."

He shook his head.

"We should just hand you over to them and be done with it", he growled through his clenched teeth.

"Jeff, please", the old man interjected, before turning his attention back to Tom.

"Thomaās, you need to understand. As much as I'm always open to more supplies, and information is the most precious commodity that I ever purchase, I need to know what's your side of the deal, and if the barter is worth it. So let's start with what you want."

"I want you to transport me and my daughter to Frankia."

Both men fell quiet. Their eyes snapped wide open in surprise before a second later a guttural guffaw of their laughter swallowed the room.

"Thomaās, I'm not a travel agent. You came to the wrong place, I'm afraid. If you want to see other countries, go and apply for the Party permission to leave the country first, have interviews and whatever else they do to their citizens, before they allow one to leave the country. But I'm not your man."

"I'm sorry, what's your name? Sharík? Should I call you that?"

"My apologies. I hadn't introduced myself properly. Yes, my name is Sharík, but friends call me Shar. And as we're all friends here, you're free to call me Shar too."

Tom nodded.

"Sharík, I'll give you information", Tom said, ignoring the offer of shallow friendship. "I'll provide you with something that you haven't heard before, and never will, because the Party is making sure it remained sealed. Nobody knows about it and no one will, and anyone who ever comes across it will be dead. They'll make sure of it. At least before they'll cover it up... That's why I can't go back. I want transportation for myself and my child across the border."

Sharík leaned forward and rested his arms on his desk.

"I appreciate your plight, Thomaās, and it sounds like you have a great piece of information, but you're seeking services we don't provide. Can you imagine if we organised boat trips across the Channel into Calais? That would be crazy. We would be like... people smugglers, or something.

Can you imagine the heat it would bring? And I'm not even mentioning the undermining of the leadership of the greatest country in the world. Oh, never!"

The old man shook his head and slammed his fist on the desk. He spoke with conviction, and Tom struggled to read him.

"We're just dock workers, who occasionally find sugary treats and cigarettes in foreign boats, but that's about it."

Sharík spread his arms and gave Tom an apologetic smile.

The silence stretched.

Tom interrupted it first.

"Fine. Then, there will be no exchange, and there will be no deal. No food provision location and no information, and trust me, with information that I hold, a lot will change. The way you work, the way you live. The country will find out eventually, hopefully...maybe...but they might not. But irrespective of that outcome, you'll be covered. You and your people won't die."

Sharík narrowed his gaze on Tom, before swinging his gaze to Jeff.

"How about you tell us what you know, and we'll see what we can do."

Tom shook his head.

"No go. If you can't help me, I'll find someone else who can."

Sharík leaned closer and dropped his voice.

"And who that might be, Thomaās? Who else might be there, able to help you? Where would you go? Do you have a directory of people smugglers and outlaws of the country?"

"I'll figure it out."

Tom was bluffing. He didn't know where else to turn and he didn't have time for more research and procurement. Besides, could the meeting of a man from his past be a sign?

Sharík reclined back in his chair and, holding Tom's gaze, shook his head.

"You don't have the scope."

"I'll figure it out", Tom repeated.

He picked up his daughter and rose from the chair.

"And you think we'll let you leave?" Sharík asked, his gaze following Tom's rise.

Tom glared at him without a word.

The old man smiled and raised his hands, his face softening. But Tom wasn't buying the soft smiles from these types of people.

"Okay, Tom, go and rest for a moment", Sharík said. "I want to speak to Jeff."

He turned to the door.

"Mort, Mort!"

The earlier orang-utan of a man appeared through the door.

"Can you please show our guests to the captains' room? Please arrange food, water, anything they might need."

"Food from our satchels... and water", Tom interjected.

"You heard the man."

Sharík gave a short nod, dismissing them.

"Follow me", Mort said, issuing the same instruction for the second time since he and Tom met.

Chapter 23

Tom was running out of time and he knew it.

Once Tilly, exhausted and fed, had fallen asleep under a woolly blanket on the double bed, Tom rolled up the sleeves on his shirt.

He sat alone, in the silence of the room lit by a single weak light bulb, inspecting the watery domes over his skin.

Tom stared at them, his mind drifting to the body of his wife on the white gurney, then to his daughter, asleep on the bed. Memories of his past were cutting through his thoughts of the empty future.

He remembered the day they received the impregnation permit, remembering years of paperwork prior, how many endorsements he had to do, how many favours he had to ask for and return.

Finally, they had a child, a healthy pink child, half him and half his wonderful wife.

The moment he held his daughter's tiny body in his hands was the greatest moment in his life. The day Tilly was born was the happiest day. He was the proudest. He was complete. He had found the plenitude he didn't know existed. He found something, he didn't know he didn't possess. That feeling was new, unique and... scary, scary because it ran so deep, *too deep*.

Tom tried to wrap his mind around the fact that he will be dead in a matter of days, wiped off this world as if he never existed, and he struggled with it.

The human mind is not prerequisite for contemplating one's mortality. It's hotwired by nature to avoid it.

The human ego cannot imagine the world after one's death. It is too fragile for that. It can't imagine that life would go on, untouched by our demise. Our world starts and ends with us. The human mind can't handle the weight of the thought that once we are dead, the world would continue spinning, unaffected by our death, unaware, as if nothing happened. Our egos are so large that the thought of the world going about its business past our death, with new births and loud laughter, feels like desecration, sacrilege. The human mind is too small and frightened to process it or to venture beyond it. And Tom struggled with it too.

He struggled to push past it: to accept it, to really acknowledge it.

Disbelief and shock were the only two feelings that swam in his head at the sight of the spots, along with mild denial, which with cool waves of wishful thinking kept asking if it could be something else, an unrelated rash and not the disease that took his wife.

Tom sat in the glum room, suspended in his own mind, stroking the layer of blistered domes, careful not to pop them, morbidly fascinated by them.

He brought his arm to his ear, moving it, tilting, listening to the blisters. He smelled them. But there was nothing, only their silent odourless shapes.

Tom unbuttoned his shirt, inspecting his stomach. It was still clean. He remembered the bleeding blisters on his wife's back, but he had no mirrors to inspect his own. So he tentatively reached and stroked his lower back. It felt smooth and clean.

He had time, but probably not much.

He rolled his sleeves down. He buttoned his shirt and tucked it inside his trousers, forcing his mind to concentrate on his daughter, on her survival beyond this country.

A knock sounded on the door.

Tom rose from the bed and opened it. Jeff stood past the threshold.

"Sharík wants to speak to you."

Tom glanced at Tilly, curled up under a rough blanket.

"Mort will stay next to the door. Just leave it open."

They walked back to the room with the desk. Sharík was already waiting for them.

"Jeff seems to think it's a trap", Sharík started, once Tom slid into a chair, "whereas I'm not sure. I'm not going to promise you anything, but let's say that many things are possible to me, especially on the docks. I can make a lot of wishes, most coveted and almost impossible wishes, come true."

Sharík held Tom's gaze, waiting for Tom to catch the innuendo and read between the lines.

"But I need to hear your information first", he continued, "to weigh up its value and act on its worth. I need to know what I'm buying."

Tom shook his head.

"No. First, we're going to talk about your side of the agreement. Can you help me or not?"

Tom wanted to hear the man's words. He needed to look into the man's eye as he issued his confirmation or promise.

Sharík leaned in, and resting his arms on the leather top of his desk and holding Tom's gaze, he gave a short nod.

"I can. We do provide that kind of service, but it comes at a cost."

"I can't believe we're even talking about cost", Tom said. "Aren't we all friends here?"

He spread his arm, raising his eyebrow at Jeff.

"There will be no cost", Tom clipped, faced by Jeff's glare.

And turning his attention back to Sharík and retiring his feigned happiness, he added: "I'll provide you with the location of food, along with an idea of where to obtain more and of the same quality. Trust me, that alone would be enough to cover the cost of the tickets. But out of the kindness of my heart, I'm throwing in the classified information as well. The combination of these is more than sufficient payment for your transportation services. It will be more than enough for the tickets."

"You have the steel of a great negotiator, Thomaās. Seems like Jeff's original appraisal of you wasn't as accurate as he thought."

Tom glanced at Jeff. He could imagine that appraisal: weak, not a fighter, avoids conflicts, subservient, all in all by the measures of these men, a pathetic twat. That's fine too. He didn't care.

"Tell me about your "service"?" Tom continued, taking control over the conversation. "How does it operate? How safe is it, and when will we be able to leave the country?"

A lighter clicked, as Jeff lit another cigarette, its smoke whirling around the light and scratching the back of Tom's throat.

"Thomaās, as you can imagine it's not like a scheduled crossing. These trips take place when we can do it. Currently, with everything that's going on in the country, we weren't planning to run one for a month, maybe two, hoping for the dust to settle..."

"That's too late. We need to cross in two days."

Shock took over Sharík's face, as Jeff huffed somewhere to a side.

"Wow", he breathed out. "You're delusional, man."

Sharík coughed and shot a glare at Jeff.

"Delivering the same notion softly", Sharík said, nudging his head at Jeff, "those are very unrealistic expectations, Thomaās. Two days is far too soon and too dangerous. We need to wait for a lull in security on the water, and currently is not the time for these operations."

"We'll sail within two days. That's in your interests."

Silence descended over the room.

"What do you mean?" Sharík asked softly. His forehead gathered, as he inclined his head and studied the man in front.

"In two days the State Security Armed Rapid Response Team will be here", Jeff said. "It has been arranged. And when they'll come, it would be better for everyone, especially you, if we were long gone. Because if we were found here... Well, you can imagine what will happen to you for harbouring a fugitive and a child, and I'm not even mentioning how that will affect your business."

The old man's face steeled. His lips thinned into a loathing line and his eyes narrowed.

He leaned across the desk.

335

"You", Sharík hissed. "I can drown both of you in the sea and that would be the end of it."

"I wouldn't advise that either. It wouldn't work as well as you'd hope. For someone who runs such a dangerous enterprise, you're too sloppy... the pair of you. Nobody's guarding your water systems. Where does the water you drinking come from? Probably from that water tower a couple of miles away. Unless I'm mistaken, and you're drinking sea water like seals. So, if you don't want to die in two days and for the State Security to find the village full of dead bodies on arrival... Well, if you want to avoid these sad outcomes, you'll do better listening to me."

Tom leaned closer to the desk.

"Think about it. What I'm offering you? What's my payment? A stock of provisions..."

Tom lifted his finger.

"... *quality* provisions, and the State Security level classified information, all in exchange for a measly trip, a trip which you'd be running anyway. I'm just asking to do it earlier. If you ask me, it's an absolute bargain. In fact, like the pirates that you are, you're robbing me blind."

Tom smiled.

"No? Bad joke?" He asked the silence. "My apologies in this case. You probably prefer the term "sea entrepreneurs"."

"Two days?" Sharík asked, glaring at Tom. "We have two days, for everything?"

Tom nodded.

"And water supplies?" The old man demanded.

"I'll remove what I've placed. There will be no danger."

"But State security still will come?"

Tom shrugged his shoulders, reclining back in his chair.

"So what? You know they're coming, so you'll prepare. You'll arrange everything. They'll come, find nothing and they'll leave. At least then, you'd have a few months of peace, before they'll drop in on you again. In that time, you'd probably be able to run two or three smuggling sessions. That must be what brings you the real money... and not the cigarettes and sugar."

Sharík reclined too, folding his hands on his stomach.

"I kinda like you. There's something about you... a gambling edge, valour with a bit of crazy. And I can't kill you?"

The old man smiled, but the smile didn't touch his grey eyes.

"Unless you want to die in two days", Tom answered, spreading his arms, the answering smile dusted his lips.

The old man laughed.

"Fair enough. Consider yourself and your daughter transported. I'll make the arrangements today, and you will be on a boat within forty eight hours."

"We'll be on French soil in forty eight hours."

"Okay, okay. That's the details. You have yourself a deal."

Sharík's gaze held Tom's.

"As I prepare your trip, you have to give me something. I need to know that your mystery classified information and food provisions are not a fluke."

"I won't give you the information, not yet", Tom cut the man off. "But, to aid our cooperation so to speak, I'll tell you where you can find food, a lot of food. It will prove to you that I'm telling the truth, and then we'll talk again."

The old man nodded.

"D'accor. I expected as much."

"But", Jeff interrupted from his side of the room, "you're coming with us to collect that imaginary food. And if you lied, or if it's a trap, I'll kill you right there."

Tom shook his head at his old acquaintance.

"I can't leave my daughter alone."

And as he said those words, he suddenly realised that he will. He *is* about to leave her, soon and forever, forever alone. And that thought scared him.

"She will be fine. I was told I'm good with children", Sharík piped in from his seat. "I'll make sure she's safe."

He looked at Tom, his gaze from under his bushy eyebrows heavy.

"Do you want her out of the country?"

Tom sighed.

"Of course."

"Well, that's the process. We all have to sacrifice something at one time or another, and your time is now."

"Fine."

"Très bon. Jeff will lead the raid, and you're going with him. Bring me what you promised, and we'll finalise the details."

Tom nodded, and without waiting to be dismissed, and to show who is in charge of this conversation, he got up from his chair and walked out of the room.

He marched to their small room, to the room where his daughter slept, and after walking in, he slammed the door shut in front of Mort's face and climbed into bed.

He didn't hug his daughter. He was afraid to disturb her sleep. Instead, he curled up next to her, listening to her soft breathing, as he dozed off.

Tom and Tilly spent the day sleeping, the softness of the bed claiming them after the week of turmoil.

Hours later, as dusk embraced the ground, a demanding knock rattled the door, waking Tom.

Mort stood past it, two plates loaded with food in his hands.

"Eat and get ready. Jeff will be here soon."

He shoved the plates at Tom, turned and walked off.

Half an hour later another knock vibrated the door, angrier this time.

Jeff stood behind it.

"Come on, it's time."

He threw a luminescent yellow wad of fabric at Tom. The fabric slapped Tom in the chest, Tom catching it before it fell to the ground.

"Kate will stay with your daughter."

Tom turned his attention to the woman past the door.

She gave him a short nod, but there was no smile.

Although the woman wasn't tall, she was wide in the shoulders under her grey shawl. She looked, as if she had stepped out of a Party poster. She looked sturdy and strong, a living embodiment of the Party endorsed image of a woman and a mother – strong and steely in body and mind, with no pity to give to anyone who failed. Petite and weak women were seen as useless in Federation Britannia. They were unable to lift things, to do heavy work on the farms or in factories or to bear healthy children.

According to the Party, weak citizens, whatever sex they might be, had no purpose in the new society. She was as far away from soft and intelligent Judy, as it were possible.

Tom turned to his daughter.

"Daddy has to go", he started, but seeing the panic in his child's eyes, he added quickly, "but I won't be long. I won't be long at all. This citizen will stay with you. She'll play with you. If you're hungry or thirsty, you ask her, and I'll be back before it's time to go back to sleep."

Tom watched Tilly's trembling lips, reading rather than hearing her words, which came in a barely audible murmur: "Daddy."

Dropping to his knees, Tom hugged his daughter tight and whispered: "Daddy will be back. I promise", and blocking the ripping of his heart, he watched Tilly's wet face for a second, committing it to memory – fat tears rolling out of her shining eyes, her round face and red lips – before turning and leaving the room under her accusatory gaze.

"You shouldn't promise something you can't guarantee you can deliver", Jeff said next to him.

Tom stopped and turned to the man.

"Who knows what might happen to you during the raid", Jeff finished.

They glared at each other for a few long seconds, before Tom turned away, his attention shifting to the yellow fabric in his hand.

Tom unwrapped it.

It was a worker vest. The "Sewage services" was written on its back in the black minimalistic font, favoured by the Party.

"Sewage?"

"How else did you think we get into town under curfew?" Jeff huffed. "Not many officers are willing to jump into sewers with us or take approval papers from our shit covered hands."

Tom followed Jeff out of the building, leaving the same way he was brought in.

Chapter 24

A utility yellow truck rumbled outside the basement door, spewing diesel fumes. The large black letters on its side, under the two coloured flag with a star, stated: "Emergency response".

Jeff pulled open the cab's door.

The two men sat inside, the familiar Mort and a young man, who was tapping something into the computerised book on his lap, without paying attention to the new arrival, or anything around him for that matter.

"Alright, we're all here", Jeff said after Tom took a seat in the cabin next to him. "Where are we going?"

"The Old Centre."

"And more precise?"

"I'll tell you once we're there."

"Okay, then." Jeff shrugged his shoulders. "Mort, you heard the man: The Old Centre."

With a jerk and screeching of its old engine, the truck turned, its headlight pulling out sleepy buildings, and picking up speed, the truck rolled down the dark street, leaving the docks behind.

They flew through the empty black streets. The trip that took Tom with Tilly two days was completed in an hour.

"Where to now?"

"Forestry ministry building."

After a second of confusion, Jeff barked a bright laugh, slapping himself on the thigh.

"That's not bad thinking."

He shook his head and then turned to Tom.

"And what, no security?"

"Apart from the regular patrols in the area, which are more common than in your neck of the woods, there's nothing."

The yellow truck puffed out smoke, as it swapped streets and turned corners, before pulling to a stop by the side of the familiar building.

The following drill looked practised and well-rehearsed, possibly even previously executed.

Without a word, Mort and the boy jumped out, the small lights on the shoulders of their yellow vests waking.

They tugged warning signs, polls, metal rods and yellow tape out of the cab, propping those around a nearby sewage manhole. They yanked the lid off it and dropped it close by.

"Now, we're working."

Jeff gave Tom a smug smile.

"Where to now?"

"At the back, behind the bins. One of the bottom windows is broken."

The young man stayed behind, surrounded by the tape and signs. Tom led the way around the back, and Jeff and Mort followed.

The broken window was as Tom had left it.

"Go!"

Jeff waved at its dark hole, telling Tom to go first, and following the instruction, Tom dropped onto his stomach, just as he did before, and slid into the familiar kitchen, hitting his back on the cooker upon landing.

"It's fine", Tom whispered up, towards the window.

Under the accompaniment of low mumbling and faint swearing, the two more heavy bodies fell through, knocking over the pans. Their

343

caught at the last minute cries and muffled curses bounced within the tiled room. The torch light on Mort's vest rolled with him.

"Are you trying to kill us?" Jeff hissed.

"If I did, you'd already have been dead", Tom rebuffed.

A bright light of a torch clicked in Jeff's hand. Its white circle slid along the walls, stopping at the large cabinet doors that Tom left open, illuminating the stocked shelves.

Mort whistled.

"Clearly, that's what we'll be doing for the next few weeks – raiding the ministries."

Mort reached into his pocket, and pulling out and unclipping a few foldable bags, he threw them open on the floor. Then, diving into the cupboard, he began loading them with the stock.

Ignoring Mort's happy whistling and the shining of his butt crack, Tom walked deeper into the kitchen, towards the door in the opposite corner.

"Where are you going?"

Disregarding Jeff's question, Tom arrived at the coveted door.

The door was still closed, held by the meat hammer threaded through the handle.

Tom slowly pulled the hammer out, holding the door closed, expecting the manic jump of the prisoner.

But the burst didn't come. Screams or kicks at the door didn't follow.

"What's there?" Jeff asked behind Tom's shoulder, but instead of answering, Tom pushed the door.

Jeff's light glided along the bare walls, sliding down to the bed and stopping at the body on it, at the brown curly hair spilled over the pillow.

Tom took a step forward then stopped. Then, as if in a daze, while keeping his eyes on the body ahead, he shuffled closer, until he was next to the bed.

The angry girl didn't jump at him.

She didn't move at all.

Tom kneeled next to her. He reached out, and after moving a strand of her hair, he gently turned her head.

Her eyes were sunken and closed, her skin wrinkled. A weak hiss of air escaped her cracked lips.

As if burnt, Tom pulled his hand away, and losing its balance, her head lolled to the edge of the pillow, hair falling, brushing the floor.

"Your work?"

Jeff's voice and harsh words made Tom jump. Watching the girl, he forgot that Jeff was in the room with him.

It *was* his handy work. He did it. But he wasn't about to admit that to this low life.

"No."

Jeff huffed.

"Yeah. Whatever, mate."

The light left the room with Jeff's footsteps, submerging Tom in the darkness, and when he knew that no one would hear him, he leaned in and whispered: "I'm sorry."

The sounds of slamming of cabinet doors, the soft rattling of pots, the shaking of grains in the packets and the metal songs of the tins hitting tins resonated through the open door, bouncing off the tiles and metal of the kitchen.

Tom walked into the kitchen lit up by the torches and noise.

"Can you be quieter?" he growled.

"We're as quiet as mice", Mort chortled, throwing the loot into the bags then stuffing it tight.

"Where's Jeff?"

Mort shrugged his shoulders.

"Don't know."

Suddenly, a sound of a struggle dimmed by the distance and coming in shreds through the broken window snaked into the room.

Tom pulled to a stop. Mort paused his whistling and throwing the loot into the bags.

Both looked at each other and listened.

Another wave of noises came, and this time Tom could hear curses, grunting and muffled exclamation weaving through the sounds of a tussle.

Mort dropped the cans he held, and with a few long steps, he reached the window and was climbing out.

Tom stood in the kitchen for a second longer, weighing up his options. But he climbed out of the window too. His own and his child's lives were tied to the lives of the dock criminals, their death or premature raid on the port before the end of this week, being the end of Tilly.

The noises of the brawl were louder outside, and as Tom turned the corner, he pulled to a stop at the sight of the black figure of a State Security officer lying on the ground, the body of the young dock criminal sprawled next to him, and Jeff wresting a rifle out of the hold of the second officer.

Mort reached Jeff and the officer before Tom, and without slowing his manic run, he jumped up on the last step and laid his meaty fist into the side of the officer's head.

Something cracked.

The officer's knees buckled, and he collapsed sideways. The rifle dropped out of his hands.

Tom strode closer.

The street was quiet, its silence only interrupted by the heavy breathing of the two men and the dull mumbling of the radios on the officers' shoulders.

"What the hell?!" Tom hissed.

He tried to keep his voice quiet, but anger and fear were yanking it up.

"What the... *fucking* hell?!" he growled, pulling out the word favoured by the men like Jeff, which he knew would relay his outrage better than any other words that he could find.

"Imbeciles! Two dead officers, in the middle of curfew. What the fucking hell?!"

Tom was livid.

He wasn't about to sabotage his and his daughter's survival for these two morons.

"Relax", Jeff huffed, as he stood folded over, catching his breath. "They didn't report the robbery."

Tom moved forward, and the closer to Jeff he came, the angrier he grew, his fury of the last few days spilling over. And when he was within the arm's reach from his old pal, he threw his fist forward, making a connection with Jeff's head.

"You, fuck! Fucking asshole!" Tom roared, as he threw punches.

"Fucking moron! Fucking inbreed! Simpleton!"

Tom's fists were flying, as he made a connection after connection, filling Tom's vision with a fuzzy red.

A sudden punch at a side of the face rocked Tom.

He stumbled, his dropped hands missing another punch, which this time connected with his jaw.

Tom shook his head, stumbling backward, the red in his eyes replaced by the dark swirls.

"Don't you fucking ever touch me, arse licker. Next time, I won't be so gentle", Jeff roared next to him, and as if unable to stop himself, or maybe to add weight to his words, he threw his right arm wide, sinking his fist into Tom's cheekbone.

Tom fell to his knees. His mouth filled with blood and his ears with ringing.

He turned his head to Jeff, and spitting blood, he held his gaze on the criminal.

"You, morons, just made two dead bodies, *officers'* bodies, in the lockdown."

Tom shook his head.

"Fucking morons and losers", he mumbled.

"They're not going to be found", Jeff growled, stroking his buffeted head.

Grabbing hold of the wall of a nearby building, Tom rose to his feet, swinging and blinking through the swirling darkness in his eyes. Or was it just the night? But if so, what was that tolling then?

"And you think that will help?" Tom answered, rubbing the left side of his face. "Of course you fucking do! In your simple way, you think that if we get rid of the bodies, it'll all be honky-dory. Fucking moron! They'll be looking for the missing officers. Their radios are tracked, you fucking twat."

Tom held his head.

"I can't believe I got involved with twats like you, can't believe that I'm counting on *you* to take me out of the country!"

"Even officers go missing sometimes", Mort piped from the side.

"Deary me", Tom mumbled, before turning to Mort.

"And what do you think will happen when a squad rolls in here, looking for missing officers? Do you think they won't search the surrounding streets *and* buildings? And they won't find the broken window and missing food? And they won't connect these two incidents? Of course, why would they?" Tom huffed, pulling a sarcastic smile. "Why would they connect the missing street-beaters with the crime committed next door?"

Tom walked to the bodies sprawled on the ground within a tight perimeter of the yellow tape.

The manhole stood open. Its lid rested next to it. The body of the young boy was folded nearby, blood pooling underneath him.

Tom turned.

"Mort, go and finish collecting the food. We're about to leave."

Mort raised his eyebrows at Tom, surprise spilling onto his face, before he turned his head to Jeff, who nodded, allowing Mort to proceed under Tom's instruction.

Mort dived behind the corner.

Tom walked to the body of the officer, and after bending over, he turned him.

"What are you doing?" Jeff asked Tom's back.

"We have two choices for staging: accident or murder. Were it not for the blood from your colleague, I would've gone for an accident, but with blood already here, there's only one way..."

He turned his head to Jeff.

"We'll cover that blood with more blood."

"You're insane", Jeff mumbled.

"Better than being an imbecile", Tom huffed.

Tom walked around the area, picking up and folding the warning signs of the sewage works, rolling up the yellow tape. He pushed the lid on the manhole closed.

Mort appeared around the corner, loaded with the burgeoning bags, tins rattling in them in time with his steps.

"There are a few more", he huffed through his gritted teeth, as he walked past Tom and Jeff and threw the bags into the open door of their yellow truck.

"We need to take the boy with us", Tom said, turning to Jeff.

"Agreed."

The two men came over the boy's body, and picking him up by the arms and legs, they carried him to the yellow truck and loaded him on top of the fat rolls of sewage pipes and yellow tape.

Tom wasn't a police officer or state official of any kind, but even he knew where eventually the investigation into the dead street-beaters would lead. Eventually, they'll come to the docks. All that he wanted was to buy some time, two days precisely.

"What now?"

Jeff's strained breathing swallowed the ending of his words.

"More blood", Tom replied, striding back to the murder scene. "We'll use their rifles on them, but once those are fired, we need to be gone immediately."

Tom bent over the officer Jeff had tussled with, inspecting his belt. The radio unit, a holster with a handgun, an electro-shocker, a pocket with a set of keys, a flask with liquid splashing inside and a folding knife.

Tom unclipped the sheath and tugged the knife free, when suddenly, the officer moaned. His head turned, and his eyes fluttered open.

With a dry click of a button, a blade flew out, doubling the size of the knife in Tom's hand, and without slowing or stopping to think, Tom sunk the knife into the officer's chest.

The eyes above the black mask snapped open. The hands reached upwards, the moans and the gurgling of blood choked by the mask.

Tom pulled the knife out and drove it in again, this time higher, in the shoulder, pulling it out and sinking it again.

Tom had to call on his self-restraint, stopping himself from stabbing the body over and over, as every time he plunged his knife, pushing it deeper with the weight of his body, he felt a weird pleasure, a relief, happiness at watching the scared eyes locked on him, knowing that the man below suffered.

Tom yanked the blade out and sank onto his heels, admiring his work.

The black figure was lifeless. The rifle next to it, maybe the one that was pointed at the children, maybe even fired at them, has failed to protect its owner.

"That will do."

Tom rose to his feet, and grabbing the body by the uniform over its shoulders, he dragged it over the pool of blood.

Mort galloped somewhere behind Tom, the tins rattling with him.

"That's the last of it", he called.

But Tom was busy. He shoved the knife's handle into the already freezing grip of the first officer and closed his hand over the bloody handle.

He lifted his eyes to Jeff.

"Block the broken window with the bins, and let's go."

Jeff's stunned gaze met Tom's, lingering on Tom's face for a moment, before giving him a wooden nod.

Tom picked up a rifle.

The metal wheels on the bin rattled past the corner.

The engine coughed, woke up and clanged, finding its laborious rhythm, as the headlights lighted the side of a nearby building, and drowned by the arrhythmic sound of the engine, Tom fired a shot.

Chapter 25

"Jeff filled me in on your unexpected visitors and your little adventure, including your tête-à-tête."

Sharík lifted his eyebrows, scanning Tom's bruised face and the swollen eye.

Tom sat in the familiar chair, in the familiar room in the docks, with Sharík sitting behind the desk and Jeff standing next to him, in his usual manner leaning his shoulder on the wall.

The ride to the docks was quiet, and more often than not, Tom would catch Jeff's studious gazes on him, and he didn't like it.

"I have to say, I'm more surprised than I'd like to admit", Sharík continued. "Very unexpected... Very unexpected, indeed. Qui savait... The initiative you've shown... and the cold-bloodedness with which you stabbed that officer?"

Sharík shook his head.

"I did not see that coming."

"But, returning to our negotiation", he added brighter. "Revenons à nos moutons. So far your information was solid. The food was there. There was plenty of it, and it was nice quality. Not surprising, really, nomenclature fat cats would've been eating it. Based on the procured goods, and carrying our agreement forward, while you were away, I've made a number of arrangements. A boat is being prepared, as we speak. I'm sending one of my best captains to sail it. It will leave the shores within the next two days."

The man outstretched his hand across the table for a handshake.

Tom gave it a long look.

"Less than two days."

"That won't be a problem either", Sharík said, smiling.

Tom took the man's hand and shook it.

"Now, I believe it's your time to share the information", Sharík said.

Tom nodded.

"Can we have something to drink?" he asked. "I mean... not water or tea. I feel like some sort of "pick me up", and you might need it too."

"Bien! Mort! Mort!"

The orang-utan man appeared through the door.

"Bring us a bottle of cognac, from my cellar."

Mort disappeared.

"Okay, the information."

Tom wasn't sure how to start. His findings were more of logic weaved through snippets of given information and remarks, through observation and examination. It was not supported by facts or evidence, and if Tom was right, there would never be any evidence. They won't be allowed to surface.

"The gossip... the information about children", Tom started, "I don't know what the Party told people, I no longer have access to a Broadcasting Unit or news, but I can assure you that what they say is not the truth... Well, it's not the whole truth. It's certainly a *specific* truth that fits Party's agenda. I don't know what they told their citizens, how they dressed it up, how they managed to twist the country, so that mothers were forced to give up their children, and those who didn't, were hounded by neighbours and family members, but somehow they did it. I don't know how they sold that one to their free citizens, but they have. Because currently, the Party's staging the extermination of an entire generation to cover up the mess *they* created, a mess that has run away from them. And now they're covering that too: no evidence – no crime."

Mort came through the door, carrying a bottle. Three glasses were stacked upside down on its top. He placed it on the desk.

Jeff reached, and taking the glasses off, he opened the bottle and poured a heady dose of the golden liquor into each tumbler.

Tom took a glass.

"For decades now, the Party controlled the population numbers: shortage of land, resources, food... You know, the usual drill. But the decades of that control divided the country. Our otherwise unified and equal in every other way nation is divided on the basis of the parenthood. The country is divided into "parents" and "non-parents". The resentment towards children and their parents had been stirring for a while, but now, it has been given the green light.

"With less than twenty percent of the population approved for a procreation licence, many men and women die without having children of their own, without experiencing the joy of parenthood. The people, who were denied a licence, are bitter. The children that they see on the streets, their smiling parents - it brings out the worst in them. I see it, and I can understand it. So, the Party have found the perfect scapegoat for their fuck up – the country's children. They announced that the children carry a new disease. And now, the earlier hunt that applied only to the children born without a permission licence is extended to them all. The entire generation is being hounded and exterminated like badgers."

Tom gave a sad bark of a laugh.

"Panic and fear are the best soil to work on, as they grow obedience and hide dirty deeds and tarnish the truth", Tom recited a quote, he once heard. "In the eyes of the entire country, the children and their parents are finally receiving what they deserved."

"I'm confused", Sharík said, picking up the conversation after a pause. "Are you saying that the Party is lying about children carrying the disease? Another stunt of disinformation by our great freedom-seeking fathers?"

"Yes and no. I think some of them do, but not all."

Tom watched the men's faces. It took a few moments longer, but the penny finally dropped.

"But some children *do* carry the disease?" Sharík demanded. "What disease?"

"I don't know what disease, what it's called or how it can be treated. I don't know any of that. I only know that some of them do. I've witnessed it."

Sharík and Jeff stared at Tom.

"Your child... Is she... Is she sick?" Sharík pushed, and Tom noticed how the man pulled his hands off the desk.

"No, I don't believe so. I don't have any way to test her, but I don't think she carries the illness."

Sharík's eyebrows were knitted. His studious gaze was on Tom.

"Bon, let's get this straight, and let's start slowly. Is there an illness affecting children?"

Tom gave a short nod.

"Yes. A few children are affected, but not all of them."

"What about your kid?" Jeff cut in from the side.

Tom turned to Jeff.

"She's fine. She's not showing any symptoms."

"The disease could be dormant..."

"It wouldn't be. It manifests quickly enough – "

"How do you know?

"I just do", Tom roared, before slamming his mouth shut.

He took a deep breath.

"Listen, she is not sick. But what you need to know is not *if* the children carry disease. As is most of the country, you are not asking the important question."

"And what that question might be, Thomaās?" Sharík asked.

"The question is *"why"*? Why the children suddenly fell ill? The entire generation. The whole lot of them, out of the blue and suddenly. That's what you should be concerned with."

"And you know the answer to that question?"

"I do."

"And?"

Tom drew in a deep breath.

He was about to give away his most precious and most lethal possession. After sharing that news, he might become redundant to these men. The disclosure might scare them, and they might pull out of the deal. Tom hoped that they won't though. He hoped that the insurances he put in place will ensure his and his daughter's safety for the next thirty six hours.

"Synthetic food", Tom eventually said.

"The children, and adults, are infected by the Party's flagship development – synthetic food. It was initially distributed through the country's nurseries, and I think it's where it was tested. I didn't have a clue until I met a man, a biologist, and suddenly, it all clicked. He told me that he had warned the leadership of its danger for years, but no one listened. The need to feed people, to keep people placid and calm, subsequently preserving rule, are more important than the possible outcome. Maybe, they hoped it would never arise. Maybe, they hoped it would be decades, or generations, before it would happen. Maybe, they didn't expect it to be so sudden and severe... I don't know. But synthetic food is the cause of the disease. The nurseries and schools were the first line of testing. Then they moved it into factories. They fed the synthetic food to millions of workers, and now, as the bodies begin to drop, they're pinning it on those, who can't argue back... those, who were already disliked by millions."

The memory of Tilly complaining about her nursery food came to Tom's mind. She cried that weekend in their flat, refusing to pack her clothes for the fresh week at the nursery, upset at being forced to eat the food she didn't like. But she went to the nursery at the end of that week, and she ate her food for many months after, because there was nothing else on offer.

The silence that followed lasted minute upon minute, interrupted only by the swirling of the cognac in the glasses and occasional slurping.

"Synthetic food?" Sharík eventually asked.

"Yes."

"They were pushing it hard", Sharík muttered. "Of course, not for export – no one wants that crap outside our country – but within, it was all synthetics lately. And there was always plenty of it..."

Sharík lifted his gaze to Tom.

"How does this disease progress? Do you know? Is it contagious?"

"I don't know, but I don't think it's contagious", Tom lied. Although, would it be a lie, if he didn't know it for certain himself?

"I believe it manifests only after the regular consumption."

Sharík narrowed his gaze on Tom.

"If it's not contagious, why are the government looking to eliminate the entire generation? That's a bit harsh, even for them. Plus announcing it via the news, admitting it to the public, then hounding the sick?.."

Sharík shook his head.

"They need to be seen doing something", Tom said, "handling the issue. If they act with dedication and enthusiasm, no one would suspect them. No one would think that they are the ones, who *created* the disease."

"True, true. Yet still..."

"For that."

Tom pointed at Sharík.

"They're doing it exactly for that! For this doubt, disbelief, for that crazy implausibility, shying anyone, who would suggest such crazy, far-fetched idea. That's why no one would believe that they were the ones to blame. No one would suspect the good guys behind bad deeds, let alone the impeccable Party of the Federation Britannia. And who are they trying to swindle? The biddable ones, those, who are left behind after decades of their leadership. They would believe these lies without a second thought. And this?"

Tom waved his hand to the side, indicating a country-wide curfew and the Party's latest directive.

"That's the perfect way to eliminate the evidence. It's a clean cut. The government can have another generation, bred by the ones, who were refused the licence prior. It's no skin off their nose. They can sacrifice this generation, wipe out the mistake and move on. They tweak the synthetic food a bit. Maybe releasing it later, when it's ready..."

A sudden thought, that hadn't crossed Tom's mind, pushed to the fore.

"Or... Or they can practice on those children. They can research antibodies, and if not, then at the very least and by a happy coincidence, they have developed a biological weapon. They can turn that mistake into a win, a huge win, a win on a global scale."

Agitated, Tom jumped up from his chair.

This possibility hadn't crossed his mind until now.

"These children could be sent to fight wars that the Party has been itching to start for a while now, looking at the rich lands on the continent..."

"You said, they're not contagious", Sharík interrupted Tom's hot rumination.

Tom pulled his gaze to the man.

The deep wrinkles riddled the man's face, eyebrows drawn, as he was trying to catch up with Tom's galloping thoughts.

"No. Not now", Tom agreed. "But once they progress, it might change. From now on, a lot can change. Little perfect soldiers, dying, as they're infecting others..."

Tom strutted to the corner of the room, mumbling to himself.

"It could be through blood or touch, depending on how far they've developed it. Could it be airborne? Potentially, if they were to tweak a few things. And they wouldn't need to announce that war. It will spread silently... By the time half of Europe is infected, it would be too late to act. The war would be won..."

"Thomaās", Sharík's voice pulled Tom back.

Tom spun towards the man. For a second, confronted by Sharík and Jeff's gazes, Tom couldn't remember where he had left off.

"That's why I need my child out of the country", he said.

Silence hung in the room. Sharík twirled his glass then gave another slurp.

"In light of that information, your plight makes a lot of sense, and weighted with this disclosure, your gift of the food supplies is even more generous."

Tom nodded.

"Now, about the water supplies..." Sharík started.

"I'll tell you where it is, and how it can be removed, once we are on the boat", Tom interrupted the man.

"You leave nothing to chance, Thomaās. Very admirable. But you see, while you and Jeff were out, procuring the physical part of your offer, I did my homework too. I looked into you, Thomaās."

Tom shrugged his shoulders, trying to appear nonchalant, but as of late, he didn't like it when people "looked into him".

There was nothing in his past he needed to hide or couldn't acknowledge. Up until the last few days, his life was an open book, written under the dictation of the Party. There was nothing illicit or illegal in his past. There was nothing noteworthy at all.

"You didn't tell me, you're an electrical engineer. Right now, you're a project manager, but you rose up by studying hard and working even harder, working with wind turbines, ventilation, electricity supplies. Half of the country's energy implementations and testing are yours. You're behind it all. You're a very humble man indeed."

"There's nothing to tell. Besides, it has no bearing on what I'm here for."

"Au contraire."

Sharík reclined in his wide chair.

"It has a very direct influence on your future path..."

Sharík smiled at Tom, and Tom reciprocated.

The man thought he had outplayed Tom, his smile said as much, and Tom wanted to laugh. This man didn't know that if taking the timeline of Judy's death into consideration, from the point of infection to the point of death, Tom's future was due to come to an ugly and abrupt end in two days, four at the very best, unless a miracle came around, with antibodies sprinkled over him by magical old deities.

But Tom didn't expect miracles. He knew where he lived. Tom lived in The Federation Britannia, with the Ordained Liberating Party ruling it, and not in a magical kingdom.

"What's so funny?" Sharík asked.

"I hear a proposition coming."

"It is."

Sharík leaned across the desk, picked up the bottle and poured more cognac into Tom's glass.

"I'll have many uses for a man of your talents, Thomaās. In fact, it would be a crime to dispose or lose a talent like yours. So, I have, as you rightly said, a proposition for you."

He paused, gathering dramatism for his offer.

"I'd like you to stick around after our transaction is complete. Of course, we'll send your daughter into Frankia within the agreed timeframe", Sharík pre-empted Tom's objection, raising his hands, "whilst you remain here, with us. I'm offering you to work for me."

Watching Tom's surprised face, Sharík rushed to add: "You'd be able to stay in touch with your child. We have a few captains who can bring letters. Of course, those fees I will cover, as well as offering you a monetary incentive. I'll provide you with safe harbour, food and all of the respect that your knowledge undoubtedly commands. I have many plans, and let's just say that your arrival is more than a gift from God."

"God? You still speak of God?"

Sharík shrugged his shoulders.

"Of course. Unlike the rest of the country, we are free here, free to worship false gods, if we please, and free to choose our paths."

Tom held Sharík's gaze.

"As much as it's very generous of you, I won't leave my child", he said. "She is too small to make that difficult journey on her own."

"I'll send my best captain with her", Sharík pushed. "I can assure you, she will be taken care of, and once there, I have a lovely family, who would be more than happy to look after your little angel."

"I'm sorry. I can't do that."

Tom wanted to know what Sharík's play would be to his rejection of the offer. Tom wanted to see, what the man had on him, and sure enough, it came.

Sharík shook his head.

"Well, that's a shame, a real shame, because as I said, I really appreciate, and value, smart people when I see them. Smart, educated and determined people are what keep our little world going, withstanding troubles that shake the country beyond our gates. I really, really hate doing it to nice people. I really hate seeing them die. It would be such a waste."

There it was: simple and unimaginative – a death threat.

Sharík's heavy gaze drilled into Tom, waiting for the innuendo to register, as if it were another test of his smartness.

Tom understood. He understood that once he is dead, Tilly would be discarded, possibly handed over to the authorities.

"Have you forgotten about the water supply?" Tom asked, holding Sharík's gaze.

The man smiled.

"You know, I sent people to check on it, and I think you're bluffing."

"Your people wouldn't be able to find it, because they don't know where to look."

"Thomaās, I can assure you, they looked, everywhere. You see, first, they looked at the base of the water tower, next to the water supply pipes and drainage, and luckily for us, it was raining the day before your arrival. And could you imagine their surprise, when they couldn't find any footprints near the water tower, anywhere? None. There are no footsteps, Thomaās. The ground is clear. So, unless you flew to the tower, I think you're bluffing."

Tom sat quietly. His narrowed gaze was on the smiling man.

"The State Police are still coming though", he insisted.

"Well, now. You see, I'm not so sure they will. I think you're lying on that matter too."

"They will", Tom repeated. "And when they come, they kill me and put you away for harbouring a wanted fugitive."

Sharík threw his hands up, folding his face into a soft smile, as if arguing with a toddler.

"Say, you're not lying. Say, they are coming."

He nodded in agreement, placating Tom.

"If they're coming, then you're absolutely right – they will kill you... which would be a travesty, to lose such a brilliant and bright mind. But... C'est la vie. Worse things are happening every day. Oh, yeah, and don't worry about me. I'll make sure to dump your body outside the docks, so we won't be implicated."

Sharík paused, allowing Tom to imagine that possibility in full, before dropping his voice and adding: "But if you work for me, then you're my family. And I look after my own. The daughter of my brother is my kin, and I'll never harm my blood. I'll do my utmost to protect her. Unlike the ruthless Party, I don't want the blood of a child on my hands. I'll send her across the channel, just as agreed. I'll make sure of it. I fear you might be right, and there's a danger to children in this country. For all we know, she might be the last child of her generation, and then preserving her life becomes my duty, as a citizen and human. As a free citizen and an honest man, I can't stand by and watch those idiots from State Security slaughtering her. I think they have enough children already."

Tom took another sip of the gold warming liquid.

"So, she will travel, but not me?"

"Yes, but only for now. Once we've done everything that I know you are capable of, should you wish to reunite with your daughter, that ticket will be on me."

Sharík puffed his chest, the smile of his generosity masking his blackmail.

Tom looked at the man in front of him, and the man held Tom's gaze.

Unlike Tom, he wasn't bluffing.

"Please, don't force my hand, Thomaās. I deliver you to State Security, I'll get a commemorative plaque and a blind eye from the state to my dealing for a year or so. I keep you here, and I've acquired myself a brilliant engineer. I'll come out on top no matter what, and I'd rather you realise that, so we can move on and avoid unnecessary bloodshed."

Tom smiled. He knew he only had a few days, but Sharík didn't. He knew that he was infected, but Sharík was oblivious to that threat.

Sharík's blackmail was robbing Tom of the last moments with his daughter, but maybe it was a good thing that she won't see him die. He wouldn't want her memories of him being the same as of her mother: a stiff body under the murky plastic.

It was Sharík, who forced Tom's hand, threatening, whilst pleading for Tom's charity and talent.

Tom's smile grew wider. He didn't have any more forgiveness to give. Whatever crumbs were left, were stolen by the callousness of his Party and the cruelty of its people.

"You strike a hard bargain, Sharík. I guess I have no choice, but to drop my anchor here."

Sharík laughed.

"Drop anchor", he repeated Tom's words. "Good one. I think we'll get along just fine."

"But she must be gone within a day", Tom interrupted their mutual appreciation. "The state officers are coming. And it's not a bluff."

Sharík placed his hand on his chest.

"You have my word. She will sail within the next twenty four hours."

He reclined back in his seat.

"I have to say, I'm relieved that you agreed to work with me. I was a bit worried. Although, I knew you were a smart man, Jeff was telling me that you're quite unbending in your beliefs, and I feared we might have one of those situations here... You're burning at the stake with the little one, rather than working for a criminal."

Sharík rolled his eyes with the last word, indicating that he doesn't believe that it's a fair assessment of him.

"No. I'm smarter rather than a martyr."

"And it rhymes", Sharík pointed, his mood high, as he had secured the transaction he needed.

Tom lifted his glass.

"To my new employment."

"To our cooperation", Sharík echoed, raising his glass.

Chapter 26

There was a day to go.

The last day Tom would have with his daughter.

Under the cover of night, the small motor boat will depart from the docks, leaving the soil of The Federation Britannia behind, driving full speed towards the coast of Frankia.

Tilly would be on board, but not Tom.

Within the last day Tom had grown weaker.

The midnight escapade within the city took more out of him than he liked to admit. The haze that descended over his vision in the last five minutes was strong. It was covering the image in the greying film, making it hard for Tom to see.

But Tom pushed through, careful not to show that he is unwell. Until his daughter leaves this country, and ideally touches Frankish land, he will stand tall, forcing his voice to ring strong.

Tom marched down the narrow corridor, remembering, rather than seeing, where their room was.

"Daddy."

Tilly jumped off the bed. She rushed to him and hugged his legs.

"Hi, darling. Told you I'd come back. Never worry. Daddy will always make sure you're okay. I will always protect you."

He kneeled on the floor, listening to the door closing behind the woman.

"Daddy will always love you, even when I'm no longer with you. Even if you don't see me anymore, you must know that daddy's always with you. Daddy loves you more than anything, more than his life and will do anything for you. I will always protect you. Always."

Tom mumbled into her hair, as he stroked her back, hugging her. Emotions wrung his throat, lodging something alien in it, through which he struggled to speak.

He held back tears for as long as he could, but eventually they spilled, and unable to say another word, he crushed her body against his, his body shaking and pathetic whimpers pushing past his strength. That will be the last time he would hold her, the last hours he will spend with her.

"Daddy?"

Her little voice cut through the stench of his dying body and his misery.

"Daddy?"

"It's okay, darling. It's okay. Daddy's just a bit sad, but that's okay. He won't be sad for long."

He lifted his face, wiping it with his arm. He changed his face into something that he hoped would look like a smile.

"Do you want to go on a holiday? Just like the holiday we took with mum last year, only this time on a boat? That would be fun, right?"

Tom was breaking inside.

Judy, Tilly... his whole life that he had spent so many years, so much love and patience building, was crumbling around him. The happy future that he cultivated so tirelessly, protecting, careful to obey the rules was taken away from him.

The pieces of his broken life lay under the boot of the Party. The shards were too small, good for nothing, not even for gathering or gluing. That was the end of him, of his dream, of his life. Something that was his entire world was not that world any longer. It was taken from him, taken because someone, somewhere had made a decision, made a call that broke Tom's life. Someone, somewhere took it upon himself to dictate how much will be taken from him. They never contemplated Tom, or anyone else for that matter. They made the decision that suited them.

Tom always believed that the Party had his wellbeing at heart, that it cared for its citizens, for each and every one of them. But the course of the last week had shown what a fool Tom had been.

During that time, Tom's feeling for the Party had progressed from confusion and disbelief to resentment, now hitting a foreign to him level of pure hatred that burned in his chest like acid.

How could they take it away from him?

Why?

The last question spun on repeat in his mind.

Hasn't he served them well? Was the dedication of his life to them not enough? Hasn't he done everything that was asked of him, and more? Hasn't he proven himself, ten times over?

He knew he had. He knew that he was a devoted little dog, an obedient lapdog that danced around the table to the tune of his owners. He grew to resent himself for that over time, as his eyes grew blinder to the last few years.

He was naïve. His hopes and trust, the excuses he uttered to himself and others, believing their lies, excusing their methods, wishing for the arrival of the bright future that was promised, confident that the methods implemented would now be forgotten.

But one can't build a white tower with bloodied hands. Blood stains everything.

Tom was dumb to expect anything less.

Now, he had no more life left, no second chances. All that he had left was bitter regret.

Sitting in the room with Sharík, he felt blood running in thin streams down his back. He felt it and said nothing, hoping it would remain unnoticed.

A sudden impatient knock on the door startled Tom.

Buttoning up the jacket to hide the blood-soaked shirt, Tom rose to his feet and opened the door.

Jeff barged into the room without invitation, coming face to face with Tom.

"You're full of shit, Whicker. Once an obedient rat, always an obedient rat. The whole act is not like you, not like you at all, and Sharík... He knows people; he sees people, I won't take it from him, but there's something about you... something ain't right, and I can't put my finger on it. This act of the lost truth-seeker with a child..."

He shook his head.

"Sharík might be buying it, but I can assure you, he is the only one. I trust you about as far, as I can throw you. You're full of shit, Whicker. Full of shit! Always were and always will be!"

Tilly clung to Tom's leg tighter.

"Would you mind watching your voice? You're scaring my daughter."

"Your daughter", Jeff mumbled, narrowing his gaze and scanning Tilly. "Something ain't right with her either, with the whole story, with both of you. You, running away from the state, who gifted her to you? That's not the Whicker I knew."

"A lot of things happened, Jeff. I would say a lot of time has passed, but what had changed me didn't take much time. The change, of which you are so afraid, took only a week. But there's no way back for me. Now, I'm an outlaw, just like you. Actually, thinking about it, even more than you."

Tom smiled.

"Who would've thought that I'd become a bigger criminal than Jeffrey Huston? I would've punched you, if you'd told me that."

Jeff narrowed his gaze on Tom.

"And you did. Remember when I ripped that Party poster that they hung in the main hall for Liberation Day? You went crazy. All I remember was standing, ripping the paper one minute, and the next, I was flying and you're laying into me... Kinda like a few hours ago. Your temper hasn't changed..."

He stepped closer, leaning into Tom.

"And I think you haven't changed either."

He paused.

"I don't know what game you're playing, or if you think that this is a game, but I can assure you, it's not, and if you think you can get away with whatever that is, whatever you're doing here, you're sorely mistaken. If you think that the Party doesn't forgive, wait 'til you cross Sharík. If you fuck him over, I'll be the first to carve your eyes out and make you eat them. Do you get me?"

Tom threw his hand to his head, saluting to his childhood enemy.

"Loud and clear."

Jeff shook his head and was about to leave, when Tom called after him: "Jeff", and when the man turned, Tom continued, "I am sorry for everything that I did to you, directly and inadvertently. I'm truly sorry."

Without a word, Jeff walked out, the door slamming the frame.

Tom spent that day with Tilly outside, out in the sun. He didn't hide, knowing that he was safe in the docks as long as Sharík needed him.

Tom and Tilly stood by the water. She was throwing pebbles, as he stared into the hazy horizon, wishing he could see the Frankish coast, as if it would help him to see her future.

He imagined her sailing across the channel.

Alone, she would cry. She would sit at the bottom of the boat, calling for him, for Judy, until she realised that they aren't coming. Her crying and screams would grow harder. Hiccups would come next, raking her small body and stealing her breath. She would be scared.

She will be alone, but she will be alive.

That was the end of Tom's life.

It was his time to reap.

He had sown many mistakes, many misjudgements, but he sowed love too.

He glanced at his daughter.

Her loose braid that he plaited with such inexperience had unravelled, most of the hair falling out of the plait, its wisps floating around her face and her shoulders, stroking her rosy cheeks, as she watched the pebbles hitting the surface, laughing every time it made a plopping sound.

He began preparing himself for their goodbye.

Steeling himself against it, he imagined how it would go.

He knew she would throw herself at him, hugging him tight, wrapping herself around his legs, as she had done so often in the last two weeks, refusing to let go.

He knew that her face would be awash with tears, her large eyes frightened and sad.

He knew that he would have to pry her hands open, maybe even yell at her – anything to put her onto that boat.

He would grow strict, short with her, as the moment of separation will loom.

He would want her to part with him with ease. He would want to ensure that she would walk onto the boat, hopefully without turning back, without calling and pleading for him. He knew he would have to be strong. But he was afraid that if she pleaded, he might break, selfishly allowing her to stay.

No. He won't allow it.

He will stand, and he will watch her.

He will let her go. He will push her away if he had to.

Tom reached out and stroked the top of her head, memorising that feeling of the silkiness of her hair against his palm.

He leaned in, inhaling the soft scent at the base of her neck.

The scent of his life is the scent of his child.

The scent of his final day is the scent of her and sea spray.

Tom knew that when the State Security comes – and they will; he made sure of that – he will come out to greet them. He will tell them his name. Armed with the handgun of the dead street-beater, he knows they will kill him.

He imagined how the bullets would fly, ripping at his flesh, stopping his heart, bringing his death forward.

At least that death will be fast. At least, it would be on his terms.

Their arrival and his death would tie up the final loose end that Tom had with this country. It will get rid of Sharík, hopefully Jeff too.

There will be no more people left who knew of his daughter, and where she went. There will be no one left who knew that she existed.

The last witnesses to her escape would be gone.

Epilogue

Le Parisien 24.

Breaking news.

For the last few days we have been receiving unconfirmed reports of the deaths of thousands in the capital of The Federation Britannia, New Bristol. All that we currently know is that most of the deaths occurred within the same area of New Bristol, in one of its new developments. But alongside these reports, we have received yet again unconfirmed information of the mass disappearance of children of age of twelve and under.

At this point, we cannot confirm if these two reports are connected.

We believe that the situation is on-going. However the information remains unverified and our requests for comments remain unanswered by the Central Liberated Media Service and its Party representatives.

About author

Olga Gibbs was born and raised in USSR, had participated in many Soviet annual parades, wore a red tie around her neck, over her state issued school uniform, and at one point she was a "Pioneer".

She lived and survived through the "lawless 90-s" and in 2002 came to the UK.

Whilst sharing her life experiences, the author wanted to voice a warning, a caution against an unopposed regime, no matter who they are, against the environmental toll of human actions on nature, against the acquisition of farming lands in the hands of very few, rich individuals and against people's compliance. These issues will threaten the lives of our children, if we don't address them now.

Olga Gibbs is a mental health expert who has experience of working with disturbance in adolescents and young people. Using her Masters in Creative Writing, she explores taboo topics such as borderline personality and social effective disorder, effects of abuse and insecure attachment in young people.

Please visit www.OlgaGibbs.com.

Printed in Great Britain
by Amazon

75626854R00225